$ .50

JOHN LUTZ

"Lutz knows how to make you shiver."
—RIDLEY PEARSON

IN FOR THE KILL

D0089193

DON'T MISS THESE EXPLOSIVE THRILLERS BY JOHN LUTZ

PINNACLE
U.S. $6.99
CAN $9.99

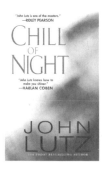

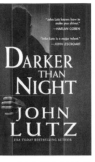

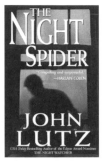

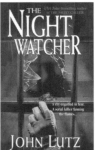

Praise for John Lutz

"Lutz can deliver a hard-boiled P.I. novel or a bloody thriller with equal ease. . . . The ingenuity of the plot shows that Lutz is in rare form."
—*The New York Times Book Review* on *Chill of Night*

"Lutz keeps the suspense high and populates his story with a collection of unique characters . . . an ideal beach read."
—*Publishers Weekly* on *Chill of Night*

"John Lutz knows how to make you shiver."
—Harlan Coben

"John Lutz is one of the masters of the police novel."
—Ridley Pearson

"A major talent."   —John Lescroart

"I've been a fan for years."   —T. Jefferson Parker

"John Lutz just keeps getting better and better."
—Tony Hillerman

"Lutz ranks with such vintage masters of big-city murder as Lawrence Block and the late Ed McBain."
—*St. Louis Post-Dispatch*

"Lutz is among the best."   —*San Diego Union*

"Some writers just have a flair for imaginative suspense, and we all should be glad that John Lutz is one of them. *The Night Spider* features elegant writing enveloping exotic murder and solid police work. . . . A truly superb example of the 'new breed' of mystery thrillers."
—Jeremiah Healy

In
for the
Kill

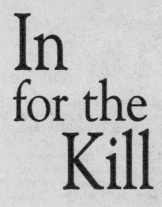

JOHN LUTZ

PINNACLE BOOKS
Kensington Publishing Corp.
www.kensingtonbooks.com

PINNACLE BOOKS are published by

Kensington Publishing Corp.
850 Third Avenue
New York, NY 10022

All Kensington titles, imprints, and distributed lines are available at special quantity discounts for bulk purchases for sales promotions, premiums, fund-raising, educational, or institutional use. Special book excerpts or customized printings can also be created to fit specific needs. For details, write or phone the office of the Kensington special sales manager: Kensington Publishing Corp., 850 Third Avenue, New York, NY 10022, attn: Special Sales Department; phone 1-800-221-2647.

This book is a work of fiction. Names, characters, businesses, organizations, places, events, and incidents either are the product of the author's imagination or are used fictitiously. Any resemblance to actual persons, living or dead, events, or locales is entirely coincidental.

ISBN-13: 978-0-7860-1843-7
ISBN-10: 0-7860-1843-7

First printing: November 2007

10 9 8 7 6 5 4 3 2 1

Printed in the United States of America

At the cross, her station keeping,
Stood the mournful mother, weeping,
Where he hung, the dying Lord.
—Anonymous

A mother is a mother still,
The holiest thing alive.
—Coleridge, *The Three Graves*

If I were hung on the highest hill,
Mother o' mine, O mother o' mine!
I know whose love would follow me still,
Mother o' mine, O mother o' mine.
—Kipling, *Mother O' Mine*

1

Did she suspect?

Have even an inkling?

He wondered about that as he watched the woman stride along the sidewalk, then shift her purse slightly on her hip as she turned and took the three concrete steps leading to the vestibule of her apartment building. She seemed tired this evening, as if something weighed on her, some of the bounce gone from her step.

No surprise there, he thought. Surely there's something in us that lets us know within minutes, at least seconds, when the world is about to end.

Up? Down? Stop? Go?

The elevator couldn't seem to make up its mind.

Janice Queen stood alone in its claustrophobic confines and felt her heart hammer. Not that this vertical indecision was anything new to her. There was only one elevator in her apartment building, and only one way to get to her unit if she didn't want to trudge up six flights of stairs, so it wasn't as if she had much choice. But she'd always had a fear of being confined in close places, elevators in particular. She could never escape the grim knowledge that if there were a serious malfunction—nothing that hadn't happened before to *someone*—beneath the thin floor under her feet was a black shaft that would lead to sudden and almost certain death.

At least two times a day, at least five days a week, she rode the elevator up or down the core of the old but recently refurbished apartment building.

Ah! Finally the elevator settled down, having more or less leveled itself at the sixth floor. When the door slid open, it revealed a step up of about four inches, enough to trip over if you didn't notice, and to provide a glimpse into the black abyss. A kind of warning.

Janice was living her life contentedly, going back and forth to her job at the bookshop, going out on the occasional date, or to hang out with friends at Bocco's down the block, or to pick up some takeout at the corner deli. Hers was a life like millions of others in the city.

The elevator could end it in an instant.

Ridiculous, she thought, as she stepped up onto the soft carpeting of the sixth-floor hall, nevertheless feeling uneasy while momentarily astride the abyss.

Her apartment door was only a few feet away from the elevator, which meant she could hear, even late at night, the device's cables strumming soft and somber chords just behind her walls, as well as a muffled thumping and bumping as it adjusted itself at each stop. Which meant she thought about the damned elevator too much, even dreamed about it, and had become reasonably convinced that death by elevator was her destiny.

She unlocked her way into her apartment and went inside. Dim. She flipped the light switch, and there she was in the full-length mirror that she paused in front of to check her appearance each time she came or went.

There was the rumpled, wearier version of the Janice she'd said good-bye to this morning on her way to work, not quite forty, still slim, with generous breasts, passable legs, and shoulder-length brown hair framing a face that was sweet rather than classically beautiful. Too much jaw, she thought. *And those damned lines.* They were only visible if the light was cruel or you looked closely enough. Fine lines like drool extended down from the corners of her lips. Crow's-feet threatened to appear at the corners of her dark eyes. Intimations of a lonely future. She still attracted men, but of course it was easier to attract than to keep them. Or, sometimes, to get rid of them.

The mirror was mounted on the door to a small closet. She looped her purse's leather strap over the doorknob, then removed the lightweight gray blazer she'd worn to work over her dark slacks and white blouse, and hung it in the closet between her heavier coat and a blue Windbreaker. She might drop the blazer off at the dry cleaner's tomorrow morning, wear the Windbreaker if it was cool enough outside and looked like rain. The bookshop's owner, Dee, was out of town, supposedly on business but actually seeing a married man with whom she was having a hot affair. Janice wasn't supposed to know about it, so she pretended right along with Dee. So there Dee was, getting her brains screwed scrambled while Janice, who now and then felt a spasm of jealousy, was dutifully opening the shop early every morning this week.

Not enough sleep for Janice, since she was addicted to late-night movies on television. Her lessening love of the moment, Graham, was also traveling, as he often did in his sales job, and wouldn't be back in town until tomorrow. They'd almost but not quite argued when she said good-bye to him at Bocco's. Janice knew their relationship was winding down and had decided to end it herself rather than wait for Graham. As she grew older, she more and more felt the need to exercise control in her life. Always before, she had waited. Not this time. Maybe the pain would be less severe.

She did know from experience that sooner or later another Graham would enter the bookshop, or use some time-worn pickup line at Bocco's.

As she closed the closet door, the intercom buzzed, startling her.

She went to it and pressed the button. "Yes?"

"Federal Parcel," said a male voice, made distant and metallic by the intercom. "For a Janice . . . Queeler?"

"Queen?" she asked.

"Queen. Sorry."

Janice pressed the button to buzz in the deliveryman.

A few seconds later the elevator cables began to thrum in the wall. He was on his way up with her package.

She opened the door and stepped out in the hall to meet him.

The elevator did its laborious dance, its door hissed open, and out he stepped, a medium-sized guy, dark hair, kind of handsome, wearing wrinkled khakis and a sweat-stained blue T-shirt, white joggers. He was carrying a long white box that looked like the kind used to deliver long-stemmed flowers, only made of heavier cardboard. He smiled, glancing down at the box to double-check the label.

"Janice Queen?"

"Yes." She saw no pocket in his shirt, no protruding pen or pencil. Other than the box, there was nothing in his hands, either.

Should have brought a pen from the desk. There's one in my purse, just inside the door.

No clipboard?

None of this struck her as wrong until a second too late.

As she reached forward to accept the package, he shoved her violently backward into the apartment. She bumped hard against the mirror, hoping it wouldn't break.

He was suddenly inside, the door closed behind him. Now he was reaching into a pocket with his free right hand, drawing out what looked like a partly wadded sock, a sap.

Is this happening? Is it real?

Somewhere in her stunned, panicked mind she decided to scream, and she'd inhaled to do so when the object from the man's pocket struck the side of her head.

She was on her hands and knees, sickened by the pain.

Someone else. This is happening to someone else. Please!

There was another starburst of pain, this time at the back of her skull.

The floor opened beneath her, and she was plunging down a dark shaft toward a deeper darkness.

Pearl Kasner trudged up the concrete steps from her subway stop and began the three-block walk to her apartment. She was short and buxom, curvaceous in a way her gray uniform couldn't conceal. A few men walking the other way fixed their stares on her breasts then quickly looked away, the way men do. As if the wife might be around somewhere watching.

She was tired and her feet were sore. There'd been a cash pickup at Fifth National, so she'd worked after hours. Helping the Brink's guys make sure the depositors' money was safe. Not that there was really much danger the place would be robbed.

But some danger. Enough. And enough pay.

Hard on the feet, though. Pearl spent a lot of time standing around. And being nice. That could be tiresome.

No job was perfect, and all things considered, she liked this one. Liked wearing the gray uniform instead of the blue. Easier hours. Fewer complications. And flat feet in middle age either way.

A couple of suits walking toward her stared at her breasts, then one of them lifted his gaze to her face. He smiled.

None of the men said anything, though. Because of the uniform.

Or maybe because she was wearing a gun.

* * *

Cold.

Pain.

Janice Queen couldn't move. Not a muscle.

Where?

Janice opened her eyes to bright light and a familiar gray tile wall. She knew she was in her bathroom. Uncomfortable. Cramped. She tried to raise her head but couldn't. She raised only her eyes and saw the chromed showerhead.

Knowing now that she was seated leaning back in her bathtub, she let her eyes explore. She was nude, her body textured with gooseflesh where it showed above the water.

Water?

That was why she was so cold. Water was running from the spigot. Only cold water. It was well above her waist.

Her arms were crossed just beneath her breasts and bound so tightly she couldn't move them, couldn't feel them. Straining hard, she glanced toward her feet, which she at least could barely feel. Her calves and ankles, even her thighs, were bound together tightly with gray duct tape. Janice could wriggle her toes—underwater—but that was it.

Her head was throbbing so that the pain was almost unbearable.

She tried to call out and discovered she couldn't make a sound. She couldn't move her lips. Her probing tongue found rough surface when she managed to part her lips slightly. The roughness and tackiness of tape. There had to be duct tape across her mouth.

The deliveryman entered the bathroom. He was nude, as she was. He only glanced at her, which frightened her even more because it was as if she no longer mattered much to him. Not alive.

He turned his back on her, stooped, and began searching through the cabinet beneath the washbasin, pulling out liquid soap, a large bottle of shampoo. He placed the containers on the edge of the tub, then left the bathroom. She heard him rummaging around in the kitchen, banging cabinet doors, opening and closing drawers.

The water was almost up to her armpits now. She panicked for a second, then made herself remain calm. What was he going to do with the soap and shampoo?

Is he going to wash me? Is this some crazy sexual thing? Will he do something to me then go away?

It's possible. It could happen. It must happen!

She was part of the singles world and knew about the kinky things that went on in Manhattan. The hard-earned knowledge was something to cling to for hope. He might satisfy whatever oddball compulsion drove him, then simply leave.

When he returned he was carrying boxes of dishwasher soap and laundry detergent from the cabinet beneath the sink. And he had his long white box, which he placed on the toilet seat lid. The dishwasher soap and laundry detergent he put next to the other cleaning agents.

The water was at the base of her neck now. In the lower edge of her vision she could see long strands of her brown hair floating on the surface. It reminded her of seaweed she'd seen fanned and floating like that years ago when she was on a Caribbean vacation.

If only she could scream!

He gave her another glance, then leaned over her and turned off the water.

The sudden silence after the brief squeal of the faucet handle seemed to herald her salvation.

She wasn't going to drown!

Thank God!

He straightened up slowly, then abruptly yanked the clear plastic shower curtain from its rod. He'd had the curtain draped outside the tub so it would remain dry, and he was careful to keep it that way. He crouched down and carefully spread it over the tile floor by the tub.

When he was finished spreading the plastic curtain, down on his knees now, he reached over and lifted the lid of the white cardboard box.

She only caught a glimpse of what was inside: knives, a cleaver, and something bulky gleaming bright orange with an arc of dull, serrated extension. Her mind flashed back to weekend days in her father's woodworking shop in the garage. A shrill scream of steel violating wood—*a cordless power saw!*

Even taped tightly as she was, she created tiny ripples as she trembled in the cold water.

The man remained on his knees on the shower curtain. He reached toward her feet—no, toward the chromed handles and faucet. She heard him depress the lever that opened the drain, and water began to gurgle softly as it started to swirl from the tub.

Still trembling with cold and fear, Janice saw the man stand up and was shocked to see for the first time that he had an erection.

He leaned over her, staring into her eyes in a way that puzzled her.

And she was puzzled in her terror. *What?* She screamed the simple question silently through the firmly fixed rectangle of tape.

What are you going to do to me?

He bent lower and worked an arm beneath the crook of her bound legs, the backs of her knees. Hope sprang up in her. He was going to work his other arm beneath her back so he could lift her from the tub. Then do what? Carry her into the bedroom? Rape and torture her?

She glanced again toward the white box and felt a thrill of terror.

But instead of reaching beneath her shoulders, he placed his hand at the back of her head and forced it forward so she exhaled noisily through her nose. With his other arm he lifted her legs, causing her upper body to slide down so her head was beneath the water.

Her bound lower legs began pumping up and down, but he held them high enough so that they contacted only air. While they flailed frantically, they were the only part of her moving even in the slightest. The way he had her head, she couldn't breathe out, only in.

Only in!

Cold water flooded into her lungs. She could do nothing but welcome it.

She watched him watching her on the other side of the calm surface as she drowned.

2

The day Frank Quinn's life was about to change unexpectedly, he had a breakfast of eggs, crisp bacon, and buttered toast at the Lotus Diner. Afterward, he leisurely read the *Times* over a second cup of coffee, then strolled through the sunny New York morning back to his apartment on West Seventy-fifth Street.

He thought, as he often did, that there was no other city like New York, no place like Manhattan, with its sights and sounds and smells. With all its flaws, it had become a part of Quinn.

He didn't mind at all.

As soon as he got home, he sat down in his brown leather armchair for a smoke. A guy who called himself Iggy supplied the Cuban cigars Quinn favored. Quinn didn't ask where they were from other than Cuba. A spot of minor misdemeanor wasn't that great a stain on the fabric of justice. Quinn had thought that way as a homicide detective, and now that he was retired at age fifty, after taking a bullet in the right leg during a liquor store holdup, he'd become even more lax. So he smoked his Cuban *robustos*. And at times, for convenience, he parked his aged and hulking black Lincoln in No Parking zones, propping an old NYPD plaque in the windshield.

These two infractions were about the only transgressions he'd engaged in after retirement, but then there hadn't been much opportunity to do more.

He sat now in the worn and comfortable chair that had become formed to his body, feeling lazy and watching pedestrian traffic on the sidewalk outside the ground-floor apartment. The window he was looking through had iron grillwork on the outside, to keep intruders out. But sometimes Quinn saw its black bars as prison bars, to keep him in, and had to smile at the irony. All the people he'd put away, the murderers—several of them serial killers—and here he sat comfortably behind bars smoking Cuban cigars.

Quinn could afford better digs, after his lawsuit against the NYPD contesting a false child molestation and rape claim had resulted in a six-figure settlement. But he was used to living on a cop's salary and used to his apartment. And it didn't make sense to drive something newer and more stealable than the reliable old Lincoln he'd bought cheap from a friend and fellow ex-cop. He'd even gone back to work as a homicide detective for a while, until the liquor store shooting. He knew then it was time to leave the party.

He settled back in the oversize chair and watched a man and woman hurry past outside. They were huddled close together, stealing glances at each other. Quinn let himself jump to the conclusion they were in love.

He drew on the cigar but didn't inhale. Didn't want lung cancer.

Nobody here to warn him about that now. Berate him. Threaten him. Maybe get so infuriated she'd kick him in the leg. The leg that had been shot.

It was okay to smoke cigars in the apartment, now that Pearl had moved out. That was about the only thing good about Pearl's absence, as far as Quinn was concerned. He missed her small but vivid presence.

Not that Pearl couldn't be acerbic, insulting, too intense, hyperactive, even violent.

Well, he wasn't perfect.

Some people said they were a good match. Quinn was tall, rawboned, with a battered nose and disconcerting flat green eyes. He had straight and unruly gray-shot brown hair that made him look as if he had a bad haircut even when he had a good haircut. Women liked the package. He was one of those men homely enough to be handsome. A rough-hewn sophisticate. He came across as laconic, when he wasn't laying on phony Irish charm.

Pearl usually had plenty to say. She was an inch over five feet tall, compactly and sexily built, and so full of energy that if you stood close you might hear her humming like a transformer. She had black, black hair, dark, dark eyes, and a broad and ready white, white smile behind red, red lips. She looked too *there* to be real.

But she was real, too real ever to lay on any kind of phony charm.

That might have been the thing about her that charmed Quinn. No wheels within wheels with Pearl. She was one big wheel that might roll right over you. Maybe even back up, if she really didn't like you.

She still liked Quinn, he was sure. Trouble was, she no longer seemed to love him.

Pearl was the one who'd decided to move out.

She'd quit the NYPD shortly after Quinn retired, before she could be fired for insubordination. Fired ten times over. Pearl had moved in with Quinn, who had a more than adequate income, between his pension and interest and dividends from the settlement. It had taken years to get the settlement and full exoneration. It had been worth it.

They'd been happy for a while, then Pearl had gotten restless. She missed the action. Now she lived across town and was a bank guard. Some action there. Stand around and look stern for the depositors. But she seemed content enough. Maybe it was the gun on her hip. Quinn wondered.

He was a great reader of people, but he truly didn't understand Pearl. Another facet of her charm.

The buzzer over the intercom blasted away like a wasp whirring menacingly nearby.

Pause, then again.

No pause.

Whoever was leaning on the button wouldn't let up.

Hell with them. Let them get tired and go away.

Quinn drew on his cigar, exhaled, studied the smoke.

The buzzing continued unabated. *Must be hard on the thumb.*

Who'd be doing this? Trying to aggravate him, if he did happen to be home and not seeing visitors, which was his right. Legal right.

He glanced at his cigar, then propped it in the ashtray on the table alongside the chair and stood up. He was wearing faded jeans, a wrinkled black T-shirt, worn moccasins, needed a shave, and looked more like a motorcycle gang member than an ex-cop. Lean-waisted, broad-shouldered, and ready to rumble.

Whoever was outside leaning on the button didn't seem to care what he was stirring up. His mistake. Quinn didn't go to the intercom to answer. Instead he opened his door to the first-floor hall and took a few steps so he could look through the inside glass door and see who was buzzing him.

The man leaning on the button was big but sagging in the middle, with a dark blue suit that didn't fit well. He was fat through the jowls, balding, had purple bags beneath his eyes, and looked one part unhappy and two parts basset hound.

Deputy Chief Harley Renz.

Quinn strode down the hall to the glass door and opened it.

Renz smiled at him and leaned back away from the buzzer.

In the abrupt silence, Quinn said, "Get in here."

Renz's smile didn't waver as he followed Quinn into the apartment.

Renz looked around, sniffed the air. "You're still smoking those illegal Cuban cigars."

"Venezuelan." Quinn motioned for Renz to sit in a small, decorative chair that no one found comfortable.

"If I had a beer," Renz said, "I'd tell you a story."

"Could it be told by phone?"

"You'd miss the inflections and facial expressions, and sometimes I use my hands like puppets."

Quinn went into the kitchen and opened the refrigerator. He found a very old can of beer near the back of the bottom shelf and opened it for Renz. He didn't bother with a glass.

Back in the living room, Quinn settled again into his armchair, held but didn't smoke his cigar, and watched Renz take a pull on the beer and make a face.

"That your breakfast?" Quinn asked.

"Brunch. This beer must be over five years old."

"Close."

"You still off the booze?" Renz asked.

"Down to just the occasional drink. I was never an alcoholic."

"Sure. Well, I can tell by this brew you aren't chugging it down soon as you buy it. Besides, I know you're off the sauce in any meaningful way. I checked."

"Must've been disappointed."

"Yeah. I wanted to be your enabler." Renz glanced about casually. "Pearl around?"

Another question whose answer you already know.

"Pearl doesn't live here."

"Oh. I forgot. Hey, you got another one of those cigars?"

"Only one. I'm gonna save it for later."

Renz shrugged. "I don't blame you. What the hell, all the

way from Venezuela." Another pull of beer. No face this time. The stale brew was growing on him. "Reason I asked about Pearl is I thought she might be interested in hearing this, too."

"I'll pass it on, but without the hand puppetry."

Renz looked around. "Not a bad apartment, but it smells like it could use a good cleaning. And it looks like it was decorated by Rudyard Kipling. Needs a woman's touch." He pointed toward a framed print near the old fireplace that wasn't usable. "Ducks flying in formation in front of a sunset. That one never goes out of style."

"I hope this is a one-beer story," Quinn said.

"Ah! Your tactful way of suggesting I get to the point."

"Get to the point."

Renz leaned closer in the tiny chair that looked as if it might break under his weight. "Dead women are the point. Two of them." He lowered his voice conspiratorially, as if they might be overheard. "Only you and I know about them now, plus a few trusted allies in the NYPD."

"And the killer."

"Did I say they were killed?" Renz shrugged. "Well, I'll let you make up your mind. The first was Janice Queen, here on the West Side. The second Lois Ullman. Both single, attractive, in their thirties, brunettes—what you might call the same type."

"So you think it was the same killer?"

"Oh, yes. Both women were drowned in their bathtubs, and there were traces of the tape that was used to bind and gag them beforehand. Then they were dismembered with surgical precision, their body parts stacked in the tubs in the same ascending order: torsos, thighs, calves, arms, and heads. The killer ran the showers, using whatever liquid shampoos or other cleaning agents were available on the body parts, until every visible trace of blood disappeared down the drains, leaving only the pale remains of the victims." Renz leaned back. "I see I have your rapt attention."

"Rapt," Quinn admitted, and drew thoughtfully on the cigar, feeling like a character in a Kipling story.

"The killer sent me a brief note, taunting several of our city's homicide detectives, even included your name. I guess he didn't know you retired. He assured me there would be more such victims."

"If anybody in the NYPD knows this," Quinn said, "it's sure to explode in the media soon like a hand grenade."

"We need to be ready for that."

"We?"

"I've decided you are the man," Renz said. "Serial killers are your specialty. You brought down the Night Prowler, and you can bring down whatever the media decide to call this sick creep."

"You left out the part about me being retired."

"I can work it out so you and your team will be doing work for hire. It'll be the way you like it, with all the resources of the NYPD at your disposal, through me, and all the advantages of working outside the department."

Quinn knew what Renz meant—the advantages of being able, if necessary, to work outside the law.

"Who's on my team?" Quinn asked.

"The same people who helped you nail the Night Prowler. Pearl and Fedderman."

"Pearl's working as a bank guard. Fedderman's living down in Florida, learning how to play golf."

"They'll say yes to you, Quinn. Just like you'll say yes to me." Renz waved an arm toward the window that looked out on the sidewalk. "Ever notice how much that ironwork resembles prison bars?"

"Never." Quinn looked at Renz through a haze of cigar smoke. "You thought you'd be chief by now."

"Instead I was demoted, but I'm back up to deputy chief."

"I heard. Also heard that's as far as you're going."

"I'm like you, Quinn. I don't quit. I don't stop climbing. What the hell else is there in life? I think you understand."

"Sure. We nail this sicko, and you get the credit and promotion. Life's been breathed back into your career."

"And you save the lives of the killer's future victims."

"Don't go altruistic on me, Harley."

"Well, okay. Then your answer is yes."

"Was that a question? I didn't hear a question."

"Since we both know the answer, a question isn't necessary."

"Have you talked to Pearl or Fedderman?"

Renz smiled. "I thought I'd let you do that. One way or another, you can talk anybody into anything."

"Not Pearl," Quinn said.

Renz thought about that and nodded.

"I'll talk to them," Quinn said. "But no promises."

"Good!" Renz was careful to place his beer can on the table where it would leave a ring, then stood up. "I'll get the murder books to you, then try to find you some office space near the closest precinct house. Something without dust and mold where you won't feel at home."

Quinn didn't get up. Far too busy with his cigar.

At the door, Renz paused. "I'm serious about nailing this asshole, Quinn, or I wouldn't have put a hellhound like you on his track. We've both seen a lot, but mother of God, if you'd seen those two women . . ."

"Is this where you cross yourself?" Quinn asked.

"Oh, I don't blame you for being skeptical, keeping in mind your devious nature and coarse cynicism." Renz bowed his head, closed his eyes, and for a second Quinn thought he actually might cross himself.

"You do compassion really well."

Renz gave him a sad and sickly smile. "We're gonna find out how well you do it."

When Renz was gone, Quinn settled back in his chair to finish his cigar before he phoned Pearl and Fedderman.

He glanced over at the print of ducks flying in a tight V formation against a vivid sunset and decided he still liked it.

The cigar was only half gone when he picked up the phone.

3

"Something's different," Pearl said.

"You took a lot of the furniture with you," Quinn said. "I had to move a few things around." He was seated in his leather armchair, not smoking a cigar.

Pearl was in the chair she used to sit in all the time, but it was on the other side of the room now. She had on jeans and a jacket this morning, Saturday, when the bank was closed. Her hair was blacker than anything Quinn had ever seen. Raven-colored, he guessed they called it. Not much makeup, if any, but still her dark eyes and lips were in sharp contrast to her pale skin. "You redecorated," she said.

"More like made do."

"I smell cigar smoke, Quinn."

"I have one infrequently."

"Not good for you."

You not being here isn't good for me. "I stay within limits."

"Not like you." She sat back and smiled with her large, perfectly aligned, very white teeth. "So what did you want to see me about?"

"Harley Renz came by yesterday and talked to me."

Her smile disappeared. "He still such an asshole?"

"More than ever. I was thinking he should be our boss again."

Pearl gave him an odd look, as if he'd just spoken in an unfamiliar language.

"That's not gonna happen," she said. "But go ahead, try to talk me into it."

He told her what Renz had said, watching her closely as he described what the killer had done to his victims. The odd look never completely left her face.

"What if I say I want no part of this?" she asked, when he was finished.

"I forge ahead with Fedderman. He wasn't cut out for golf in Florida. Last time I talked to him on the phone he said the game was driving him crazy."

"And you think he'll throw away his irons and woods and fly up here and join forces with you and Renz to hunt down a serial killer?"

"That's his real game," Quinn said, "not bogies and birdies. It's yours, too. Not standing around Fourth National—"

"Fifth."

"—with a gun you'll never fire."

"And never want to fire. Fedderman will tell you exactly what I'm going to tell you."

"His wife left him, you know."

"I know. Last year."

"He's lonely."

"How do you know?"

"I know."

Pearl looked away from him. "Don't try that crap with me, Quinn."

"Well, think about it before you give me a definite answer."

"Okay. I've thought about it. Answer's no. There's a time for everything, Quinn, and the time for us to track a killer who slices and dices his victims is way past."

"You have to feel for those women."

She let out a long sigh, he thought a bit dramatically. "Feeling. That's something else I'm past."

"Pearl—"

"I'm content, Quinn. Screw happiness. Contentment is enough. I get up and get through my days in a pleasant enough way, do my chores, live my life, not pulled this way and that like a . . . I don't know what."

"Like you were with me?"

"Yeah. Like that. I need to be self-sufficient, Quinn. So do you. That's why we didn't make it together. Why we shouldn't work together. I want no part of Renz's operation."

"Sounds almost final."

She smiled and stood up from her chair, then walked over and leaned down so she could kiss his forehead. "What a hard case you are, Quinn."

"You, too."

She didn't deny it.

He watched her walk out the door.

Before calling Fedderman in Florida, Quinn fired up a cigar and sat down at the desk in the spare bedroom that had become his den.

He leaned back and listened to the phone ringing in what was probably an empty condo in Boca something or other, Fedderman being out on the golf course, dazed and chasing a little white ball in the sun.

He was about to hang up when Fedderman picked up.

"Quinn?"

"How'd you know, Feds?"

"Caller ID. There's a widow I'm trying to avoid." Fedderman had been alone since his wife left. Their grown kids had moved out several years before. If Quinn remembered right, the girl was working in Philadelphia; her brother was one of those people who never wanted to leave college and was away somewhere on a scholarship working on yet another degree.

Quinn propped his cigar in the square glass ashtray on the desk corner. The ashtray was from the old Biltmore Hotel, maybe a collector's item. "I thought you'd be out on the golf course."

"I gave up golf. It was driving me insane. Now I'm deep-sea fishing, but that's driving me nuts, too. You ever see the shit you pull out of the ocean? Most of it doesn't even look like fish."

"Harley Renz came to see me yesterday."

"He still such an asshole?"

"That's what Pearl asked. The answer's yes."

"How is Pearl? You two still—?"

"We're not together. She's still Pearl."

"Hmm. Who did the leaving?"

"Pearl."

"Hmm. So what'd Renz want?"

Quinn told him.

"I'm in," Fedderman said.

Quinn was surprised by how quickly the answer had come. He'd thought Fedderman liked at least some part of retirement and would prefer it to looking at dead bodies and maybe being shot at.

"So when can I expect you?" Quinn asked.

"Soon as I can catch a flight to New York. That's the thing about condo living, you can turn the key in the lock and leave. Don't have to worry about the weeds taking over the lawn. I'm looking forward to seeing you and Pearl."

"Pearl's not in."

"You serious?" Fedderman sounded amazed.

"She said she's happy being a bank guard."

"Banks don't need guards. She knows that. Time I get to New York she'll have changed her mind."

"Pearl doesn't change her mind."

"She did about you."

Quinn felt a stab of annoyance. On the other hand, this was what he liked about Fedderman. They'd worked together a long time and were completely honest with each other. Fedderman had a way of driving to the truth and to hell with the cost.

"I'll call you when I get into town," Fedderman said. "Meantime, you work on Pearl."

He hung up before Quinn could reply.

Quinn replaced the receiver in its cradle and picked up his cigar from the ashtray on the desk. It had gone out. He relit it and settled back in his chair, thinking about what Fedderman had said. Thinking about Pearl. He'd worked with her, slept with her, lived with her, knew her.

Pearl doesn't change her mind.

He watched the smoke rise like a spirit and catch a draft up near the ceiling.

Pearl doesn't change her mind back.

4

Ida Ingrahm had a date.

Normally she wouldn't have made one with somebody she'd just met in a bar, but Jeff was different.

No, *really* different.

Seated at her mirror in her West Side apartment, she smiled at her reflection. Not *un*attractive, she thought. Full face with dark brown hair worn in bangs that made it look fuller. Not fat, mind you. And the rest of her was slim, except she didn't have much of a waist. Small breasts, legs okay. Especially with the right shoes.

Why do I have to appraise myself like this?

Ida knew the answer. Once they'd slept with her, men tended not to stick around. And she was way, way over thirty now. On the slide.

Time to panic?

She gave her reflection a brighter smile and decided, not yet. Hope lived. It wasn't that she wanted to get married. A lasting relationship was her goal. Modest enough, she thought. She saw other people achieve them. Meanwhile, life wasn't so terrible.

She liked her job as graphic designer for Higher Corporate Image, a company that produced promotional and motivational material for retail chains. It paid on the low side, if you didn't figure bonuses that were no sure thing, but there was a future. There was no glass ceiling at HCI. She could see her life ten years out, and it was okay, and would be better than okay if she had somebody steady. Somebody who cared about her.

She could learn to care about him.

I could learn . . . Stupid attitude.

Her smile faded, and for an instant her blue eyes did flash panic. Perhaps that was her problem, why men left her; her desperation shone through. Thirty-eight and alone in New York—scary. Then again, she knew there were millions of unhappy Midwestern housewives who'd give up their drudge lives in a New York minute for her situation.

Independence! Wa-hoo! She told herself, *Quit being such a wimp.*

She put on a sapphire pendant with a long silver chain that formed a V so her neck looked longer, her face thinner. Then she unfastened the top button of her blouse to reveal a suggestion of cleavage that wasn't there.

She wasn't a wimp. She was doing just fine, sticking in the big city, date with a guy like Jeff, living the life unlike the one she would have led back in Fort Taynor, Arkansas.

She'd thought she'd gotten rid of her southern accent completely, but Jeff had picked up on it right away and said he found it charming. Some of the other women in Loiter, the lounge where a crowd younger than Ida hung out, had glanced with envy at her, seeing her with Jeff. He was easily the best-looking man in the place, and he hadn't come in with a bunch of leering buddies whose goal for the evening was to score. He was nicely dressed in a dark blue suit that looked expensive. He was even the kind of guy who wore cuff links.

Nobody back in Fort Taynor wore cuff links.

She fumbled trying to fasten the clasp on her knockoff

retro wristwatch, and almost dropped it when the intercom buzzed.

Ida squinted at the watch's tiny face. It was difficult to make out the time without her reading glasses.

Almost seven o'clock. Jeff was early. If it was Jeff.

She gave a final try to engage the miniature latch of the watch's silver-plated chain, and smiled in surprise when she was successful. A good omen? She hesitated, considering slipping into her high-heel pumps, then padded in her nylon feet toward the intercom. If it was Jeff, she'd have enough time to put on her shoes while he was coming upstairs.

A final glance in the mirror behind the sofa.

She winked at herself and whispered, "Hot!" Letting her tongue show.

Believing it a little.

As she moved toward the intercom, her gaze roamed around the tiny apartment, hoping it was neat enough, clean enough.

Being judged. Always being judged.

She pressed the button and tried to sound casual and sexy. "Who's there?"

"Jeff Davis."

Ida decided to hold her silence and simply buzz him in. Not make herself seem too interested and available. Too eager.

Be cool. Like he is.

As she struggled into her shoes that for some reason seemed too small, she imagined him standing in the elevator, rising to her floor.

One of her toenails that needed trimming cut painfully into the toe next to it.

Damn it! Feet swollen again. Should have taken a water pill.

The left shoe wasn't completely on, and she almost turned an ankle, as she hurried to answer his knock.

5

Renz was true to his word. Always a bad sign.

He'd found them office space on West Seventy-ninth Street, not far from the two-oh precinct on West Eighty-second. It had been used as a child welfare reporting center until the city budget had forced its closure. On one side of the old brick building was a dental clinic, Nothing but the Tooth. Renz had laughed about that one over the phone when he called to send Quinn to the address, thinking it a riot that a cop shop should share the building with a dentist with a sense of humor. Quinn didn't think dentists should joke about their work.

The entrances to the two office suites faced each other across a cracked concrete stoop, three steps up from the sidewalk. Quinn and Fedderman didn't know what the dentist's digs looked like, but their "suite" consisted of two adjoining rooms and a half bath. Gluts of truncated cable and smaller wiring protruded like weird high-tech vegetables out of the hardwood floor, Quinn guessed for phones and computers. Ghastly illumination was provided by dangling flourescent fixtures.

"We'll get you desks and stuff tomorrow," Renz had assured Quinn.

That had been two days ago. Quinn and Fedderman were still working out of Quinn's apartment, or sometimes the claustrophobic room Fedderman had rented in a residence hotel in the Nineties.

They were in Quinn's den today, the contents of the murder files arranged in something like chronological order before them on the floor. Quinn was seated in his desk chair, which he'd rolled out from behind the desk, leaning out over the mess on the carpet with his elbows on his knees, gazing down like God at His miscreants. Fedderman was sitting on the floor with his back against the wall. He'd become almost bald on top, his graying hair too long on the sides and curling over his ears. His pants were wrinkled, and his brown suit coat was wadded in a chair. Fedderman had no respect for clothes. They didn't like him, either. He was tall and narrow-shouldered, and nothing seemed to fit his thin, awkward body, with the potbelly and abnormally long arms.

"What we know," Quinn said, "is both victims were brunettes, in their thirties, attractive though not raving beauties. They both were drowned before they were butchered. No signs of sexual activity. No semen found in the bodies or anywhere at the scenes."

"Probably untaped after death," Fedderman said. "He wouldn't want them splashing all over the place in the bathtub while he was holding them under."

"And he took the used tape with him."

"Neatnik," Fedderman said.

"Trauma to the heads of both victims before death."

Fedderman nodded and nudged one of the morgue shots with the unpolished toe of his brown shoe. "Sequences probably the same. No indications of forced entry into either apartment. So he's let in, whaps them in the head, and undresses them and tapes them up while they're unconscious. Then he carries them into the bathroom and places them in the tub. He makes sure the stopper's engaged and turns on the water."

"That's probably when they come to," Quinn said.

Fedderman thought about that. "Yeah, the cold water. Then they realize where they are, the fix they're in. Jesus!"

"When the water's high enough, he turns it off and drowns them," Quinn said.

"Thank God for that, considering what comes next."

"He wouldn't let them just sit there and drown. Their heads would be too high, anyway, and he wouldn't want them struggling, even taped tight like they were. They'd still be able to splash around some. Maybe work loose the tape over their mouths and make some noise."

"So he holds them under," Fedderman said.

"Then, when they're dead, he removes the tape and uses the tools he's brought with him to start carving."

"Ignores the knives in the kitchen?"

"Has so far."

"Must have brought his tools in a box or a bag of some sort."

"Uh-huh. Maybe somebody noticed. Something to check."

"Gets together all his cleaning agents first," Fedderman said. "Before he starts to carve. No blood in the kitchen. None in the cabinets where the stuff would have been kept."

"Yeah, sounds right. He uses the shower curtain to protect the floor, so he won't be walking or kneeling in blood while he's . . ." Quinn paused and gave his cigar a George Burns look, even the faint smile. It occurred to him how good it felt to be having one of these give-and-take conversations with Fedderman again, homing in on the facts, or at least the hypothesis, and nudging ideas alive. "No, Feds, he's got to undress. He'd be working nude, even before he drowns them. Wouldn't want to get his clothes wet. Somebody might notice when he leaves."

Fedderman nodded. "Shower curtain keeps whatever mess there is outside the tub contained. I'd say he opens up his victims and sits there a while and lets them bleed out in the tub, much as possible without a heartbeat, then washes the blood down the drain and begins his carving. Probably just gets residue blood on his hands and arms, maybe upper body; easy to wash off, while he's cleaning the body parts."

"Then he cleans his tools."

"After stacking the severed body parts in the tub." Fedderman looked disgusted, maybe a little scared, his features as mismatched as his clothes. "What the hell have we gotten ourselves into, Quinn?"

"Nothing we haven't been in before."

Or is it?

"Body parts stacked exactly the same way," Quinn said, pressing on, "in the same order."

"And everything washed so clean," Fedderman said. "Like maybe he was trying to wash away his sins."

Take me to the river . . . Quinn sat back in his chair. "It's still too early to get inside this one's head. We can't make any assumptions. Other than he's one sick cookie, and he's got a thing about brunettes."

"Lots of us have a thing about brunettes."

"I talked to the ME," Quinn said. "Near as he could make out, sharp knives, and probably a cleaver or hatchet of some kind, were used to disassemble these women. But some body parts would be too difficult to remove with a knife or cleaver. The severed large bone ends suggest a saw was used. Because of the finely serrated blade, most likely a power saw."

"Dangerous to use one of those around water, even a portable with a battery. Might get your ass electrocuted."

"Still, my guess is he used a portable. They're quieter. And they make them plenty powerful enough for the job now. He'd be using it after the water was gone from the tub, and most of the blood and other body fluids were drained from his victims."

"Like in a butcher shop." Fedderman made his disgusted face again.

"Exactly like, Feds. He did butcher them." Quinn sighed and let his gaze roam over the photographs, statements, and reports arranged on the carpet. "Apparently the two victims didn't know each other and had no friends or acquaintances in common."

"That's ground we can go over again," Fedderman said. "They might have frequented the same bar or restaurant, shopped at the same store."

"One lived on the East Side," Quinn pointed out, "one on the West."

"They had one thing in common, anyway. The killer."

"Yeah, they—"

The phone rang, interrupting Quinn.

He scooted with his feet so his chair rolled closer to the desk, then stretched out an arm and lifted the black plastic receiver. Said, "Quinn."

After a while: "Uh-huh." He rolled the chair even closer so he could reach a pen and make a note on a pad on the desk corner. "You sure about the address?"

Apparently, whoever had called was sure.

"We're leaving now," Quinn said, and hung up.

Fedderman knew better than to try a guess at what the conversation was about. Quinn was always the same on the phone, calm, almost mechanical. He'd tell Fedderman when he was ready.

"Better straighten your tie, Feds," Quinn said, standing up from his chair. "That was Renz. We've got a third victim, woman named Ida Ingrahm, 197 West Eighty-second Street, apartment six-B."

Fedderman jotted down the name and address in his own note pad. "Not far from here." He stood up slowly, unfolding in mismatched sections, gave his tie a tug, and shrugged into his wrinkled suit coat.

He pulled down his right shirtsleeve and rebuttoned its cuff. Something about the way he wrote, or maybe the cheap shirts he wore, made his right cuff button always come undone. He was adjusting the baggy coat so his shoulder holster didn't show, when he suddenly stopped and stared at Quinn.

"You positive about that location?"

"I had Renz repeat it," Quinn said. "Pearl's old address."

6

The victim's was a small, corner apartment that looked a lot neater than when Pearl had lived in it. For one thing, it was completely painted. Pearl had always been in the process of painting the place, never finishing. There were no newspapers or magazines strewn on the floor, and the furniture looked . . . well, arranged.

There was also a disturbing odor. Quinn had encountered it before, but not to this degree. So had Fedderman.

"Smells like a butcher shop," Fedderman said. "Lots of fresh blood, fresh meat."

"He is a butcher," Quinn said.

"A real one, maybe."

The thought had occurred to Quinn. "He'd have the skills, as well as the tools of his trade."

There was a uniformed cop in the apartment, standing and staring out the window. He hadn't turned around when Quinn and Fedderman entered. Now he did. He was a middle-aged guy with a gray military haircut, his cap in his hands, over his crotch. His face was so white Quinn thought the man might faint any second. Quinn and Fedderman flashed the shields Renz had provided, and the uniform pointed toward a short hall that Quinn knew led to the bathroom and only bedroom.

"Maybe you oughta sit down," Quinn said.

"I can stand okay," the cop said. Point of pride.

Quinn nodded and led the way down the hall. He and Fedderman both slipped latex gloves on their hands as they walked. Quinn was a little surprised by how effortless and automatic it was, an old task still familiar.

There was no way to prepare for what was in the bathroom. In the center of the tub, Ida Ingrahm's head lay propped on its side on the stack of torso and limbs. Her damp brown hair had been smoothed back so her face was visible. Her eyes were open, darkened by blood from capillaries ruptured as she'd drowned, but they didn't so much look dead as expectant. As if she'd been waiting for somebody to come into the bathroom. Maybe Quinn and Fedderman.

"Some sight," said a voice behind them.

Quinn turned and saw Nift from the Medical Examiner's office, not one of his favorite people. Nift was a pigeon-chested little guy with thick black hair that dangled in short bangs high on his bulging forehead. He had an imperious attitude, a smart mouth, and appeared to be strutting even when standing still. Always a meticulous dresser, he seemed to be dolling up even more for his work. Today he was wearing a black three-button suit, white shirt, and a black silk tie. Quinn thought he looked like Napoleon gussied up as a mortician.

"Some stench," Fedderman said.

"Smells something like the morgue on a busy day," Nift said. "I knew you guys were on the way, so I didn't touch anything, just tippy-toed in and looked at the poor woman. I determined that she was dead."

"Cut up like the others?" Fedderman asked.

"I wouldn't know if she had a sense of humor," Nift said.

"I might throw you into that tub with her," Quinn said.

Nift stared at him. "I believe you just might, Captain."

"Maybe you oughta give us a straight answer," Fedderman said.

"As near as I can tell, without having moved the body parts, she seems to have been dissected in the same manner as the two previous victims. She also fits the killer's type."

"Now you're doing detective work," Quinn said.

Nift smiled. "My weakness. Too many TV cop shows, I suppose. But I really can't tell you much more than the obvious until after the postmortem." He shrugged. "Cut, hack, saw."

"Drowned first," Fedderman said.

"Yes, I can about guarantee you that. Just like the first two. And like with the first two, I doubt if there'll be any indications of recent sexual activity." He smiled. "Wanna take a closer look?"

"We'll take your word for it," Quinn said. "Was her hair pulled back from her face like that when you arrived?"

"Sure was. Just as the killer wanted you to find it. Or maybe it was simply a gentle gesture after the beheading."

There was a flash behind them. The police photographer had arrived, armed with a digital camera about the size of a cigarette lighter. There were three techs beyond him, nosing around the living room for prints or stray hairs or dying messages or whatever. Quinn figured they wouldn't find much, if anything, of use. This was a clean and careful killer they were hunting. Cleanliness and caution were deep in his methodology and would be essential in his psychology. The police profiler should be having a ball with this guy.

"I'll finish my preliminary," Nift said, "then get out of the way."

Quinn and Fedderman moved aside so Nift could squeeze back into the almost sanitarily clean bathroom. Chromed faucet handles glittered. The ceramic tiles gleamed. Admirable.

Except for what was in the tub.

"Let's go into the bedroom," Quinn said.

Fedderman followed. "We'll look for clues where it's less crowded and the light's better."

Quinn was glad Fedderman was recovering his cop's sense of humor that helped to keep him sane. Like Nift, maybe, only without the mean streak.

Fedderman knew why Quinn wanted to examine the bedroom—to get a better sense of Ida Ingrahm, who she was before she became victim number three.

The bedroom was neatly arranged, the bed still made. The room didn't seem to have been touched by the crime except for the odor. Their bed had been against the other wall when Quinn and Pearl had slept here. He tried not to think about that.

Ida Ingrahm seemed to have fit the mold of thousands, maybe millions, of single women in New York. On her dresser was the framed family photo, a man and woman and two teenage girls, posed smiling in front of a lake ringed with trees that looked about to surrender their leaves to autumn. The females in the photo looked quite a bit alike. Quinn figured he was looking at Mom, Dad, Sis, and the future murder victim. There was nothing in the smiling faces of either of the daughters that portended an early, violent death.

Ida's closet held an assortment of mix-and-match black clothing, a rack of shoes. Near the foot of the bed was a small TV on a white wicker stand. There was a bookshelf that held mostly self-help and diet books, a few paperback mysteries. On the lamp table next to the bed, a pair of glasses was folded atop a Stuart Kaminsky novel. Pearl used to read Kaminsky's series about a cop named Lieberman, and Quinn wondered if she'd left behind the book when she moved out. It bothered him that the dead woman had read the same book as Pearl, maybe even turning down page corners the way Pearl did to keep her place. He went to the glasses and, careful not to touch anywhere that might obscure prints, examined the lenses. Single power and weak. They looked like drugstore reading glasses.

"Lots of shoes," Fedderman said behind Quinn, still staring into the closet.

"Lots of women have lots of shoes," Quinn said, glancing over at him. When he turned back, he saw something he hadn't noticed before because it was mostly hidden behind the lamp base. A cell phone.

Maybe with speed dial numbers, information, a log of recent numbers called or received. Maybe with a recorder, a calculator, a digital camera with a stored photo of the killer. Well, who knew, these days? It looked like an ordinary cell phone, but who could tell? Quinn couldn't keep up with technology.

He left the bedroom and went halfway down the hall, then summoned one of the techs, a bright looking young guy with dark-rimmed glasses and a bow tie. Quinn had always thought that men who wore bow ties were a separate breed, understood only by themselves. Probably had a secret handshake.

Like Quinn and Fedderman, the bow-tied tech was wearing white evidence gloves. Unlike Quinn and Fedderman, he was under thirty and would understand cell phone technology.

"Do what you want with this so we can check out any information stored," Quinn said, pointing to the phone.

The tech nudged the phone with a gloved fingertip, then began dusting for prints.

After a few seconds, he looked up at Quinn, smiling. "Something you should know about this phone, sir."

Quinn liked it when a tech called him "sir." Very rare. He put it down to youth. "There something different about it?"

"Yeah."

What happened to "sir"?

The tech carefully lifted the phone between thumb and middle finger, then lightly squeezed. It began to buzz.

Quinn was just about to tell the tech to let him answer the phone, when the buzzing stopped.

"It's not a phone, sir. Only looks like one. It's a vibrator."

"That's to let you know you got a call when you don't want people to hear it ring," Fedderman said.

"It's not a phone. Really, it's a vibrator."

"Huh?" Fedderman said, finally getting it, interested.

The kid pushed another button and the buzzing got louder. The little cell phone became a blur.

"Whoa!" Fedderman said.

Quinn didn't know what to say.

"It's not the kind of vibrator you'd use on your sore back," the tech said. He was still smiling, but looking thoughtful. "I guess it's so women can carry it around, maybe use it when they travel, and it won't draw attention and embarrass them if security or customs root through their luggage."

"What a great idea," Fedderman said.

The tech turned off the mock phone and placed it back down exactly in its original position. "I think I know whose prints'll be all over this for everyone to see."

"She's beyond embarrassment," Quinn said.

"What are you doing in my bedroom?" demanded a woman's voice.

Startled, all three men turned to look.

Pearl.

"Who's guarding the bank?" Fedderman asked, after Pearl had been filled in and had looked around the apartment. They were outside on West Eighty-second, standing in the shade near the building's concrete stoop.

"Someone else," Pearl said. "I'm on a leave of absence."

Quinn looked closely at her. She was simply Pearl. Compact, buxom, and beautiful. She had on her usual deep red lipstick today, so stark against her pale complexion that her generous mouth seemed to have been painted on by some manic, inspired artist. With her large dark eyes, perfect white teeth, black hair, she was so vivid she often reminded Quinn of some kind of cartoon character. But she was real. Quinn knew she was real.

"Renz call you?" he asked.

"Even before he called you."

"I thought you weren't interested in this case."

"This sick asshole killed somebody in my old apartment. Somebody who might just as easily have been me. That makes it personal."

"Also makes it coincidental," Fedderman said.

"Doesn't it, though?" Pearl said.

A brisk summer breeze kicked up and moved a crumpled white takeout bag along the sidewalk. Quinn stood his ground, merely lifting a foot to let the bag pass and continue along the pavement.

"We need you, Pearl," Fedderman said.

She smiled. "Thanks, Feds."

"You one of us again, Pearl?" Quinn asked.

"The smart one," she said.

They spent the next several hours talking to Ida's neighbors, some of whom remembered Pearl. No one had seen or heard anything unusual. Those who knew Ida Ingrahm said she was quiet, and worked as some kind of artist or graphic designer at a company in midtown. She rode the subway back and forth to work.

All the detective team's time and effort left them right back where they'd started hours ago, standing on the sidewalk just outside the building. Ida Ingrahm's remains had long since been removed, and the crime scene unit had pulled out. A uniform remained in the hall outside the apartment, with its door yellow-taped, and would be relieved in a few hours by another cop who would remain there all night. Sometimes criminals really did return to the scene of the crime. Especially if they forgot something incriminating.

Quinn unwrapped a Cuban cigar and lit it. The butcher shop stench had stayed with him and become taste. The acrid scent of burning tobacco helped. A few people walking past on the sidewalk glared at him as he exhaled a large puff of smoke. *So arrest me.* Neither Pearl nor Fedderman complained; they'd been upstairs like Quinn. It seemed to them that the entire building smelled like a slaughterhouse, but Ida's neighbors didn't seem to notice. Maybe the death stench had grown on them slowly, and they became accustomed to it.

Or maybe it was mental. The other tenants hadn't been in Ida's apartment to bid her farewell.

Ida nude. A three-dimensional Picasso. In pieces like a disconnected puzzle doll, chalk white and eerily pure in her drained bathtub.

Ida clean.

Her sins washed away?

Quinn knew better, but he wished for Ida that it worked that way. He felt an overbearing sadness not only for her but for himself and the entire human race.

The things we do to each other . . .

"You cab over here?" he asked Pearl.

Pearl nodded. Did a thing with her lips so she could take in some secondhand smoke.

"That's our unmarked across the street," Quinn said.

"I know," Pearl said. "It's the only car that looks like it should be wearing a fedora."

"Since you're on the case, come with us back to the office and we'll bring you up to speed."

"We have an office?"

"Such as it is," Fedderman said. "And not far from here."

"Has it got a coffee machine?"

"No."

"Then it isn't an office."

"Let's move," Quinn said, already starting to cross the street.

"Vroom! Vroom!" Pearl said behind him.

Smart-mouthing me already, Quinn thought. Hiding behind her wisecracks where no one could touch her soft spots. *Well, who doesn't? At least sometimes?*

A car pulled out of a parking space and had to brake hard to keep from hitting the three of them. The driver leaned on the horn. Pearl made an obscene gesture, otherwise ignoring the man.

Quinn thought this wasn't going to be easy.

So why, whenever he looked at Pearl, did he feel like smiling?

7

The office: three gray steel desks (as if Renz had known Pearl would be joining them); four chairs; a file cabinet; and a wooden table with a lamp, computer, and printer on it. The printer was the kind that copied and faxed and scanned and did who knew what-all that Quinn would probably never figure out. The table was directly over one of the outcroppings of wire on the floor, everything mysteriously connected to it via another tangle of wire emanating from computer and printer.

"This thing work?" Pearl asked, walking over to the computer. It was an old Hewlett-Packard, gigantic.

Quinn pulled a cord that opened some blinds, letting natural light in to soften the fluorescent glare. "Yeah. And some computer whiz from the NYPD's gonna set us up with more of them. Update our system. We're coded into the NYPD and various data banks. Codes and passwords are on a piece of paper under the lamp base."

Pearl grinned, the brightest thing in the gloomy office. "Everybody hides their passwords under the lamp base. First place burglars and identity thieves look."

"Nobody's gonna break in here," Fedderman said. "And

far as I'm concerned, somebody else is welcome to my identity."

Quinn settled into the chair behind his desk and rocked slightly back and forth. The chair squeaked. The other two chairs at the desks were identical—cheap black vinyl swivel chairs on rollers. The fourth chair was straight-backed and wooden, presumably for an eventual suspect.

Pearl and Fedderman rolled the other two chairs up close and sat down. Quinn's desk was strategically placed directly beneath one of the fluorescent fixtures, so there was plenty of light even if it was ghastly. He slid open one of the rattling steel drawers and handed Pearl the murder books on Janice Queen and Lois Ullman.

"You can look them over now, if you want," he said, "then take them home and study them."

Pearl rested the files on her lap, and opened the top one. Quinn watched her scan each piece of paper or photograph inside, then move on and repeat the process. A tune from *Phantom of the Opera* was seeping over from the Nothing but the Tooth side of the building. *Music to fill molars by?* That, the hum and swish of traffic outside, and Pearl leafing through the files, were the only sounds for a long time.

Then Fedderman said, " 'Music of the Night.' "

Pearl, not looking up, said, "Uh-huh."

Along with a ballpoint pen and the glass ashtray with BILTMORE HOTEL on it, was a telephone on Quinn's desk. It wasn't a rotary, but it was old and black with a base and receiver.

And it was ringing.

Quinn lifted the receiver and pressed it to his ear.

The caller was Nift, with a more detailed autopsy report.

"Death by drowning," he said. "Probably carved up by the same cutting instruments used on the previous victims. Looks like a power saw was used on the larger bones and tougher ligaments. Tightly serrated blade, like an electric jigsaw or maybe a circular. Her family should be glad she was dead at the time."

"A portable saw?"

"Could've been a portable. It'd almost have to be, wouldn't it, not to make too much noise? And they make them powerful these days."

"That's how we figure it," Quinn said.

"No signs of sexual activity of any kind around the genitals or on any of the body parts. No traces of semen anywhere at the scene. A residue of adhesive on ankles and arms, and around the mouth, from when the victim was taped in such a way that she wouldn't have been able to move anything but fingers and toes. In short, Ida Ingrahm died just like the first two victims. And she was a brunette, like the first two. If there was any doubt before that you're on the trail of a serial killer, there shouldn't be now. The beautiful if disassembled Ida was number three."

"You think it coulda been a doctor or a butcher? The way the work was done and he cleaned up after himself?"

"Coulda been almost anyone," Nift said. "It only took rudimentary knowledge, maybe gained from animals. Coulda been a fastidious janitor."

Quinn didn't say anything for a few seconds.

"Anything else I can help you with while I'm on the phone?" Nift asked.

"You called me," Quinn said. "Most of the time medical examiners wait for the detectives to call."

"I find this killer interesting," Nift said. "You know me, how I like to play cop. Also, I thought I should call and let you know there's a journalist from *City Beat* hot on this story. Woman named Cindy Sellers. She's a hard charger, and serial killers make for big news. These murders take 'if it bleeds it leads' to an extreme."

"I never heard of *City Beat*."

"It's fairly new, not much circulation yet. But you know

the way it works: One wolf gets the scent, then the whole pack's on the hunt."

Quinn knew. He thanked Nift, then hung up and relayed the information to Fedderman and Pearl.

"No surprise there," Pearl said. She leaned forward and placed the murder files on the desk, then rolled back a few feet in her chair so her gaze could take in both Quinn and Fedderman. "But there is something."

Quinn waited. "No dramatic pauses, Pearl. Please."

"I'm not being theatrical," she said. "I'm just thinking, trying to decide if it's plausible."

"Let us decide along with you," Fedderman said.

Pearl looked at Quinn. "I think the killer chose you as his opponent."

"That might be plausible," Quinn said, "except Renz did the choosing."

Pearl kept him trapped with her dark eyes, wouldn't let him go. "The last victim, Ida, was killed in my apartment. You think that's some wild coincidence?"

Quinn had to answer honestly. "No. But that doesn't nec-essarily lead me to your conclusion."

"It wouldn't me, either," Pearl said, "except for the vic-tims' last initials, in the order of their deaths: Janice Queen, Lois Ullman, Ida Ingrahm."

"*Q, U, I,*" Fedderman said, staring at Quinn. "Almost spells—"

"It does," Quinn said, standing up from behind the desk. He started to pace, but tripped over one of the wiring-clump mushrooms growing on the floor and almost fell.

"The next victim's name will start with an *N,*" Pearl said.

"She's right," Fedderman said.

Quinn didn't have to be told. Pearl wasn't always right, but almost always.

She was almost surely right this time: The killer was choos-ing victims whose last initials spelled out Quinn's name.

"Think we oughta tell the media?" Fedderman asked. "Be our asses if we don't."

"He's got a point," Pearl said. "Women with *N* surnames have a right to know."

Quinn picked up the phone again.

"Who you calling?" Fedderman asked.

"Renz. Then Nift. He knows a journalist who's already been on this, a woman named Cindy Sellers, with *City Beat*."

"Never heard of her or it," Fedderman said.

"You will after they scoop this story," Quinn said.

As he was pecking out Renz's number with his forefinger, Pearl got up from her chair and stood with her hands on her hips, looking around.

"We gotta get a coffee machine."

Pearl arrived at the office early the next morning with a sack containing a bag of gourmet ground Columbian beans, a pack of filters, and a brand-new Mr. Coffee that was still in the box.

Under her other arm were the murder files, which she'd taken home for a closer read last night.

She placed the Mr. Coffee on the computer table, the beans and filter next to it.

The files she laid on Quinn's desk. Ida Ingrahm's was on top.

"I wish you'd told me yesterday about that vibrator phone," Pearl said.

Quinn and Fedderman looked at each other. Fedderman, slumped in a chair in front of the desk, said, "Pearl, Pearl."

"I don't have one," she said, not blushing, "but I happen to know where they're sold. A little shop in the Village. Intimate Items."

"How would you know that, Pearl?" Fedderman asked.

"I shop there sometimes, asshole. The place isn't as

risqué as you might think. It's erotica that's mostly for women."

"Ah," Fedderman said, "no whips and chains."

"Well, some. But mostly stuff like those Dial In phones."

"Dial In?" Quinn asked.

"That's the brand name, even though they're not really phones and have a fake keypad. I haven't seen them anywhere but in that shop. We can check and see if they have a record of Ida buying one there, or maybe they'll recognize her photo."

"How would that help us?" Fedderman asked.

"She might not have been alone when she bought her phone."

Quinn tried not to smile. Pearl a step ahead of Fedderman. Old and familiar patterns taking form. They were again becoming a team.

"Drop Feds and me off at Ida Ingrahm's apartment," Quinn said, "and we'll reinterview some of her neighbors, see if anybody's memory can be jogged. Then you drive the unmarked down to . . . what's it?"

"Intimate Items," Fedderman reminded him.

"Yeah. Talk to the clerk, or whoever." He handed her a morgue photo of Ida Ingrahm. "Nift faxed this here this morning."

"It's a head shot," Fedderman said.

Pearl looked at him in disgust. "Jesus, Feds." Her expression was unchanging as she glanced at the photo. She reached for the murder files she'd laid on the desk. "I'll take photos of the other victims, too. Just in case."

"No coffee this morning?" Fedderman asked, looking over at the packages Pearl had piled on the computer table.

"No time," Pearl said. "You guys can make some tomorrow."

Quinn stood up from behind his desk .

"I'll drive," Pearl said, "since I'll be going on down to the Village."

"Seat's all the way back," Quinn said, "so I might as well drive to the apartment." *So we get there alive.*

He and Fedderman knew how Pearl drove—as if she'd learned by watching *The French Connection.*

Fedderman glanced over at Quinn, smiling slightly, but like Quinn, he held his silence.

Familiar patterns.

8

On the drive to Ida Ingrahm's apartment, Fedderman tried to talk Quinn into sending him along with Pearl to follow up on the cell phone lead. Quinn knew this would be more for Fedderman's amusement than anything else, so he'd nixed it and told Pearl to take the unmarked and return to pick them up later. So here Pearl was alone, without having to cope with Fedderman and vibrator cell phones simultaneously. Pearl considered it a gift.

Intimate Items was a block off Broadway, and wasn't the kind of blatant sex shop its name might suggest. The merchandise was varied but mostly ran toward sexy lingerie, massage potions, aphrodisiac incense, romantic CDs, and other mood makers. Pearl thought the mannequin in Intimate Items' display window was dressed more for a romantic night at the Hilton than a session at an S&M club. Satin rather than leather, lace rather than Velcro. Make the mannequin's see-through gown more opaque, her panties bikini instead of thong, and she might fit right in flaunting her stuff in the windows of midtown department stores.

Opening and closing the door set off a soft chime somewhere in the shop. A hidden sachet made the place smell faintly of cinnamon. The design and decor were those of an upscale boutique, racks of clothes down one side, harder merchandise and a sales counter on the other. Changing rooms and full-length triple mirrors up on a low, carpeted podium were at the far end. Vibrators were kept out of sight beneath the counter. The shop's customers were almost exclusively women.

At the moment, Pearl was the only customer.

A young, primly dressed woman in a high-necked white blouse, with a sweet face that looked swollen from too much sleep, smiled puffily at her from behind the glass counter.

"May I help you?"

"Cell phone vibrators," Pearl said.

The woman, maybe still in her twenties, appeared faintly surprised by Pearl's request. Then the puffy smile widened, doing something to her eyes and making her appear Asian. "Dial Ins?"

"Those are the ones."

"I'd like to help you, but you're too late."

"I'm not even forty," Pearl said.

The clerk ducked her head and looked embarrassed. "No, ma'am, I didn't mean that."

"I know," Pearl said, then dipped into her purse and flashed her shield. "My job infects people with a strange sense of humor."

"You think mine doesn't?" the clerk said, glancing at the badge before Pearl put it back out of sight.

"Point taken. What about those vibrators?"

"We haven't handled them for a few months. Not that they didn't sell, but we got a few customer complaints. Some people thought they'd also bought functional phones."

"Yuck," Pearl said.

"I thought the phone-vibrators were a great idea for the shop. They let you travel without being embarrassed by some security or customs character rooting through your luggage and coming across a vibrator he just *knew* wasn't for your stiff neck."

"Seems like an item that'd be right up your alley," Pearl agreed.

The woman frowned.

"A discreet, intimate item," Pearl explained.

The sales clerk seemed satisfied that Pearl hadn't been exercising cop humor.

"So you returned them to the manufacturer?" Pearl asked.

"Not actually. We sold them at wholesale price to Nuts and Bolts. It's a lounge on East Fifty-second. A pickup place but respectable. Lots of single professional women hang out there, the sort with jobs where they have to travel. The boss knows the lounge's owner, so that's where the cell phone vibrators went."

"How many?"

"Oh, two cases and a partial, about fifty of them. I bought one myself before we let them go. I think they're such a super idea. And they really do look like cell phones."

Just in case, Pearl showed the clerk photos of the first two victims, then the gruesome morgue shot of Ida Ingrahm, and asked if she recognized any of the women.

"I don't think so," the clerk said, swallowing. "But the first two look vaguely familiar. This last one, is she . . . ?"

"Dead," Pearl confirmed. "They all are."

The clerk's puffy features registered dismay. Was she about to cry? "God! That's horrible!"

"They're all victims of the same killer."

"That's why the first two look familiar. I must have seen them in the paper or on television news."

"Are you sure they never came in here? Maybe bought mock cell phones."

"Oh, I'm positive. I'm here during all our open hours, so I sold all the phones."

Pearl slid the photos back in her blazer pocket and thanked the woman for her time.

"May I interest you in anything else?" The clerk was sud-

denly very professional, a reaction to distance herself from
the Ida Ingrahm photo by grounding herself in the normal
world. "We have all sorts of products that aid in relationships with men."

"Thanks anyway," Pearl said. "I already carry a gun."

But as she left the shop, she glanced again at the display-
window mannequin in the transparent nightgown and thong
underwear.

She thought she could bring it off. Probably.

Nuts and Bolts was on the ground floor of a gray stone
office building, flanked by an office supply store and a mar-
itime insurance agency. It was closed, but it served food as
well as booze, and Pearl could see through the tinted glass
door that several people were bustling around inside in the
dimness, preparing for the lunch crowd.

She rapped on the glass with the cubic zirconium ring on
her right hand, making a lot of noise. The last guy she'd
dated had given her the ring, telling her it was diamond. It
turned out to be as genuine as he was.

A chubby, bald kid peered curiously through the glass at
her. He made exaggerated shrugging motions while he
shook his head back and forth violently to signal that the
restaurant-lounge was closed. He held up all his stubby fingers, then two, indicating that she should return at noon.

As he turned away, she rapped on the glass again and
pressed her shield to it.

He turned back, stared at the NYPD detective's badge,
then faded away in the dimness.

A few seconds later, the door was opened by a potbellied
man in a white T-shirt, wearing a stained white apron over
jeans. He was about forty, balding, jowly, and with a double
chin. Pearl guessed he was gaining middle-age weight steadily
and it would eventually catch up with his beer belly. He looked
somewhat like the kid who'd answered Pearl's knock, and

she wondered if they were father and son. His tired blue eyes moved up and down, taking in all five-foot-one of Pearl and registering nothing.

Thanks a lot.

"Something wrong?" he asked.

"You tell me." Pearl smiled when she said it, trying to steer the guy from neutral to friendly. Why make things difficult?

He did smile back, making him look younger and less fleshy, a glance at an earlier version that wasn't the kid who'd first come to the door.

"I don't think we've broken any laws," he said, wiping his hands on the apron and stepping back so she had room to enter.

"Maybe the soup yesterday," the kid said. He was leaning on a broom about ten feet away, grinning. He was wearing a black Mets sweatshirt with the sleeves cut off, baggy stained chinos, and looked as if he had an erection. Pearl felt alternately amused and flattered.

"Get back to work, Ernie," the potbellied guy said wearily.

Ernie kept his dreamy smile trained on Pearl for a full five seconds, then turned away and began sweeping. Pearl decided she kind of liked him.

"Is the owner around?" Pearl asked.

"I'm him," potbelly said. "Lou Sinclair."

"Good. I want to talk to you about vibrators that look like cell phones."

Ernie continued to sweep, but was moving toward them now so he could hear better.

"I bought those phones from somebody I know," Sinclair said. "Somebody honest. If they're stolen, neither one of us knows about it."

"Me, either," Pearl said.

"We get lots of traveling businesswomen in here. I let Victoria, my female night bartender, tell the ladies about the phones. If they're interested, she shows them one and maybe makes a sale."

"You sell a lot of them?"

"Yeah. I'm gonna try and get some more. Damned things really look like phones. You wouldn't believe it, but we had a woman here thought she could make a call and—"

"I believe it," Pearl said.

"Get busy, Ernie," Sinclair said. Ernie began sweeping harder, moving away from them this time.

"Victoria your only night bartender?"

"Her and me," Sinclair said. "She comes in at eight, and I'm here from nine to closing."

"How can I get in touch with her?"

"Easy. She's in the kitchen."

"She works days, too?"

"As well as nights? No, only the owner works those kinda hours. She came in to get her paycheck."

"Ah, my lucky day."

"Is it hers?"

"Far as I know. She's not in any kinda trouble. I just want to show both of you some photographs, see if you recognize any of the women in them, then talk to her about the phones. Maybe Ernie, too."

"Ernie goes home after we close for lunch and he's done busing tables. He's my brother's boy. A teen klutz. Knows from nothing."

"He's gotta grow up sometime," Pearl said.

Sinclair gave her a curious look, then said, "Wait here and I'll go get Victoria."

Pearl sat at the end of one of the booths, looking around. The floor was carpeted except where Ernie was diligently sweeping. There were round tables with white cloths, crystal chandeliers, a long bar inlaid with polished brass, fancy stools with high, curved backs. It wouldn't be a bad-looking place if they turned up the lights. Probably they didn't want passersby glancing in and seeing them cleaning up. Pearl couldn't read the lunch menu behind the bar, but it didn't look like much.

Sinclair returned within a few minutes with a tall, dark-haired woman in a tight tan pantsuit. Or maybe she wasn't so tall. She looked as if she'd just had her hair done, or overdone. It was piled improbably high and made her look as if she were about to play a country-western singer in a bad movie. When she was closer, she gazed with charcoal dark eyes from beneath dense bangs at Pearl.

Pearl introduced herself, then removed the photographs from her blazer pocket. "Ernie," she said, "put down your broom for a minute and come over here."

"Yes, ma'am." Still with the spacey smile. Did the kid ever stop grinning?

Pearl found the brightest spot on the table and spread out the photos. "Do any of these women look familiar?"

Ernie stopped smiling and pointed. "That's one's dead, ain't she?"

"She's dead, Ernie."

"Cool."

"Those two," Victoria said immediately, and pointed with a long red fingernail. "Janice and Lois. I don't know their last names. They come in here all the time."

"They who I think they are?" Sinclair asked.

"Depends," Pearl said.

"The women the Butcher killed?"

"Huh?" Victoria said.

"That's what people call him," Sinclair said, "the Butcher. Because of the way he carves up his victims and puts their parts on display. The meat. Don't you read the papers or watch the news?"

"No, I spend most of my time dealing drinks here. That's the only way I know Janice and Lois. They work in the neighborhood and come in sometimes in the evening."

"Together?"

Victoria wrinkled her nose, thinking. "No, I can't recall ever seeing them together. Or even here at the same time. But I could be wrong."

"I don't think I've ever seen them," Sinclair said.

"Ernie?" Pearl asked.

"I don't know any of 'em," Ernie said. "That dead one's gross."

"Yeah. There oughta be a law." Pearl looked at Victoria. "Ever sell either of them a cell phone?"

Victoria appeared startled behind her bangs. She glanced worriedly at Sinclair.

"It's okay," he said.

"I sold both of them cell phones," Victoria said. "One to Janice about two months ago. Then, maybe six weeks ago, one to Lois."

"Was either woman ever here with a man?"

"Not that I can recall. Not that they weren't flirted with. They're—they were—both real attractive. And for all I know they left with somebody from time to time. That's the kinda place this is at night, a social spot for people to meet one another."

"Do you recall either woman saying anything unusual?"

"We didn't have those kinda conversations. I mean, I only knew them from when they ordered drinks and we exchanged a few words. Then, when we began pitching the cell phones, I talked to them some more, but only about the phones." Victoria looked worried. "I'm not gonna have to go to police headquarters and make a statement or anything, am I?"

"No, we'll send somebody around. Nothing to it."

"It'll be okay, Vicky," Sinclair said, resting a hand gently on her shoulder in a way that made Pearl wonder. It could be a small, intimate world.

Pearl scooped up the photos and returned them to her pocket. "I want to thank both of you. You've been a big help."

She left them the way she left most people she interviewed, looking slightly confused and concerned. Pearl guessed everyone had something to hide.

As she was going out, she heard Ernie say behind her, "Phones? I never knew we sold phones."

9

Before the papers, even *City Beat,* had a chance to break the news about Ida Ingrahm, local TV had it. It had been leaked to them by one of their many sources at the NYPD, an organization that fortunately wasn't a ship.

Florence Norton saw it first thing when she got home from work, kicked off her shoes, and lazily clicked on the remote.

The TV was still on NY1, from when she'd checked the temperature this morning before leaving for her job as sales rep for Best of Seasons salad dressings. Florence was good at her job, and had just about convinced one of the hottest restaurants on the West Side to increase its weekly order of special ranch with bacon and beef bits. She was over forty and had bad feet, and the calls she had to make, along with the subway rides where there were no available seats were taking their toll. She had to lose weight, she knew, but she also, deep down, knew she was only fighting a holding action.

The volume came on slightly before the picture on her old TV: ". . . the Butcher again . . ."

Then there was the pretty blonde anchorwoman, Mary

something, looking concerned but still sexy, as if someone were pinching her slightly too hard.

Florence watched and listened as the woman explained how police thought it possible that the Butcher was murdering women whose last initials spelled out the name of the lead homicide detective assigned to catch him, a guy named Quinn. Of course, police reminded, this could be a coincidence, and there was no need for public panic. Still, it was wise to take precautions.

"Victims *Q*, *U*, and *I* have already been found," Mary said with pained concern, which means—"

Holy Christ!

It suddenly occurred to Florence that she was an *N*.

A potential victim. All of a sudden, the Butcher didn't sound simply like a corny name for a killer on television news.

For a while her feet stopped hurting, and she was infused with so much nervousness that she almost got up from the sofa.

Calm down . . . Calm down . . . You're not some flighty ingenue. You're a grown-up, self-sufficient woman. Maybe even too self-sufficient. So Dad always said.

The police were right; there was no need for public panic.

Unless maybe you were a woman and your last initial was *N*. Unless maybe you were Florence Norton.

She turned up the volume and sat forward on the sofa, while the pretty blonde woman reminded viewers that the Butcher killed slim, attractive brunettes.

Reassuring, Florence thought, with bitter irony. She was breathing easier. While she had mousy brown hair, it was a comfort to know she was middle-aged, dumpy, and nobody had ever thought of her as attractive. Passable at her younger, thinner best, but that was years ago.

Directors would hardly cast her as the delectable prey of a psychosexual serial killer.

Florence had long ago stopped worrying about not being

a beauty. Despite being overworked, she was quite happy doing her job, going to art exhibits, and dining out with friends of both sexes. It was a narrow life, perhaps, but she found it a contented one.

She used the remote to switch channels. The national news. Now here were people with real problems. In some city where there were palm trees, flames and smoke were curling into the sky above a fire-ravaged building. Several cars parked nearby were also on fire.

The picture cut to a helicopter shot of a distant white van speeding the wrong way along a freeway; apparently the vehicle contained the arsonist who'd set the fire. This was something, Florence thought. She peered at the screen, trying to read the crawl without her glasses, and figured it all had to be happening in LA.

The intercom buzzed, and she muted the TV and rose from the sofa. It took her several seconds to cross the room on her sore feet, press the painted-over button, and ask who was there.

She felt not the slightest sense of danger when the voice from the lobby fifteen stories below told her there was a Federal Parcel package to be delivered to her address.

A present? Something she'd ordered from a shopping channel and forgotten?

Whatever, it was sure to brighten her mood.

Pearl had removed her practical cop shoes and sat with her feet propped on the coffee table, watching TV news. Another California car chase. Was that all they did out there, when they weren't hauling in junkie celebrities?

Maybe that was what she should do, she thought, watching the white van being pursued by an orderly procession of LAPD cars with flashing lights. Leave New York and become an LA cop, join the parade of police cars. Forget about Quinn and the NYPD and this noisy, dirty city with the accelerated heartbeat. Forget about all her frustration. LA looked clean and sunny and sparsely populated—at least compared to New York. It looked manageable. Being a cop in la-la land might even be fun.

She took a sip from her can of diet Pepsi and watched the driver in the white van slow down and cut across a grassy median, then wave at the cops and lead the pursuit in the opposite direction. Police cars on the other side of the highway politely got out of the way as the van passed.

The hell with that, Pearl thought, and wondered how far the asshole in the van would get in some good old New York traffic with NYPD radio cars on his tail.

As she watched, two cops by the side of the road stood helplessly with hands on hips as the van sped past.

Pearl shook her head.

The hell with that!

If it hadn't been her TV, she might have thrown the soda can at it.

10

Darkness had fallen.

Nine-year-old Sherman Kraft lay on his sagging mattress in his bedroom in the ramshackle house on the edge of the deep swamp. His door was open about a foot, and he'd scooted over on the bed so he could see out into the hall, where from time to time his mother appeared and peeked into the bedroom of their boarder, Ernest Marks.

His mother's hair was darker than the shadows, unkempt and hanging to beneath her shoulders, exaggerating the eager craning of her neck as she opened Marks's door a few inches to peer in. Sherman knew what she was looking for, waiting for.

He was a skinny boy but with a good frame, and as handsome as his mother was beautiful. He had his father's blue eyes but his mother's firm jaw, her high forehead. His thin lips were a slash that curled downward slightly at one corner, like his mother's. Maybe like his father's, too. Sherman had no idea what his father looked like, only that his name was George, he was what Sherman's mom called a con man, and he'd deserted them both five years ago and been shot to death by a woman's angry husband in South Carolina.

Chickens coming home to roost, Sherman's mom had remarked a few times, and that was the end of conversation about her late husband and Sherman's late father George.

George the forgotten man.

The hinge on Mr. Marks's door squeaked again, not loud, almost like the plaintive cry of a mouse surprised by a trap. Marks was a big man, in his late sixties, but he still looked strong. Sherman's mom was being careful.

Sherman let his gaze slide to the side in the dim bedroom. It took in his wicker desk, where he was homeschooled. His bamboo fishing pole, propped gracefully against the wall in the corner. His threadbare armchair, where he loved to sit and read, whenever he could buy or steal a used paperback. Sometimes, when he had nothing to read, he simply sat and did math problems in his head. It was funny, the way the world could be broken down into numbers and mathematical equations. Everything neat and orderly in its place, if you concentrated hard enough and made things fit. If you questioned things enough. Sherman was always questioning. Not out loud, of course, but questioning.

How many heartbeats to the minute? He considered taking his pulse. His heart was surely racing. He'd read somewhere that seventy-six was normal. He placed his fingertips over his pulse for what he thought was ten seconds, then did the calculation.

Much higher than seventy-six.

He knew why.

The door hinge squealed louder out in the hall. His mother, no longer being careful, opening Mr. Marks's door all the way.

Much, much *higher than seventy-six. Like a bird trapped in my chest and beating its wings.*

Footsteps in the hall, bare feet on the plank floor. His mother, coming toward his room.

She pushed his door open all the way and looked in at him. He could see her only in silhouette, dark and almost without substance, like a shadow.

Sherman rolled onto his side, facing away from her. He didn't want to do this. He didn't.

He never did.

"Sherman, I know you're awake. I need your help."

He knew there was no point in arguing. He simply didn't disobey. It was always easier if he did as he was told. Always.

He rolled over and sat up in bed.

"Go into Mr. Marks's room and wait for me," his mother said. She wasn't whispering.

"Mom . . ."

"This isn't any fun for me, either, Sherman."

He nodded to the shadow in his doorway and watched it disappear into darker shadows. Then he climbed out of bed, slipped on his jeans that felt stiff and cool even though the night was warm, and walked reluctantly into the room across the hall.

The conch shell lamp by the bed was on, too dim to read by. Next to it on the table was a cracked saucer with a snubbed out filter-tip cigarette in it. Mr. Marks was in bed, lying on his back, his right hand raised about a foot off the mattress, as if he were about to reach for something. Not looking at it, though. Staring at the ceiling. Not breathing. So still. Dead.

The light was on in the hall now, and Sherman's mother came into the bedroom. She was carrying a long-bladed pair of scissors.

"We'll undress him here," she said in her crisp voice that meant business, "then you know what to do."

Sherman knew.

Mr. Marks hadn't been dead long enough that he was starting to get stiff. Sherman had been told that was why they had to act soon each time, before rigor mortis set in.

He'd looked up the term in his old dog-eared dictionary and knew what it meant, though he didn't quite understand why it happened.

Like the dead cat I found that time out in the swamp . . . Didn't bend when I picked it up by one leg. Its claws were out, though, sharp, hurt . . .

Sherman, thinking of other things, any other things, wanting to be in some other place, any other place. Pretending this was happening to somebody else. A different Sherman altogether.

While his mother snipped away with the scissors, Sherman yanked and tugged, and the tattered gray T-shirt and underpants Mr. Marks slept in came off and away from his heavy body. Sherman tossed them into a pile alongside the bed. He knew his mother would burn them later. She rolled Mr. Marks off the bed and he landed on the woven throw rug with a terrible soft muted sound of flesh-padded bone hitting hard.

Sherman and his mother each grabbed a corner of the rug near Mr. Marks's head, and then pulled with all their might to get him moving. Then it wasn't so difficult to drag his body on the rug along the hall floor to the bathroom.

It was more of a struggle to wrestle him into the big claw-foot bathtub. As if he felt the need to resist even though it was too late.

An elbow bonked loudly against the tub. "Damn you!" Sherman heard his mother say, but he knew she was talking to Mr. Marks. Sherman worked harder to get a long, uncooperative leg into the tub, his own bare foot slipping on the plastic his mother had spread on the tile floor, making him almost fall.

Then Mr. Marks's big soft body with gray hair all over it settled down in the tub, his feet at the end with the faucets, his head resting on the slanted porcelain at the other end. His expression was peaceful. He might have been relaxing, taking a bath.

There was no need for words now between Sherman and

his mother. She tugged the plastic shower curtain around the freestanding tub so it shielded the back wall, then went into the kitchen while he went out to the garage and got George's old tools—a handsaw, jigsaw, cleaver, and a power saw with a long coiled cord.

He carried them into the house in a burlap sack, then removed them and placed them carefully on the floor next to his mother's kitchen knives.

His mother began to undress, which was his signal to leave.

He went out to the hall and closed the door behind him, but he stooped and peered through the keyhole, as he always did.

There was his mother, her leg, the rest of her, looking so much paler, smoother, and larger than she did with her clothes on. The shower was running and she was bending over the tub, using the knives and heavier tools. Sherman knew that when she was finished with the knives, cleaver, and handsaw, she'd turn off the shower before using the power saw. Water and electricity were a dangerous mix, she'd warned him. Setting a good example.

She never once glanced toward the keyhole, but he was sure she knew he was watching.

It was the power saw's lilting whine that he could never forget.

When she was finished, Sherman's mother called for him to come back into the bathroom. He waited a few seconds, so they could both pretend he'd been in his bedroom, then he opened the bathroom door, knowing what he'd see.

There was his mother, fully dressed. Everything in the bathroom was meticulously scrubbed. All the fluids from Mr. Marks had been washed down the drain to the septic tank. His pale, clean parts were neatly stacked in the tub, his torso, thighs, calves, arms, then his head. His sparse gray hair was wet and matted, but his face wore a peaceful expression, as if he might be dreaming of his childhood.

The black plastic trash bags were folded in the tiny closet with the towels. Sherman's mother got them out, separated plastic, then snapped a bag in the air to open it out. Sherman helped her to stuff the pieces of Mr. Marks into the bags, arms and head in one, two bags for thighs and calves, one for the torso. The bag with the head in it was always surprisingly heavy, so Sherman carried that one. Always the gentleman, or he'd be scolded.

He and his mother lugged the bags out to the cedar-plank back porch that faced the deep swamp. The alligators were conditioned to being fed from there, everything from fish heads to . . . everything. They'd be waiting in the darkness, all of them, hungry and expectant; as if they recognized the sounds and knew what they meant. Maybe the whine of the power saw.

Sherman and his mother removed one by one the pieces of Mr. Marks and tossed them to the alligators beyond the porch rail. Some of the pieces the gators dragged back into the depths of the swamp. Some they ate right there. One of the big gators always made primitive, guttural noises along with the crunching of bone. That was another sound Sherman would never forget. A sound that was older than the human race, and might be in the collective memory and needed only reminding.

It wasn't until years later that Sherman understood what it was all about. The elderly boarders would disappear from the isolated shack on the edge of the swamp and be missed by no one. Before renting them a room, Sherman's mother always made sure they had no family. Their Social Security checks would continue to arrive, and be endorsed by Sherman's mother. One of the few useful skills her con man husband had taught her, before leaving her so she could toil alone with child and poverty, was forgery.

She made the most of it, and wasted little time.

Tomorrow she'd place another classified ad in the papers under Rooms for Rent. She knew there'd be plenty of replies. Florida was full of pensioners, lonely and poor and closing fast on the end of life, people who had no family and needed a final place to stay before being claimed by death or the dreaded retirement homes.

There! Dessert.

There was a final grunting and stirring and rippling of water in the moonlight, a parting splash in the darkness beneath the moss-draped trees.

Sherman's mother leaned down and with his help began folding the now-empty plastic bags.

They were the thick kind that could be washed out and used again. Over and over.

Fifteen minutes later Sherman was back in his bed, listening to the night sounds outside his window. A loon cried off in the distance. Closer by, there was the rustling of something moving through the brush. Insects droned and shrilled constantly so that you got used to them and only now and then realized you heard them. The swamp seemed peaceful but wasn't.

The swamp was a dark place that held its secrets close.

11

Florence barely had time to go to the kitchen and have a drink of water from a plastic bottle before the Federal Parcel deliveryman knocked on her door. It must have been a straight shot for the elevator.

She placed the water bottle back in the refrigerator. The cold air that tumbled out felt good on her stocking feet. And the hall carpet felt soft after the tiled kitchen floor.

She opened the door to find the deliveryman smiling at her. A nice-looking guy with a nice smile. That was the word he brought to mind—*nice*. Regular. And he was cradling a long white box of the sort flowers came in.

"Florence Norton?" he asked, making a show of looking at something on his side of the box, an address label, probably.

"That's me," Florence said, returning his nice smile, wondering if the box contained flowers, wondering if this guy was married or otherwise attached.

He used a balled fist between her breasts to shove her hard back into the apartment, then stepped inside, closed the door, and lifted the box's lid a few inches so he could reach in and withdraw a gun.

The room spun and her chest ached where he'd pushed her. Anger became fear became paralysis.

"Keep your head," the man said. "That might keep you alive."

Florence felt herself nod. The muzzle of the small, blue-steel gun looked like a tunnel to death. Which was what it would be, if she didn't do what this nice man said.

"Step to the center of the living room," he said.

Keeping the gun low for a moment, he moved to the window and closed the drapes.

"If this is a robbery—" Florence began.

"Keep your mouth shut or I'll shut it with a bullet."

That got through.

"Now you can undress."

Not robbery. Something more. Something worse.

Her dread was like a drug, slowing her motions. Florence undressed slowly and deliberately, keeping her elbows in close, movements tight, trying to make what she was doing look like anything but a striptease.

"All the way," he said, when she was down to panties and bra. "Leave your clothes on the floor. I'll pick them up and fold them for you later."

She felt more naked than she ever had in her life, yet strangely she wasn't embarrassed. Maybe because the stakes were so high. Or because of her terror. She would cling to any hope. She told herself the nice man was right. *If I keep my head and do as I'm instructed, I might get through this. Might.*

It was all she had, all she could allow herself to believe.

"Sit down on the sofa."

She obeyed, keeping her knees pressed tightly together, her arms crossed over her breasts.

He laid the white box down alongside the sofa, where she

couldn't see its contents, then straightened up holding a thick roll of wide silver-gray duct tape.

Useful for so many things.

Quickly and skillfully, with the practiced motions of someone who'd rehearsed or done it countless times before, he taped her wrists together, then her ankles, then her knees. It had happened almost before she started to panic, aghast at her sudden immobility. She strained against the tape. He seemed to expect this and hurriedly ran a length of tape around her back and taped her wrists so she couldn't raise her arms from her lap.

She was about to scream when a rectangle of tape was slapped painfully over her mouth. Her lips were parted about half an inch and stayed that way. She began breathing noisily through her nose and realized she was crying.

She panicked and began to squirm desperately.

He smiled and patted her gently on the head until she was calm enough to sit still.

"It's going to be all right," he said. "I promise."

She nodded.

"There's nothing to get excited about," he assured her.

But at the same time he pulled the white box out where she could see its contents—gleaming steel, and what looked like a portable electric drill or saw.

Yes, a saw!

Meticulously, with a lazy kind of precision, he undressed before her, standing directly in front of the sofa so she'd have to look at him.

He had an erection, but how could he violate her, with her legs taped so tightly together? The inaccessibility of her position was some small comfort to Florence. If only she could move something other than fingers, toes, or her head. If only she could make some noise, attract someone's attention. Anyone's attention. She needed help.

Any kind of help!

Without glancing at her, the intruder turned his back and sauntered toward the hall, toward her bedroom and the bathroom.

Then came a familiar sound; pipes clanking in the walls.

Water. Preparation!

Florence knew that the man in her bathroom must be the Butcher.

Panic took her again and her body shuddered as if she were freezing. Her tears blurred the room around her. Her rapid breathing through her nose sounded like a small animal nearby panting.

A warmth spread beneath her and she knew she was urinating on the sofa cushions. An acute humiliation cut through her panic, only making it worse.

There was no hope here. None.

She attempted mightily to scream, but the only sound in the apartment was that of running water.

12

Pearl almost fainted when she was hit with the familiar charnel house smell as she, Quinn, and Fedderman entered the victim's apartment. Sickening images of the previous Butcher victims flashed through her mind. She felt them in her stomach.

It was another white-glove affair. The crime scene unit was still at work, dusting, photographing, picking, probing, bagging, choreographed to stay out of one another's way in the crowded apartment.

Fedderman started talking to the uniform who'd been standing by the door, someone he knew, or possibly the first officer on the scene. Pearl followed Quinn toward a hall and what figured to be a bathroom. The meat market stench grew stronger, along with the perfumed disinfectant scent of soap and detergent.

Only Nift, from the Medical Examiner's office, was in the bathroom with the victim. Though it was hard to think of Florence Norton as a victim, because a victim was a person. Florence had become a blanched stack of body parts in the bathtub. Pearl remembered what Sinclair had said at Nuts and Bolts:

*". . . the way he carves up his victims and puts their parts
on display. The meat."*

The Napoleonic, annoying little bastard Nift was dressed
today as if on his way to apply for a banker's job. His shave
was so close he'd nicked himself, and his sleek black hair
was combed straight back. Stooped low next to the tub, he
had his chalk-stripe blue suit coat unbuttoned. His red silk
tie was tucked into his white shirt, so it wouldn't dangle and
contact any blood or anything else that might stain it. He
glanced up at Quinn and Pearl, flashing his nasty smile.

On the floor was an assortment of bottles and boxes,
empty cleaning agent containers. The shampoo was Swan,
the brand Pearl used—used to use.

The body parts were stacked in the same ritualistic order,
the severed head resting on top, its facial expression one of
pain even though the eyes were closed. The victim's brow
was furrowed, cheeks and mouth drawn tight as if braced for
more agony to come. Agony that had mercifully ceased.

It was obvious to Pearl that Florence was older than the
other victims, and though it was unfair to judge in death, she
hadn't been a particularly attractive woman. Not the usual
sort of Butcher prey. Pearl wondered why the deviation from
type.

"The guy would make things easier if he'd shrink-wrap
the meat," Nift said.

Pearl felt like kicking him.

"What I'm wondering," Quinn said, "is if you'll find any
water in her lungs."

"Haven't gotten that far yet." Nift began parting the victim's matted hair with his fingertips, exploring for head in-
juries. "Haven't even gotten down to finding out whether she
had good boobs. It's a science, you know. The blood stops
flowing and they don't look so great, but I can tell."

Pearl felt herself flush. If this wasn't bad enough, a horrible little prick like Nift could make it worse.

"You're sick," was all she said. Admirable restraint.

"She's right," Quinn said. He didn't want Pearl getting out of control. Her temper was what had hamstrung her in her career, even before the missing knife incident that had resulted in her leaving the department.

Even awkwardly stooped over as he was, Nift somehow shrugged and made it look nonchalant. "Well, whatever I have, it isn't fatal."

He straightened up all the way and stretched his back, sighing and sticking out his stomach. Like a lot or short men, he stood with rigid posture, as if to make every inch count. Pearl saw that he was getting a little paunchy. He was wearing suspenders so his suit pants draped well. "To answer your question," he said, "my guess is we'll find water in her lungs, like with the other victims." He pointed at the mottled bleached skin, some with bone protruding. "You can still find traces of adhesive from where he taped her." He shifted around the aim of his index finger. "There, and there."

Quinn nodded, but Pearl looked and saw nothing.

"The width is right for duct tape," Nift said. His vision was better than Pearl's. Also, he knew what to look for.

"She looks older than the other three," Quinn said. Like Pearl, he was wondering about the variance in type.

Nift nodded. "She was well into her forties. And good tits or not, she wasn't a looker. I think what really killed her was her name started with an *N*. Funny how serial killers like to play games. This one even went out of his way to murder a woman not his preferred type, just so he could spell your name right, Quinn."

"Maybe, but there are plenty of attractive young brunettes whose surnames start with the letter *N*."

"So something else could have attracted the killer to this victim. Maybe he's a guy can't resist a great rack. We might know more when we get to those boobs."

Liking Nift less and less, Pearl backed out of the bathroom and left Quinn to deal with the obnoxious little medical examiner. As she did so, she couldn't help but notice

Nift's shoes, gleaming black and as meticulously clean as what was left of Florence Norton. Strange how images stuck in the mind. Pearl knew that when she was an old lady she'd be able to recall those polished black wingtips contrasting with the clean tile floor and chalk-white body parts stacked neatly in the tub.

"Did you close her eyes?" Quinn asked, as Pearl backed into the hall.

"Sure did," she heard Nift answer. "I didn't like the way she was looking at me."

So sensitive.

Pearl walked over to a small desk that was situated near a window so Florence would have natural light to work by during the day.

"Done with this?" she asked one of the techs.

He nodded. "We got what we can. Your turn."

Pearl put on her evidence gloves anyway, before opening the top desk drawer. Maybe Florence knew who'd killed her and had his name in her address book. It had happened.

But not this time. There was a dog-eared address book, but it contained almost exclusively the phone numbers of merchants or fellow employees. Or women. It seemed Florence Norton hadn't had much of a love life.

Still, the numbers would prove useful.

Other than the book, the desk contained only the usual pens, pencils, stamps, stationary, paid bills, and canceled checks for utilities or credit cards. There was a self-inking stamp with the victim's name and address, a stack of old checkbook pads (which Pearl placed off to the side with the address book and checkbook), and a tangle of rubber bands and paper clips in a plastic drawer divider. Unpaid bills indicated that Florence still owed more than five thousand dollars on her MasterCard.

One way to beat them, Pearl thought, reminding herself that her own monthly payment was due.

Staying out of the techs' way, she moved across the room to where Florence's obvious Prada knockoff purse lay on a table near the door. Fedderman and the uniform, who were standing nearby, glanced at her, then moved away to give her room. They were still conversing in low tones. Pearl heard Fedderman say something about an Italian restaurant where the two men used to eat, asking if the place was still in business.

Good investigating, Feds. You're sure to come away with something.

She caught the same tech's eye and pointed to the purse. He nodded, then ignored her as thoroughly as did Fedderman and the uniform.

Pearl carefully unzipped the purse and began examining its contents: wadded tissue; a small folding umbrella that didn't look as if it could be more than a foot in diameter when opened; loose change; a tiny round mirror; comb; lipstick; wrapped condom (Florence living in hope?); half a box of lemon-flavored cough drops; and a bulging red leather wallet.

It continued to bother Pearl that this victim wasn't in her thirties, like the other victims, and she wouldn't be regarded as a beauty. She'd died simply because of her last initial. And Quinn was right; there were lots of younger, more attractive brunettes whose last names began with the letter N, so why Florence?

Pearl decided to look through Florence's wallet.

She withdrew it carefully from the purse, then opened it.

Lots of credit cards, way too many. Pearl wondered what the dead woman had owed on them combined. Or did she merely carry the extra cards as backup, as many women did? A plastic security blanket. Or were they in her wallet simply to make her feel richer?

The bills in the wallet added up to twenty-seven dollars. An old theater stub from a play called *I Love You, You're Perfect, Now Change* was stuffed in among them. There were no photos, but there was a New York Public Library card, a small plastic calendar from an insurance company, a Metrocard, and a medical insurance card that had been laminated.

Pearl held the med insurance card up and squinted at it. Florence had belonged to an HMO Pearl had never heard of. Pearl, who was barely insured.

The card had Florence's account number and the expiration date—six months from now. On the flip side of the card was some general information about the insured. She'd been five-foot-two and would have been forty-four in December. She—

Pearl felt a chill on her neck and stood motionless, staring at the card.

If she hadn't once loved and lived with Quinn, she might not have noticed.

She returned to the bathroom, carrying the insurance card.

Quinn was still watching Nift work. Some of the body parts were spread out in the tub now. The head was near the drain. Quinn looked over at Pearl, his face completely without emotion—holding his feelings at bay like the pro he had been and still was. His dreams, the sudden unbidden images, would come later.

Fedderman had finished his conversation with the uniform and had come to stand in the bathroom doorway. He was looking over Pearl's shoulder. "Jesus H. Christ," he said softly, staring at what was in the tub.

"I guess He's here someplace," Nift said, still leaning over the tub, his voice echoing faintly against porcelain. "You want I should call Him?"

"We want you should go see him personally," Pearl said.

She handed Quinn Florence's medical insurance card.

He glanced at it, then looked inquisitively at her.

"The victim's date of birth," Pearl said. "December fourth. The same as yours."

That caused Nift to pause in what he was doing. Pearl instantly regretted having told Quinn about this in his presence.

Nift turned only his head. "You and the victim shared a birthday?"

"It looks that way," Quinn said.

"That's why the killer couldn't be so particular about looks," Nift said. "He wanted one with your birthday *and* the last initial *N*. That's why he killed such a dog."

Pearl couldn't hold it in. "You little asshole!"

Quinn gripped her shoulders, pulling her away from Nift, out of the bathroom. Pearl heard Nift chuckle.

"He's such a . . . a . . ." Pearl sputtered.

"But he's right," Fedderman said somberly. "First there's the note to Renz about Quinn, then the dead women whose last initials are spelling out Quinn's name, and now this victim, whose birthday's the same as Quinn's. She had two criteria to meet. The killer couldn't be his usual particular self, which is why he settled for Florence."

"Feds, why don't you—"

"Ease up, Pearl." Quinn handed her back Florence Norton's insurance card. "And don't forget the 'coincidence' of one of the victims living in your old apartment."

"So what's it all mean?" Pearl asked, still too angry, primarily at Nift, to think clearly.

"It suggests the killer maneuvered the police into assigning Quinn, and us, to track him down," Fedderman said. "Spelling out Quinn's name, he's finishing what he started, and he chose a victim with Quinn's birthday so we wouldn't have any doubt about what he's doing."

"And so we know he's in control," Quinn said. "Moving us around like pawns."

Pearl did some deep breathing, feeling her rage at Nift dissipating now that she had something else to occupy her mind. The person she should be mad at, the killer. "You really figure that's what this is about?"

"It's at least a possibility," Fedderman said.

"We all know when we can be positive," Quinn said.

"She did have pretty good boobs," Nift called from the bathroom.

Pearl started toward him, but this time Fedderman held her back.

"Ignore the little prick, Pearl. He just wants to get to you. We've got other things to think about."

They both knew what Quinn had meant. There was little doubt that the killer knew how to spell Quinn's name: with two *N*s.

13

Manhattan was like a kiln that had been shut down, but only temporarily and not for long. It was another morning already uncomfortably warm because of yesterday's heat still permeating the city's miles of concrete. Day after day, the heat built pressure. Off in the distance a siren wailed, bemoaning the meteorological injustice of it all.

"There was never much doubt he was jerking our strings," Harley Renz said. "We just didn't know how hard and how many strings."

They were in Renz's office at One Police Plaza, where it was at least cooler than outside. The office was small and looked as if it had been decorated by Eliot Ness. An old Thompson submachine gun was displayed in a glass-fronted case on the wall behind Renz's desk. Also on the wall were framed certificates and awards Renz had accumulated through wile or war; a photo of him shaking hands with the mayor; another, older, photo of the two of them on a dais in a similar situation. In that one the younger, less saggy-faced Renz was holding up his right hand as if about to inhale from a cigarette he was smoking, only the cigarette had been airbrushed from the photo, leaving Renz looking like he was signaling someone somewhere that the number was two.

Quinn, seated between Pearl and Fedderman before Renz's wide desk, glanced around and noted that everything in the office was either functional or laudatory, no doubt exactly the impression Renz wanted to project. Quinn recalled that he'd never been here when there wasn't an open file with some fanned papers on Renz's desk, as if he'd just been interrupted while pondering a case. This time maybe he really had been pondering, because the file was the autopsy report on Florence Norton.

"The killer must have gone to a lot of trouble to find a victim who shared Quinn's birth date," Pearl said. Renz was important enough to have an office with a window; light shone through the blinds and illuminated her black hair as if it were a raven's wing.

Renz said, "Our guy's resourceful, like you people are gonna have to be in order to catch him."

Pearl didn't figure there had to be a reply to that.

"Did the lab find anything he left behind on this one?" Quinn asked. He noticed something new on Renz's desk, a small silver picture frame propped at an angle to face the chair where Renz sat. Quinn knew Renz was unmarried and had no children. He wondered who or what was in the photo, or whatever the silver frame contained. Maybe a romantic interest.

Renz swiveled a few inches this way and that in the brown leather chair while he shook is head no. "Forensics has got nothing to work with. Nothing left behind but death. Our sicko is pathologically neat." He stopped swiveling and leaned forward in his chair; fitted small, rimless reading glasses onto his nose; and surveyed the Florence Norton file's contents. "Postmortem indicates this one died by drowning, like the others. Sucked in almost half her bathwater. She was dismembered by a knife or knives, a hatchet or cleaver, and the same or a similar saw used to sever those joints too resistant for smaller cutting instruments."

"Power saw?" Fedderman asked.

Renz nodded without looking up. The reading glasses picked up the light from the window and made him appear owlish and scholarly. "Same as with the other victims. Kind of saw you'd buy at Home Depot to build your deck."

"Ah," Fedderman said. Pearl couldn't imagine Fedderman building a deck without cutting off at least a finger.

"The cleanser found on Florence's body parts," Renz continued, "was Whoosh, a common dishwasher detergent. The empty plastic container was found on the floor behind the commode. A bottle of carpet cleaner, also empty, and devoid of prints like the Whoosh squeeze bottle, was lying on its side in the hall outside the bathroom. An empty bleach container was in the kitchen, its cap in the sink. Apparently all three cleansers and purifiers were used, the dishwasher detergent last. Our neatnik makes do with whatever's at hand."

"All these containers wiped?" Quinn asked.

"Signs of wiping. Also signs that the killer wore rubber or latex gloves."

"Consistent with the other crime scenes," Pearl said.

"What else is consistent," Renz said, removing his reading glasses and tucking them in his shirt pocket, "is that we've got nothing to work with."

"We can be pretty sure he'll be looking for another *N* victim," Fedderman said. As usual, one of his white shirt cuffs was unbuttoned and dangling, the shirt's arm too long for his coat sleeve. Fedderman unconsciously buttoned it as he spoke. It came immediately unbuttoned.

"Which leaves us with a question," Renz said. "How much should we tell the media?"

"What they're going to find out anyway," Quinn said, "which is everything. The more information that's out there, the more it's liable to shake something loose."

"And we have an obligation," Pearl said.

"Obligation?" Renz seemed puzzled as if by some foreign term.

"To warn dark-haired women with last-initial *N*s that they're in particular danger."

"Don't they already know that?" Renz asked.

"Not all of them. And not how much danger."

Renz looked inquisitively at Quinn. The sun glanced off his glasses again, giving him the same owlish expression.

"Pearl's right," Quinn said. "We've got an obligation to warn them. This psycho finishes what he starts, and he's going to finish spelling out my name."

"We've gotta make damned sure they're warned." Pearl pressing her point. Maybe too hard, judging by the expression on Renz's face. She knew she had the reputation of getting too passionate about her cases, sometimes losing her cool. She glanced at Fedderman for support.

"Sure," he said daringly.

"It's the politically smart thing to do," Quinn said, coming to Pearl's rescue, "as well as the right thing. That combination happens seldom enough you oughta take advantage of it, Harley."

"Now you're talking sense," Renz said. "I'll issue a press release making it clear that the Butcher's next victim will likely be a brunette between twenty and fifty with a surname beginning with *N*."

Pearl smiled, pleased. If most New York women hadn't already heard or caught on, by this time tomorrow they'd be in the know. Brunettes all over the city would be going blond.

"What about the birth date?" Fedderman asked.

"Let's not mention it," Renz said. "There's no guarantee the killer will use it again, and it might cause women not born on Quinn's birthday to be complacent."

Everyone agreed that made sense.

As they stood to leave Renz's office, Quinn made a thing of maneuvering his chair back into some kind of alignment.

It enabled him to sneak a look at who or whatever was in the silver frame on Renz's desk.

It was Renz.

No cell phone vibrator had been found among Florence Norton's possessions, but Pearl was bored, so she figured why not?

It might not be a bad idea to return to Nuts and Bolts this evening. The lounge was, after all, the one thing other than last initials that seemed to connect at least two of the killer's victims.

As Pearl had suspected, the place looked better when open for business, illuminated and full of customers. The soft lighting from the rows of dim crystal chandeliers helped obscure imperfections in the ambience and the patrons. And there was music. The background kind. A woman was diddling melodically and faintly on a piano that Pearl hadn't noticed on her previous visit, seemingly letting her imagination prompt her fingers over the keys without any planning whatsoever, somehow making it work to create a pleasant, restful mood.

Most of the tables were occupied, and all but a few of the stools at the bar. Behind the bar stood Victoria, looking much more beautiful in the flattering light, wearing a paisley blouse that allowed for some cleavage. Her highly piled hair didn't look so structured now, and her dark bangs were parted in the middle and pushed to the side, making her overly made-up eyes seem larger.

Pearl walked over and stood alongside an empty stool, near where a white towel was spread out on the bar. It was where the servers bustled over to pick up the drinks Victoria concocted.

"Busy place," Pearl said, when Victoria noticed her and moved to stand by her.

Victoria smiled. "We do a lively business, despite Sinclair's bitching."

"Bitching is what bosses do," Pearl said, one working girl to another.

"Mostly. Get you something? Or are you on duty?"

"Yes and no. I'll have a Bud Light."

"Beer drinker, huh?"

"You know it," Pearl said. "Beer and doughnuts. All part of being a cop."

Victoria drew the beer from a tap and placed the glass in front of Pearl on a coaster on the bar. "I don't believe in stereotypes."

"Me, either," Pearl said. She glanced around. "Most of your customers are women, well dressed, respectable looking. Same way the men. Thirties and forties, mostly. Old enough to have good sense while having a good time. At least you'd think it by looking at them. But it's surprising what they can be up to."

"You would know, being a cop." Victoria forgetting all about her stereotype ban.

She excused herself and moved down the bar away from Pearl to wait on a man and woman who'd just come in. They both ordered what looked like martinis. The woman sampled hers and smiled. Pearl took the time to listen to the music. The woman at the piano was still playing nothing Pearl could identify, and she was reasonably sure the music was impromptu. Still, it was mesmerizing. It always amazed her how in New York there was so much talent to be found in unexpected places.

When Victoria returned, she said, "Most of our customers are single, or pretending to be. If they come in alone, connections are sometimes made. That's one reason we're in business."

"God bless connections," Pearl said, lifting her frosted glass in a toast before sipping draft beer that felt icy and good going down.

"Amen," Victoria said. "The ones who stay late, they're the ones most likely to be troublesome."

"Late and alone?"

Victoria seemed to think about that. "Yeah, maybe pissed off because they're not gonna get laid."

Pearl lifted her glass again. "God bless getting laid."

"I like to think He does," Victoria said.

A man on the good side of forty edged up to the bar, almost pressing against Pearl. She could feel the vibrancy of his presence, smell his cologne or aftershave. She looked at his reflection in the mirror behind the bar—regular features, average size and build, well groomed, tailored blue suit with white shirt and nondescript tie. Not much for a woman to complain about. Not on the surface, anyway.

Their eyes met in the mirror and he smiled at her—nice smile—then turned his attention to Victoria and held out something gold. Pearl diverted her gaze from the mirror and looked at the object. A cigarette lighter, knife-thin and expensive looking.

"I found this wedged down behind a seat cushion," the man said. "Somebody must have lost it."

"There's no smoking in here," Victoria said.

"I know, but I figured somebody might want this back anyway."

Victoria accepted the lighter. "I'll put it on a shelf where it can be seen. Maybe somebody'll claim it. Nobody does, you can have it."

"I don't smoke," the man said. He pushed back away from the bar. As an afterthought, he turned and said, "Thanks."

"You're the good Samaritan," Victoria said. When the man was gone, she grinned at Pearl. "You shoulda spoke up. You could've had a nice lighter."

"At least," Pearl said.

Victoria laughed. It was a loud laugh that held nothing back.

"But I don't smoke, either," Pearl said. "Do you?"

"Secretly. Like a lotta people." She winked at Pearl. "Cops are secretive about some things, right?"

"Meaning why am I here?"

"I guess so."

"I wanted to see what kind of place two of the victims spent time in," Pearl said, "so it might give me more of an idea of the kind of women they were."

"Can I ask if you're married," Victoria said, "or if you've got a special someone?"

"Yes, you can ask. I won't be secretive. Answers are no and no."

"Then you should understand. We just get your average career woman in here. They're from the office buildings in the neighborhood. Average working guys, too. White-collar drones. Tired from a long day at the office, needing a drink, maybe some understanding the wife doesn't give them. I guess what I'm saying is, there's probably not much you can learn about those two victims here, other than that they led more or less average lives."

Pearl knew about *average* lives. "Sure, and they happened to stop in at Nuts and Bolts."

"And probably some other places around here."

"And bought Dial In cell phones from you."

"Yes, they did. How many grown-up women do you know who don't have a vibrator?"

"We're back to that secretive thing again," Pearl said.

Victoria emitted another loud laugh. The place seemed to be getting more crowded, more alive with conversation. The piano was louder and playing something identifiable. "Night and Day." One of Pearl's favorites. She wouldn't have minded sitting for a while and listening, but she knew she shouldn't. And Victoria was right, there was probably nothing to be learned here. It was simply another Manhattan nightspot, someplace she and Quinn might have frequented when they were together.

Quinn.

Why am I thinking of Quinn? He's still interested, and he knows I'm not. Over. It's over.

The music was insistent and hypnotic.

"Want another?" Victoria asked.

Pearl looked down and noticed with some surprise that her glass was empty.

"No, thanks," she said. "Early day tomorrow."

She placed some bills on the bar and stepped away to leave.

"I thought maybe you'd learned something," Victoria said. "You looked so thoughtful, like maybe you were detecting."

"I wish it worked that way. Drink a beer, then detect. What you took for detecting was just my mind wandering."

Cops are secretive about some things, right?

"See you."

"Maybe," Pearl said.

Victoria watched her leave. She kind of liked Pearl the cop, and felt sorry for her. There was something sad about her. Maybe because, with her job, she saw mostly the worst in people.

A man three stools down ordered a scotch rocks, and Victoria went to the back bar to pour it, noticing the gold lighter somebody had lost. It did look pretty expensive, like real gold, and even had some engraving. A fancy letter *N.*

14

The subway system lay like arteries just beneath the city's flesh.

A fanciful thought, but those weren't uncommon for Marilyn.

Marilyn Nelson loved riding the subway. She relished the cool breeze of an approaching train, the piercing twin lights down the long dark tunnel, then the great rush of wind and the metallic creak and strain underlying the train's roar. Car after car would flash past, the illuminated windows like personal instant tableaux that were here then gone. There was no sign of slackening speed. Surely the train was going to roar on beyond the station. But it didn't. Instead it slowed smoothly but with surprising abruptness, like a living thing suddenly drained of energy, and came to a complete stop. A pause, and the doors would hiss open with an urgent whisper that seemed to spur on the people spilling out onto the platform or wedging their way into the cars.

She'd been in New York a little over four months, after spending most of her adult life in Omaha, Nebraska. Omaha was a nice enough city, she thought, but it had nothing like Times Square, the Village, or Central Park—or the subway, which to Marilyn was the very essence of her newly adopted city.

She emerged from underground at West Eighty-sixth Street near the park, as impressed as she always was by how quickly she'd made it here by subway from her apartment near Washington Square. It was late afternoon, Sunday, and as she entered the park the dwindling sunlight lancing between the buildings highlighted her long dark hair. A slim, attractive woman in a white blouse with large patch pockets, and jeans that were tight everywhere except for the bulging cargo pockets on each thigh, she drew the attention of almost every man she passed. The thick leather belt and fringed boots didn't detract from her appeal, either. The belt and boots were black, and the belt had a large silver buckle that glittered like the matching studwork pattern on the boots.

The farther into the park she got, the quieter it became. Marilyn stepped off the asphalt trail onto soft earth that was easier on her feet, and began crossing the grassy area toward where the concert would be held.

Ross Bossomo was going to play here soon, along with his backup musicians. Marilyn had grown up listening to Bossomo's hit records, then followed his career as he became less mainstream and more experimental. A free concert! She'd read about it in the *Village Voice*. Not much like this happened in Omaha. At least, not very often. But here, in New York, there seemed to be surprises every day. Serendipity, she told herself, smiling. Serendipity city.

She could see the raised platform that would be Bossomo's stage. There was already sound equipment set up, even speakers mounted on the trunks of some of the surrounding trees. Straps and ropes held the speakers so there'd be no harm to the environment. This would be something, once the sun went down. Maybe people would hold up candles or cigarette lighter flames the way they used to all the time at concerts, even though New York was practically a total no-smoking zone.

She picked up her pace. Her hair swung in rhythm with

her switching hips; fringe dangled as her long legs stretched her stride, and her buttocks rode against taut denim, emphasized by the blossoming cargo pockets. She was the only one wearing such jeans now, or anything resembling her sleeveless blouse with the oversized patch pockets and large brass buttons, but soon that would change. It was part of her job to change it. Part of her job to be seen in the Rough Country line.

The speakers began to hum. So did Marilyn, an old Ross Bossomo hit, "Love Goin' to Pieces."

The Butcher turned to see what so many male heads had swiveled to look at, and she took his breath away. He'd never seen that kind of motion in a woman. It was a shame he was being so choosy these days, or she'd be one of his for sure.

He had to have her. But he was extremely disciplined and didn't always partake of what he *had* to have. He prided himself on that.

She'd changed direction and was striding up a gradual rise, her body leaning forward slightly to compensate for the grade, coming toward him where he stood along with several dozen people who'd arrived early for the concert. There was a faint smile on her face, lips pressed together, as if she might be humming.

He was probably the only one more interested in the concertgoers than the music. He'd barely heard of Ross Bossomo.

"Joe?"

He turned toward the slight, dark-haired woman he'd been talking with in an attempt to draw out her name.

He smiled at her. "Sorry, I didn't mean to daydream."

She glanced at the woman in the fringed boots and shook her head. "I know what kind of daydreaming you were doing." She seemed miffed.

He beamed his charm at her. "You never told me your last name."

The woman gave him a knowing smile and moved away. "I never told you my first. And I don't think I'm going to."

Screw you, he thought.

He turned his attention back to the woman in the fringed boots. If he'd already been penalized for looking, he'd have another look.

Like many beautiful women, especially ones who dressed so distinctly and obviously relished being observed, she seemed used to being stared at. It didn't offend her. It was, in fact, homage to her very being.

Some getup she's wearing.

But she made the extreme, outdoorsy outfit work. With a body like that, rags would look good on her.

The sun's glitter off the studded boots and oversize belt buckle drew his eye.

And held it.

He felt the way he had one time when, while playing high-stakes poker, he'd been dealt a straight flush. Such luck he couldn't believe!

The large buckle was definitely in the form of a fancy letter *N.*

A monogram. Her initial.

He calmed himself. A straight flush and then this? Nobody was *that* lucky. And the *N* might be for her first name, Nancy or Norma, or maybe it was simply the logo of the belt manufacturer.

He quickly regained his composure, his smile, his style, and approached the woman.

Four heavily tattooed men who looked like motorcycle types were standing nearby talking. One of them—a weight-lifter, no doubt—had his shirt off and tied by the arms around his waist. His sculpted torso was marked with the crude, faded blue tattoos that suggested prison time. They all paused and looked at the Butcher and smiled slightly, as if they knew he had no chance with a woman like the one he was moving in on.

You don't know me, assholes.

"Nadine? Is that you?"

She regarded him with appraising brown eyes. They had an intelligence in them that made him decide on caution. He knew exactly what she was seeing: a handsome man in his thirties, average height, regular features, neatly styled dark hair, blue eyes. He was well dressed (not like the tattooed geeks), and had a reassuring smile. Always he possessed a vision of himself, as if he were another self looking on.

"Sorry," she said, "I'm not Nadine."

He put on a crestfallen expression. Then his smile was back. "Well, I'm sorry, too. I haven't seen Nadine in a long time, and you look a lot like her. Then I noticed your belt buckle, the big letter N, and I thought . . ."

"It's for Nelson," she said.

He laughed. "You don't look like a Nelson."

She met his laughter with her own. She laughed so easily and naturally, an innately friendly girl. A people person. They were so easy. "That's because it's my last name."

"Ah! And your first?"

"Marilyn."

"Nice name." He feigned awkwardness, but for just a few seconds, letting it register on her.

"Who's Nadine?" she asked.

"Someone I was very fond of a long time ago in another place."

"I'm sorry to disappoint you."

He took a step away, then turned back. "Maybe it was fate that I thought you were Nadine."

"Fate?"

"You know. Destiny."

"I'm not sure I believe in destiny."

"What do you believe in?"

"Well, I believe you're trying to pick me up."

He put on the awkward act again, standing with his body square to hers, hands jammed in pants pockets. "I'm trying too hard, I guess. I apologize."

"Accepted."

"The pickup or the apology?"

The easy laugh again. "Maybe both."

The speakers *yeeeowled!* as a sound technician adjusted them. People laughed, groaned, or cupped their hands over their ears.

The handsome man grinned at her. "That noise they heard was me expressing pleasure at your answer," he said. *Don't be too smooth yet. Not with this one.*

Marilyn thought it was one of the nicest things anyone had ever said to her. And there was one thing they had in common already—they were both Ross Bossomo fans.

"I don't know your name," she said. The speakers screeched again, and she winced and repeated what she'd said.

"Joe. Joe Grant."

"Grand?" The speakers again.

"Grant," he said. "You know, like the Civil War general. Ulysses."

"I know," she said. "The one on the winning side."

He glanced down. "By the way, I like your boots."

She gave him a wide grin. "Good. What I'm wearing is clothing from Rough Country. They're a Midwestern chain, except for a small trial store in Queens, and they're going to enter the New York market in a major way. That's why I'm here. I'm an interior designer specializing in retail space. I'm going to lay out their stores for them."

"Talented woman."

She waited, as if giving him a chance to tell her what line of work he was in, but he remained silent, raising his head and glancing at the trees. Dusk was just beginning to close in. Enough people had gathered to constitute a crowd. Their collective conversation and laughter was louder now. Half a dozen scruffy-looking young guys with musical instruments were filing up onto the stage. A warm-up band.

After a few seconds, Marilyn said, "There's gonna to be a mob here soon. Do you want to see if we can get closer?"

"That's a good idea," he said. "Let's get closer."

15

In the course of his mission, it was essential that he control events, and he had events by the balls.

Things were going so smoothly that he tended more and more to take time in order to contemplate and enjoy. The Butcher sat in his leather recliner, his feet propped up, a Jack Daniel's over rocks in his hand, and gazed out his high window at the lights of the city he felt was his. Or if it wasn't his, it soon would be. Because the city was only beginning to experience the terror he'd inflict on it. The control he would exercise. Before he was finished, he'd own New York in a way no one searching for him would have imagined possible. In the world's greatest city, he would be the world's greatest nightmare.

It had been so simple to manipulate the police into bringing Quinn out of retirement. Then it was easy to see that his former partner in and out of bed, Pearl Kasner, would join him in the hunt. All it took was research and a modicum of personal involvement. People like Pearl and Quinn took personally the knowledge that a serial killer was operating in what they considered *their* city. It was born in them; they had to set things right.

The killer understood what compelled them, because he gloried in and was burdened by the same obsession. The only difference was in the definition of right. That was subjective. And that was where he and Quinn and his team clashed, which was precisely why they were perfect adversaries.

The Butcher hadn't intended Pearl's involvement at first, but when he was doing his research on Detective (then bank guard) Kasner, he discovered where she'd lived during the last case she'd worked with Quinn, and been pleasantly surprised to find the apartment now occupied by a rather pretty young brunette. Pretty enough, anyway, so that it would be a pleasure using her to send a message to Quinn and Kasner. They'd know the death of the apartment's present occupant hadn't been coincidental. Cops didn't put much stock in coincidence.

Neither did killers who didn't get caught.

The Butcher took a sip of Jack Daniel's and smiled at his reflection in the dark window. There he was, outside himself, observing himself, a transparent figure in a reflective world between where he sat and the jeweled and glimmering nighttime cityscape beyond the glass. That was how the world was, really, layer after layer like coats of paint upon reality, and if you were smart enough you could move from one layer to the other. Live in more than one. He'd learned to do this at a young age because he'd had to in order to survive. Some lessons you never forgot. And if you never forgot them, you could put them to good use. You could control the game.

The last letter *N* had been a matter of expedience. The next one he would fully enjoy.

After the bland Ross Bossomo concert, he'd accompanied Marilyn Nelson home to her apartment, but he hadn't gone in. He wasn't ready yet. Didn't have his equipment. Didn't sense, as he always did, the proper time. Marilyn had told him she didn't believe in destiny. She was a fool. He knew her destiny, even if she didn't.

One thing for sure: meeting and moving toward the moment with Marilyn was instructive as well as pleasurable. He hadn't considered monogrammed or initialed clothing and accessories, like Marilyn's oversize belt buckle, as an aid to identifying prospective victims. Many women indulged in that simple exercise in ego. However it might work in the future, he thought it had been much more precise and productive than following strange women and scanning apartment mailboxes. That was how he'd found Florence Norton—and wasn't Marilyn Nelson a brighter trinket?

Everything had gone so well he decided he'd enjoy her for a while before the time was right to end their affair.

To end Marilyn.

Quinn and his team were in their office a few blocks from the precinct house. The window air conditioner was humming and rattling away, not doing a bad job of cooling the place because it was still morning and the sun was low. The aroma of roasted beans from the Mr. Coffee brewer Pearl had bought wafted in the air. Now and then, just outside the door, they could hear another door closing and soles shuffling on concrete, people coming and going at Nothing but the Tooth, the dental clinic that occupied the other half of the building.

"So the owner and both employees at Nuts and Bolts didn't recognize the other victims," Quinn said. "And of course we only have two victims we know frequented the place and bought those kinky cell phones."

Pearl was sure his tone was accusatory.

He was sitting behind his desk, leaning dangerously far back in his chair. Pearl and Fedderman were pacing, each with a mug filled with coffee. The mugs were from a home decorating store on Second Avenue and had their individual initials on them so nobody would mix them up. When Pearl had handed Fedderman his, he commented that initialed mugs seemed like something the killer might send them. Pearl had said maybe that was so, and seemed thoughtful.

Fedderman thought she might be contemplating nudging Quinn's chair the rest of the way over.

"It was never my idea that the place was the one and only hunting ground for the killer," she told Quinn. Why was Quinn like this, critical of what they both knew was basic, solid police work? Maybe he was jealous that he hadn't thought about further checking out the pickup lounge.

"On the other hand," Fedderman said, "the killer might have picked up *all* his victims in Nuts and Bolts, and the owner and employees don't remember."

"Somebody would have recalled the other victims," Quinn said, "or remembered the same man with at least some of the women. Most likely two of the victims simply happened to work in the same neighborhood and frequented the same lounge sometimes after work or in the evening."

"On the third hand," Fedderman said, "the killer might never have set foot in the place."

"Still, it's a connection," Quinn said, giving in and allowing for the possibility.

"And remember both victims bought cell phone vibrators," Pearl said.

"They sold a lot of those to women who haven't been murdered," Fedderman reminded her.

"My gut tells me it means something," Pearl said. She sipped her coffee from her initialed mug, thinking Mr. Coffee had done a pretty good job. "Could be the killer lives in the neighborhood and goes into the lounge often."

"Kind of a leap in logic," Quinn said, "but if you want to go to Nuts and Bolts from time to time to check it out, that's not a bad idea."

"It's a pickup place," Fedderman said. "Maybe you'll get lucky."

"Maybe you'll need somebody to pick you up," Pearl said.

Fedderman tried not to smile. Quinn thought it was a good thing he controlled himself. His two detectives were bitching at each other the way they had in the old days. He didn't mind, as long as it didn't get out of hand. Agitation wasn't all bad. It required an active mind of the sort that was valuable in a murder investigation. It could create the pearl in the oyster, even a necklace of evidence pearls.

"How strong's this gut feeling of yours about the cell phone vibrators?" he asked Pearl, artfully veering away from the subject of pickups in singles' lounges.

"Not very strong, I admit. I guess it's more hope than anything else."

Quinn looked over at Fedderman. "What's your gut tell you, Feds?"

"Tells me I'm hungry." Fedderman put down his mug on the desk nearest to Quinn's and glared at Pearl. "And it tells me not to drink any more of this coffee."

The Butcher slept late, having worked much of the night at his computer. He'd then spent most of the morning at the Rough Country store in Queens. So busy had he been that he hadn't had time to check the news on the Internet or read any of the morning papers.

Now he slouched in his leather recliner and read again the piece in the *Times*. The Florence Norton murder had been dropped from the front page but had never left the news entirely.

He greatly enjoyed the inside feature story on the Butcher murders. It provided brief biographies of the victims and time frames of their deaths, but concentrated mainly on Florence Norton. Perhaps in everyone's death there were fifteen minutes of fame. The features section, or obituary page, as curtain call.

As usual, if anyone astutely read between the lines it was obvious that the police were mystified. They simply had nothing to grab hold of that might lead them to the killer.

The Butcher.

It was so apropos. Every time he read the sobriquet the media had chosen for him, he had to smile. In fact, almost everything he'd read or heard in the media pleased him. Everything was falling into place. The re-formation of Quinn's detective team especially gave him satisfaction. The NYPD without Quinn and company were easy opponents, but the three detectives specifically assigned to hunt him down were top-notch and had a track record. They would at least make the game interesting.

He let his right arm drop and laid the folded paper on the floor, then adjusted the chair at a lower angle and rested the back of his head against the soft leather headrest. Though he didn't require much sleep, it wasn't unusual for him to nap during the daytime in the recliner. It was because he often worked most of the night.

He glanced at his watch. Not even three o'clock. There was plenty of time before he had to shower and dress for this evening. He settled deeper into the chair, closed his eyes, and thought about Marilyn Nelson. His right hand, the one that had held the folded paper, moved to his crotch.

Pearl's phone was ringing when she entered her apartment that evening, and she made the mistake of picking it up without looking at caller ID.

"Pearl, it's your mother. You're finally home. I've been calling and calling."

Pearl's mood darkened, as it did whenever her mother

called from where she lived in the Golden Sunset assisted living apartments in Teaneck.

"Sorry, Mom. Busy working." She stretched the phone cord so she could move halfway across the room and start the window air conditioner. It would soon cool down the apartment and chase away the musty smell that often permeated the place.

Her mother said something she didn't understand, so she moved away from the humming air conditioner. "Say again, Mom."

"The Butcher murders. Why haven't you caught the animal yet?"

"He's smart, Mom, like the papers and TV say."

"Still, you have Captain Quinn."

"He's not exactly a captain anymore." It rankled Pearl, the way her mother was a sucker for phony Irish charm and remained so fond of Quinn. She could still hear her mother's confidential whisper after meeting Quinn the first time: *"He's the one. A keeper. A real mensch, that one."*

"But the television news—"

"Not a permanent captain, anyway," Pearl interrupted. "He's more a civilian temporarily out of retirement."

"Like yourself, dear?"

"Not unlike."

"I never approved of you in that dangerous occupation."

Or any other. "I know, Mom."

"So why haven't you phoned your apartment from time to time to check your messages? You'd have learned your mother was calling from nursing home hell."

"It's not a nursing home, Mom. It's assisted living."

"I need assistance to breathe?"

"Not for that, thank God." *Not yet.* Pearl lay awake sweating in bed sometimes, thinking of even more oppressive days to come. "For other things."

"Oh? Such as?"

Pearl remembered the time her mother had warmed up a can of chili by placing it in a pot of water on the stove—neglecting to open the can—and heating it until it exploded, sending boiling water and chili all over her kitchen. Pearl remembered because it was she who'd had to clean up the mess. "I'm thinking about the chili on the ceiling, Mom."

"You mean the cans they don't make like they used to."

"If you say so."

"No, it's not what I say. It's whether they're making paper-thin cans these days, and they are."

Pearl moved over a few feet so she'd be in the flow of cool air from the window unit. "You might be right, Mom." *Just let me get off the phone!*

"Your mother's always right, dear." Violent coughing. Dramatic pause.

Pearl played along. "Mom?" She was surprised to hear real concern in her voice.

"I'm right about this, too, dear. It's something mothers can feel. God willing, you'll know someday."

Pearl worked her feet out of her shoes and wriggled her toes. "We still talking about the chili?"

"My reference was to Mrs. Kahn's nephew, Milton."

Huh?

Pearl knew Mrs. Kahn, a seventy-six-year-old woman with a walker with tennis balls on it, was in the assisted living unit next to her mother's. "I don't think I know him, Mom."

"But you should, Pearl, which is why I called."

"Nine times," Pearl said, "according to the message count on my answering machine."

"The machine you should have remotely checked to see if you had any messages at all."

"Why would I want to know this nephew Milton?" But Pearl knew why.

"Because he's eligible in every way, and newly single."

"I don't have time right now to search for a husband, Mom, being busy searching for a killer."

"What search? I'm dropping him into your lap."

"I want my lap empty for now."

There was a long silence on the other end of the connection. Then: "Speaking of your lap, so how is that nice Captain—excuse me—Mr. Quinn?"

"Jesus, Mom!"

"Pearl!"

"Sorry for the language. Mr. Quinn's fine."

"You didn't preface his name with 'nice.' "

"No, I didn't. He isn't nice all the time."

"So who is, dear? Did he ever beat you?"

"Never."

"Then he was nice enough to you and would be again. He's quite handsome in a manly way and is a person of substance, Pearl. There will come a time when you won't want to chase criminals, or stand in one spot in a bank developing varicose veins just to earn a small paycheck. There will come a time when you might be in assisted living."

Pearl hated these phone conversations with her mother. They almost always ended in arguments, and this evening Pearl was tired. She'd worked hard. She didn't feel like bickering with anyone, much less her mother. And she especially didn't want to argue about her status as a divorced single woman. It simply was not in her at this time to foster her mother's delusion that her daughter was actively seeking a husband.

"Whether or not you say so, Pearl, Mr. Quinn is a fine man."

"He's an obsessive psychopath."

"They can be good providers, dear."

Pearl hung up.

Hard enough that her mother wouldn't call her back tonight.

But maybe tomorrow.

* * *

The Butcher prepared himself to go out. He took a shower, not a bath, then put on clean blue silk boxer shorts. He brushed his teeth with Crest, combed his hair, and leisurely dressed in his new clothes.

All the time he was doing this, somewhere in his layered and partitioned mind he was thinking about Marilyn Nelson; the rhythmic roll of her hips when she walked, the mischievous glitter like dark tinsel in her eye when she turned and ducked her head to glance at him. As if on some level she *knew.* And maybe she already did know. Like some of the others, maybe from time to time she caught a glimpse of destiny that transcended conscious thought.

His second *N* woman.

Florence Norton had been a matter of expedience. This one he would take his time with and relish. He owed her that, as he owed himself. They were in this together now, whether she realized it or not. Partners in crime and time and players in the game that could only end one way for Marilyn Nelson.

Finished dressing, he stood before the full-length mirror attached to the closet door and appraised himself. He could smell his expensive spicy aftershave. It was much too strong now, but he'd recently applied it and knew that within a short while it would lose much of its potency.

He turned this way and that, striking poses like a confident and playful catalog model, observing how he looked in the outfit he'd bought that morning at Rough Country in Queens.

Marilyn would be pleased, but it wasn't his usual style. He wasn't crazy about the square-pocket jeans and rough piped cotton shirt with its flap pockets and dull brass snaps instead of buttons. The essence of Rough Country style seemed to lie in the liberal use of metals and coarse material. He preferred tailored conservative suits, custom-made shirts of Egyptian cotton, and silk ties. But since he had on the shirt and jeans, he didn't so much mind the boots. They were surprisingly comfortable.

He did flatly like the hat. It was like a cowboy hat but with a narrower, raked brim. Like something Glenn Ford might have worn. He was partial to Glenn Ford movies, and fancied that he bore some resemblance to the late movie star, which was enhanced by the hat.

He laid the hat on the bed (knowing some people thought doing so brought bad luck, but the hell with superstition if you were smart), then adroitly dusted his dark hair with aerosol spray.

Posing before the full-length mirror again, he placed the hat on his head carefully so as not to muss his hair. He adjusted the hat, touched a finger to the curved brim, and shot himself a smile.

Then he switched off the light and left in something of a hurry.

He had a date.

16

Quinn had finished his impromptu late dinner of hash and eggs, and was enjoying a cigar at his desk in the den, when there was a knock on his apartment door. This didn't surprise him, as the building's security system allowed most anyone with an IQ higher than a rabbit's to find a way to enter without being buzzed in.

He propped the cigar in an ashtray so it wouldn't go out, and made his way into the living room. With a glance at his watch, he saw that it was past nine o'clock. He'd spent most of the evening reading over the murder books on the Butcher's victims, hoping something might snag his attention and open new vistas of investigation. It seldom happened, but happened often enough to warrant tireless scrutiny of file information. It hadn't happened this evening.

Peeking through the round peephole he saw only what appeared to be the shoulder of someone not very big. He opened the door to the hall.

A young woman of about eighteen stood staring in at him. What drew his eye was the glitter of a tiny glass or diamond stud in her left nostril. Then there was the general impression of build, average if a bit fleshy, five-feet-four or so, stuffed into a tight aqua-colored top made of some kind of stretch material. Her dirty, faded jeans were too tight and rode low, revealing between waistband and blouse an expanse of stomach that showcased a navel pierced by a small silver ring. She had brown hair combed in a practical short do, a slightly turned-up nose, wide, generous mouth, a strong chin, and green eyes exactly like Quinn's.

She smiled and said, "Hi, Dad."

Astounded, Quinn actually backed up a step or two. This almost stranger was his daughter Lauri, whose mother May and her present husband, Elliott Franzine, lived in California, where Lauri lived with them.

Should be living with them.

Only Lauri wasn't in California. She was here. Quinn was seeing her for the first time in a little over a year. The change was astounding.

He said, "Lauri?"

Still smiling, she came in and dropped an overstuffed backpack he somehow hadn't noticed on the floor, then glanced around. "Your place is nice."

"You're . . . here," he said, still stunned. She was so much older, grown-up. A full-sized . . . person.

"Sure am." She came to him, wrapped her arms around his neck, kissed his cheek, and was gone before he'd had a chance to hug her back.

"May . . . Your mother . . ."

"I decided to leave California. Saved up some money. Rode buses all the way. That Port Authority place is like wild. Got anything to eat?"

"Sure." He led the way into the kitchen, his mind atilt. "You're supposed to be in school."

"Summertime, Dad. Graduated anyway. High *B* average. Coulda done better." She opened the refrigerator. "Hey! New York stuff! That fatty red meat."

"Pastrami," Quinn said. "They have it in California, too."

"Not where I been. You like it?"

"Sure. You graduated from *high school*?" His guess would have been that she was a junior, maybe a sophomore. Time working its malicious magic.

"Yep."

Drawers opened, twisties were untwisted, jars unlidded; the refrigerator door was worked, and a squeeze bottle of mustard *squeeched*! A pastrami sandwich with pickles on rye appeared incredibly fast before Quinn. The fridge door opened and closed again. *Hisssss!* Lauri was seated at the table with a fizzy cold can of Pepsi, attacking the sandwich.

"Does your mother know you're here?" Quinn asked, embarrassed to sound like a character in an old TV family sitcom.

"I think not." Through a huge bite of sandwich.

"What about Elliott?"

"He's a dork."

Quinn remembered her calling *him* a dork not that many years ago. It had stung. "Elliott's not such a bad guy."

Which was true. Quinn had himself at first thought Elliott a dork, but eventually, when he finally accepted that it was over forever with May, he came to appreciate the home and consistency that real-estate attorney Elliott provided for his family—that used to be Quinn's family. Quinn, who any day or night at work might have been shot, had never been able to provide that kind of security at home. A cop's wife leaves him—who doesn't understand and sympathize?

"Does Elliott know you traveled to New York?" Quinn asked, amazed by how quickly the sandwich was disappearing.

"Nobody but you knows I'm here, Dad. This stuff is great. I'm looking forward to New York. Don't worry. I'm gonna get a place of my own soon as I find work."

"Huh? Place? Work?"

"You got a spare bedroom, Dad, right? Place to crash. Extra bed? I don't snore, most of the time."

"Listen, Lauri . . ."

She stopped chewing pastrami and looked up at him with those green eyes. Smiled big. *Ah, God . . . May.*

Memory was physical pain.

"There's a spare bedroom," he said. "I'll have to move out a few things I've got stored in there."

She took a big bite of sandwich and stood up. "Let's go. I'll help you."

"Doesn't have to be right now," he said. "Finish your sandwich. Make another one if you're hungry."

She settled back down and began eating in earnest again. She said, "I don't have any tattoos."

He smiled. "Fine."

"Do you mind if I get one?"

"Does it matter what I think?"

"Sure. I asked, didn't I?"

"Yeah. Will you not get a tattoo if I say I mind?"

"Wouldn't go that far."

"I've gotta say I don't have an opinion on you getting tattooed," Quinn said honestly. "I never gave it much thought. I mean, I never figured it was a question I'd have to wrestle with."

"I'll wait, then. Till you get it straightened out in your mind."

"Thanks."

"Wouldn't be right away anyway. Your place. Your rules."

"Really?"

She grinned. "I wouldn't go that far."

He stared at her, befuddled.

"Make yourself another sandwich if you want," he said. "And there's more soda in there. I'll be right back."

He left her and returned to his den. His cigar had gone out. He relit it, then walked over and shut the door and called May and Elliott Franzine's number in California.

Elliott picked up almost immediately.

"It's Quinn," Quinn said. "I've got Lauri here."

"Thank God!" Elliott said. "She's been gone four days.

We thought she was at a girlfriend's house until yesterday. We called the police, and they're about to list her as a missing person."

"Well, she isn't missing. She's here. Said she rode buses in from California."

"May's not here, Quinn. She's out talking to the girlfriend's parents. We've worried out of our skulls."

"I guess so. Lauri get upset about something?"

"Didn't seem to. Well, we did have a bit of a tiff about where and when she'd go to college. A few harsh words. But we've had those discussions before and everybody's cooled down. We didn't think she was mad enough to leave home. Though she's been talking about not liking California, seeing more of the world. We didn't think there was anything to the talk, just Lauri venting, but it seems we were wrong."

"She's planning on going to college?"

"Eventually, she says. After gaining what she calls true life experience, whatever that is."

Quinn knew what it was. It could be painful. Even fatal.

"She intends to stay with me for a while and try to find a job in New York," he said.

"How do you feel about that?"

"Like I've got no choice."

"Well, she is eighteen."

"That's an age when you can get in a lotta trouble," Quinn said. *And be a lot of trouble.*

"May and I both know she'd be safe with you."

"If I put her on the red-eye to California, she might bounce right back here," Quinn said, thinking out loud.

"Probably would. Or go someplace else altogether. Like Minnesota."

"Why Minnesota?"

"I don't know, but I've always had a bad feeling about Minnesota. It's a place where you can get in trouble if you're eighteen."

"Like plenty of other places," Quinn said.

"If she's really made up her mind to leave California," Elliott said, "she'll go someplace else. Lauri's awfully stubborn. Once she's made up her mind, she usually doesn't change it."

"Stubborn, huh?"

"Very."

Quinn picked up his cigar and toyed with it. Studied it. No sign of an ember. He mentally pronounced it dead.

What a screwed-up world it was.

"We can try it for a while," Quinn said. "On a trial basis. Maybe she'll see how tough it is here and get New York out of her system."

"This is great of you, Quinn."

"Not really. She's my daughter."

"Yeah, she sure is."

"Have May call me when she gets in."

"Okay. Tell Lauri we love her out here in California."

"You wanna talk to her?"

"Of course."

Quinn went back to the kitchen and returned a few minutes later and picked up the phone.

"She said she doesn't want to talk to you," he told Elliott. "Said you were a dork."

"That hurts."

"Tell me about it."

Quinn hung up the phone, smiling around his dead cigar.

17

"You drank just the right amount of wine during dinner," he told Marilyn, as they strolled along the sidewalk toward her apartment. Even though Marilyn was wearing high heels, he was slightly the taller of the two in his Rough Country boots, and he knew the hat added another three or four inches. They were walking very close together and presented a kind of unassailable front that prompted people approaching to veer around them. *Power prevails,* thought the Butcher.

Marilyn laughed. "I'm afraid to think what you might mean by that."

"I mean you showed restraint."

"And you admire restraint?"

His turn to laugh. "Up to a point."

He rested his right hand lightly on her shoulder as they walked, raising his head slightly and smiling as he let his senses take in the moment. The mingled scents of the city rode on the sultry summer evening. Headlights of approaching traffic starred in the humidity. The slightly sweet smell of curbside trash waiting to be picked up in early morning was like perfume to him. He enjoyed the subtle but persistent wafting of exhaust fumes; the rumble of a bus or truck; a cacophony of blaring horns echoing from far away.

And something else . . . a delicate hint of nearby scent.

Her shampoo.

"Did you wash your hair just for me?"

She seemed surprised and pleased. "Of course I did. It's perceptive of you to notice."

"There isn't much I don't notice." He realized at once he'd sounded a note of arrogance and moved to temper it. "I'm afraid my job makes me like that."

"You never told me what you did for a living," she said.

I can tell her anything now, on this, her last night.

"I'm a historian."

"You teach?"

"Not now. I'm writing a book on the Civil War."

"About your ancestor."

"General Grant wasn't exactly an ancestor."

"You know that for a fact?"

"Well, no."

"Then maybe you and he are related. Or maybe not. You drank just the right amount of wine for dinner, too. Showed restraint. I don't think General Grant often did that."

They'd reached the entrance to Marilyn's building and stopped walking at the base of the concrete steps up to the stoop.

"You know your history," he said. "The general did enjoy his liquor. Lincoln once said—"

He fell silent as he noticed a woman approaching. As she passed from shadow into brighter light, his glance took her in quickly—medium height, slightly overweight, short blond hair, white joggers, dark slacks, untucked sleeveless blouse, a purse of glittering green sequins slung by a strap over her right shoulder. When she got closer, he saw that she was in her thirties, had protruding teeth, was moderately pretty, and was wearing half a dozen jangling silver bracelets on her left wrist. A necklace. Rings. *In love with jewelry. Presents to herself.*

The woman smiled. "Marilyn?"

Beside him, Marilyn took a step toward the woman. "Ella? Is that actually you?"

"Of course it's me!" Smiling with her toothy mouth wide open, the woman hobbled toward Marilyn on her high heels, her arms spread like inadequate wings. She reminded him of one of those birds that couldn't fly but because of Darwinian memory still ran and flapped about as if they might take off.

The two women hugged while he stood by awkwardly, making himself smile, putting on the amused and tolerant expression that he thought appropriate. *Play their game.*

"You did something to your hair," Marilyn was saying. She stood back, hands on hips, and looked perplexed.

"Made it blond," the woman said. "It's something I always wanted to do, and since I lived in New York, I thought it'd be a smart time to do it."

"Oh, you mean because of that Butcher creep."

His smile stayed firm. *Only a matter of time. Destiny is on rails, and gaining speed and momentum. Sixty miles an hour. No whistle. No stopping it. No avoiding it.* He was the engineer and he knew.

"I thought I saw you on the street a few days ago," the woman said, "only I couldn't be sure. But I decided to try and find you."

"How did you?"

"Called Rough Country. I'd heard some time ago you worked there. They gave me your address."

"If I'd known you lived here—" Marilyn suddenly gave a start. "Excuse my bad manners, I was so excited to see you. This is my friend Joe Grant." She made a sweeping motion toward him with her hand. "This is Ella Oaklie, Joe. She's an old college friend from Ohio State."

He shook the woman's damp hand, feeling the pain of a sharp ring. "Any relation to Annie Oakley?"

"Not hardly," Ella said, grinning. "Spelled differently. And about the only thing I shoot off is my mouth." She cocked her head to the side, appraising him. "Hey, I like your hat. Not to mention the boots. Kinda cowboy, but also big city. Sexy. Must be the Marilyn influence."

He suddenly felt ridiculous in his new outfit. "It sure is. She's good for me, and having a startling effect on my wardrobe."

"Well, you look right at home in New York, wrangler."

"We were just on our way out to have some drinks," Marilyn lied. Her way of letting Ella know Joe was hers. He liked that. "Join us, why don't you? Joe won't mind."

"Sounds great," he said, trying to show adequate enthusiasm.

Ella shrugged. "I really can't . . ."

Good. Why don't you mosey along.

"Then come on upstairs. I know you'd like to see the place," Marilyn insisted. "And I'd like to show it off. Really."

Damn it! This is going to happen.

Roll with it. Social ju-jitsu.

"Listen," he said, "why don't you two go up without me?"

"Joe—"

"I really don't mind, Marilyn. You're obviously good friends and haven't seen each other for a long time. You'll have plenty of news for each other. You don't need a third party around who doesn't recall old times."

"Really—" Ella began, flapping her arms. She really did resemble an awkward, overweight bird.

"So go ahead. I'll leave you two to catch up, long as you don't talk about me."

"It'll all be complimentary, Joe," Marilyn said.

"I'll try to believe that."

"Call me?"

"Speed dial."

"I can see you've made a good impression," Ella said,

aiming her indomitable toothy grin at him. "And I can see why."

Interested? He gave her a shy smile. "I try."

"Not enough men do."

"Amen," Marilyn said.

He kissed her lightly on the cheek. "Night." He smiled and backed away.

"Night, Joe."

He assured Ella it had been a pleasure meeting her, then deftly touched the brim of his Glenn Ford hat before turning and making his way down the sidewalk.

Near the corner, he glanced back and saw the two women entering the building.

For a second he considered following them inside, then he told himself that wouldn't be right. That wasn't part of the game.

Maybe someday he'd make it part. Two victims in the same tub. Mix and match. Wouldn't Quinn be confused.

He laughed out loud, then noticed several people on the street staring at him and immediately arranged his features in a solemn expression.

Laughing on the inside, though.

"Your *daughter* is living with you?" Fedderman seemed unable to comprehend this.

"Temporarily," Quinn told him.

They were in their office, drinking morning coffee from their initialed mugs. Quinn was seated behind his desk. Pearl and Fedderman were perched on theirs. The coffee was aromatic this morning, strong and slightly bitter. From the dental clinic next door, seeping faintly through the wall, came the faint but unmistakable shrill sound of drilling.

"Lauri," Pearl said thoughtfully. They'd never met, but he'd told Pearl about Lauri, not all of it good. "She'd be eighteen now, right?"

Quinn took a sip of coffee, noticing that his hand was shaking. The Lauri factor? "Eighteen," he confirmed. "Graduated from high school. She's in New York looking for a job."

"What kinda job?" Fedderman asked.

"She isn't sure."

The drilling next door paused, then resumed louder and shriller.

"She on the outs with mom and stepdad?"

"Only mildly. She mostly just wanted to head out on her own. You know kids."

Fedderman did. He had two of his own, grown and gone. Pearl didn't know kids.

"Lauri must be a young woman now," she said, then looked at Quinn. "She could have struck out on her own in any direction, you know."

"Meaning?"

Pearl smiled. "She wanted to be with you. She missed you."

"She wouldn't say so."

"Of course not. But that's why she's here."

"Maybe partly," Quinn said.

Fedderman looked thoughtful. Pearl was grinning.

Quinn said, "Let's think about murder."

But by that evening, when he entered the apartment a little after six and saw how excited Lauri was, all thoughts of the Butcher murders case fled his mind, something just a few days ago he would have thought impossible.

"Got a job!" she practically yelled, bouncing around the living room. "Doesn't pay much, but it pays. Starts tomorrow." She sat down on the sofa, sprang out of it, stalked to the window, hitched up her low-riding jeans. Her smile hit him in the heart.

"Doing what?" he asked.

"Waiting tables, mostly. Bussing them sometimes. Helping out in the kitchen. Cleaning up after closing. That kinda stuff."

"This would be at a restaurant?"

"Sure is. Down in the Village, on Fourteenth Street. The Hungry U."

Quinn had never heard of the place but thought he'd better not say so.

"They serve Pakistani food. And there's live music there sometimes at night. Not open for breakfast, so I can sleep late."

"Very important." Fourteenth Street in the Village. He made up his mind to check out the Hungry U tomorrow.

"I go in at eleven," Lauri said. "Help get set up for lunch."

"What about dinner?"

"I told you, Dad. I just—"

He grinned. "I mean us. This evening. We should celebrate."

She gave him another smile that cleaved his heart. "You know, we really oughta!"

"So what are you in the mood for? Pakistani?"

She paused, thinking. "I wouldn't know."

"I guess you're gonna find out," Quinn said. "You'll learn fast."

"Pizza! I noticed a place down the street, right near the corner. Looked neat."

He knew the restaurant. About a year ago, he and Pearl thought they might have gotten food poisoning there.

"Sounds great!" somebody else said.

No, it had been his voice. Some girl—woman—had him by the arm. He was headed for the door.

He played it cautiously, waiting almost a week before phoning Marilyn, then dropping by her apartment.

He wore well-pressed black slacks and a gray pullover

golf shirt; not very Rough Country, but he had on the faux-battered semi-cowboy hat with its artfully curved brim.

When she opened the door, smiling out at him, she was a surprise.

"Your hair," he said.

"You noticed."

"Hard not to. You're blond." She was also barefoot and wearing a pink silk robe, though he'd called fifteen minutes ago to let her know he was in the neighborhood and would soon be at her door.

"You don't like it?" Her smile threatened to fade as her right hand floated up to touch her newly colored hair.

He instantly slipped into pleased mode. After all, what did it matter? "I *do* like it. You just surprised me."

She did a neat pirouette, flashing bare calf and ankle beneath the robe, and the smile was back at full radiance. The abrupt turn had stirred the air and left it perfumed with the scent of roses. "The new and improved Marilyn Nelson."

"I like you blond, Marilyn, but it'll take a little getting used to. And there's no way to improve on the basic you."

You with the dark roots.

"Come in, Joe. I didn't mean to leave you standing in the hall."

When he entered, she seemed to notice for the first time the box beneath his arm.

"You've brought something," she said, using a lilting tone to demonstrate her pleasure.

"For later, actually."

"It's too big a box for wine. Flowers?"

"It'll be a surprise." He touched her robe with his free hand. The material was so soft and smooth it felt almost like flesh. Definitely more Frederick's of Hollywood than Rough Country. "Did I interrupt you getting dressed?"

"No. Getting *un*dressed." She gave him a look impossible to misinterpret: Marilyn coming around. He could guess what wasn't beneath the robe.

"I was about to take a shower," she said. Her smile went from shy to conspiratorial. "Maybe you'd like to join me."

"No, thanks."

Just as her features began to register surprise and embarrassment, he kissed her forehead. Then he pulled her close and kissed her mouth, feeling her immediately respond with her tongue. Her breath was sweet and warm. Heat emanated from beneath the robe. Marilyn was ready.

When they separated, he saw her breasts rising and falling beneath the taut material of the robe. She bit her lower lip, trying not to breathe so noisily.

"I was going to suggest a bath," he explained, standing close and smiling down at her.

She thought for a second. "Sounds wonderful, but maybe kind of cramped."

"We'll work something out." He kissed her again.

"Promise no bruises?" she asked, gazing at him with eyes that told him she was his.

Promise them anything . . . "You can trust me."

Her gaze remained locked with his as she unfastened the sash about her waist. With the slightest whisper, the delicate silk robe dropped to puddle at her feet.

On the way to the bathroom, he stepped on it.

18

Quinn didn't want to embarrass Lauri, so he'd waited for her night off before visiting the Hungry U.

It was one of those Village restaurants that tried too hard for bohemian décor, as if the owners were still in the thrall of Kerouac and Ginsberg. There was a small bar near the door, and beyond it round tables surrounded by mismatched chairs. The walls were different colors. On the blue wall was a doorway with beads hanging in it rather than a door. On the mauve wall was an arch, also beaded, that apparently led to another room with more tables. Each of the walls had movie posters mounted on them advertising films that had been set in Hollywood's idea of exotic places. Sidney Greenstreet, wearing a fez, smiled jovially behind a pointed gun. Peter Lorre sweated profusely in a desert setting. There was Bogie, suave in a white dinner jacket. Lauren Bacall wore a silky evening gown. Quinn knew most of the films had been shot in and around Los Angeles.

A woman who looked like an Eastern version of Madonna smiled at Quinn and led him to a table on the other side of the arch. This room was more expensively and tastefully decorated. The chairs around the tables matched, and there were framed landscapes on the walls rather than old movie posters. At the far end of the room was a slightly raised stage, and in front of it a small dance floor. There was a microphone and some sound equipment on the stage—two gigantic speakers—and a taped-up white banner on the wall with THE DEFENDANTS spray-painted on it in red block letters like gang graffiti.

Most of the tables were occupied. The Eastern Madonna led Quinn to a table toward the end of the room farthest from the stage and supplied him with a tall, narrow menu.

A small man of indeterminate ethnicity and wearing a pointed dark beard appeared and took Quinn's order. Soon Quinn was settled in with a glass of Pakistani beer and something called *roghni naan,* from what he assumed was the appetizer section of the menu.

It turned out to be bread sprinkled with sesame seeds and was tasty. The beer could have been colder, but it was good, too. The clientele appeared respectable enough and typical of the Village. A democratic mix of ages, races, and sexes, neighborhood people with a few obvious tourists here and there.

When the server with the pointed beard returned and asked if Quinn wanted dinner, he said the *roghni naan* would be plenty and it was delicious, but he'd have another beer. The man smiled as if privately amused that Quinn had mispronounced something, and it wasn't "beer."

"You're here for the band," the man said.

Quinn glanced at the stage, where a scroungy-looking young black man in a sleeveless T-shirt—his muscular arms covered with tattoos—was tinkering with the speakers.

"The Defendants," the server said.

"Ah!" Quinn said. "Sure. What time do they start to play?"

"About ten minutes."

Quinn hadn't quite finished his . . . bread, and he'd just ordered another beer. He was stuck.

Halfway through beer number two, there was a smattering of applause, and an older man with graying hair who might have been one of the owners introduced the Defendants with a good-natured flourish, as if they were opening at Vegas for Wayne Newton.

There were four of them: a drummer, two guitarists, and a guy with some kind of keyboard attached by a strap slung around his neck. Wires ran from the keyboard to the speakers. Wires ran everywhere.

Then a fifth member of the band arrived, to heightened applause. Apparently this band was having a good run at the Hungry U.

Quinn figured the new guy must be the front man and singer. At first he appeared almost shy, then he seemed to shake off any inhibitions and took his place at the mike. He grinned, signaling with his skinny right arm to the backup musicians poised behind him.

Quinn had never seen anyone skinnier. The kid, who probably wasn't even in his twenties, was about six feet tall and had shoulders and waist of about the same narrow dimension. What there was of his chest was concave beneath his faded red T-shirt, and his torn jeans clung to long, pipe-cleaner legs. He had wide blue eyes and a head of corkscrew red hair that lent him an amiable, startled expression. Quinn thought he resembled an anorexic Harpo Marx.

Unlike Harpo, he could talk. He confidently introduced the band's first piece, something called "Lost in Bonkers."

The band tore into it like starving men in a lifeboat, and the skinny kid began to sing.

Quinn wished he could arrest them for auditory assault.

The kid shouted incomprehensible lyrics while bounding around the stage as if there were springs in his feet, as if *he* were a spring, his long, skinny body rhythmically contorting in an undulating S shape. Then he produced a harmonica and began to play, somehow getting the instrument to make wheezing sounds like a damaged bagpipe.

But "Lost in Bonkers" was getting to the crowd. They

were clapping in time and stamping their feet. Quinn caught some of the lyrics:

Lost in Bonkers on familiar ground.
Lost in Bonkers an' I don't wanna be found.
Gone pure crazy lookin' out for you.
'Cause I know you're lost in Bonkers too.

What the hell did it mean? Quinn wondered, and took a swig of Pakistani beer.

His shirt pocket came alive.

His cell phone was there, the ringer set to vibrate so it wouldn't make noise and disturb anyone in the restaurant. Hah!

He drew the phone from his pocket and flipped it open. Said hello. Didn't even hear himself.

"Quinn, that you?" Renz's voice.

"Me."

"Where the hell are you? What's that racket?"

"Lost in Bonkers."

"Yonkers?"

Quinn turned his face toward the wall and talked louder. Still didn't make much of a dent in the din. "I'll explain later, Harley."

"I want you outta Yonkers and on the Upper West Side. I got a call . . ."

"Hold the line," Quinn said. He laid down enough money to cover his check and tip, then stood up and edged his way between tables and off-key notes toward the beaded arch. After getting slightly tangled in the strings of colorful beads, he freed himself and avoided the crowded bar to make a circuitous detour to the door. The smiling, exotic-looking woman who'd led him to his table nodded a good night to him and Quinn nodded back, the phone still pressed to his ear, and made his way outside into the quiet night.

"Harley?"

"Yeah. Wherever you are, get your team here." He gave Quinn a West Side address. "Uniforms are there already, got the scene frozen."

"The Butcher?"

" 'Fraid so. Another victim. An anonymous call came in twenty minutes ago."

"Sure it was our guy?"

"Take a barf bag."

"I'm beyond that, Harley. And I'm on my way."

"Where *are* you? What was all that goddamn noise?"

"I'm not sure myself," Quinn said, and broke the connection.

On familiar ground but in Lauri's new world, feeling lost.

19

"Sherman, is it? You got a great name, so you got a responsibility to live up to it. Know that, boy?"

"I guess," Sherman said. He'd had some history and remembered the name, but even though it was his name, he couldn't quite recall who it was the new boarder, Sam Pickett, was talking about.

They were sitting in cane-backed chairs out on the plank porch, leaning almost too far back with their feet up on the rail. Sherman had his ankles crossed and was sipping a warm pop. Pickett was messing around with the big, dirty briar pipe he smoked. Before them the swamp loomed green and lush, buzzing with life and smelling of rot. Something moved out there, causing dozens of blackbirds to rise screaming in a panic, and then settle down near their point of takeoff.

"My feelin' is he was the greatest Civil War general of 'em all," Pickett said, using his yellowed thumb to tamp tobacco firmly into the bowl of the odorous briar. "Ol' William Tecumseh Sherman."

That was why he hadn't stuck in Sherman's memory.

Sherman was his *last* name. Would Pickett remember everybody famous named Sam?

But Sherman liked it that Pickett must have realized Sherman didn't know who they were talking about, yet he hadn't pointed out Sherman's ignorance or made fun of him, just went on talking as if they both knew.

"Marched through the south tearin' up Ned all the way, burned an' killed an' left nothin' to eat neither on nor in the miles of scorched earth left behind him." He glanced over and gave Sherman a slight smile and a look that might have meant anything. "You think that was great?"

"Dunno," Sherman said. "Maybe. He was a general, so that was his job." He was choosing his words carefully, wary of Pickett, who seemed smarter and more interested in Sherman than any of the other boarders. Pickett was always doing this when they talked, asking questions right out of the blue, as if testing to see if Sherman was paying attention. Sherman didn't mind. Even kind of liked it.

"You got the truth of it," Pickett said, grinning at Sherman as if proud of him. "Ol' Sherman's hated—that's the general, not you—'cause of all the death an' destruction he created, but the fact is, if people'd just read their history, his march to the sea shortened the Civil War by months or years and saved a lot more lives than it cost."

"He kill women and kids, too?"

Pickett stopped in the process of raising his pipe to his mouth and looked over at Sherman, his bushy gray eyebrows raised in curiosity and surprise. "That's a damn—a darned good question, Sherman. Let's just say he did what he had to do. You could make the argument that the southerners started the war 'cause the people wanted it, so it was the southern people—not just the soldiers—to blame, an' it was only in the way of justice that they should have to pay the price of their lives."

Sherman looked out at the swamp, thinking of all the

death out there. "Seems like you know a lot about that kinda thing."

"I'm a student of the Civil War, all self-learned but well-learned. I understand what Sherman had to do, an' I think he was a good man. Now an' again you gotta do what ordinarily would turn your stomach. That's what life comes down to sometimes, Sherman."

"Yeah, it does."

The sun was going down. They listened to the crickets trilling away for a while. Pickett struck a book match and got his pipe fired up. The burning tobacco smelled good to Sherman. Better than the swamp.

Sherman liked Sam Pickett. Though he looked almost as old as the previous boarders, maybe in his fifties, there was a kind of energy about him. It was like he was younger even though he had a lot of lines in his face, and gray hair and a gray mustache. He wore his long hair in a ponytail, but Sherman never thought he looked womanish at all. In fact, if he didn't have such a big belly, Sherman could imagine Sam Pickett in a Civil War Union blue uniform, maybe even an officer's.

Pickett was the first boarder who didn't have his own room. Maybe because it was full of all the books he'd brought in his big trunk and some cardboard boxes. Or maybe it was because he was the first boarder who didn't have to pay. Sherman had heard Pickett and his mother talking about that one night when they were in the kitchen and didn't know he was listening. And what surprised Sherman was when his mother flat-out told Pickett he shouldn't have to pay any board. Pickett had said they'd work out something, that he'd pay for the groceries and whatever the boy might need. Sherman figured he was "the boy."

So books were piled on the bed where the other boarders had slept, and Pickett slept with Sherman's mother. Sometimes he and Myrna, Sherman's mom, would argue, and

Sherman would hear them other nights making noises as if they were fighting in the bedroom. Now and then there were bruises on Myrna, but Sherman never heard her complain.

Though he never dared call his mother anything other than "Mom," Sherman began to think of her and Sam as a pair, thinking of how they called each other—Myrna and Sam.

Sherman guessed Pickett did pay for things, but it was Myrna who took the truck into town most of the time and bought them. She said she was the only one who knew how to drive the balky old pickup, and Pickett seemed happy enough to stay behind and read, then help her unload groceries, beer, or firewood and carry the heavy stuff in when she returned.

Pickett read more often than anybody Sherman had ever met. It was how he passed the long hours, just sitting there concentrating, like he was breathing in information. Sherman thought of Sam always with a book in his hands, and his pipe clenched between his teeth. Which was how he almost always was. There was even a notch in his stained teeth worn there by the briar's pipe stem over the years. And Sherman guessed Pickett might have calluses on his fingers from turning pages.

"Ever fished?" Pickett asked, sucking and puffing noisily on the pipe to get the bowl glowing bright red.

"Sure. Some. Got a good bamboo pole."

"Know how to use a rod and reel?"

"Never had the chance."

"You got it now. I got one broke down in one of my boxes."

"You mean someday we can go fishing?" Sherman asked.

"Someday hell! Excuse my French. Don't wait for someday, Sherman. Let's get up outta these chairs an' go fishin' now. Unless you got somethin' better to do."

Sherman was grinning wide. "Can't think of a thing better."

The removed their feet from the porch rail, and the front legs of their chairs thumped on the plank floor in unison.

Over the next several weeks Pickett taught Sherman how to find where the fish might be biting, the bluegill around the weeds near banks where insects bred, and the big catfish that were bottom-feeders out farther from the banks and twisted banyan and cypress roots. He taught him how to cast side-arm so as not to hook low branches or Spanish moss, and drop the bait or fly within inches of where he aimed. After the first few times fishing, Sam always used the bamboo pole and let Sherman use the rod and reel.

It was a great summer for Sherman. When he wasn't fishing or talking with Sam Pickett, he was reading some of Pickett's books. Sam told him he could read any or all of them without asking, only had to put them back when he was finished.

Sherman soon understood why Sam knew so much about the Civil War, because that was what most of the books were about. Some of them looked so old they might have been written *during* the Civil War. Sherman got to know all about William Tecumseh Sherman and some of the other famous generals and other personalities on both sides of the great conflict. And he learned about the battles, how sometimes their outcome turned on little things, like which troops needed boots and shoes, or maybe on the weather that might turn open fields into deep mud that mired down troops and made them easy to slaughter with artillery. Death meant something in the Civil War, Sherman decided. Every death.

The Civil War became Sherman's obsession because it was Sam Pickett's obsession. And Sam became like a father to Sherman—at least the closest thing to a father Sherman had ever known.

Once when he was lying quietly in the warm dark and listening to Sam and Myra talking in the kitchen while they drank beer, Sherman heard Sam remark on how uncommonly smart Sherman was for a boy ten years old, how quickly he caught on to things. That was news to Sherman. He heard his mother say that was news to her, too.

Sherman just lay there in the night, smiling, while they drank more beer and changed the subject.

Sometimes, years later, he'd lie in his bed in the dark and recall that conversation and smile. He might drift off to sleep while mentally re-creating that long-ago time and Sam Pickett.

It truly had been a great summer.

For a while.

20

It was beginning to feel like a recurring nightmare to Quinn. Here he was again with Pearl and Fedderman in an apartment crowded with cops and techs, the bleached stench of death and dismemberment made somehow obscenely sanitary. More and more he was asking himself the question cops asked when they'd seen too many dead bodies: What was the value of life, if it could come to this?

"I wish we didn't have to look at this one," Pearl said, probably thinking the same thoughts as Quinn.

"Want me to check with the uniforms, then the neighbors, as usual?" Fedderman asked Quinn.

"Go to it, Feds."

Fedderman gratefully disappeared from the apartment.

Quinn eased past two techs who were diligently dusting and tweezering, then made his way down the short hall to the bathroom. Pearl was right behind him.

There wasn't much room for both of them in the bathroom, so both stood in the doorway looking in. Nift the ME was bending over the tub. An empty detergent box lay on the floor near a plastic bleach bottle. The box proclaimed in bold text that the soap contained bleach. A lot of bleach here, Quinn thought, but the smell of corruption somehow seeped through to lodge in the nostrils and lie like a dull taste on the tongue. He swallowed and only made it worse.

"Jesus!" Pearl said in a hushed voice behind him.

"No, only me," said the smart-mouthed little ME, still facing away from them. He'd known they were there. He duckwalked aside slightly in his crouch, maybe to allow them to see the severed head of Marilyn Nelson lying on top of her bone-white crossed arms. Marilyn was staring back at them with an expression of alarm, as if they'd interrupted her in an intimate moment, which in a manner of speaking they had. Quinn wished Nift would close her eyes.

"This one is really a shame," Nift said, probing pale dead flesh with a bright steel instrument.

It wasn't like him to show anything other than callousness or dumb wit toward his job. Was he developing human feelings? Sensitivity?

"They're all a shame," Pearl said.

"Yeah, but this one especially. You put all the pieces together, at least in your mind, and she was built like a sex machine."

"Dr. Frankenstein Nift," Pearl said in disgust.

Nift glanced back and up at her. "Franken*steen*!"

"This one like the others?" Quinn asked, trying to head off a verbal confrontation, not to mention more mundane drivel.

"In almost every way that matters," Nift said. "Looks like the same kind of cutting instruments, then the same draining and immaculate cleansing of the body parts. She's stacked—no pun intended—in the same ritualistic way. Adhesive residue indicating that tape was recently removed from her wrists and ankles, as well as from across her mouth. I can't say for sure before the postmortem, but my guess would be death by drowning. Then chop, chop. And just as in the other cases, the killer left the bathroom cleaner than my wife ever could."

Pearl stared at him. "You've got a *wife*?"

"I was speaking metaphorically."

Quinn gave Pearl a warning look. He knew how she felt about Nift and didn't want her going ballistic at a crime scene.

"You said this one was like the others in *almost* every way that mattered," Quinn pointed out. He knew that Nift liked to put off whatever of value he might have to say, savoring the suspense and then the moment.

"I meant that mattered to the victim," Nift said.

"How about what matters to us detectives?"

Nift appeared to give the question some thought. "C'mon in all the way so you can get a closer look," he said. "Just you, not the cop with the curves."

Pearl showed admirable restraint, clamping her lips together.

Quinn moved farther into the bathroom, unconsciously holding his breath against the ungodly stench, and saw for the first time that the victim's wet and slicked-back hair was blond. That must be the difference Nift had referred to, what mattered; the other victims were brunettes. And there was something stuck to Marilyn Nelson's left cheek, a few inches in front of her ear. At first Quinn thought it was a dead insect. He leaned closer and saw that it was a clipping of dark, curly hair.

"That what I think it is?"

Nift smiled. "Uh-huh. Dark pubic hair. Not a clipping, though. The follicles are still attached. These hairs were yanked out, then placed on her cheek on display. The victim was a dyed blonde."

Quinn leaned closer to examine the blond hair. "It would figure, but I don't see any dark roots."

"That's because it's a very recent dye job. She's a brunette." Nift chuckled. "Take it from me, I checked." Nift shot a look back at Pearl. "Wish I coulda checked when she was alive."

Pearl had her jaws clenched so tight in her effort to remain silent that Quinn thought she better be careful or she might break a tooth.

He straightened up, leaving Nift down in a crouch to finish his preliminary postmortem.

But Nift also stood up. He had on his creepy smile. "Know what I think that display of pubic hair means, Quinn?"

"What it might mean," Quinn said, "is that our killer who prefers brunettes was acquainted with the victim well enough to know she wasn't a real blonde."

"No might about it," Nift said. "He wouldn't have killed her in the first place if he didn't know she was actually a brunette—his type. I think he knew this one personally."

Pearl had to admit to herself that Nift had a point, but she still maintained her silence, biting down on her anger and fierce dislike for the nasty little ME. If she started in on him . . . Well, there was no reason to consider that.

"It's a recent dye job," Quinn said. "But that doesn't mean the killer knew his victim personally. He might have stalked her for weeks, even months, when she was a brunette."

And because her last name began with an N, Pearl thought.

Nift chewed on the inside of his cheek, then nodded. "Possible," he admitted.

Good, Pearl thought. *The little prick's been squelched. Teach him to cross swords with Quinn.*

"Another thing," Nift said. "My guess is Miz Nelson hasn't been dead more than three hours."

That interested Quinn. It meant the killer must have made his anonymous call to the police shortly after murdering Marilyn Nelson, his second *N* victim. The bastard had probably planned on the phone call. Didn't want to wait for the body to be discovered by someone other than the police. He wanted Marilyn Nelson to be viewed by Quinn and company exactly as he'd left her so the strands of dark pubic hair were sure to be found. Playing his gruesome game.

Quinn took a careful look around, and then started to back out of the bathroom so he and Pearl could talk to the first uniforms on the scene, then to the crime scene techs, to see when they'd be finished. Then they'd help Fedderman interview Marilyn Nelson's neighbors. She'd been dead only a few hours. Maybe someone would remember actually seeing the killer come or go.

As they were leaving the bathroom and the immediate presence of violent death, Pearl decided to mention calmly to Nift something to the effect that from now on he should concentrate on his job and let the detectives concentrate on theirs. She really did intend for it to be calm and measured. A relatively polite parting shot.

What came out was, "Hey, Frankenstein, you really are an insufferable little asshole."

Far from being insulted, Nift grinned and glanced wide-eyed at Quinn. "She's *alive!*"

Quinn wrapped an arm around Pearl's waist and turned her away from Nift, then gripped her elbow tightly and got her out of there.

"Sorry," Pearl said, when they were back in the living room. "I couldn't resist."

Quinn smiled at her. "Considering the provocation, I thought you did well."

Still avoiding the CSU techs, who assured them they were almost finished, they crossed the room to a small desk where a phone sat. A tech told Quinn the phone had already been dusted for prints, so it was okay to touch. Quinn touched. He pressed the redial button on Marilyn Nelson's phone and got a number that gave out time and temperature and an offer for expense-free checking. So the killer hadn't called the police from the apartment. At least not on this phone.

A cursory search of Marilyn Nelson's apartment wasn't very revealing. There was no sign of a cell phone, vibrating or otherwise. Maybe she'd had a cell and the killer had taken it with him, used it to call the law.

Quinn had to smile, thinking maybe the killer had tried to use the cell phone and it only vibrated.

They left the apartment and stood out in the hall, more to get away from the stench of bleached death than for any other reason.

Quinn said, "Nift is probably right. This one might have been chosen because her last initial was *N,* but the killer probably got to know her first as a brunette, or had known her all along."

"Maybe it's her brother," Pearl said, glaring back into the apartment in the general direction of Nift. Once someone got under her skin she simply couldn't let it go. She fumed for a long, long time, maybe unto eternity. Quinn thought it might be part of what made her such a good detective and such a bad cop.

He was familiar with the white splotches at the corners of her mouth, the pugnacious thrust of her chin. In truth he'd always found these manifestations of her righteous rage oddly attractive, though he'd never told her so.

He shook his head slowly and with sad knowledge. "Pearl, Pearl . . ."

The look she gave him might have scorched his clothes.

The sanitized stench of death stayed with them the rest of the evening and followed them home.

Quinn shared Pearl's rage, but in a quieter way and directed at the killer. Pearl was a hothead buffeted by her emotions. Quinn's rage was constant and controlled and patient, a laser beam probing the darkness, obsessively seeking its target.

Pity the target.

21

Quinn had no idea who had knocked unexpectedly on his apartment door. He was peering out at an emaciated kid in his early twenties, over six feet tall but not more than a hundred and forty pounds. He had on incredibly narrow Levi's, a stained gray T-shirt lettered IMAGINE REALITY across the chest, and untied, worn-out jogging shoes held together with duct tape. His red hair looked like a mass of unruly springs. It was the hair, and indeed something springy in his slightest movement, even as he stood what in his mind must be still, that triggered Quinn's memory. The lead singer of The Defendants at the Hungry U.

"I'm Wormy," said the human Slinky.

"They've got pills for that," Quinn said.

The kid's grin spread wider, so wide for his narrow face that it pushed his cheeks way out. "I've heard that one. Wormy's my name."

"Is that French or something?"

"No, it's a nickname, actually. I'm a singer-musician."

"I've seen and heard you," Quinn said, noticing the odd tattoos on Wormy's arms, twisting, twining designs that apparently represented nothing while adding to the impression of constant movement. There seemed to be, for Wormy, nothing akin to a state of rest.

"I know," Wormy said. "I remember you 'cause you walked out in the middle of my big number."

"It had nothing to do with the music," Quinn said. "I got a phone call."

Big smile. Bounce, bounce. "That's good to know." Wormy looked up and down the hall, then back at Quinn, as if waiting for Quinn to invite him in.

Quinn simply regarded Wormy as if his name represented what he was.

"I'm here for Lauri," Wormy said.

"I was afraid of that."

Quinn moved back and Wormy slithered in. Well, he didn't exactly slither, but his long body's repetitive *S* motion seemed to propel him forward.

"Hi, Worm." Lauri, who'd been in her bedroom changing clothes, was now in the living room. She looked tentatively from Wormy to her father, then back. "I see you two have met."

"Formally for the first time," Wormy said, "but your old— your dad—was at the Hungry U having dinner the other night. I guess to listen to the music. He's a fan."

"Great!" Lauri said, pleased but puzzled.

"I wanted to check out where you worked," Quinn said. He saw anger cloud her face, and for a second she looked remarkably like her mother.

Wormy touched her arm. "Don't be hard on him, Lauri. It's a dad thing. He's concerned about his daughter's all."

Lauri took a deep breath and seemed calmer. "So what did you think of the Hungry U?" she asked Quinn.

"Food was good."

No one spoke for an awkward few moments.

"You two are going out?" Quinn said finally, as if the possibility had just entered his mind.

"On a date," Lauri said, bearing down on the last word.

Quinn told himself he was being tested. He had little control, maybe none at all, over whom Lauri dated. But this human single-cell creature . . .

"I'll have her home 'fore she turns into a pumpkin," Wormy said, still with the grin.

Quinn wanted to scare him stiff then hurl him like a javelin, but he restrained himself.

"I understand your dad's concern," said Wormy. "You're his dear daughter, an' he don't know a thing about me other than I've got musical talent."

I do know about you. I've seen thousands of you.

Lauri moved toward the door, and Wormy seemed rooted though moving, continuing to grin at Quinn.

"Where are you two going?" Quinn heard himself ask. He thought he sounded casual, only remotely interested. Tried, anyway.

Must have failed.

Lauri clouded up again. "Look—"

"Zero down," Wormy said good-naturedly to her. "We're gonna take in a band down in the Village, Lauri's dad. Some band thinks it's better'n mine, if you can believe it. No drugs, and no . . . drugs."

"You didn't say no—"

"Dad!"

Quinn knew he was helpless. He willed his stiff facial muscles to arrange themselves in a smile that couldn't have fooled anyone. "So have a good time. You got a key?"

"Got my key," Lauri said. Impulsively, she came to him and pecked his cheek, grinning up at him. "Don't worry so much about me, Dad, really."

"I'll try not to."

"She's with me," Wormy said reassuringly.

"I'll try not to," Quinn repeated.

Then they were gone into the world, his little girl and the human worm, and the door was swinging closed.

"I like your dad," Quinn heard Wormy say, just before the latch clicked.

* * *

Some kind of telepathy, Quinn thought. May and Elliott lived all the way on the other side of the continent, and still May chose that night to call Quinn.

"How's Lauri doing?" she asked, after they'd traded hellos.

"Doing well," Quinn said. *I hope.* He hadn't gone to bed and was slumped on the sofa, worrying while watching four lawyers on a quarter-split TV screen argue over a murder that had happened in some other state, maybe Minnesota. The victim had been an attractive young woman. He'd muted the lawyers but hadn't been able to stop watching.

"New York hasn't corrupted her, has it?"

"I won't let that happen," Quinn said. "Besides, she's more grown-up than I imagined. She's smart."

"Not street-smart. You don't get that way here in the burbs of LA."

Quinn wondered if May read the papers. If you were a teenager, anyplace you were had the potential to make you wiser but sadder—or worse. His gaze wandered back to the attorneys jabbering silently on the muted TV. "I think she's taking care of herself pretty well. She's got a job."

"You're kidding. The Lauri I know couldn't hold down a job."

"She's held it down so far. She's a waitress at a restaurant down in the Village."

"Servers, they call them now, Quinn. And I'm not sure I like it that this place is in the Village."

A dapper gray-haired man who used to be the chief medical examiner in New York was on the screen now, holding up a chart with a skeleton printed on it and using his manicured forefinger as a pointer.

"The restaurant's Pakistani," Quinn said, watching the former ME point at the skeleton's pelvis. "At least it claims to be. The food seems kind of eclectic to me. Lots of barbecue."

"You've been there?"

"Damned right."

May laughed. "Good. That's comforting. She's still working there, so you must have thought the place was okay."

"It's a job," Quinn said. "A start."

"Can I talk to her?"

"She's not home right now."

"It's eleven-thirty, Quinn."

Damned Worm! "She's on a date."

May didn't say anything for a moment. Then: "Oh. It didn't take her long to get into circulation."

"She's a beautiful girl, May. Like you're a beautiful woman."

"Spare me the Irish bullshit. Who's she going out with? Another of the food servers?"

"A musician from the band that's playing at the restaurant. There's a bar there, too, with live music."

"Pakistani music?"

"For all I know," Quinn said, remembering the high-decibel onslaught of "Lost in Bonkers." "I've met the guy. He seems . . . safe."

"Is that what your cop's instincts tell you?"

They tell me what to tell you. "He's a scrawny young kid, looks like he's never had real sex. If you could see him, May, you wouldn't worry so much."

"What's his name?"

"Wormy."

"God! Is that a nickname?"

"I don't know. I think it's French and I might be pronouncing it wrong."

Quinn heard noises in the hall, then the key ratcheting in the lock.

The door opened and Lauri came in alone. A vague, S-shaped shadow behind her writhed and flitted away in the hall.

"She just got home," Quinn said, trying to sound reassuring. He mouthed to Lauri, *You're late.*

"Close, though," she whispered back.

Quinn studied her. Clothes not too mussed, lipstick unsmeared, pretty much the same Lauri who'd left with the human worm.

"She all right?" asked the voice from California.

"Fine, fine . . ." Quinn held the phone out toward Lauri. "It's your mother. She wants to talk to you."

Lauri seemed to think about that, then shrugged and walked over to where Quinn sat on the sofa. He handed her the phone, then stood up and diplomatically left the room.

In the kitchen, he opened a cold Budweiser and for a brief moment considered listening in on the extension, then thought he'd probably be caught at it.

Sitting at the table, sipping his beer, he couldn't make out the contents of the conversation in the next room, but it didn't take long, and Lauri's tone was curt.

After a few minutes of silence, she appeared in the kitchen doorway.

"Your mother still on the line?" Quinn asked.

"No. I guess she didn't have anything more to say to you." She smiled at him. "I'm going to bed. Unless you wanna chew me out first for being forty-five minutes late."

"You were close enough," Quinn said. "Besides, eleven-thirty wasn't a promise, it was just something Wormy mentioned." He took a sip of beer. "You like that guy?"

"Not nearly as much as he likes me."

Quinn tilted back the bottle for another sip. "You'd better get used to that kind of thing."

Lauri looked at him. "Fatherly wisdom, along with a compliment. I like that. Thanks." She waved languidly to him. "'Night."

"'Night," he said, not sure whether she was kidding.

He sat for a while absently peeling the label from the beer bottle, trying to sort through how he was feeling, not getting anywhere. Probably like a lot of fathers of teenage girls. Unknowing. Unsettled.

He decided he'd ask Pearl to talk with Lauri, to just sort of get acquainted. Maybe she could figure things out and enlighten him.

Then maybe Lauri could explain Pearl.

22

"It somehow makes the murder more intimate," Renz said.

He unmistakably winked at Pearl before he glanced around. It was the first time he'd been in the office space the city had rented for Quinn and his team, and he was obviously thrown by the idea of the place as an ersatz squad room. It looked more like the scene of a boiler room operation that had folded only minutes before the police arrived.

Zzzziiiiiiiiiii, went a drill at Nothing but the Tooth.

Renz winced.

"Murder itself is as intimate as it gets," Quinn said. "The fact that the killer displayed some of the victim's pubic hair after dismembering the body doesn't make it any worse."

"No," Pearl said, "Deputy Chief Renz is right. There's something especially intimate about that kind of thing that gets to people—especially women. But men, too, if they have any sensitivity." She was perched on the edge of her desk, where she could usually be found instead of in her chair.

Quinn gave her a dark look from behind his desk. Was she ticked off at him over something? And Renz was at least sensitive enough to know he was being played.

But Renz was smiling; Pearl was playing his game. "Officer Kasner has it figured right, Quinn. That's why the chief and the commissioner and everybody who ever so much as ran for office in New York is on my ass."

"Which is why you're here," Quinn said.

"Yep. Pass the potato. You and your team have gotta start showing some results, or the entire NYPD will be in so much deep shit with the pols it'll be traded for Boston's police department."

"Or Mayberry's," Fedderman said. Pearl figured he must have seen Renz's earlier wink.

Renz grinned. "I like that. Your team's at least got a sense of humor, Quinn. Like a lot of losers, they've learned to laugh at themselves."

"I was thinking the same thing," Quinn said.

Now Renz was laughing. They were all laughing. Oh, it was a jolly world.

Renz wiped his eyes. "I was told by the chief to come here and shake a knot in your tail. I'm going easy because I know how it is, how clean this bastard works, so there's nothing you can grasp that doesn't slide right outta your mind. All I'm saying is, remember who hired you. We're working together while you're working for me."

"And we *are* working," Pearl said, having lost track of who was doing the kidding.

"And hard," Fedderman added.

"Don't I know it?" Renz said. "This visit is just a political necessity." He studied Quinn. "So what ails you? Have a bad night?"

"Real bad," Quinn said. He wondered if Renz would have a sense of humor if he had Lauri for a daughter.

"Anything I can help with?" Renz asked sincerely, probably putting on Quinn again.

"No. It's family stuff. Kinda thing you've gotta shake off so you can get to work."

"So I was about to say," Renz told him.

There was a sudden, muffled yelp.

Renz appeared startled. "What the hell was that?"

"Could be a root canal," Quinn said. "At the dental clinic on the other side of the building. That was the drilling you heard earlier."

"Ah. I thought maybe the Butcher was killing somebody right next door. Just the sort of thing he'd do to make us look bad."

"Different kinda sadist over there," Fedderman said, smiling with bad teeth.

Renz looked around again at the cluster of desks and workstations, the walls that were bare except for occasional nails or screws and clean rectangles where frames had been hung, the hardwood floor with clumps of tangled wiring jutting up from of it. "Place is a minefield. What happens if you step on one of those wiring masses? You get zapped?"

"Maybe," Pearl said.

Renz hitched his belt up over his belly and glanced down to make sure the drape of his pants was right. Quinn knew it was a sign he was about to leave.

Renz said, "Well, you people can consider yourself chewed out. Far as the chief knows, that's what happened here this morning."

"Thanks," Pearl said. She thought somebody should say it so Renz would leave believing his line of crap had been a sale.

Renz nodded to her, let his gaze slide over Quinn and Fedderman, then turned and went out the door.

"Man's some piece of work," Pearl said.

"Piece of something," Fedderman said. He got up from behind his desk and sauntered across the minefield to pour himself a cup of coffee.

Pearl waited until he was out of earshot. "What kind of family problem?" she asked Quinn.

"The Lauri kind."

She looked simultaneously sympathetic and amused.

"From what I know of her, which is very little, she seems like a nice kid."

"She is. And a naïve one. She's got some misconceptions that I'm afraid make her vulnerable."

"We talking about a boyfriend?"

"If you can call him that."

"Well, I think I understand the situation. She's probably not as naïve and vulnerable as you imagine, Quinn."

"That's what I'd like you to find out."

Pearl raised her vivid eyebrows in surprise. She wasn't sure what to think of this. Family was sticky.

God! I really should call my mother, after hanging up on her the way I did.

"Just meet and talk with her," Quinn implored. "Get to know her a little. She might tell another female stuff she wouldn't tell her father."

"Oh, she might," Pearl said. What must it be like to have Quinn for a father?

"Will you do that, Pearl?"

"Sure." But she knew from the expression on Quinn's face that she hadn't sounded sufficiently enthusiastic.

They both fell silent as Fedderman returned with his coffee.

"Mayberry," Fedderman said thoughtfully. "Things *are* quieter there. Remember Floyd the barber?"

"What you both oughta know," Quinn said, "is that Renz isn't to be taken lightly just because he's talking like he's one of us. He'll act all buddy-buddy, but he'll jam us up in a minute if it'll help him get promoted."

"We know it," Pearl said. "We were only putting you on, Quinn."

"Still," Fedderman said, "Mayberry . . ."

"New York," Quinn said. "Marilyn Nelson was the second *N,* but that doesn't mean she was the final victim."

* * *

Searching the weeds again. That was what Quinn called it, and that was what Pearl was doing here in Marilyn Nelson's modest West Side apartment that still held the disinfected scent of death. Searching the weeds again. Hoping to find something, anything of use, on ground already covered.

Pearl walked around slowly in a second, more careful search of the apartment, paying closer attention. It was cheaply but tastefully decorated. Probably Marilyn Nelson had thought she earned a pretty good salary but found out it didn't go far in Manhattan. The bedroom closet contained some interchangeable black outfits—Marilyn catching on—and some great outdoorsy-looking items. They would have suggested Marilyn was a hiker or rock climber, if Pearl didn't know she worked for a clothing chain, and the rough-textured, riveted clothing and heavy boots were more for style than hard use.

There was nothing noteworthy in the refrigerator—an unopened bottle of orange juice, some leftover pizza in a take-out box, a half-gallon carton of milk well past its expiration date and almost empty, some bagged and sealed lettuce for salads on the go, the usual condiments. Pearl leaned close and breathed in some of the cool air before closing the refrigerator door.

Nothing new in the bedroom, either, but she went through drawers and the closet, even checked between the mattress and box spring, making sure a Dial In cell phone vibrator hadn't been overlooked. It would have been nice to tie Marilyn Nelson in with two of the other victims. Tidy. Clean. Pearl swallowed. Clean was beginning to seem like a nasty word to her.

She made herself spend more time in the bathroom than was necessary, as if testing herself. The gleaming old porcelain tub was to her more disgusting than if it had been stained with the victim's blood.

Sickened, she left the bathroom, then quickly made her way through the hall and living room toward the door. She would replace the yellow crime scene tape she'd untied from the doorknob, then get back out into the fresh air and the wider world where death wasn't so near.

After a last, sad glance around the living room, she opened the door to the hall.

Her breath caught in her throat.

23

Sherman was dreaming, and suddenly he was awake and unable to recall the dream.

It had frightened him, though. He was drenched in sweat, and his heart was pounding in his ears, the loudest thing in the night other than the buzz of insects in the nearby swamp.

Then the voices. *Like the ones in the dream.* Sam's deep voice, and Sherman's mother's. His was calm; hers higher-pitched, faster-paced. It sounded as if Sam and Myrna were arguing in the bedroom down the hall, where they slept in the sagging double bed. Sherman's body grew rigid and he realized he was squeezing his thumbs in his clenched fists, a habit he'd pretty much gotten over since Sam arrived.

There was a sound that might have been a slap. Flesh on flesh—hard.

Sherman's grip on his thumbs tightened so that they ached.

His mother's voice, then, much louder. Even though Sherman couldn't make out the words, he was sure she was furious, cursing at Sam.

Sam's voice was softer but not as calm, as if he didn't want to wake Sherman, trying to get Myrna to regain control of herself. Another slap. Then another, terrible sound Sherman had never heard. He was sure his mother was weeping.

Sam again, speaking angrily but softly, in that slow, reasoned tone he used when patiently teaching Sherman to fish or telling him something interesting about the Civil War.

There was a war going on in his mother's bedroom, Sherman thought. One he wanted no part of.

He lay motionless for a long time, waiting for more noise from the bedroom down the hall, but there was only the buzzing of the swamp in the night. He could smell the swamp through his open screened window, the rotting death scent of it, the fear and the fight of it within its lush green beauty. Thousands of cicadas were screaming now; Sam had told Sherman it was their mating call. It sounded desperate. Amidst the shrillness came a faint splashing and a deep, primal grunt. Something moving in the blackness not far away from the house. Not far away at all.

In the bedroom down the hall there was only silence.

The next morning, Sherman thought he was first up, but when he padded barefoot down the hall, there was his mom in the kitchen. She was lighting the butane stove to cook some eggs that were lying on the sink counter. Her hair was wild and there was a thoughtful expression on her face, but she didn't look upset. She had on her old pink robe, its sash yanked tight around her narrow waist. Like her son, she was barefoot, the way she liked to be most of the time. Her toenails were painted red and one of them looked broken and as if it had been bleeding.

Sherman didn't think she'd seen him. He changed direction and trudged toward the bathroom, seeing through the inch-wide crack where his mother's bedroom door was open. There was Sam's bare lower leg and foot on the bed. He must still be asleep.

Sherman thought that maybe last night—everything he'd

heard—had been a dream. It was possible. Dreams and reality sometimes met and became entangled in his mind.

He urinated and then flushed the leaking old toilet so it would drain to the septic tank buried alongside the house. The washbasin's ancient faucet handles squealed when he rotated them. He washed his hands and dried them carefully before leaving the bathroom.

The plank floor was cool beneath his bare feet as he returned to the kitchen. He noticed that now his mother's bedroom door was closed all the way. He slowed so he might try the knob, see if it was locked.

"You want some eggs?" she asked.

"Toast is all," Sherman said, picking up his pace.

"You go get some pants on first."

Sherman was wearing only his Jockey shorts. He nodded and went back to his bedroom and put on his jeans. The morning was already hot and humid. He tried wrestling back into the T-shirt he'd worn yesterday, but it stuck to his damp skin so that it was difficult to pull down in back. He peeled it off and tossed it on the floor, then went shirtless back to the kitchen, this time not pausing near his mother's bedroom door.

There was a slice of buttered toast and a glass of milk where Sherman always sat at the table. His mother was being nice to him this morning; usually he prepared his own breakfast.

She'd cooked up some eggs for herself. Now she used the rubber spatula to slide them onto a plate. Next to them she plopped down the second slice of toast from the old toaster.

Without speaking to or looking at Sherman, she sat down across from him at the table and began to eat.

"Sleep okay?" she asked, through a bite of egg she'd forked into her mouth.

"Always do." Sherman took a big bite of toast.

"You're young and you got no troubles," she said, smiling.

"Got some."

"Yeah, I guess ever'body does."

They continued to eat, not looking at each other.

Then Sherman became aware that he was the only one eating.

His mother slowly raised her fork with a bite of egg halfway to her mouth, then set it back down on her plate. The expression on her face changed, like she was aging right in front of Sherman. She slid her chair back with a loud scraping sound, stood up from the table, and hurried into the bathroom.

She hadn't even taken time to shut the door. Sherman could hear her retching in there.

Absently carrying what was left of his toast, he got up and walked to where he could see into the bathroom.

His mother was kneeling on the tile floor, her head hung over the yellowed porcelain toilet bowl so that some of her long brown hair dangled down into the water. Her face was as pale as Sherman had ever seen it.

She made a horrible grunting sound like the one Sherman had heard last night from the swamp, then retched and vomited into the toilet bowl. Sherman saw that a lot of what she was bringing up was blood. There was a smear of blood on the floor near her broken toenail.

So last night had been real, not a nightmare. There'd been a fight for sure. At least it had sounded like a fight.

Sherman moved closer to the open door, still staring into the bathroom.

"Mom . . . ?"

"G'way!"

"You want me to wake up Sam?"

"Let him sleep," said Sherman's mother into the yellowed bowl.

She stayed the way she was, kneeling and staring into the toilet, for a long time. Sherman didn't move, either.

Finally his mother reached up and worked the lever to flush the bowl. She scooted back away from it, lowered the wooden seat, and swiped the arm of her robe across her mouth.

"You okay, Mom?"

"Gonna be. Gotta be."

She twisted her body to the side, then reached up and used the washbasin for support to haul herself back to her feet. Her breathing was deep and loud. Leaning with both arms on the basin, she looked into the medicine cabinet mirror, then quickly looked away.

The faucet handles squealed.

For a long time Myrna stood hunched over and holding her wrists beneath cool running water. This wasn't like her because, as she often reminded Sherman, there was a limited amount, mostly rainwater, in the holding tank, and the pump water smelled bad and was unfit for washing or drinking.

Finally she turned off the water and looked over at Sherman. It gave him a chill, the way her eyes were, so sad and at the same time . . . something else. Something that frightened him.

"You and Sam were goin' fishin', as I recall."

"Yes'm." He couldn't look away from her eyes.

"You go ahead, and he'll meet you when he's been up and had some breakfast."

Her eyes.

Sherman didn't move.

"Sam know how to find you?"

"Yes'm. We been goin' to the same place."

"Then you go on, Sherman. Sam'll be along. You take your toast with you."

Sherman took one hesitant step. Two. Her stare was like heat on his bare back.

"Sam'll be along," his mother said again.

*   *   *

Sherman could feel her eyes following him as he went out onto the porch, munching the last of his toast. He brushed his hands together to get rid of the crumbs and wiped his buttery fingers on his jeans.

He reached for the fly rod Sam had been letting him use, but on second thought took his old bamboo pole from where it was leaning against the house. It was already rigged with a line, bobber, and hook, and he could find some worms or bug bait where he'd be fishing. Let Sam use the rod and reel and colorful fly bait this morning.

Sherman went to where they'd been having luck lately, near the gnarled and twined roots of an ancient banyan tree, and sure enough he had no trouble finding worms in the moist soil.

But his luck didn't hold. The fish weren't biting this morning.

Sherman listened to the muted sounds of the swamp, thinking he could almost hear things growing. A mosquito buzzed very near. Hundreds of gnats glittered in the light and lent motion to a slanted sunbeam. There was no breeze, and yet foliage rustled. He watched water spiders adroitly traverse the dark surface near the shore, saw a brown-and-gray moth the size of his hand flutter into the dappled shadows beneath the trees.

He stayed there a long time, standing in the shade and staring into the water at his cork that never bobbed in any way meaningful, looking into the dark ripples, thinking about his mother's eyes, waiting for Sam, hoping Sam would show up grinning with his rod and reel balanced and resting easy in his right hand, knowing he probably wouldn't.

Thinking about his mother's eyes.

24

Startled by how close the man was standing when she opened the door to leave Marilyn Nelson's apartment, Pearl automatically backed up a step.

Quickly regaining her composure, she assessed the man in a cop's glance.

His right hand had been raised shoulder high; he'd been about to knock. He was medium height, dark-haired, good looking. Even features, amiable brown eyes, a nice smile. His clothes told her little—khaki pants, short-sleeved blue shirt with the top button undone, brown loafers. There were no rings on his fingers. His wristwatch looked more expensive than the rest of his clothes. Not unusual these days. People were into watches.

"I was expecting Marilyn," he said, obviously puzzled.

Pearl didn't say anything immediately. Let him stew. She wanted the advantage.

"You a friend?" he asked. Curious and still amiable, as if open to making new friends himself. The heart of a golden retriever.

She flashed her shield and introduced herself as NYPD Homicide.

"Are *you* a friend?" Pearl asked.

He was the one who was slightly rattled now. "Yeah. Yes, I am. Name's Jeb Jones."

Pearl didn't recall the name from Marilyn's address book.

His brown eyes slid to the side, then back. "You said 'homicide.' This yellow tape really what I think it is?"

"I'm afraid so."

"Not a gag?" He seemed deeply upset now, and genuinely surprised. He didn't want to believe.

"No gag. You look at the papers or check the news on TV, Mr. Jones?"

"Not for a couple of days. Tell you the truth, I stay away from the news. It gets me depressed."

"Marilyn Nelson was a victim of the Butcher," Pearl said.

Judging by the stricken expression on his face, Jones had heard of the killer. "Holy Christ!" He raised a hand and pinched the bridge of his nose, closing his eyes and trying to adjust to the news that was even worse than he'd thought.

"C'mon inside," Pearl said, stepping back. "Marilyn's . . . gone."

He entered slowly, looking left and right as if expecting to see bloodstains or other signs of violence. If he noticed the odor of death he gave no sign. He walked unsteadily to the sofa and sat down on it with what Pearl took to be a kind of familiarity.

She took the wing chair opposite and got out her notepad and stub of a pencil. "How good a friend of Marilyn's were you?"

He pinched the bridge of his nose again, the way people do sometimes when they have a bad headache. Closed his eyes again, too, only they were lightly closed and not clenched shut like before. "We dated twice. We got along well, I thought. Last time we parted, about a week ago, I told her I was going to drop by sometime." He lowered his hand, trained his blue gaze on Pearl, and shrugged. "Here I am."

"Your name is really Jones?"

"Of course."

His indignation seemed genuine. "I had to ask," she said.

"I guess you did."

"Where did you and Marilyn meet?"

"In a lounge, a couple of weeks ago."

"Nuts and Bolts?"

"Pardon?"

"It's a lounge on the East Side."

"No. A place called Richard's, near Lincoln Center."

Pearl knew it. A respectable stop for the after-show and concert crowd. Not a pickup parlor like Nuts and Bolts. "Where'd you and Marilyn go on your two dates?"

"We went out once to dinner, the other time to an old Woody Allen movie at the Renaissance Theater over in the next block."

"*Bananas*," Pearl said. She happened to be a big Woody Allen fan and knew what was playing at the Renaissance.

"Huh? Oh, yeah. South American dictators and all. I forgot the title."

"On the other date, where'd you have dinner?"

"The Pepper Tree, right down the street." He looked around. "We talked by phone, and we met where we decided to go. This is the first time I've ever been inside her apartment. And now she's . . . I mean, Jesus!"

Pearl made a show of folding her notepad and putting it away with her pencil. She sat back and made herself look relaxed; it was time for a friendly off-the-record conversation. She'd seen Quinn use this tactic to lull someone he was interviewing, pretending the *real* interview was over. "I'm interested now not so much in facts as in your impressions. So tell me, what kind of woman was Marilyn?"

Jones gave it some thought before answering. "She was

always upbeat, optimistic. At least when I saw her. Also bright and ambitious. She thought she was going someplace in this world, and she probably was. She hadn't been in the city long and was doing some sort of consulting work for a chain of clothing stores."

"Rough Country?"

"I'm not sure. That coulda been it."

Pearl smiled as if slightly embarrassed. "Now I'm sorry to have to ask you an intimate question, Mr. Jones."

He understood. "She and I were never intimate." He looked at Pearl with direct honesty. "Like I said, this is the first time I've ever been in here. And she never came to my place." He glanced down at his shoes, back up. "I did have hopes."

"Sure," Pearl said. "What else can you tell me about her? I'm just trying to get a feel for who she was." *And who you are.*

"She laughed so easily," Jones said. "I liked that about her more than anything. She had the kind of sense of humor where she didn't say much that was funny, but she enjoyed what other people said." He actually seemed about to tear up. "The truth is, I guess we didn't know each other all that well, but I'm going to miss her, so I guess that's the kind of person she was." He glanced about. "This is such a waste. Such a goddamned shame!"

"It is," Pearl agreed. Two dates and no sack time, and this guy was about to cry. Well, it was possible. Pearl wondered who'd cry over her if she were murdered. It was the kind of question her mother might ask.

She really should call her mother.

"I mean, a woman so wonderful and still young." Jones sniffed. "Well, I guess in your job you see it all the time."

"Too often." She waited a beat, then: "What do you do for a living, Mr. Jones?" Abrupt change of subject. It might cheer him up even if it didn't throw him off balance. His grief did seem real.

"I'm a freelance journalist."

Great!

Her alarm must have shown on her face.

"Not a newshound," he assured her. "I'm in New York working on a book about the intersection of politics and economics and its influence on the functions of each."

"Sounds fascinating."

A faint smile passed across his features. "I try not to make it too dry. I'm still looking for a publisher."

She got out her pad and pencil again. Official cop time. "And your address?"

Pearl dutifully wrote it down, the Waverton, a residential hotel over on the West Side. It was a place that showed its age but was still respectable and had reasonable rates. Pearl thought it was exactly the kind of hotel where a freelance journalist with intermittent income might stay.

She put pad and pencil away again and thanked Jeb Jones for his time; then she stood up, waiting to see how anxious he was to leave.

Not very.

"We finished?" he asked.

Pearl had the impression he might prefer to hang around for a while and chat, as if he were lonely.

"Maybe," she said. "I might be in touch." She smiled. "You've been a help."

"I hope so." He stood slowly and looked around again, almost as if expecting to see Marilyn Nelson. He didn't so much as glance toward the bathroom.

"What do you know about the bastard who did this?" he asked. "Are you going to find him?"

"Not much yet, but we're learning. And you can bet we're gonna find him."

Jones nodded, but he didn't seem satisfied.

When he was gone, Pearl used her cell phone to call the Waverton and ask for Jeb Jones.

She waited while his room phone rang over and over, until finally it stopped and someone Pearl assumed to be the desk clerk came on the line and informed her that Jones wasn't in his room but she could leave a message.

Pearl told him no message, then thanked him and broke the connection.

So Jones was real, what he'd told her was at least true up to a point, and he wasn't in two places at once. Progress?

Who the hell knew?

She glanced at her watch. She was a long way from the Village, but there was still plenty of time to get to where she was having lunch with Lauri Quinn.

Quinn's request that she talk to his daughter nagged at Pearl, but she could understand why he had to ask.

Family! Pearl thought. *River of blood. Sticky.*

Call Mom.

The hell with Mom! Trying to run my life. Trying, for Chrissake, to marry me off like I'm some kind of virgin in Fiddler on the Roof*!*

Don't call Mom!

The Hungry U was a bit of a joint, but Pearl had seen worse. And it was in a part of the Village where "joint" was . . . well, chic.

Inside, the restaurant was one of those places with a décor that tried too hard. Pearl thought it was like a movie director's low-budget idea of how a Pakistani restaurant should look.

Wafting on the aromatic air was repetitious recorded music played on an unfamiliar instrument, maybe a zither. Pearl thought the music might be Pakistani, but how would she know? The cooking scents titillated her appetite but made her eyes water. She was led by an exotic-looking woman to a table next to a wall.

Lauri must have seen her come in and was waiting for her to be seated, because she appeared right away and shook hands with Pearl before sliding onto the chair opposite.

A waiter also appeared. He was a handsome guy in his twenties with a sharply pointed dark goatee. He was wearing cutoff jeans and a baggy-sleeved white shirt. Maybe that was what waiters wore in Pakistan.

He smiled at Lauri. "Can't stay away from the place on your day off?"

"It's the saffron," Lauri said. She looked at Pearl. "That's like this orange-colored spice that's from flowers."

"Ah!"

The waiter took their drink orders, diet Pepsi for Lauri and iced tea for Pearl, then left them.

Pearl studied Lauri. She definitely had her father's eyes and chin. It was odd how the feminine version of what made Quinn look like a thug was somehow beautiful on his daughter. Her hair was blond and worn short in a don't-give-a-damn cut. There was an obviously fake diamond stud in her nose. She was attractive now, but if she somehow managed to grow up in this crappy world, she might be stunning.

"You know about me," Pearl said. Not a question.

"Yeah. You're the one who was shacked up with my dad."

Pearl sighed. Was this going to be difficult? "That's me, all right. He thought we should have this conversation."

"So he'll understand me better, I suppose."

"I suppose the same thing," Pearl said.

"Think it'll work?"

"Yes. I'm intuitive."

Lauri gave her a frank look. A Quinn look. "You're pretty much what I expected."

"Is that good?"

"Not bad. I'm not predisposed to dislike you."

Predisposed. Girl's got herself a vocabulary.

"I'm glad," Pearl said. "I'm not sure what I'd do if you disliked me."

"You're joking?"

"Not entirely."

"Mom said Dad loved being a cop and he also hated it.

She said you were the same way and you and he deserved each other."

"Mom had it right."

"So what happened between you two?"

"That isn't the conversation your dad wanted us to have," Pearl said. "But I've gotta tell you, that question was so your father."

Lauri laughed. Quinn's rare laugh only without the low thunder.

Pearl smiled and opened a menu, buying time to think, beginning to enjoy this.

"So what's good here?" she asked.

Lauri grinned brightly and shrugged, at the same time glancing around what was just another tired ethnic restaurant in a tired block of the Village. "Everything's wonderful."

Pearl was beginning to see Quinn's problem.

25

Pearl often thought about why moths were drawn to flame. The problem wasn't that she couldn't figure out the reason. It was that she knew. She wondered if the moths knew, too, and didn't give a damn.

That evening she phoned the Waverton Hotel again and asked for Jeb Jones. This time he was in his room and picked up on the second ring.

"I'm the homicide detective you talked to earlier in Marilyn Nelson's apartment," Pearl said. "I have a few more questions to ask. Is this a good time?"

"I'll make the time for you." His voice was mellower over the phone; he seemed more in control.

Pearl was in her apartment, slouched on the sofa with her bare feet up on a hassock. There was a scotch and water in her left hand. Her second in the last hour. The TV was on mute, showing convincingly wrought animated dinosaurs pursuing people through a phony-looking forest. She didn't need her scotch hand. It wasn't as if she were taking notes.

"Did you ever meet any of Marilyn Nelson's friends?" she asked.

"No. I don't think she had many yet. She'd only been in town a short while."

"Did she ever happen to mention anyone? A name?"

"Not that I can recall."

"Had her behavior changed in any way the last time you saw her? Specifically, did she act afraid, or mention anyone who was in any way threatening?"

"No, she was her usual bright self. She didn't act at all like she thought she might be in any danger. She was the kind of girl—woman—that seemed to trust everyone. What happened to her . . . I think it must have come as a total surprise."

Pearl found herself without a next question. She knew why she'd really called. There was something about Jeb Jones she couldn't get out of her mind. Maybe it was simply that she felt sorry for him. He did seem genuinely crushed by Marilyn Nelson's death. Pearl knew she was a sucker for a bird with a broken wing. Even one who, when nursed back to health, might peck her eyes out.

But the guy wasn't a suspect. The Butcher wouldn't knock on the apartment door of a woman he'd recently murdered.

Unless he returned to recover something he'd forgotten.

Or was the type with a compulsion to revisit the scene of the crime.

Pearl pushed these possibilities to the far edges of her mind and took a sip of watered-down scotch. This wouldn't be the first time she'd become personally involved with someone on the periphery of an investigation. Flirting with a man and with disaster simultaneously. Once burned, twice shy didn't apply to moths.

She'd been quiet for a while, prompting Jones to speak:

"Officer . . . Kasner, is it?"

"Pearl Kasner."

"Pearl, listen. I know I was a little emotional yesterday. I'm not usually like that. I mean, such a wimp."

"You didn't come across as a wimp." She wanted to help him, soothe and rebuild his ego. "Anyway, it's not as if you burst out crying. And it isn't against the rules for men to show emotion in front of women. In fact, some women count that in a man's favor."

"Some women say that."

There was a silence that was definitely awkward.

Again, Jeb was the first to speak. "I'm ready for more questions."

"I don't have any right now. But I might have to talk to you again."

"I wish you would."

"Try to get some sleep and you'll feel better." *Dumb thing to say. Shouldn't have called.*

"You, too, Pearl. You must be awfully busy these days."

"Busier than I'd like," she said. "Good night, Jeb."

" 'Night, Pearl."

She hung up the phone but kept her hand on it. She wasn't trembling. Not quite. And she was a little angry with herself.

No, more than a little.

What an idiot you are!

Idiot full of scotch!

The phone sprang to life beneath her hand and jangled, starling her. She didn't pick up, didn't feel like talking to anyone else. She'd already made an ass of herself on the phone. Let the machine take it.

"Pearl?" inquired her mother's voice from the machine.

God! There was no one she felt less like talking to now.

"Pearl, are you there? Of course you aren't. Busy making the world safe when you gave up a steady job to put yourself in danger. I thought you were finished with the police and were planning on a normal life. Speaking of which, I talked to Mrs. Kahn, and it's true her nephew Milton is at the moment between relationships after his regrettable divorce from a woman who didn't deserve him. What she put him through you wouldn't believe. Mrs. Kahn says the divorce was a long time coming and, if you'll excuse the expression, financial rape. Of Milton, not the hellion wife. Mrs. Kahn says Milton says he would like to meet you, and I can tell you he's a presentable and kind person and with prospects. I saw him when he came here to visit his aunt, and I will confirm to you that he's a hunka-hunka. There'd be no harm in you two getting together to break bread and break the ice and see what's beneath it even. You should consider, dear. The clock is ticking, and faster than you think. Your mother knows, Pearl. Call your mother."

The machine clicked off.

Maybe not such an idiot.

When Quinn arrived at the office the next morning Pearl was already there, perched on her desk with her arms crossed. Fedderman hadn't yet arrived. The coffee was on and smelled fresh and pungent. Someone thumped three times, hard, on the dividing wall between the office and the dental clinic, possibly a patient attempting escape.

Quinn touched his chin where he'd nicked himself with his razor. This thing with Lauri and Wormy . . .

"I met Lauri for lunch yesterday," Pearl said.

Quinn sat down behind his desk, the chair cushion hissing beneath him as a reminder that he should lose some weight. "And?"

"We had a long talk. She really is an exceptional girl."

Quinn smiled, then became more serious and began lightly tapping a pencil on the desk. "What I'd like is for her to give herself a chance."

"She's trying to do that," Pearl said. "Her workplace seems okay except for the food."

"And the music."

"What I heard was recorded," Pearl said.

"A mercy."

"I don't know, Quinn. I'm not a parent. But I'd feel okay

about Lauri. Life teaches its lessons gradually, and I can see why a father would be impatient, especially if he's . . . impatient. My advice to you is to stop worrying so much."

"What about that musical geek she's been dating?"

"Wormy? Him I didn't see. Does he have a real name?"

"If he did, no one would use it. Wormy's too apropos. Or maybe it's his show business name, for when he sings and fronts his band at the restaurant."

"Have we got a sheet on him?"

"I'm going to check on that," Quinn said. "I need for you to find out his name nobody uses."

"Me?"

"It might be too obvious if I ask Lauri. And if I ask at the restaurant, somebody, some worm, might recognize me and mention it to her. You could go by the Hungry U when she's not there and ask around in an unofficial capacity."

Pearl stood up from her perch on the desk. "Get hold of yourself, Quinn. You're liable to get that boy fired."

"What if he has a sheet? Deals in drugs, steals cars, or assaults women?"

"You suspect any of that?"

"All of it."

Pearl stared at him and shook her head. "You're overplaying your role as a father, Quinn. I was glad to talk with Lauri, but I'll be damned if I'm going to spy on her or delve into her personal life."

"Personal life?"

"Sex life."

"Damn it, Pearl!"

"Damn what?" Fedderman asked. He'd just come in. The morning was heating up and he already had his suit coat slung over his shoulder, holding it Frank Sinatra–style, hooked on one finger. His tie was crooked and there were crescents of perspiration beneath his arms on his white shirt that was partly untucked.

"Nothing," Quinn said. "I want you to call a restaurant in

the Village, the Hungry U, and tell them you're a journalist for *Spin* magazine. Ask for the real name of a guy whose band is playing there, goes by Wormy."

"That French?

Quinn explained and spelled it for him.

Fedderman had played journalist before and didn't find the request all that unusual. "What's the band called?"

"The Defendants."

"Cute," Fedderman said. "What're we gonna do when we find out who this Wormy is?"

"We're gonna find out who he *really* is," Quinn said.

26

Bocanne, Florida, 1980

It was deep into the night, and Sherman had been unable to sleep. His light was on and he was lying in bed reading about the battle of Lookout Mountain and trying not to think about Sam, when his mother opened his bedroom door. She had on an old dress and apron and was holding some trash bags.

He lowered the open book to his chest.

"Come when I call," she said to Sherman.

His heart fell as he watched her lay the folded trash bags on the corner of his dresser. He knew what they were for. She knew he'd bring them when she called.

"Mom . . . ?"

"It's not time for questions, Sherman, it's time for doin'. And what you're gonna do's what I tell you."

"I know, Mom." He propped up his book again and watched the print swim before his eyes.

He didn't hear her leave, but he knew she was gone.

Ten minutes later she called his name and, wearing only his Jockey shorts, he trudged into her bedroom.

Sam was lying nude and dead still on the bed. He had a peaceful expression on his face, though his mouth was a bit crooked.

"He didn't suffer none," Sherman's mother said, noticing how Sherman was looking at Sam, not at all like Sam was any of the other lifeless hulks he'd seen. "Pick up his stuff." She pointed to a pile of Sam's belongings she'd built in the middle of the floor. Next to it were his boxes of books.

"Can we keep the books?" Sherman asked.

"Ain't you read 'em all?"

"I could read 'em again."

"They go into the swamp with the rest of Sam's things, Sherman. Every part of Sam's gotta be gone."

He didn't argue. Instead he stooped by the pile of old clothing. Next to it were an empty leather wallet and tobacco pouch, and an old pipe with a tooth-marked stem. Sherman began to cry as he stuffed it all into one of the black plastic trash bags.

When he was finished, his mother said, "Go put that bag on the porch, then come back here an' give me a helpin' hand with him."

Sherman did as he was told, then returned to help her move Sam into the bathroom.

Myrna gripped Sam beneath his arms, and Sherman clutched him just beneath the knees. They'd done this often enough that unconsciously they'd established a system.

"Shut up your cryin'," Myrna said to Sherman, as Sam thumped off the bed onto the floor. "Now come grab an arm."

But Sherman was already on his way. Sniffling and choking back sobs, he gripped Sam's right wrist while his mother gripped the left, and they began dragging him over the plank floor toward the bathroom.

Rigor mortis had come and gone in Sam, so it wasn't too difficult to wrestle him into the big clawfoot tub.

"Go out an' git your father's tools," Myrna said.

Sam silently obeyed. He knew which tools to select from the old wooden shed.

When he'd returned to the bathroom with the tools, the water was running. His mother had already removed all her clothes so as not to get blood on them, and had begun on Sam with a knife.

"He weren't a bad man," Sherman said, observing.

"Bad don't figure into it, Sherman. It's about survival." She began working the knife back and forth in a sawing motion to cut through a small tendon. "Someday you'll understand."

Sherman wondered if he would.

"Turn that tap water down some," Myra said, "then go fetch the rest of them bags."

Sam obeyed, then he stood and watched the water mixed with blood swirling down the drain. *Sam's blood.* He began to cry again.

"The bags, Sherman!"

He left the bathroom, glancing back as his mother scooted across the tiles to the dry end of the tub opposite the taps, her bare breasts swinging pendulously with her smooth but hasty movement. He knew how she worked, keeping everything dry as possible until finally it was drained enough to use the power saw on what was too big or tough to cut with a knife. The stench, the sound of the gurgling, bloody water, went with Sherman as he returned to his mother's room and got the rest of the plastic trash bags.

When he came back he watched his mother work with her usual speed and economy, and before long Sam's parts were stacked neatly in the tub in the familiar, orderly fashion. There were cleaning agents and bottles of bleach nearby, most of them already empty.

Myrna turned the cold tap water on full blast, then reached over and worked the lever that diverted it to the showerhead. The shower hissed and spat before breaking into a steady spray.

Sherman and his mother watched the shower water run on the tub's contents for a while, then Myrna turned off the squeaky tap and said simply, "Sherman."

He knew precisely what to do.

Their system was fast and efficient. Myrna and Sherman stuffed the damp, pale body parts into the plastic bags and carried them out to the back porch. Sam had been a big man, so it took several trips, and when they were finished they were both breathing hard. Myrna stood with her hands on her hips for a few seconds, staring out at the black night. Then she sighed and turned around. She got a short bamboo rod from where it was leaning against the house and rattled it back and forth over the wooden porch spindles, the way a child would run a stick across a picket fence.

Within a few minutes, Sherman and his mother heard and saw movement in the dark swamp. The gators were conditioned to respond to the rattling sound that carried on the night through the black swamp, just as Sherman was conditioned to respond to his mother's commands.

Sherman helped his mother remove the body parts from the bags and toss them into the darkness beyond the porch rail. He tried not to cry, tried not to listen to the splashing and the grunting, grinding sounds. He knew alligators usually carried their food back to their nests in the banks to let it rot some before they ate it, and he wished these would. But some of these gators were too hungry to wait, and the swamp was theirs at night.

When all of the bags were empty, Myrna looked at her son in the faint moonlight and nodded. He watched her as she refolded the plastic bags so she could wash and reuse them. The boxes of Sam's books, and the bag containing his clothes, would remain on the porch and she would bury them in the swamp when it was daylight.

And Sam would be gone.

Like the boarders before him. Old men who didn't have long to live anyway.

But Sam was different.

Sherman's mother would never again mention his name, and Sherman knew better than to utter it even to himself.

"You go back to bed," Myrna told him. "I'll clean up."

Without a word, he turned and went back into the house, aware of his mother staring at him. Behind him the dark swamp continued to stir. Off in the distance, a night bird cried.

Sherman lay in bed thinking he'd sob himself to sleep. Only he didn't sob. And he didn't sleep. His eyes were open and dry.

He lay quietly listening to the sounds of his mother down the hall, scrubbing the bathroom. When she was finished there, she'd return to her bed, alone.

Sherman knew that if he could cry it would relieve some of the pressure in him that was making it difficult for him to breathe. And maybe his heart would stop crashing around in his chest as if it wanted to get out. If only he had Sam to talk to . . .

Sam was gone. But what would Sam tell him to do?

Sherman got out of bed and slipped into his stiff and damp Levi's cutoffs, then the T-shirt he'd worn that day. Moving quietly, he rummaged through his dresser drawers and pulled out what clothes he'd need, including some socks and his old joggers. He'd go barefoot for now, for silence. He stuffed the wadded socks into the shoes, then wrapped his clothes around the shoes and fastened the roll tightly with his old leather belt.

All he had to do now was remove the screen from his bedroom window and slip outside, and he could be miles away by morning.

Miles away! Free!

"Sherman."

His mother's voice was soft and neutral, almost lazy. He was too terrified even to move from where he was crouched facing the other way.

"You plannin' on leavin' me, son?"

He moved only his head, craning his neck so he could see behind him.

She was standing in the doorway, not frowning, not smiling, her dark eyes fixing him where he crouched. In her right hand she clutched the bamboo rod she used to summon the alligators. Slowly, she raised it high.

She moved fast toward Sherman, crossing the room like a tiger.

27

The printed note was sent to Quinn via the NYPD:

> *Red blood on blue tile. Fools rush in.*
> *So do the police.*
> *The Butcher*

"It came in the mail yesterday," Renz said, seated behind his desk. He was wearing his reading glasses, and the sun piercing the blinds glinted off their lenses. The office was too warm and smelled faintly of cigar smoke again. Renz the addicted couldn't keep away from whatever cheap brand he smoked. How he must long for one of Quinn's illegal Cuban *robustos*. He knew damn well they weren't Venezuelan, as Quinn claimed.

Renz held up note and envelope. "Lab's already gone over it. The paper's cheap stock, sold all over the place. Same with the envelope. It's the kind people buy by the thousands to pay bills and send letters. No DNA on the flap. Nothing remotely like a fingerprint. And two handwriting experts agree the printing is almost drawn and there isn't enough of it to be distinctive or provide material for a meaningful match. The killer used a number-two lead pencil, the most common kind."

Quinn said, "You've got it pretty well covered."

Renz peeled off his glasses so he could focus long on Quinn. "Doing my job."

Quinn was seated in one of the chairs angled toward Renz's desk. Pearl and Fedderman were standing on either side and slightly behind him. "You might have told us about this yesterday," he said.

Renz shrugged. "I wanted to have something to tell, so I waited for lab and handwriting analyses." He squeezed one hand with the other, as if someone had given him a high five way too hard. "What do you think this means?"

"Can we run a computer check and see if the tile color in Marilyn Nelson's bathroom was mentioned to the press and repeated?"

"Did that," Renz said. "No matches. No mention. The note's genuine."

"The bastard's toying with us," Pearl said.

"So the profiler tells me," Renz said.

"Nothing unusual in that," Qunn said. Like many cops who'd been on the job a long time, he had little faith in profilers; they could easily head an investigation off in the wrong direction. "It's all part of what drives sickos like the Butcher. He wants to engage in a game and prove he's smarter than we are. He wants this note released to the media."

"That'd be your call," Renz said. "Why I hired you. And of course, you take the heat if it turns out to be a big mistake."

Quinn shifted a few inches in his chair so the sun wasn't in his eyes. "You asked what the note means, and I don't know the answer. But apparently it was written after Marilyn Nelson's death, and it means *something*. We have to figure it out. I say release it to the media. Call Cindy Sellers at *City Beat,* give the little rag a scoop."

"How will that help us?" Renz asked.

"We might need a favor from her someday."

"No, I meant what good will it do to release the note to the media?"

"If we don't figure out what the killer's trying to tell us, maybe somebody else will."

"You think he wants this figured out."

"Yes, but only when it's too late. In fact, if we don't figure it out, he'll tell us. But not in time to have stopped him from taking his next victim."

"Maybe the key is colors," Fedderman said. "Red and blue."

"And gold," Pearl added.

The three men looked at her.

" 'Fools rush in.' Fool's gold. The gold rush."

"Somebody whose last name is, or starts with, the word gold," Fedderman suggested.

"If the killer's still focusing on his victims' initials," Quinn said.

"There's that question," Pearl said, "Maybe he's spelling out something else. I mean, not necessarily a person's name."

"It better be the word *apprehended*," Renz said, looking at each of them in turn. "And soon."

Quinn considered telling him to stop playing the hard-ass, then he decided to let it pass. It was part of Renz's persona. He needed to flex his bureaucratic muscles now and then to remind himself they were still there. The important thing wasn't that Quinn knew what made Renz tick; it was that Renz knew that he knew.

Pearl, however, looked as if she were about to say something. He could tell by her eyes, by the way she was tensing her lips.

"We're on it, Harley," Quinn assured Renz, figuring Pearl would be less likely to spout off to a superior who was on a first-name basis, who was one of them rather than simply an authority figure. Before she could cut into the conversation, he added, "We'll go to the office, run computer searches on the colors mentioned in the note. If you don't mind, I'll take it and the envelope with me so we can put it in the file."

"That's the place for the original," Renz said, handing the items to Quinn. "We've got copies."

As the three detectives filed from the office, Renz motioned for Quinn to stay behind and close the door.

"Are you staying on those two?" Renz asked.

"They don't need it, Harley. They're solid cops. And remember, you chose them just like you chose me."

"But I had some reservations."

"About who?"

"You and Pearl together, if you know what I mean."

Quinn knew. "It isn't any of your business, but that relationship's been over for a long time."

"Then why do you look at her the way you do?"

"Start worrying, Harley, if she looks back at me that way."

Renz smiled. "I haven't noticed that. She looks terrific in that outfit. If boobs were brains she'd be a genius."

"How come you have to keep trying to irritate people?" Quinn asked, pushing his anger away.

"I dunno. How come the Butcher keeps killing and chopping up women?"

"Maybe it's the same answer," Quinn told him.

"Hey, screw you!" Renz said, as Quinn was leaving.

Quinn couldn't help smiling. It wasn't easy getting over on Renz. He'd have to tell Pearl about it.

As it turned out, the decision to release the note to the media wasn't relevant. It was featured on the front page of the *New York Post.* The killer had sent copies to all the New York papers and TV news desks.

When Renz released the information that the tile in Marilyn Nelson's apartment was indeed blue, the media was on the story even hotter. Red blood on blue tiles. Cindy Sellers wrote it straight, but a columnist in *City Beat* speculated that if the bathtub and commode were white, there might be a patriotic slant to the killings.

At the office, Pearl continued to work the computer, double-checking Renz to make sure no one had mentioned the color of Marilyn Nelson's bathroom tiles before the note arrived.

She found no mention. The only way the author of the note could have known the colors was if he'd been in Marilyn's bathroom, unless someone in the NYPD had leaked the information to him. That last was one Pearl didn't want to think about.

Quinn was at his desk rereading the murder files, while Fedderman was on line with his own computer, using the Internet to tie everything possible to the colors red, blue, and gold.

Beneath the hum of the air conditioning, the only sounds were Quinn shuffling pages, and the rattling of keyboards. Pearl raised her head for a moment and looked around, thinking they were all probably doing precisely what the killer intended.

She considered returning to the victim's apartment again. Maybe she'd missed something unobtrusive, or too obvious. Or maybe Jeb Jones would turn up again.

Not that he had a reason, she thought.

Or he might. She might be the reason.

The possibility made her blood rush. It also made her realize she wasn't thinking straight or professionally. This was the kind of thing that had gotten her in trouble throughout her career. It was a bad idea to return to the Marilyn Nelson apartment on the unlikely premise that Jeb might be there.

Not only am I flirting with disaster, but I'm making everything all too complicated.

She put returning to Marilyn's apartment out of her mind. Easier simply to phone the Waverton.

28

Anna Bragg emerged from the dimness of the subway stop's narrow concrete stairwell into slanted, early evening sunlight. A compact, shapely brunette wearing a tight skirt and blazer, she drew admiring male glances as she strode along the sidewalk in her four-inch heels toward her apartment. Anna would have preferred wearing joggers back and forth to work like most of the other women at Courtney Publishing, but she was conscious of her height deficiency and thought it might be affecting her prospects for advancement. By chance or design, most of the other women at Courtney were built like, and in fact resembled, tall twelve-year-old boys.

Anna had decided that for health reasons as well as how she wanted to appear, it was a bad idea to diet relentlessly and exercise away your hips and boobs. Anyone looking at her would have applauded the decision.

Pedestrian traffic piled up at the corner, and Anna waited with everyone else for the light to change. She had a clear complexion, large brown eyes, and a way of holding her head always cocked to the side as if she were straining to hear a slight, distant sound.

Usually she was thinking. Right now she was considering "Greenlander's meal on the wing" as a crossword clue for "puffin." Anna's job at Courtney was to edit their monthly crossword puzzle magazine. While the puzzle writers submitted clues and answers together, it was the clues that most often needed editing. Some were too vague, some too suggestive, some simply irrelevant or downright dull. The clue for "puffin" was one that definitely had problems. It might be too obscure. There were subscribers who didn't even know what puffins were, much less that Greenlanders ate them.

The traffic light changed, and Anna stepped off the curb and moved with the mass of pedestrians across the street. A van making a right turn honked at her, though the vehicle wasn't nearly close enough to hit her. The guy driving it might have been leaning on the horn as a way to compliment her. Anna preferred to think of it that way rather than contemplate what else might have been on his mind.

Something, maybe a small pebble, worked its way between the sole of her shoe and her right foot. Anna moved to the side and stopped walking, then raised her leg bent at the knee so she could work a finger beneath her foot and remove whatever was bothering her. The pose she had to strike showed a lot of thigh and brought a lot of male looks, and an especially long look from a handsome, dark-haired man in a blue sport coat and gray slacks. He was average-size—not too tall for Anna—and his regular features almost but not quite formed a smile as he glanced at her and walked on.

It occurred to her that he looked somewhat familiar. Had she seen him around the office? Maybe he worked in her building.

On the other hand, he had the kind of regular, everyman features that were probably often mistaken for someone else's. He was like a catalog model—handsome, but you tended to remember the outfit.

She'd forgotten about the man by the time she turned a corner and walked two more blocks to her building.

Like the buildings on either side, it was a redbrick, three-story walkup in the middle of the block. Anna took the four worn marble steps to its entry and pushed into the vestibule. The familiar mingled scents of stale urine, disinfectant, and cooking spices told her she was home. White was showing in the fleur-de-lis cutout in her brass mailbox. She fished her key ring from her purse, opened the box, and drew out two pieces of mail.

It didn't take her long to glance at them and decide she'd throw them in the trash when she got upstairs. She hadn't won the lottery, or gotten a job offer, marriage proposal, or free vacation. She keyed the mailbox locked and told herself she also hadn't received an eviction notice or jury summons.

Cheer up, Anna.

She used another key to open the security door from the vestibule to the rest of the building's interior.

Her legs were twenty-three years old. Even in high heels, she barely noticed climbing the three flights of creaking wooden stairs to her corner unit apartment.

Twenty-three. For all she cared, it might as well have been a ten-story walkup.

The Butcher was pleased when he entered the vestibule of the attractive brunette's building. He had no trouble finding the mailbox he'd watched her open as he observed her through the long window in the street door. And just in case he couldn't trust his eyes, the tarnished brass box appeared to be one of the empty ones—only darkness beyond the carved fleur-de-lis. Second row end, he was sure, apartment 3-B.

The slotted card above the mailbox read *A. Bragg*. She was cautious, like most single women in New York, and simply used her first initial. He smiled. He'd seen what office she'd emerged from and followed her down in the elevator and then to the subway and home. While he only knew her first initial and last name, he also knew where she worked and where she lived.

He was also glad to see that, while the building had a sturdy security door between the vestibule and the first floor and stairwell, the intercom looked newer than the mailboxes, and workable.

He was whistling when he left the vestibule and took the marble steps down to the sidewalk, betting that, like most businesses, Courtney Publishing had a website.

Only fifteen minutes after sitting down at his computer, his search engine located Courtneypub.biz.

He clicked on *Divisions* on the home page and saw that Courtney published half a dozen magazines as well as a line of paperback romance novels. Back to the home page, where he clicked on *Personnel.*

Courtney's employees were arranged alphabetically. *Bragg, Anna* was third down.

Wonderful. This was much easier than constructing a puzzle note and then finding a suitable victim. Better to select the victim then construct the corresponding puzzle.

He clicked on her name and found that she was the editor of *CrossWinds*, a monthly magazine of crossword puzzles.

Small world, puzzles.

Fate.

Destiny. His and hers.

Anna Bragg. What might he do with that name? A literary allusion. Sports? Politics? Show business? He knew that while Quinn looked like a kind of handsome thug, he in fact was rather cultured and enjoyed the theater, reading, and dining out. The Butcher had followed him more than once to Barnes & Noble, and had sat directly behind Quinn one night in the theater and enjoyed a performance of an Edward Albee play, one of the playwright's more enigmatic endeavors.

After the play he'd studied Quinn's rugged face briefly in a lobby mirror. Quinn did seem to have understood the play.

The killer concentrated again on Courtneypub.biz on the screen of his laptop.

There was Anna's photo alongside her brief profile. She was smiling, head tilted to the side, looking beautiful. Her company profile didn't reveal her age, but she was younger than he might have wished. She'd graduated from Sweetbriar with a journalism degree, been with Courtney Publishing two years, and loved her work because she loved all kinds of puzzles. Her ambition was to set the world on fire, but not so the flames couldn't be controlled. Her likes were red convertibles and gin martinis with olives. Dislikes were dogs that bit and people who deliberately insulted.

The Butcher noted that the profile didn't list her fears.

29

Alone and lost and lonely.

That was how Sherman felt.

Sam had been gone for three days, and Sherman hadn't been the same. He didn't go fishing by himself, and of course there was nothing to read now that the swamp had claimed Sam's Civil War books. He tried to watch television, but reception wasn't good, far as they were from town, and he didn't want to see quiz shows and soap operas anyway. His days were hot and boring, and he felt so strange, like something was about to happen, like he was on a speeding train and another one was on the same track, headed toward him so they were bound to meet.

They *would* meet at night sometimes, in his dreams, and he'd spring awake wondering if he'd screamed out loud and stirred his mother from sleep.

The worst part was, he was afraid and wasn't sure why.

Evenings TV reception was better, and whenever they were on, Mom would let him watch *The Rockford Files* or *Magnum, P.I.,* but none of it seemed as real to Sherman as the Battle of Gettysburg. He knew none of it *was* that real. There was a special on PBS once about the Civil War, but soon as she noticed what he was watching, Sherman's mother made him switch channels and watch some quiz show. He knew all the answers the contestants missed, but he kept quiet so as not to rile his mother.

Sherman thought about what she'd said the night they gave Sam to the swamp: *"Bad don't figure into it, Sherman. It's about survival."*

Sherman guessed she was right. A person first of all had to do everything possible just to survive. But it seemed to him they'd been doing that okay with Sam alive.

If there were only somebody he could talk to about how he felt inside, somebody like Sam, it would sure make things easier. He knew he couldn't talk to his mother. He'd considered it a few times, but then he'd see her standing with her fists on her hips, looking at him in a funny way that scared him. Other times he'd think that maybe if they talked about things, whatever was in her eyes that was scaring him would go away.

Or maybe it would get more scary.

He'd seen that look in her eyes before and knew what it might mean, though he didn't want to admit it to himself.

On the fifth night after Sam was gone, when Sherman was undressing for bed, he saw that he'd soiled his underwear. This was about the only situation that prompted Sherman to voluntarily change Jockey shorts, so he removed the shorts he was wearing and tossed them in a corner with some dirty socks, then went to his dresser for clean underwear to sleep in and wear tomorrow.

But he was out of underwear. His mother had fallen behind in the wash, and there were only clean socks and T-shirts. Sherman remembered stuffing some not-too-soiled underpants into his closet with some other dirty clothes, and he decided to retrieve them.

Rumpled and dirty clothes were piled two feet high on

the closet floor, and the Jockey shorts were buried somewhere in there. Sherman got down on his hands and knees
and began digging.

His fingertips slid over a surface unexpectedly smooth.
He scooted deeper into the closet and pushed away some of
the rumpled clothing and saw something glistening and
black. More digging through the clothes revealed black plastic trash bags and his dad's power saw.

This was odd. Other than trash, there was only one use
Sherman knew of for the bags. And he was the one who was
always sent to the toolshed to get the saw.

He drew in his breath, and his heart broke like fragile
glass as meaning came to him.

Sam . . . the look in his mother's eyes. She knew Sherman
understood what she was doing—at least most of it—and
after Sam died he'd questioned her about it as he never had
before. She knew Sam had been different, had changed
things forever, and Sherman would continue to question her.
Sherman was getting older, getting ideas of his own.

Dangerous ideas.

After his initial attempt to escape into the swamp, his
mother had caught him, whapped him over and over with the
bamboo rod so hard he could *still* feel it, and made him
swear an oath to obey her without question.

He'd sworn the oath when the pain was at its worst, meaning it at the time with all his heart.

He knew he had to break that oath now.

It was about survival.

Forgetting about underwear, he quickly struggled into his
jeans and moccasins, a dirty T-shirt from the closet floor.

It was well past sundown, plenty dark outside. This time
he wouldn't wait until the middle of the night when it was
more likely his mother was asleep. She was in the living
room watching a quiz show now—she loved quiz shows because just like him she usually knew the answers ahead of

time—and she wouldn't want to leave even to check on him. And concentrating as she was on the TV, she wouldn't hear Sherman remove the screen and climb outside.

More quietly than last time, he worked the screen loose and leaned out to prop it against the house, well alongside the window where it wouldn't trip him up when he was leaving.

As an afterthought, before climbing out the window, he arranged some wadded clothing and his pillow so it looked at a glance as if he might be sleeping in his bed. He'd seen it done plenty of times on TV, and it might work.

Making only a soft scraping sound as the sole of his right moccasin slid over the sill, he wriggled from the window and lowered himself a few feet to the ground.

Ahead of him loomed the blackness of the swamp. Though his heart rattled up into his throat, he didn't hesitate. He began walking toward the dirt road that wound between the lush foliage and the canopy of vines and moss-draped branches. The night sky was cloudy, with only a sliver of moon, so the swamp was almost at its blackest. This morsel of luck buoyed Sherman's spirits as he passed into darkness.

Behind him there was an explosion, and something like a flight of birds rushed through the leaves very near him.

Sherman knew it wasn't birds—it was buckshot.

"Sherman, you come back here!"

His mother! With the shotgun!

He bolted and ran down the narrow road, now and then splashing through spots where the swamp had spread fingers of water across it. His back muscles were bunched so he could barely move his arms. Any second the old double-barreled twelve-gauge might loose another load of shot his way.

But there was no second shot.

He heard instead a grinding sound, and the engine kick over on the old pickup. The truck had a poacher's searchlight mounted just outside the driver's side window, and he knew his mother would use it to locate him.

There was a loud roar, then a metallic grating noise, like a mechanical monster clearing its throat. Sherman knew what it was. First gear.

The truck was coming.

The roar of the truck engine drowned out the other sounds of the swamp. Headlights played over the trees and undergrowth. Sherman's heart was a banging drum in his chest. The only reason the headlights hadn't picked him up was because the road was curved. He knew he had only seconds.

Without hesitation he veered off into the darkness of the swamp. The water was at his ankles and he had to slow down. His mother wouldn't hear him over the roar and rattle of the truck, but she might see any ripples he stirred up.

Still moving swiftly, he was careful to lift his feet high and place them easily almost straight down to minimize roiling the water. Soon he was in deeper water, and foliage that grabbed at his legs and scratched his face, as he moved faster, plowing ahead.

The truck motor dropped to a rumbling idle, and the spotlight beam danced like a phantom over leaves and moss and gnarled roots. Now and then something dark and formless moved swiftly away into blackness, as Sherman must if the beam found him.

"Sherman! You come back here!"

The dancing phantom light was closer. He knew his mother was creeping along the dirt road in the old truck, checking the swamp on both sides with the spotlight.

"Sherman!"

In waist-high water now, he moved cautiously around some twisted banyan roots. When he looked up he could see only blackness. The canopy of growth obscured the moon and whatever stars were out. Pressing his back against the mossy coolness of a tree trunk, he listened to the truck engine barely turning over, the loose left fender vibrating and rattling as the vehicle tilted and jounced over ruts and holes in the road.

Movement caught Sherman's eye off to the left, and he saw the rough black hump of a gator glide away into deeper darkness. He was accustomed to gators and knew they probably wouldn't attack him if he kept his distance. Probably.

Something cool and quick darted across his bare arm and he fought not to cry out in surprise. *Snake?*

Whatever it was moved on, but Sherman had bit his lower lip so hard it was bleeding.

The loose fender ceased its rattling as the truck seemed to stop, the rumbling of its exhaust and the click and clatter of its idling engine unchanging. The spotlight darted closer, moved away, swooping back and forth like a live thing in the swamp.

Right now the blackness of the swamp Sherman had feared so much in his dreams seemed like his friend. Its thick foliage sheltered him. The snakes and gators that he knew were around him in the night were less menacing. They were in their element and so was he, because here in the dark, in deep water where the truck couldn't go, he was safe from his mother.

As long as the spotlight beam didn't find him.

The truck engine roared briefly, as if in anger.

"Sherman! You come back here! Come back to your mother!"

30

New York, the present

Anna had changed from the skirt and blazer she'd worn to work to an old pair of jeans and an untucked T-shirt lettered COMMIT RANDOM ACTS OF KINDNESS. She'd decided the skirt needed to go to the cleaners, but the blazer was good for another wearing. She'd just hung it up in the closet when the intercom buzzed.

She hurried barefoot to the hall and pressed the button to ask who was there.

She was puzzled when the scratchy voice on the intercom said there was a Federal Parcel package for her. She wasn't expecting anything. On the other hand, the shopping network where she often ordered things sometimes sent free gifts. God knew she was a good enough customer to have one coming. There was also the possibility—one she didn't like to admit—that she'd ordered something and forgotten about it. Anna didn't like being reminded that her shopping and her charge card balance were somewhat out of control.

She buzzed the deliveryman up, then returned to the bedroom and put on her slippers before going to the door to open it so she could sign for the package.

The deliveryman wasn't out of breath, as they usually were after taking the stairs. Must be in great shape. He wasn't wearing the usual Federal Parcel uniform and looked vaguely familiar to Anna. Had she seen him recently? At the office? In the subway? Nice-looking guy, worth wondering about.

But her attention was focused mainly on the large white package he held beneath one arm.

He smiled. "Anna Bragg?"

"Uh-huh." She returned the smile, focusing now mostly on his amiable brown eyes.

He extended his free hand, only it didn't hold a pencil or clipboard, and he'd made it into a fist.

Barely had that registered in Anna's mind when the fist slammed into her stomach, just beneath her ribs.

Her breath rushed out in a raspy *whoosh*!

She wanted only to curl into a ball and would have fallen, but the man deftly placed an arm beneath her and held her up, her body doubled over but her feet off the floor. He effortlessly carried her back inside her apartment.

Pain and panic were simultaneous. Anna gasped desperately, sucking in nothing because her body wouldn't respond to her mind's command. It was impossible for her to breathe out, because she had no breath to exhale. She was made mute by her lack of oxygen and by her agony.

Even in her terror, she tried to gather her thoughts. Tried to comprehend what was happening.

Who was he? Why had he done this?

What's he going to do now?

The man was maybe slightly older than she was, handsome in a regular way. Studying him through her tear-blurred eyes, she was sure they'd never met. Not formally, anyway. But there was still that feeling that she'd seen him somewhere before.

He placed her gently on the sofa and she drew up her legs even tighter and groaned as she attempted again to draw air. She was going to suffocate; she knew it.

Her cheek pressed to the sofa, she watched the intruder go to the front door and make sure it was locked, and then fasten the chain. He stooped to pick up the white box and carried it nearer the sofa, then laid it on the end cushion where her drawn-up feet didn't reach it.

Her feet were pressed together and she realized she couldn't separate her ankles. She heard a loud ripping sound.

Her clothes being torn?

No. She recognized the sound now. It had been made by tape being ripped. He'd taped her ankles together. Now she felt the tape wrapping tightly around her calves.

He propped her up on the sofa, maneuvering her so she was on her knees. She'd hurt her neck turning her head sideways so her face wasn't pressed into the soft cushion. *I don't want to suffocate! Please!* She was still gasping, making wheezing sounds, struggling to recapture the great gift of being able to breathe. She knew her rear end was jutting up in the air. Was he going to rape her? Take her from behind?

She didn't think so, not with her legs taped so tightly together. And that frightened her even more.

Something worse?

Her arms were yanked behind her back and her wrists were taped. It had been accomplished quickly and expertly.

He's done this before. More than once.

He turned her around so she was seated on the sofa, bent forward and unable to move.

Anna was breathing in great gulping gasps now, and glimpsed the man in profile. She understood why he didn't seem a complete stranger. *He looks familiar because he's been following me!*

In her new sitting position she could see into the white box at the other end of the sofa.

Suddenly she knew who the man was. Why he'd been stalking her.

She took a deep breath, managed the brief beginning of a scream, before there was another loud ripping sound and a rectangle of gray duct tape was slapped across her half-opened mouth and pressed firm.

He approached her with something metal then, worked his thumb on it, and a razor blade appeared.

She began to tremble as slowly, with practiced skill, he began slicing and removing her clothes.

The muted shrill scream of a dentist's drill in Nothing but the Tooth made its way through the wall, followed by three loud thumps.

Seated at his desk, Fedderman said, "We could give somebody the third degree in here and nobody'd notice."

"Tempting," Pearl told him. She glanced over at where Quinn was seated behind his desk, studying a sheet of paper she figured was the killer's tantalizing note.

Fedderman had been studying the same thing. "The 'gold' in the note might mean blondes," he said, making a sour face after sipping his morning coffee. "Our sicko's been killing brunettes. Maybe he's hinting to us he's gonna start murdering blondes."

"That wouldn't fit the profile," Pearl said. "He wouldn't be set off by blondes the same way he is by brunettes."

Quinn said, "Hmm." She wondered if that was agreement.

"You're assuming it's the hair that's triggering his choice of victims," Fedderman said. "Maybe he's focusing on something else about these women."

"Such as?" Quinn asked.

Fedderman shrugged. "In what other ways are the victims similar? Eyes, legs, the way they dress, their noses, height, boobs? There are lots of possibilities."

Pearl felt somewhat offended but couldn't say why. "A bit of a reach," was what she said.

"It is," Quinn agreed, "but it might be true that his next victim doesn't necessarily have to fit the profile."

Pearl knew how little faith Quinn put in profilers. She

didn't quite agree, but now wasn't the time to argue with him.

"He might have read all those books and watched those TV shows about serial killers and he's decided to run counter to type," Quinn said. With his free hand, he absently toyed with a wrapped cigar in his shirt pocket. Pearl knew he didn't dare.

"It's happened before," Fedderman said. "Blondes," he repeated thoughtfully. "Gold . . . blondes. The time when he displayed the pubic hairs to make sure we knew he'd really killed a brunette, maybe that's when he started to deliberately change his profile. First make-believe blondes, then on to the real thing. He wouldn't be the first."

"What the hell does that mean?" Pearl asked.

Fedderman sipped coffee and shrugged.

"There's enough to what you say about the possibility of some commonality we haven't struck on," Quinn told him, "that I'm going to study the morgue shots and photos of the women while they were alive to see if they might share something other than general type and hair color." He laid the killer's note on the desk. "You and Pearl take another look at where they were killed."

"Their apartments?"

"See if there might be some common denominator there. Their tastes in art, the way the places are furnished. And if it's still possible, look at their wardrobes. Maybe there was something about the way they dressed that turned them into victims."

"I thought I'd talk again to some of the victims' friends or neighbors," Pearl said. "When they get tired enough of us, they might remember something just so we leave them alone."

Quinn thought about it. "Okay. Catch up with Feds later. I'm going to worry over this note a while longer, then go see if Renz has anything new. He's got a meeting this morning with the profiler, so it'll probably be mostly bullshit."

Pearl went into the washroom and waited until Fedderman had left, then returned to where Quinn was still seated behind his desk.

"You check on that Wormy guy?" he asked, organizing the Marilyn Nelson murder book before closing it.

"We don't have a sheet on him. I contacted Buffalo, where he grew up. He's clean there, too. Might as well be an Eagle Scout."

"He looks like a damned junkie. If he's not a known user, he must be on something legal, like glue or gasoline." He bowed his head and gazed thoughtfully at the killer's note lying in the center of his desk. "Some of them just don't get caught."

Pearl didn't know if he meant junkies or serial killers. "I had another talk with Lauri," she said.

He glanced up at her, surprised. "Duty above and beyond. Thanks."

"It was her idea."

Quinn leaned back in his chair so he could see her without craning his neck and began to swivel inches this way and that, as if experiencing the beginning of uneasiness. "Lauri's idea?"

"Yeah. We met at a restaurant near the Hungry U and had sodas, then walked around the Village a while. She's a great kid, got more sense than most her age."

"But not enough sense."

"Well, at that age, no. Even thee and me. If you can remember back that far."

"She told me she likes you," Quinn said. "Really admires you."

"She used those words?"

"Verbatim."

"That's nice to know." Pearl was surprised by how pleased she felt. "It partly explains why she wanted to tag along with me while I work."

Quinn stopped swiveling gently back and forth in his chair. He looked mystified. "Tag along?"

"That's what she wanted. Why she phoned and asked to meet with me."

"You mean she wants to hang out with you, even while you're working?"

"She wants to watch and learn, Quinn. She told me she wants to become a cop."

Quinn sat stunned. Lauri? A cop? His own little girl? She had no idea what that meant. What she'd see and do, and how it would change her.

"She damned well better *not* tag along with you," he told Pearl.

She smiled. "That's exactly what I told her, Dad. Almost verbatim." She went to the door and looked back at him. "Still, I'm flattered she thinks highly of me."

"I don't want her hurt," he said helplessly.

"Neither of us does, Quinn."

"Jesus, what would May say if she knew?"

"I guess you're gonna find out."

He watched Pearl go out into the already steamy morning.

For a long time he sat staring at the closed door. Being a father—a close-by father—wasn't easy. Nothing seemed to work out as he planned. Lauri didn't act or react the way he imagined she would. Hardly ever. Turning up unexpectedly at his door, the job at the restaurant, going out with that Wormy misfit. What next, a tattoo?

He'd tried to act in her best interests, got Pearl to talk with her, the better to understand her. That had sure as hell backfired. Now his daughter wanted to be like Pearl. A cop.

Like me.

His brief flush of pride became a stab of pain.

A life like mine.

Quinn noticed he was squeezing the desk edge with both hands so hard that his fingers where white.

Daughters!

He could barely contain his frustration.

31

Pearl sat in the unmarked parked across the street from the Waverton Hotel and watched a sprinkling of raindrops dot the windshield. Rain wasn't in the forecast and she knew it would stop soon. A brief summer spritzing that would juice up the humidity and make the day even hotter.

She wasn't much concerned with the weather. Pearl hadn't yet visited any of the victims' apartments, per Quinn's instructions. She was holding her cell phone loosely in her right hand, hefting it as if contemplating throwing it.

But she didn't throw it. She used it.

Jeb Jones was in his room at the Waverton when Pearl called. When he picked up on the third ring and said hello, she said, "This is Detective Kasner, Mr. Jones."

"Ah, Pearl."

"Detective Kasner," she repeated.

"Sorry. I shouldn't have assumed we were on a first-name basis."

Pearl felt frustrated. Already she'd botched this up. "I didn't mean to sound unfriendly, just professional."

And just distant enough.

"We'll make it professional, then. I'm ready and willing

to answer all your questions." He sounded more amused than miffed.

"When can we meet?"

"You don't want to do this by phone?"

"No. I like to see people when I talk to them in the course of an investigation." She sounded like a bureaucratic prig even to herself.

"Suspects, you mean?"

"For God's sake, no."

Too fast. And I shouldn't have told him that.

He laughed, gaining confidence. "I figured you were about to tell me that at this point everyone's a suspect."

"No, it's not like on television."

"Well, I can meet with you just about any time."

"Now?"

"Sure. Where?"

"How about the lobby?"

He laughed. "You like to surprise people, don't you?"

"I guess I do. It's part of my job."

"Let's meet in the hotel coffee shop in ten minutes."

Pearl told him she'd be waiting, and broke the connection.

This wasn't all professional, and they both knew it. Odd how sexual tension could make its way across a phone connection. What life was about—connections.

She turned off the engine and climbed out of the coolness of the air-conditioned car into the heat. The drizzle wasn't enough to worry about, not much more than a mist, but it sure upped the humidity. Almost immediately her clothes felt damp and as if they were sticking to her flesh.

After waiting for a bus to rumble past, she crossed the street and used a revolving door to enter the Waverton Hotel.

Cool air again. Refreshing.

She made her way across the carpeted lobby toward a wide archway and went down two steps to the coffee shop. It was surprisingly large, with rows of tables and a long counter. The floor was oversize black and white tiles in a checkerboard pattern. The place gave the impression of being almost devoid of customers, but there were more than a dozen people at the tables, and three at the counter. Pearl noticed a street door at the far end of the counter and figured many of the diners weren't hotel guests.

She found a table where she could be seen. A placard propped next to a cluster of condiments said there was a sale on pie. She ordered a diet Coke.

She waited.

Jeb Jones took the steps down into the coffee shop with an athletic ease that bordered on arrogance. He was wearing designer jeans today, and a black blazer over a gray T-shirt. So was she.

"Jesus!" she said, taking in the fact that they were dressed almost identically.

He paused, not knowing what she meant at first, then he smiled. "Fate."

"If there is such a thing," Pearl said. She saw that he did have on brown loafers, while she was wearing her clunky black cop's shoes.

"Such a thing as fate, or Jesus?"

"Take your pick," Pearl said.

He sat down opposite her. His face looked scrubbed and unnaturally ruddy in a way that suggested he'd just shaved, and his wavy dark hair was damp and pushed back carelessly, as if he'd used his fingers instead of a comb or brush. "Fate might have it that we develop a relationship made in heaven—a professional one, of course."

The woman who'd taken Pearl's order came over and Jeb ordered a fountain diet Coke. Pearl didn't tell him that was what she was drinking.

When they were settled in with drinks and straws and no one was around to overhear, he said, "Fire away, Officer Pearl."

She gave him a mock angry look. "Not 'Officer Kasner'?"

"I thought this might be an acceptable compromise," he said with a grin.

"Let's make it just Pearl, if we have to compromise."

"All right. You've got me in a compromising position, Pearl."

So damned smooth. She felt a slight tingle of alarm, or was it something else? She sipped Coke through her straw, watching him watch her. "Have you thought any more about Marilyn Nelson?"

He sat back and seemed to take the question seriously. "I've thought a lot about what happened to Marilyn, especially after I read some of the details in the paper. From what little I knew of her, I liked her a lot, but to tell you the truth I'm not grieving as if she were an old and dear friend. She was a woman I dated twice."

That seemed to Pearl to be an honest answer. "Do you remember ever running into any of her friends?"

"On our first date we said hello to some people she knew in a restaurant—the Pepper Tree. It's right down the street from her apartment."

"How many people?"

"Four. Two men and two women."

"She introduce you to them?"

"Yes, but to tell you the truth I don't recall their names. They were seated at a table near ours and we stopped briefly and she said hello to them on the way out. I'd even have trouble picking any of them out of a lineup."

Pearl smiled. "I doubt it will come to that. Did she mention where she knew them from?"

"No, just said they were friends of hers. Maybe they live in her neighborhood, since they were eating at the Pepper Tree." He brightened. "If you and I had dinner together there, I could watch for them. You'd be working. It would be professional."

"Hmm. The food good?"

"Mine was. I'm sure it would be again, if you were across the table."

She sipped some more with her straw. "You seem to believe in getting to the point."

"I admit I don't like wasting time. In this kind of thing, there's no sense in dancing around forever unless that's what you enjoy most."

"This kind of thing?"

"There was a handwritten phone number on the back of the business card you gave me."

"My cell phone," she said. "In case you recalled something and wanted to talk to me when I was in the field."

He wasn't buying into it. He gave her a confident smile, in that way he had of being just this side of arrogant that she found attractive. "I don't believe you came here to have a conversation about Marilyn Nelson."

Okay, you like coming to the point. She drew in her breath, and then plunged. *Idiot, Pearl.*

"No," she said, "I came to see you."

"Good. I'm pleased. More than pleased."

Done. And it worked out well. The world didn't cave in on me. She was having difficulty breathing. "The dinner invitation still good?"

"Of course."

Absently toying with the wrapper from his straw, he glanced through the archway dividing the coffee shop from the lobby, toward the elevators.

Uh-oh! Pearl knew where this was going. She knew where *she* might be going if Jeb Jones had his way. *We not only dress the same; we both tend to seize the moment.*

But not this moment. You're a cop on duty.

"You're not planning on asking a police officer up to your room, are you?" she asked with a poker face.

He grinned. "I confess."

She was about to speak when her cell phone chirped.

Still looking into Jeb's brown eyes, she drew the phone from her pocket, flipped it open, and saw by the caller ID that it was Quinn.

"What's up?" she said. She could hear traffic sounds in the background; he was calling from his car.

"We've got another Butcher job. Down in the Village." He gave her the address.

"Like the others?"

"Feds said it was when he called me. He got there first. I'm on my way. Like you are."

"Like I am," Pearl said, and broke the connection and flipped the phone's lid down.

She looked across the table at Jeb. "Work," she said. "I've gotta go."

He reached across the table and his fingertips brushed the back of her hand. The contact almost hummed with high voltage. "I'm disappointed, but I understand. Duty."

When he withdrew his hand she stood up and reached for her wallet.

"On me," he said, standing also. "Dinner still on for tonight?"

"I can't promise," she said.

"I understand again."

She smiled nervously, feeling oddly as if she'd just been shot at and missed.

"I've got your number," he reminded her, as she hurried away.

Yeah, she thought.

32

Pearl flashed her shield for the uniform guarding the open door and found the victim's apartment crawling with crime scene unit techs.

As soon as she stepped inside, the familiar butcher shop stench made her stomach protest. She swallowed bile and continued past the techs busily gathering evidence in the modestly furnished living room, then continued through the kitchen and along a narrow hall to the bathroom.

She looked inside and found Quinn and Fedderman blocking her view. Pearl could see by the shape of the hips and the small black shoes that the Medical Examiner's office had sent a woman this time, who was bending over the bathtub to sort through what was left of the victim.

Quinn and Feds both glanced over at Pearl and nodded. There was no room for Pearl to enter the small bathroom, so Fedderman edged over so she could see.

Another jolt to her stomach. Even though she knew what to expect now, it was a shock.

That one human being could do this to another . . .

The detached head resting atop pale and severed arms had damp dark hair.

"Not a blonde," Pearl said.

The ME shot a look over her shoulder. She was about fifty, with puffy cheeks and carrot-red hair worn so short it was almost a buzz cut. Though Pearl was sure they'd never seen each other before, the glance seemed to satisfy the ME that Pearl belonged, because she simply returned to her work.

Quinn eased his way out of the crowded bathroom and led Pearl down the hall to the kitchen, where as yet there was no CSU activity.

"Same bullshit?" Pearl asked.

"So far," Quinn said. "When it comes to method, our guy's the model of consistency."

The ME came into the kitchen. She was wearing a man's pinstriped gray suit and tie and carrying a scuffed black leather medical bag. Perspiration beaded her puffy face and she looked tired and bored. Pearl thought that no matter how the woman felt, she probably always looked bored.

"Julius filled me in on the others," she said. Her voice didn't sound bored. It was crisp and efficient.

Quinn raised an eyebrow. "Julius?"

"Dr. Nift," she said. "This fits the pattern all the way down the line. Virtually all bodily fluids drained before dissection began. Most of the cutting done with sharp blades and a cleaver. The larger, more difficult cuts done with what appears to have been a power saw."

She might as well have been talking about carving a turkey. But then that was what the Butcher did, dehumanized his victims by making them mere meat.

Pearl must have appeared ill. The ME gave her a look without pity. "Sorry not to introduce myself. I'm Dr. Jane Tumulty."

Pearl nodded. "Pearl Kasner. Where's Nift today?"

"Dr. Nift had family business."

It was difficult for Pearl to think of Nift—Julius Nift—with a human family, but she supposed it was possible.

Tumulty turned her attention back to Quinn. "When the cutting was finished, the body parts were stacked and washed clean. Not scrubbed or rubbed in any way, though. I think the cleansing agents from the empty containers were used, along with spray from the shower, then bleach was employed. Everything liquid went down the drain with the shower water." She looked at both Quinn and Pearl. "I've never dealt with such a clean cadaver, whole or in part."

"He's a butcher who works clean," Quinn said.

Tumulty gave a swollen smile. "I don't think this was done by a butcher, and certainly not by a doctor, but whoever did it had experience with dismemberment. Maybe a short-term medical student with limited time with cadavers."

"Or on-the-job training," Quinn said.

"Possibly. Cause of death was probably drowning. I'll have more for you after the postmortem. Dr. Nift or I will be in contact." She hefted her black bag with both hands. It was obviously heavy. "She's all yours and the paramedics'. I'm finished here."

Quinn thanked her.

As she was leaving, Tumulty shook her head. "One sick bastard, this killer. I'd rather not do another of these prelims."

"We'll see what we can do," Quinn said.

When the ME was gone, Pearl said, "What do we know about the victim, other than that she's in pieces?"

"She didn't show for work," Quinn said, "so they called. They got no answer, so they asked the super to look in on her. When there was no reply to his knock, he noticed the smell, then let himself in and found her. The uniform at the door and his partner took the call. The super's down in his basement apartment, trying to get used to what he saw."

"I guess he is," Pearl said.

"Victim worked at Courtney Publishing. The super and neighbors aren't sure what her job was. We need to talk to the people at Courtney."

"What was her name?" Pearl asked, picturing again the severed head with its dark wet hair and closed eyes. She wondered if Jane Tumulty had closed the dead eyes. Nift wouldn't have bothered.

"Anna Bragg," Quinn said.

Pearl turned the name over in her mind. Quinn was watching her, smiling slightly and sadly.

Pearl struggled to connect Anna's name to the killer's note. "Bragg . . . Braggadocio . . . The victim worked for a publisher. None of it fits."

"He's more subtle than that," Quinn said. "But you're on the right track with the book connection."

It took a few seconds to dawn on her. " 'Fools rush in,' " Pearl said. "The note didn't have anything to do with gold hair or the Gold Rush."

"Rushin," Quinn said.

"*Anna Karenina*," Pearl said. "Russian. A Russian novel. It's a stretch, but that's gotta be it."

"Not such a stretch," Quinn said. "We both came up with it. My guess is she's the most famous fictional woman in Russian literature. Probably the most famous Anna in any novel."

Pearl was pretty sure they'd figured out who the Russian was in the killer's note. They didn't have to guess the identity of the fools.

"So we agree," Quinn said. His voice softened. "It can happen."

Pearl didn't like the moony way he was looking at her. "What about Feds?"

"He's not in any novel I ever heard of."

"Stop it, Quinn."

"Sorry. He might not agree with us. But I don't think Feds reads Russian novels, even famous ones."

"He's probably the better for it," Pearl said. She remembered reading *Anna Karenina* in high school. Maybe she should read it again. The killer probably had. "Do you think we're in for more victims based on female characters in literature?"

"With this killer, who knows?"

Quinn wanted a glass of water but knew he couldn't touch the faucet handles, or anything else in the kitchen, until the crime scene techs were finished.

"I'll give the paramedics the word to remove the body," he said. "Then you and Feds can talk to the super and neighbors again while I drive over and see what Anna's employers have to say about her."

Pearl watched him leave the kitchen but stayed there to wait for Fedderman.

The sad, grueling work of restructuring the last few days in the life that had ended last night was about to begin.

Nighttime. Pearl had been here before. Because of death she wanted love. Being close to the former and yearning for the latter was nothing new and she understood it. Love and sex were life and the opposite of death. Love was, anyway. Sex and orgasm . . . well, Pearl wasn't so sure.

Her blood still pounded through her veins. Jeb Jones lay next to her in his madly mussed bed at the Waverton, still breathing hard. Traffic on the crowded avenue below was the only other sound.

"You're something," he sighed.

"I needed something."

"Did you get it?"

She reached over and patted his bare, sweating hip. "It was a start."

He laughed in a way she liked.

The small room was too warm and still smelled of sex. There was a ceiling fan but it didn't work, and the windows weren't the kind that opened. Pearl didn't mind. Lust was supposed to be a sweaty business.

She was lying nude on her back, feeling the damp pillow beneath her neck. The slightest cool stirring of breeze from the inadequate air-conditioning played across her midsection. Jeb's breathing was evening out, as if he might be falling asleep.

Pearl didn't move but turned her mind loose. She knew

she might have made a mistake. But wasn't that how you won something, by risking a mistake? After what she'd seen in Anna Bragg's apartment, what happened in this room fell under the category of life-affirming, and that was what Pearl needed—her life to be affirmed.

What would Quinn think of her tryst with Jones—she had to smile slightly—other than wanting to kill Jeb? Though Quinn would disapprove because of how Pearl knew he felt about her, she didn't think he'd disapprove on a professional basis. Jeb was simply a guy who'd had a few dates with the luckless Marilyn Nelson, not a suspect. Not even a person of interest. If there was a difference. And though he'd dated Marilyn a few times, they'd always met someplace. According to Jeb, the only time he'd been in her apartment was when he showed up after she was murdered.

On the other hand, Pearl didn't even know if Jeb had a solid alibi for the night of Marilyn's death. Or for the time of Anna Bragg's.

She figured it might behoove her to ask.

She let her head fall to the side to gaze over the near white horizon of her pillow, and the cop in her took over.

There were her clothes folded neatly on the desk chair. She knew Jeb's were in a pile on the floor. On the desk were a Toshiba notebook computer, a portable printer, and a small spiral notebook with a blue cover. There was an opened package of printer paper on top of the nearby radiator cover. On a small table near the desk was a stack of books, all non-fiction on economics or politics. The largest one, on the bottom, was titled *America and Canada—Friends and Traders*. Pearl didn't think it was a threat to outsell Stephen King. Topping the uneven stack of books were a pad of yellow Post-its, a cheap ballpoint pen, and a couple of stubby yellow pencils. Though the pencils were worn down, their erasers looked fresh and unused.

A freelance journalist's room. At least as Pearl imagined one.

Pearl looked back at the ceiling and thought about Jeb. He'd proved himself a gentle but decisive lover, sometimes letting her take the dominant position, then reasserting himself. He was quite experienced, she was sure. He knew how to turn her in on herself, string her out, tease her, make her wait, and then surprise her.

Why do the erasers look unused? Does he never make a mistake?

"You had supper?" he asked, jolting her out of her thoughts.

"Forgot all about it," Pearl said, realizing she was hungry. "Been kinda busy."

"Wanna go out or do room service?"

Pearl didn't like the idea of a bellhop coming into the room. "Coffee shop downstairs any good when it comes to dinner?"

"Good enough that I eat there almost every night," Jeb said. "Not to mention cheap enough."

He swiveled his body and sat up on his side of the bed, his bare feet on the floor. Pearl studied the lean musculature of his back. He had to be a journalist who worked out regularly.

"Let's take a shower," he said.

"Together?"

"Has to be that way. There's only one cake of soap."

"Can't argue with that," Pearl said, and stretched her arms and legs before getting up out of the warm, perspiration damp bed. The air was cool on her bare buttocks and legs.

Jeb sauntered into the bathroom ahead of her and turned on the shower.

Pearl wasn't surprised that he'd gotten the temperature just right.

Half an hour later they sat in a booth in the Waverton coffee shop, showered, dressed, reasonably unrumpled, and not so obviously lovers.

Pearl had followed Jeb's recommendation and ordered

chicken pot pie. They were both having draft Budweisers in frosted glasses. Pearl enjoyed her cold beer while looking across the table at Jeb and waiting hungrily for her food. She thought life was pretty good. Rare for her.

A broad-hipped waitress with a name badge that said she was Maize arrived with their food on a large round tray and began placing plates on the table. "You must like the pot pie," she said to Jeb.

"Or maybe it's you," he said with a grin.

Maize shook her head and looked at Pearl. "He ordered the same thing for supper last night."

"You were working then, too," Jeb said, still flirting but in no way meaningful.

Maize grinned with crooked teeth. "Yet I don't think we have anything going together except as tipper and tipee."

Jeb aimed his grin at Pearl. "Maize serves humor with the food."

Maize kept a straight face. "But only if its yesterday's special. It's a distraction." She placed the last dish on the table. "Getcha anything else?"

"We've got it all," Jeb said, smiling at Pearl.

Knowing when to be silent, Maize returned to behind the counter.

"You had this same dish here last night?" Pearl asked.

Jeb nodded and poked his fork into browned pot pie crust, causing a faint curl of steam to rise. "I told you, I eat here most of the time. You'll see why. It's delicious."

Careful not to burn her tongue, Pearl dug into her pot pie and found she agreed. Maybe it was because she'd worked up such an appetite in Jeb's room. Or maybe it was because Maize had just supplied her new lover with an alibi for last night, when Anna Bragg was murdered.

Of course it was always possible Jeb had convinced Maize to lie for him. They were tipper and tipee.

Pearl told herself not to be so cynical and sipped her beer.

33

Celandra left the audition thinking she didn't have a chance, but also telling herself that sometimes those were the roles you got. This business was full of surprises. But if you halfway expected them, they weren't really surprises. But if she understood that, then she must think there was a chance.

The hell with it, she thought. It was all too complicated. All she knew was that she'd waited her turn on stage and read the lines of the mad housewife. Mad as in insane. In the six years she'd been pursuing an acting career in New York, she'd landed several off-off Broadway roles, and a few juicy Off Broadways, but she hadn't experienced what she'd define as success. And here she was almost thirty. She was a handsome rather than pretty woman, with a pale, somber face and tall, athletic build. She'd gone heavy on the eye makeup for this audition, so that her large brown eyes appeared darker and sunken, and she'd made her shoulder-length brown hair suitably mussed.

When she left the theater through a stage door alongside the marquee, she found that the heat had built to an uncomfortable level, and the humidity lay like damp felt on her

bare arms. She hailed a cab rather than ride the smelly, stifling subway to get to her apartment in the West Nineties.
The last time she'd ridden the subway, coming home from
buying a knockoff Prada purse on Canal Street, some goon
had rubbed himself against her, and as she was getting off
pinched her left buttock hard enough to leave a bruise. When
she'd turned to confront him, she was looking at the mass of
people eager to get out through the sliding doors before the
train pulled away for its next stop. Apparently her assailant
had faded into the crowded car and left by one of the other
doors. Or maybe the creep was still on the train, hunched in
a seat and hiding behind a newspaper or magazine.

Celandra didn't have the time or opportunity to find him.
People glared at her, or looked right through her, as they
streamed from the train, forcing her to exit along with them.
On the way out, she was buffeted by people boarding the
train. New York, the city that got you coming and going.

When she'd arrived home and examined the bruise developing low on her ass, she vowed never to ride the subway
again, knowing she would someday break that vow, so maybe
it wasn't really a vow. But if she was going to break whatever
it was, today wouldn't be the day. She was still in a quandary
after her audition, and there was the cab right in front of the
theater, like a consolation prize from the city.

She told herself not to be an idiot; the city wasn't God,
maintaining a celestial equality, answering prayers or handing out damnation on a whim. Though sometimes it seemed
that way.

She settled back in the soft upholstery while the cab
rocked and jerked about as the driver fought his way into
heavier traffic on West Forty-fourth. Horns blasted. From
somewhere came an angry shout. Away from the curb lane at
last, the cabbie cursed under his breath and shook his head.
". . . ing city . . ." she heard him grumble. "Hard as rock . . ."

Tell me about it.

She decided she'd take the cab all the way home unless it

got bogged down in traffic. If that happened, and she was within eight or ten blocks of her apartment, she'd get out and walk the rest of the way. Celandra liked to walk. It was good exercise and she was used to it, having spent her formative years on a wheat and soybean farm in Kansas.

Celandra had almost gone insane there, which was why she'd come to New York after her drama coach at the University of Missouri assured her she had real talent. But then she knew she was one of his favorites in another way, too. Not that she'd truly encouraged him or he ever really tried to get in her pants, but he'd made it obvious that was what he wanted. But then, if he hadn't actually tried . . .

She leaned her head back and closed her eyes. It seemed there was nothing definitive in her life. Was it that way with everyone? Weren't there some people who understood exactly where they'd been, where they were at the moment, and where they were going, and planned and noted the steps along the way? She tried to plan her life, but everything turned out to be a goddamned surprise. She'd be an old lady before she knew it, surprised to see the wrinkles. But wasn't that true of everyone?

The cab hit a pothole, jarring her so she actually rose a few inches off the seat.

A few blocks farther and it slowed to an intermittent crawl, then a complete stop. Traffic was backed up and unmoving for as far as Celandra could see through the windshield. And it was getting too warm in the cab. Maybe the driver had switched off the air conditioner so the engine wouldn't overheat in the stopped traffic, or to save precious gas. They did that sometimes. She used the power button to lower the window, and even warmer air fell into the cab. Out of patience, she plucked her wallet from her purse and told the driver she was getting out.

"I get you to the curb," he said, when he saw the bills wadded in her perspiring hand. His accent, which she hadn't noticed earlier, was one she didn't recognize.

"This is fine," she assured him, stuffing the bills into the little swivel tray in the Plexiglas divider, leaving a generous tip.

"You be killed," he said in his peculiar accent, not wanting to lose his fare. "Run flat over. Be my fault."

"I'll be fine," she insisted, thinking there was nothing moving out there to run over her.

"I want no—"

She didn't hear the rest of what he was saying, because she already had the cab's door open.

Three steps, then up on the curb, and she was on the sidewalk and striding away from the stalled cab. Horns blared behind her. Probably one of them was the cab's, but she ignored the brief but violent torrent of noise and walked on.

A medium-height, well dressed man walking in front of her turned around to see what all the honking was about, and their eyes met. Celandra looked quickly away, not wanting to give the guy ideas, but it did register in her mind that he was handsome and well groomed. More than that—there was the mysterious instantaneous something between them that everyone was always searching for. Forces had met, with undeniable potential. But in the beginning there was always a choice.

Right now, still upset over the audition, Celandra told herself she wasn't interested. And apparently he wasn't interested in her. He didn't glance back at her again as he stopped at the intersection and waited for the light to change so he could cross.

He also didn't bother looking at her as she strode past him and he stepped down off the curb to cross with a dozen other people.

So maybe he hadn't felt the magic. It didn't always work in both directions. She might have been flattering herself.

After walking another block, Celandra had forgotten the man.

It never occurred to her to look for him on the other side

of the street, where he was walking parallel to her, dipping a shoulder to ease between people on the crowded sidewalk, occasionally bumping into someone and mumbling a perfunctory "'Scuse me" as he continued at his pace.

At her pace.

Keeping his gaze glued to her.

Making up his mind.

Later, when she left her apartment, he followed her to a Starbucks where she met two other women. Hanging back, he ordered a cappuccino and watched them have Danish and coffee in a booth near a window. Not a low-calorie lunch, but a light one in bulk. All of the women had trim figures, but then they were all young.

After following her home, he'd gleaned her last name from the slot over the mailbox she'd perfunctorily checked before going upstairs to her apartment.

She hadn't seen him, and might not recognize him now if she noticed him in Starbucks, sitting only two booths away, where he could overhear the three women.

So far, none of them had called each other by name. It was amazing how, after the initial meeting, people seldom used names to address each other. He did learn from their conversations that they were actresses. That didn't surprise him, considering the beauty and bearing of the woman he'd followed. The woman he'd chosen.

So she was an actress, which meant it shouldn't be difficult to learn her given name. He smiled. Her name might even be up in lights somewhere.

All he really needed now was her name.

34

Four days later, early in the morning, Pearl was sitting on a bench in Washington Square, watching a homeless guy finding his way awake on an opposite bench. He was wearing ragged clothes two sizes too large, and he moved arthritically though he didn't appear to be older than forty. An empty can of Colt 45 malt liquor lay beneath the bench, probably his sleeping pill.

Pearl watched as the man sat up, glared angrily at her as if she'd caused his bad luck, then made it to his feet and staggered toward Macdougal Street. Lauri passed him walking the other way, toward Pearl, and gave him a wide berth. He didn't seem to notice her.

In sharp contrast to the homeless guy, Lauri strode with the sureness and lightness of youth, through about a dozen disinterested pigeons pecking about on the pavement, causing them to flap skyward with obvious reluctance. She was smiling. She and Pearl had met for lunch, or simply to walk and talk, several times, and had come to like each other. Pearl knew the teenager admired and trusted her, perhaps too much.

Lauri plopped down next to Pearl on the bench. She was

wearing jeans and a yellow sleeveless blouse, joggers without socks. The morning sun glinted off her zirconia nose stud.

"You talk to my dad?" she asked.

"Beautiful morning," Pearl said.

"Oh, yeah, I'm sorry. Inward directed, I guess."

Pearl figured the kid must have been watching Dr. Phil.

"It *is* a beautiful morning," Lauri said, applying the grease.

Pearl didn't actually think it was particularly beautiful. There was trash all over the ground, including some broken crack vials, and four or five homeless reminders of life's travails still lurked about. The pigeons Lauri had stirred up were back. Dirty things. Pearl didn't like pigeons.

"Pearl—"

"I did ask your dad what he thought about me giving you pointers on what it means to be a cop. He was okay with that. In fact, he likes us talking with each other. But he also doesn't want you to be a cop."

"Why not? He is."

"He thinks you can do better."

"Can or should?"

"Both, I would imagine."

"Mom and that Elliott geek were always pushing me to do better. Like I was some kind of Rhodes Scholar." Lauri made a face as if she were disappointed. "I didn't think Dad was like that."

"Wanting the best for his kid? Why shouldn't he?"

"Because not everybody can be a Rhodes Scholar. Some of us want to be cops. Like you."

"I don't think it's that, Lauri. Your dad doesn't want you to see certain things."

"Well, why shouldn't I see them? He has."

"Exactly. He has, and he knows. Also, he doesn't want certain things to happen to you."

"Such as?"

That one was easy. "Getting shot or stabbed to death."

"Oh."

Pearl stood up from the bench. "I'd better get going, Lauri. I've gotta meet your dad and Feds in about twenty minutes."

"I thought we were gonna have breakfast."

"No time now. You were almost an hour late."

Lauri bowed her head to gaze at a gray-and-white pigeon that had wandered close. "Yeah, I need to work on promptness."

Pearl smiled. "It'll come."

"What about the other?" Lauri asked. "Did you talk to Dad again about that?"

"He didn't seem warm to the idea of you tagging along with me while I'm working."

"How do you mean?"

"He said he'd shoot me." Pearl waited until Lauri looked up from the pigeon to her. "I think it's a bad idea, too, Lauri. This isn't a job like word processing or selling insurance. You can learn by watching, but you can also get hurt."

"I'm willing to take the chance."

"He isn't."

"And he's Dad, is that it?"

"Yeah. And he's my boss."

"I guess we both have to settle for that."

"Now you're learning."

But Pearl knew this was too easy. Lauri was, after all, Quinn's daughter, and Pearl knew a thing or two about Quinn.

"We can still meet now and then as friends," Lauri said. "Still talk."

"Wouldn't have it any other way," Pearl said.

Lauri stood up, shrugged, and smiled. "Then I guess that's the way it is. That's what life's about, settling for what you get."

"Part of what it's about," Pearl said. "Car's parked over there. Want a lift uptown?"

"No, I've gotta check in to work soon." Big smile. Made her look like Quinn. "Gotta be prompt."

"Atta girl," Pearl said. *You are so full of bullshit, like your father.*

When she reached the car, Pearl turned and saw Lauri walking in the opposite direction, away from her. Standing there with her hand on the sun-warmed car roof, she felt a sudden and unexpected fondness for Quinn's daughter, a protectiveness. Maybe even a stirring of something maternal.

Scary.

When Pearl arrived at the office, Quinn was seated behind his desk, wearing the drugstore reading glasses he used for fine print and looking at the postmortem results on Anna Bragg. They were those weird glasses that sat low on the nose and looked as if they'd been sawed in half lengthwise. Fedderman was across the room, pouring himself a cup of coffee.

"Want one?" he asked, glancing over at Pearl.

"Not this morning." Pearl's stomach felt oddly unsettled, maybe because of her probably futile conversation with Lauri and the unfamiliar maternal instinct it had provoked.

"Orange juice? I stopped and got a carton."

"Nothing, thanks." *Leave me the hell alone.*

"This is more of the same, almost down to the number of cuts the killer made," Quinn said dejectedly, tapping the report with a blunt forefinger. Pearl wouldn't have wanted to be tapped that hard.

"Cause of death?" she asked.

"Drowning. Like the others. He puts them in the bathtub, runs the water, then drowns them before carving them up."

"What about the tape residue?" Pearl asked. "Is that the same?"

"Yeah. Same kind of duct tape, sold everywhere. Same MO all the way. Taped tight as a Thanksgiving turkey, and with a rectangle of tape across the mouth. When they're dead and silent forever, he removes the tape, including the gag, before going to work with his blades and saw."

"Time of death?"

Quinn adjusted the narrow glasses on his nose and glanced down to make sure. "Says here between six and nine P.M."

Pearl thought that was about perfect. Unless Maize the waitress was lying, Jeb Jones had his alibi.

Jeb . . .

"Her colleagues at Courtney Publishing all seemed to like her."

"They always do, after they're dead," Pearl said.

"Yeah. She was an associate editor, working her way up. Her boss said she had potential. Nobody there noticed her acting scared lately, or different in any way. She'd dated a guy in sales a few times, but it didn't go anywhere and they stopped seeing each other. He's at some book convention in Frankfurt now."

"Ah, the Frankfurt alibi."

"I talked by phone to people who were with him at the time of Anna Bragg's death," Quinn said. "No possibility he flew here, killed her, then flew back."

Fedderman had walked over and was sitting behind his desk. He had coffee in one hand, a plastic cup of juice in the other. "You get anywhere with him?" he asked Pearl.

"Huh?"

"With that guy who dated Marilyn Nelson a few times."

"Oh. No, I didn't. And he's alibied up for the time Anna Bragg was killed."

"That pretty much clears him across the board," Quinn said. "Just like the other guys we connected with the dead women. They dated them, some of them had sex with them, but they've got alibis for one or more of the murders."

"*Sex and the City*," Fedderman said.

Pearl looked at him.

"I rent the videos and watch them," he explained. "That way I know what I'm missing."

"What we're all missing," Pearl said.

Quinn removed his goofy half-glasses and gave her a look she knew too well. Had he picked up something in her voice? Did he somehow know she was covering up exactly the kind of furtive sex she was lamenting not having?

Don't be a fool. He isn't a mind reader.

But she knew Quinn.

He could see through people and beyond. Sometimes, only for brief moments, she found herself feeling sorry for the people Quinn hunted.

She turned and walked toward the coffee brewer so he wouldn't be looking right at her, studying her. Damn him!

"I think I'll have some coffee after all." She needed to get everything out of her mind except the Job.

"You should have some of the orange juice instead," Quinn said. "It might cool you down."

Damn him!

The fax machine began humming and gurgling.

Though he was sitting down, Fedderman was closest. He stood up and wandered over to the machine, then loomed gazing down at it as if it were some puzzle he couldn't quite work out.

When it beeped and was silent, he picked up the two pages that had been faxed and carried them over to Quinn.

"Copies of Marilyn Nelson's charge account receipts," he said.

Quinn scanned them, and then put his glasses back on and looked at them more closely. The receipts were mostly for meals and clothes. Only one of them was for two meals, at the Pepper Tree restaurant. Quinn remembered seeing the Pepper Tree just a few blocks from Marilyn Nelson's apartment. The date on the receipt was less than two weeks before her murder. Had she been dining with her killer? Unlikely.

But maybe with someone who might be able to tell them more about Marilyn Nelson's last days.

With his huge blunt finger he pointed out the charge to Pearl. "Pay a visit to this restaurant. See if anyone recalls who the victim dined with on this date. Marilyn picked up the check, and she was a regular who usually ate alone, so somebody might remember."

Pearl thought it was a long shot, but it was something. If they were lucky, Marilyn Nelson had dined with a date that evening even though she'd picked up the check. Marilyn going Dutch out of desperation, maybe even with someone who knew her intimately. Pearl could picture it.

Death and the City.

Then she looked more closely at the name of the restaurant. The Pepper Tree. Jeb had told her he and Marilyn Nelson once dined there.

Pearl and Jeb had a date to go there.

It seemed to Pearl that nothing in her life was simple.

35

Harrison County, Florida, 1980

It was a moonless night and dark, or Sherman might have seen the danger. His time in the swamp had made him alert to such things. He'd learned hard lessons, such as how to shelter himself from the storms that blasted through the trees and raised the black water, how to find and eat things alive and dead that wouldn't make him sick, how to sleep fitfully and watchfully for what had become his natural and very real enemies.

How to survive.

Every sound in the swamp meant something to him now, as did the subtle scents on the breeze, or the irregular ripple of previously still water. He studied and learned to read these signs as he'd studied and learned from Sam's books and his long, lazy conversations with Sam. That knowledge was Sam's legacy. The swamp was Sherman's home now, dangerous, but less so than the home he had left.

The leaving had been complete. No longer did he even think of his name as Sherman, for there was no one to call him that or anything else. And there wasn't much time to contemplate the past; he had no choice but to live in and for the present. He knew that to get lost in the past was to surrender the future. He was in and of the swamp now and considered and obeyed only the laws of nature, and really there was only one law—survive.

He violated that law when he stepped on the rough, ridged surface that moved beneath his bare foot in the inky water. In an instant he knew—*gator!* And he knew he might die and would do anything if only he might live.

A long, thick tail rose into darkness and slapped down on the shallow water, breaking its surface with a sound like a rifle shot and splashing it coldly on Sherman's face. He instinctively tried to take a giant leap away from the gator, but his foot slipped and he almost fell. Teetering desperately, he went splashing sideways away from another slap of the huge tail.

Then the gator was up high on its legs, its pale belly clear of the surface. It was gigantic, at least ten feet long, and Sherman knew it could outrun him, especially in the shallow water.

The sight of the beast paralyzed him with terror. The gator was accustomed to this temporary lack of motion in its prey. It was the time to strike.

Black water foamed and roiled violently as the gator lunged. Sherman felt something hard brush his bare heel and heard the eerie clack of primal teeth. He yelped and flung himself frantically away, landing on hands and knees. Fueled by fear, he was up almost immediately, running through the knee-deep water, lifting his legs high and stretching out his strides to minimize splashing and maximize speed. Survive.

He knew the gator was coming. He could hear it between the frenetic dissonance of his own splashing. He could sense and see it in his mind, swift and graceless in its bent-legged strides, gliding smoothly at times through the dark water, then finding firm footing again and picking up speed, gaining.

Gaining!

Sherman bumped his shoulder on a thick tree trunk. Chanced a glance behind him.

Gaining!

Climb!

Though they were fast, big, strong, and armed with tooth and tail, the one thing gators couldn't do was climb. Sherman leaped, wrapped his arms and legs around the tree, and attempted to shinny higher. Up was safety. Up away from the guttural grunts and the slashing tail, the tearing teeth. Up was life!

But the tree trunk was coated with moss and slippery. He slid lower instead of gaining height and was back in the muddy water.

The lowest branch might be within his reach. He bent his knees and leaped, groping in the night air for the branch.

His fingertips brushed it.

He landed splashing awkwardly and leaped again, and this time was well short of even touching the branch.

The gator had stopped now and was angled in the water, crouched low again, watching him with a gaze thousands of years old, detached, observant, and merciless.

Sherman understood gators. He knew why this one had stopped. It sensed in its prey the knowledge that the chase was over. It had won.

Slowly, smoothly, it began moving toward Sherman, leaving the slightest V wake in the shallow water. Sherman could only stare paralyzed with fear. He knew what would happen next. The gator's jaws would close on him, then it would drag him toward deeper water where it would do its death spin until Sherman bled lifeless or drowned. The gator would carry what had become its meal to its lair in the deep mud near the waterline and store it there where it would rot and become tenderer. Those nights with his mother at swamp's edge came crashing into Sherman's memory. He remembered the doomed boarders, and Sam, dragged away in pieces into the night. He remembered the gnashing and grinding and grunting of pure gluttony and its appeasement.

He wouldn't give up—not yet. Not ever. He had to run! Had to get away!

Run, damn you!

He made himself abandon his fruitless attempts to climb the tree and began splashing away into the swamp, roiling black water with each stride, praying the gator would give up.

He slipped and fell. Splashed helplessly trying to stand up. Gained his feet. Ran, ran. Part of the swamp. Part of the struggle. One of the hunted.

Survive! Survive! That was his one and every instinct in mind and muscle. Run fast enough, far enough. *Survive!*

A branch scratched his face, breaking his stride, slowing him only momentarily.

Three awkward steps and he had his balance again, steadier now. Full speed!

Something grabbed his lower left leg and became a painful vise as he slammed down hard on his stomach and inhaled swamp water. Flailing with his arms and free leg, he fought to keep his head above the surface.

The vise tightened and became needles of incredible pain. Choking, spitting, unable even to scream, Sherman felt himself being pulled backward through the water.

He glanced back at what had him and almost died from terror. He was caught firm in the jaws of the beast. Two prehistoric, uncaring eyes met his. They were very close, darker than the night, and they were death.

Then came sudden brilliance and a roar.

Sherman felt himself sinking.

36

New York, the present

The Pepper Tree was decorated mostly in grays and blues, with one wall a wide mural of green fields beneath a blue sky. The fields were dotted with trees Pearl assumed to be pepper trees, but then, she wasn't even sure if there were types of peppers that grew on trees.

Culinary license, she thought, as a smiling African American man approached. He was handsome if a bit paunchy, wearing a navy jacket with brass buttons, white shirt open at the collar, a red ascot. A guy who had lost his yacht.

"We're not open for breakfast," he said.

Pearl looked out over the rows of white tablecloths without flatware, china, or napkins. "I can see that. You should have locked your door."

He seemed amused. "We're trusting sorts."

"I wish I were," Pearl said, and showed him her shield.

The man's smile disappeared, which was a shame. He had a great smile but without it looked rather ordinary.

"This is about Marilyn Nelson?" he asked, surprising her, and for the first time sounding as if he had a slight Jamaican accent.

"You're clairvoyant," Pearl said.

"Oh, not hardly. Marilyn ate here often. She was a pretty woman. We notice pretty women, especially if they're also as nice as Marilyn."

Pearl glanced about. She and the man seemed to be the only ones in the restaurant.

"My employee Harmon is in the kitchen cleaning up," the man said, guessing her thoughts. "I am Virgil Mantrell."

"The manager?"

"And owner. Which means I'm here virtually all the time."

Useful, Pearl thought. The prospects of her visit to the Pepper Tree brightened. Surely Jeb wasn't the only man who'd dined with Marilyn in the restaurant. "I understand Marilyn usually ate alone."

"Usually, yes. She hadn't been in the city long and hadn't had time to explore. Though she wasn't always alone. I remember her coming here for dinner with men a few times, on dates, it looked like. And another time, later, she had lunch with a woman."

"What do you remember about them?"

"The men were different. Except for one she was here with at least a couple of times."

"What did that one look like?"

"I don't remember much about him. He seemed to be in his thirties, had dark hair. I suppose you'd call him handsome, but at the same time he was very ordinary looking. I'd have trouble recognizing him if he came in here again, and I have a memory for faces."

"And the woman who dined with Marilyn?"

"Her I would recognize."

"Pretty, I'll bet."

"Not as pretty as Marilyn." The smile was back. "We don't like to quantify our customers in terms of beauty or handsomeness."

"Wise policy," Pearl said.

He nodded. "It is only polite, and politeness goes far in the restaurant business. When I made it a point to visit Marilyn's table and make sure everything was all right, she introduced me to the woman, who she said was an old college friend."

"Did she refer to her by name?"

"Yes, she did." He raised his dark eyebrows in a way that made him appear to be in pain. "I'm sorry, but while I remember faces, I don't remember names."

Pearl showed him a copy of the fax with the charge receipts and pointed to the one from the Pepper Tree. "Do you have a copy of this?"

"We do. We keep careful records. That would be from the meal Marilyn had with her lady friend."

"How do you know?"

"The price. And I remember. They were here for lunch. The time will be marked on our receipt."

"I don't see anything on the list from when she dined with the men."

"That would be because they paid cash," Virgil said. The smile flashed again. "It still happens." He looked thoughtful. "Or it's possible that there was an oversight and we haven't yet submitted a charge receipt to the bank. If so, it would still be here and wouldn't show up on your list."

"Shall we look?" Pearl asked.

"You won't need a warrant," he said, using the smile to make it a joke.

He led her through the kitchen, where a pimply teenager who had to be Harmon was cleaning or waxing the floor with some kind of sponge mop, then on to a surprisingly large office with a gleaming hardwood floor and a loosely woven carpet containing muted shades of myriad colors. Virgil Mantrell's desk was large, made of a lightly grained wood that could have been teak. There were oils of sailboats on the walls. Pearl was no judge, but she thought they were good.

Maybe her impression had been right and the man did own a yacht.

"Do you sail?" she asked, as Virgil rummaged through a black metal file cabinet behind the desk.

"Never," he said, not glancing back at her, "but I paint."

"And very well."

Virgil did look back at her and smiled at the compliment, then bent again to his task.

He found the sheaf of charge receipts he was looking for, and swiveled in his chair so he was facing Pearl across his desk. He began adroitly riffling through the receipts.

Pearl, knowing when to hold her silence, stood patiently waiting. Her gaze went to the paintings of graceful sailboats. She wondered if the one on the wall behind the desk was a sloop. She wondered what a sloop was.

Suddenly Virgil's dancing fingers stopped. "Ah!" he said, with seeming great delight.

"You found it?"

"No. The men and Marilyn must have paid cash for their meals."

"Then why the orgasm?"

Virgil looked sharply at her and seemed genuinely shocked by her language. Pearl almost apologized.

"I mean," she said, "you gave the impression you'd found what we were looking for."

"Something else," Virgil said. "When Marilyn lunched with her lady friend, she paid the check by charge. But there's another receipt for that date, time, and table. Her friend used her own charge card to pay the bar bill." He slid the thin receipt across the wide desk so Pearl could reach it.

The name on the receipt was Ella Oaklie. Pearl read it aloud. "Ring a bell?"

"I don't think so," Virgil said. "But she must be the woman I saw with Marilyn. The receipt proves it."

"Can you please give me a copy of this?"

"I'll make a copy," Virgil said, "and I'll let you have the original."

"Because I'm polite," Pearl said.

"And have an eye for art." Virgil smiled. "And are quite pretty."

And could subpoena it anyway, Pearl thought, but politely kept silent.

Pearl found Ella Oaklie's address easily enough. She was in the phone directory. Sometimes detective work was a snap.

The woman behind the counter of a small flower shop on First Avenue had let Pearl used the shop's directory. Pearl made a note of the address and phone number. Not wanting to be overheard, she thanked the woman and stepped outside into the heat to use her cell phone to call Oaklie.

She got an answering machine informing her in stilted language that there was no one available to take her call right now, but if she would please leave a message . . .

Pearl waited patiently for the drivel to end, then left her name and number for Ella Oaklie and cut the connection.

Since it was almost lunchtime, she drove over to Third Avenue and Fifty-fourth, where she knew a street vendor sold tasty and reliable food. Pearl generally lightened up for lunch, so she bought a knish and bottled water from the vendor, then wandered over to sit on a warm stone wall and people-watch while she ate.

After her second bite, her cell phone vibrated in her pocket. Setting knish and bottled water aside, Pearl picked up.

Ella Oaklie had called home and checked her messages and wanted to get in touch with Pearl as soon as possible, since it was so horrible what had happened to Marilyn Nelson. When Pearl offered to meet Ella at her office, Ella was reluctant, but might they meet for lunch? Pearl said sure, and suggested the Pepper Tree near Marilyn Nelson's apartment. She'd found that putting the witness as close as possible to the scene of the crime sometimes did wonders for the memory.

Ella agreed at once. While Pearl had Ella going, she suggested they meet in half an hour. Forty-five minutes would work, Ella said, and Pearl said she'd meet her just inside the door, where there was a small waiting area with a bench. Ella asked if she'd be in uniform, and Pearl, irritated, told her no, she'd be wearing gray slacks and a blue blazer, not to mention sensible black shoes.

Kind of a uniform, Pearl thought, as she broke the connection and slid her phone back in her pocket.

It buzzed again almost immediately.

This time it was Jeb. He wanted to meet her for lunch.

"If you can get away," he added, when he sensed Pearl's hesitancy.

"I'm going to meet someone at a restaurant for a brief interview, then we can have a bite ourselves if you want, and maybe go somewhere."

"Sure it's okay? I mean, I don't want to mess you up in your work."

"It's more than okay," Pearl assured him. "The restaurant's the Pepper Tree."

"Great. We were planning on going there anyway."

She told him approximately what time the interview would be over.

"Go ahead and eat hearty," he said. "I'll have some lunch before I turn up at the restaurant, then we can have a drink or two and leave."

And go to your room at the Waverton?

Pearl didn't have to ask him. She knew it was what they both wanted.

She said good-bye to Jeb, then again slid the phone into her pocket, hoping the damned thing would stay there for a while and be quiet.

That was when she glanced across the street and saw Lauri Quinn.

Lauri, in patched and faded jeans and a baggy red pull-over shirt, was standing near the doorway of an office supply store, pretending to look at something in the display window. Pearl figured she might be watching her in the window's reflection and averted her gaze.

She was more annoyed than surprised at seeing Lauri, because it wasn't the first time. Twice before Pearl had caught a glimpse of someone she thought might have been Lauri, but it had been so brief she couldn't be sure. Now she was sure. Apparently Lauri hadn't taken her insistence that she not accompany Pearl on the job seriously, but had decided to follow Pearl without Pearl's knowledge.

Lauri not giving up on what she wanted.

Lauri being like her father.

Pearl wasn't sure what to do about this, but decided not to do anything now. She had to meet Ella Oaklie soon, anyway, and didn't feel like confronting Lauri about being inexpertly and annoyingly tailed. And of course there was the danger of an amateur—a kid, at that—dogging a homicide detective on the trail of a serial killer. It might be a good idea to tell Quinn what was going on, find out how he wanted to handle the situation. After all, Lauri was *his* daughter.

On the other hand, Pearl did feel a certain protectiveness toward Lauri, and Quinn seemed completely at sea when it came to dealing with a teenage girl who wasn't a murder suspect.

Pearl glanced at her watch. Forty minutes until her meeting with Ella Oaklie. She had the unmarked and could get to the Pepper Tree in a hurry, so she was okay on time.

Being careful not to glance again in Lauri's direction, Pearl ate her knish.

37

Another one.

Quinn had expected it. The Butcher was going to continue taunting the police with his puzzle notes.

Renz had just faxed the newest one to Quinn, along with the expected useless results of lab tests on the note itself and the envelope it arrived in. No prints on envelope or stamp, no DNA on the envelope flap, the usual common and virtually untraceable paper stock, a midtown New York postmark, and almost mechanically neat printing in number-two pencil. Like the first note, this one was addressed to Quinn.

Pearl and Fedderman were in the field, leaving Quinn alone in the office. He carried the just-faxed note to his desk to give it some thought. It was cool in the office and quiet except for an occasional thump or muffled voice from the dental clinic on the other side of the wall. Quinn leaned back in his swivel chair and rested the note on his knee, squinting at it and trying to parse its brief and cryptic message:

A rose is a rose is a rose by any other name.
Take care,
The Butcher

Fedderman came in from helping to canvass the buildings surrounding Anna Bragg's apartment. He looked hot, his suit coat hooked over his shoulder with a forefinger as he often carried it, his shirt sweat-stained and wrinkled. His right cuff was flapping unbuttoned, as it often was. Fedderman was the only person Quinn knew whose cuff persistently came unbuttoned while he was writing with pen or pencil. Maybe it was the brand of shirts he wore. His rep-striped tie was loosened and looked as if it had been used in a tug-of-war.

He sighed, and his desk chair sighed as he sat down in it.

"Any progress to report?" Quinn asked.

Fedderman rolled his weary eyes in Quinn's direction. "How can you even ask that?"

"I wanted to get it in before you passed out."

"None of Anna's neighbors remembered anything they hadn't recalled or made up last time they talked to us. There are a few inconsistencies, but I think that's because the heat is addling their brains. I know it's addling mine."

"Maybe you oughta have a hot coffee," Quinn said. "There's a theory that if you drink something warmer than your body temperature it will feel cool on a hot day. Worth a try."

"Sadist," Fedderman said. "Lab give us anything from the paper or envelope?"

"Not a thing. We got zilch. Except for this other note he sent us."

Fedderman stopped feeling sorry for himself and sat forward, interested.

"Renz just faxed it over." Since Fedderman still looked too exhausted to stand, Quinn got up from behind his desk and walked over to the opposite desk and handed him Renz's fax.

Fedderman studied the brief printout for almost a minute, as if waiting for inspiration.

It never came.

"Woman named Rose?" he said finally.

"Kind of obvious."

"Kind of rose," Fedderman said. "We look for roses named after women, maybe we come up with the next victim's name."

"I thought you said your brain was addled."

"If I said that, I forgot it," Fedderman said. "The composer, what's his name, Cole Porter. Didn't he name a kind of rose after his wife?"

"He did," Quinn said, but I can't think of it."

"Internet," Fedderman said.

As Quinn was returning to his desk, Fedderman was already booting up his computer.

Within half an hour they had more than twenty species of roses that were named after women, including the Linda Porter, namesake of Cole Porter's wife. There were also among the multitude the Betty Boop rose, the Helen Traubel, and the Charlotte Armstrong.

And Quinn came across another possibility as he was roaming the Internet—Shakespeare: "*That which we call a rose by any other name would smell as sweet.*" A quote from *Romeo and Juliet.*

Would the next Butcher victim be a Juliet?

When he asked Fedderman what he thought, he agreed that Juliets were in danger.

"Should we warn them all?" Fedderman asked. "The Juliets and all the other rose women?"

Quinn stared at the lengthy list of rose names and thought about all the Lindas, Bettys, Charlottes, Annabels, Sonias, Michelles . . . He saw that there was indeed a Juliet rose listed. Not only that, it was the *Sweet Juliet.* He informed Fedderman.

"I dunno," Fedderman said, perusing the same list. "It seems like every woman's got a rose named after her. I still kinda like Starina. Sounds like a stripper."

"We need to make the note public as soon as possible,

and it wouldn't be a bad idea to see if we can get the media to print all of the names."

"My guess is that's what the Butcher wants us to do," Fedderman said. "That way he can terrorize more women."

Quinn thought he was probably right. Still, it was the thing to do.

"I'll call Renz," he said. "He likes to hold press conferences, especially the part where you refuse to take any more questions and strut away."

"She might already be dead," Fedderman said sadly, looking at his list. "Starina, Elle, Carla, Dainty Bess . . ."

"Christ!" Quinn said. "Dainty Bess."

He pecked out Renz's phone number, hearing Fedderman say, "I wonder if there really is a Starina out there."

38

"Gertrude Stein," Pearl said, when she'd checked in by cell phone and Quinn told her about the Butcher's latest note. She was driving fast, trying to make up for heavy traffic due to construction on Lexington Avenue.

Now Quinn remembered. "Jesus, Pearl! It was right in front of us."

"She's the one who said, 'A rose is a rose is a rose.'"

"I know. Our sicko's going to kill a Gertrude." He wondered if there was a *Gertrude* rose. Something to check.

Steering one-handed, Pearl swerved around a furniture van. "I wouldn't be too sure. There are plenty of other possibilities, including some we haven't thought of."

"But I sure like this one, Pearl. It's oblique, which seems to be our guy's approach in his little puzzle notes. I'm glad you thought of it."

She couldn't help feeling a flush of pride. Also, she had to admit, affection. Despite her present relationship with Jeb, Quinn could still get to her. You didn't live with someone, sleep with him, without a part of that staying with you.

Maybe it wasn't just Quinn. She wondered if it somehow had anything to do with Lauri. For a moment she considered telling him about his daughter following her around after being forbidden to do so, then decided this wasn't the time or place. The way was a problem, too.

"I'm pulling up in front of the Pepper Tree to meet Ella Oaklie," she said. "Gotta go."

She replaced the cell phone in her blazer pocket and double-parked, then got out of the car and used her shield to chase away some joker who was waiting for someone while parked illegally in a loading zone. When he was gone, Pearl parked there. She placed the NYPD placard on the dash, just in case some civilian couldn't read the invisible letters on the unmarked that screamed *police*, and climbed out of the car into the brilliant heat.

When she entered the comparatively cool and dim restaurant, Pearl saw a thirtyish, rather plain-looking dishwater-blond woman seated on the gaily decorated deacon's bench just inside the Pepper Tree's door. The woman seemed anxious and looked up at her inquisitively, as if she'd been sitting forever in a doctor's waiting room and Pearl might at last usher her into a tiny room and poke a thermometer in her mouth. Pearl smiled, and the obviously greatly relieved Ella Oaklie rose and introduced herself.

Here is someone, Pearl thought, *who's been often stood up.*

They were led to a table toward the rear of the restaurant, near a corner. Pearl was glad. There weren't any diners so close that they might overhear and conversation would be inhibited.

Ella ordered a vodka martini before lunch, and Pearl a Pellegrino. This was going well; alcohol might help to loosen Ella's tongue.

"So you and Marilyn were college chums?" Pearl asked.

"We were roommates throughout our freshman year, so I guess you could call us that. We hadn't seen each other in years. I don't think I can be much help to you, but I'd sure like to do anything to help catch the bastard who killed her." Her voice didn't convey anger, but she did sound sincere.

"Conversations like this help us to get as accurate an idea as possible about a murder victim," Pearl explained. "Sometimes it leads us to the sort of people they associate with. Sometimes even to a particular person who turns out to be the one we're looking for."

Ella smiled with straight but prominent teeth. Her dentist had done everything possible but it hadn't been quite enough. "You might have some difficulty there. The Marilyn Nelson I knew liked all kinds of people. She was outgoing and friendly, and I guess what you'd call democratic. I couldn't name anyone who disliked her. I always thought she'd go into sales or public relations, but she stuck to her designing."

"Good student?"

"Dean's list. Beauty and brains. If we hadn't been roommates and friends, I'd have been jealous of her."

Ha! Pearl thought. She knew jealousy when she heard it. "Do you recall her using drugs?"

Pearl saw a sudden and familiar wariness in Ella's eyes at the mention of drugs, as the woman reminded herself she was talking to a cop.

"Not in any way meaningful," she said, obviously choosing her words carefully.

"The statutes of limitation have expired," Pearl assured her with a grin. Then she winked. "Not to mention we were all young once." Become a coconspirator; an interrogation technique she'd learned from Quinn.

It worked. Ella seemed to relax. "Okay. We smoked a little weed, took some uppers when we had to cram for exams. But when I knew her, Marilyn wasn't at all what anyone would describe as a drug addict."

"When you had lunch with her here, not long before she died, did she make any reference to drugs?"

"None whatsoever. She didn't even drink alcohol, just Pellegrino water, like you are."

"So what was your lunchtime conversation about?"

"What you'd expect. What time had done to us. What's happened to old friends. Then clothes. Or her job. Same thing in this case. She was really enthusiastic about her job designing some new store here, and the Rough Country line of clothing that was gonna be sold there. She was even wearing jeans and a Western-looking shirt and jacket to impress me."

"Did it?"

"Yeah."

"Trying to sell you?"

"I guess. That's what I'd have been trying to do in her place."

Their drinks came, and they each ordered a salad, Ella because she was on what she called her endless diet, and Pearl because she'd already scarfed down a knish.

"You sound a bit defensive about her," Pearl said, when the server was gone.

Ella sampled her martini and shrugged. "I liked her. And my God, she's been murdered. I mean, I wouldn't trample all over her memory even if I hadn't liked her."

"But you did like her."

"Of course! Unless she changed a lot, you'd have to turn over a lot of rocks to find somebody who didn't like Marilyn."

"Did she talk much about her job? The people she worked with?"

"Quite a bit about the job, but not about the people. I think she was pretty much on her own here in New York, except for the one other store over in Queens or someplace. And she hadn't been in town long enough to make any enemies."

"In this city you can be murdered for looking at somebody the wrong way," Pearl said.

"Yeah, but the way Marilyn was killed . . ." Ella took another sip of martini. "Jesus! That was so awful!" She stared across the table at Pearl. "You actually saw it, what that ghoul did to her. Doesn't that haunt you?"

"Forever," Pearl said, being honest to evoke honesty. Another Quinn technique.

"And it happened just a few blocks from here," Ella said, "in the everyday world."

"That's the horror of it," Pearl said. "Everything happens in the everyday world."

"But you're a cop, so you should be used to it."

"Well, I see more of it than most people. But no matter how much or how little any of us sees, it's still happening. What goes on behind all those walls and windows out there sometimes isn't what we imagine or would like it to be. But it happens every day."

Ella seemed to think about that most of the time while they ate their salads.

They'd both virtuously decided against dessert when Pearl noticed a change in Ella's eyes, a kind of double take, as she looked over Pearl's shoulder.

Pearl turned and saw Jeb Jones approaching the table.

He smiled and said hello to Pearl, then nodded at Ella.

"Spotted you when I walked in," he said to Pearl, resting a hand lightly on her shoulder. "I just wanted to let you know I was here."

He backed away. "You're working. I'll grab a table up near the front and we can talk when you're done."

"Haven't we met?" Ella said.

Jeb studied her. "I don't think so. I'm Jeb Jones."

"Ella Oaklie."

"Sorry, doesn't ring a bell." He gave her his incandescent grin. "But now we know each other." To Pearl: "Take your time."

Pearl said that she would and watched him cross the restaurant. Watched the way Ella was looking at him.

"I thought that was the same guy I saw with Marilyn about two weeks before she was killed." She frowned. "But now that I look at him, I suppose he's just the same type."

"You saw them where?"

"Outside her apartment."

Jeb had dated Marilyn Nelson a few times, but hadn't been inside her apartment except for the initial interview with Pearl.

"They were just coming out when I interrupted them," Ella said. "We talked a few minutes and I tried to leave, but Marilyn insisted I come up and have a drink with them. I figured that might be awkward so I refused. Then the guy insisted, said we were old friends and should catch up, but we didn't need him. Then he said his good-byes and left. He was very nice about it."

Pearl put down the fork she'd been toying with. "Did Marilyn introduce him?"

"Sure." She bit her lower lip. "I'm trying to remember his name. It wasn't Jeb Jones, I'm sure." She brightened. "Joe! That was it. Joe something. Joe Grant! So it couldn't be him." She glanced toward the front of the restaurant. "Your guy, I mean."

Pearl made a show of making a note of the name. "Very good," she said.

"Is he a suspect?"

"Not really. Marilyn Nelson was an attractive woman. I'm sure she had her admirers. Most of the Butcher's victims were attractive, so we've had to routinely eliminate the men who dated them recently. Did Marilyn and this Joe Grant seem close?"

"Not particularly. At least not in the way I think you mean."

"But you did think they were more than friends."

"Maybe. I can't be sure of that. It was just that your guy, Jeb, something about him reminded me of Joe, or I wouldn't even have thought of it." She looked at Pearl over the dessert menu they'd decided to spurn. "You and Jeb, you're close, right?"

Pearl smiled. "You're intuitive." Which was true, and probably meant she'd read the Marilyn Nelson–Joe Grant relationship correctly—nothing serious. Pearl decided not to tell Ella that Jeb had also dated Marilyn. Not so odd that there'd be a slight resemblance. Like many women, Marilyn had liked a certain type.

It struck Pearl that they might be approaching this from the wrong direction; the Butcher chose as his victims a certain type of woman, but he might also have been able to get next to them because he was their type.

Ella looked again toward the front of the restaurant, where Jeb was seated alone at a table with a glass of beer before him. "Now that I think about it, there really isn't that much of a resemblance. But when your Jeb walked in and I thought he was Joe, it sure gave me a start."

"Me, too," Pearl said.

Me, too.

39

"He doin' okay?" Cree asked over his shoulder, his hands skillfully playing the jumping, jerking steering wheel.

"He ain't sayin'," Boomer shouted back through the truck's knocked-out rear window.

The old Dodge pickup rattled over the swamp trail that eventually widened and joined Palmetto Road. Cree was alone in the cab, fighting with the sweat-slick steering wheel. Boomer sat in back in the truck's rusty steel bed with the boy and the dead gator. The mosquitoes didn't seem to mind that the truck was moving. They allowed for windage and maintained their assault on Boomer and the boy with the skill and persistence of fighter pilots.

Boomer slapped at a mosquito on his sweaty forearm and brushed another of the pesky insects off the boy's cheek.

Ahead of the truck the swamp was bathed in white light, not only from headlights but from a rack of spotlights on the roof. There were maneuverable spotlights on each front fender, too, aimed straight ahead. Cree and Boomer were poachers who froze their game at night with brilliant light that was followed by sudden death. The gators were wily in their dumb way and didn't always stay motionless like the other swamp creatures pinned in the brilliance, the occasional deer, possum, or bobcat—even a panther once. Cree had opened up on the big cat with his twelve-gauge, but the panther bolted into heavy foliage along the bank and disappeared into the night. *If* it had been a panther, like Cree swore. Boomer had acted as if he believed him, but . . . well, he didn't know what the hell they'd seen. The swamp was like that. It could trick a man, make him sure of himself and then surprise the hell out of him.

Like tonight.

An hour into the swamp, loaded for gator, they'd fired at a big one and it swam away and slipped under the water just as if it hadn't been shot. Could be they'd both missed, but it wasn't likely, and they used twelve-gauge shotguns with slugs in the casings instead of pellets. A lead slug that size was usually enough to stop anything it hit anywhere.

When they'd come across the other gator, the huge one that was now laid out in the back of the truck, neither one had seen the boy at first. Then Boomer had put a hand on Cree's shoulder to stop him from firing his shotgun. "Got somethin' in his mouth!"

"So?"

Boomer was squinting into the darkness where tree limbs shadowed the wash of the truck's lights. "Whatever it is ain't dead. It's still movin'."

Water stirred and Cree focused in and saw more clearly. "Deer, you think?"

"Deer, shit!" Boomer said. "Looks like a kid."

"Mother of Christ, you're right!" Cree had said, surprising Boomer a little, Cree not in Boomer's memory being particularly religious.

Both men waded deeper into the black water to get closer, holding their shotguns high. Boomer's breath was caught in his throat.

"Don't shoot yet," Cree said. "Gotta get closer so's we don't hit the kid."

The kid, a skinny boy about ten like Cree's nephew, apparently didn't see them. They caught a glimpse of his pale face, his staring eyes that seemed to hold life yet observe nothing. He was still alive. His limbs were still moving, other than the leg the gator had hold of, but they were waving almost lazily. Boomer thought it was like the kid didn't care he was caught in the jaws of something that wanted him for a meal. The boy was resisting his fate blindly, automatically, as if he'd already surrendered to what was happening and he'd turned off his mind to the horror.

Cree and Boomer were close enough to the big gator now. They moved slowly and silently to the side to get a better angle, both men sighting down the barrels of their shotguns.

The swamp exploded with the thunder of their shots. Cree's gun was a double barrel, and he let loose with both barrels a second apart. Boomer had a pump action and he'd fired only once, but made it count. He was pretty sure his was the slug that entered the gator's head. Another had missed and kicked up a spray of water a foot away from the huge gator.

The boy went limp, and Cree prayed to Jesus they hadn't shot him. The big gator didn't thrash around, the way most of them did when they took a twelve-gauge slug. But it did release the boy, whose still body floated off to the side. That was fortunate. Even shot in the head, a gator would sometimes in its death throes bear down harder with its jaws.

The gator suddenly whipped its tail around, flailing and foaming the black water, and then rolled over on its back, its pale belly luminous in the night.

Both men splashed forward and grabbed the boy. He was still alive, staring about blankly, somewhere else in his mind.

They were pulling him toward dry ground when Boomer glanced back and noticed the gator was right side up again.

A stab of alarm went through him as he thought it might be alive, but he watched it for a full ten seconds and was pretty sure it was dead.

He waded closer to put another slug in its head, and he saw that it truly was dead. One of the heavy slugs had gone through its eye, leaving a black, gaping hole that held about as much expression as the boy's eyes.

"Leg looks like shit," Cree said, when they had the boy lying on the ground beside the pickup.

Boomer had his shirt off and ripped in strips and was wrapping the boy's leg as gently as he could. Then he used a piece of greasy rope from the pickup bed to make a tourniquet. He knew he'd have to loosen it periodically so some blood could circulate, or the kid might lose the leg.

They decided to take the dead gator for its meat and hide, and the two of them wrested it into the truck bed, then gently laid the kid next to it. Boomer climbed over the rear fender and situated himself in the bed, just behind the cab, so he could keep an eye on the kid and make sure his head didn't bounce around on the hard steel. They didn't have anything soft to lay him on.

The gator was so big they had to leave the rusty tailgate down, and Cree could feel the lightness in the front end as he steered the truck along the rutted road.

After about twenty minutes, he braked the truck then pulled to the side on a barely discernable narrow dirt drive that led to Boomer's shack, where they usually gutted and skinned their game.

It didn't take them long to drag the gator out of the truck, letting it lie where it dropped near the crude wooden hoist they'd later use to lift it.

Boomer clambered back into the truck bed with the boy as Cree reversed the vehicle along the trail that would return them to the swamp road. He tried again to find out the boy's name, where he'd come from, but the kid remained silent. He was in shock, Boomer figured, and why the hell not?

There was nowhere they could take the boy without arousing suspicion as to how and where they'd found him. What were they doing in the swamp at night? And what in God's name had gotten the boy by the leg?

Most everyone would guess the answer to that last one, and there'd be plenty of explaining to do. Eventually that explaining would have to be done to the law.

Neither Cree nor Boomer wanted any discourse with the law. They hadn't discussed the situation, but both men had been giving it a lot of thought.

"Doc Macklin," Cree called back from the truck cab.

Boomer said, "Go!"

Doc Macklin was Jerry Macklin, spelled like a man only it was a black woman. She was rumored to have once had a regular practice somewhere in the panhandle, until there was trouble involving the death of a stranger. Now she depended on herbs and poultices and other swamp remedies to treat her patients. She was short on science but long on successes.

When they reached Doc's cabin, just outside the small town, they gently lifted the boy from the truck and stretched him out near the door on the wooden front porch.

Boomer patted the boy's cool forehead. Cree stared down at the kid and crossed himself.

Boomer pounded on the door with his big fist. Then the two men hurriedly left the porch and climbed back into the truck, both of them in the cab this time.

The rattling old truck made a cautious U-turn, then kicked up dust and gravel as Cree steered it back toward Boomer's shack to deal with the dead gator. Cree leaned on the horn as they drove away.

Inside the ramshackle house, Doc Macklin lay in a stupor

from one of her powerful remedies that relieved deep sadness, and heard nothing.

Just before dawn, Sherman awoke and wondered who and where he was. He slowly stood up before falling back down and realizing there was something seriously wrong with his right leg.

He pulled himself up again, holding onto the porch rail for support. There was a throbbing pain in the leg, but he'd felt pain before and could put it away in the back of his mind. He looked down and saw bloody, makeshift bandages, and a length of rope tied around his thigh. Where had they come from? Who'd put them there? He loosened the knot and tossed the rope away, and that made the leg feel better, though the deep gouges in it began to seep blood. The boy cautiously peeked beneath the strips of bloody cloth. Chunks of flesh were missing. What had happened to his leg?

No time to wonder now. He stumbled down off the porch and limped to the nearby dirt road. The sun had just risen and lay low over the swamp, warming Sherman's face. He trudged toward the warmth, not knowing where he was going or why, only that he should keep moving. Something might get him if he didn't. Something horrible and real and dangerously nearby.

A jolt of pain ran up his leg and he almost fell. But he knew he mustn't. He had to remain upright. Moving.

He resumed his slow and limping gait along the road. It had to lead somewhere. Every road led somewhere.

The sun rose higher, and along with it the temperature.

He walked, because walking was everything. He walked away from the wooden porch where he'd found himself, away from whatever else was behind him. Walked despite the dizziness and the pain that beat with his heart. He didn't ask himself why, but he knew he had to keep moving. It was his simple and unquestioned duty, his one chance and his salvation.

He was certain in his bones that whatever he was walking toward was better than what was behind him.

What was behind him was so horrible his memory drew back and hid from it in a deep well in his mind.

He walked.

40

New York, the present

After Ella left the Pepper Tree, Pearl walked over and joined Jeb at his table near the front of the restaurant, where it was brighter and there was a view of the street.

He took a sip of his draft beer, which was in a tall, graceful glass he'd lifted from a round coaster that had the green outline of a tree on it with the name of the restaurant.

"You spooked my friend," Pearl said, settling into the chair opposite Jeb.

He smiled. "Your witness?"

"Not technically, as she didn't witness the murder, but she knew the victim."

"She thought she knew me, too. I assume that's what you mean by my having spooked her. I get that stuff all the time, people thinking I'm somebody else. It must be something about my face. I should have been a spy."

"I like your face," Pearl said.

A skinny waitress who tended to act shy and clasp her hands together came over and Pearl told her she wasn't eating but would have another glass of Pellegrino. Pearl knew it was politically insensitive to think of the woman as a waitress, but in the restaurant's white blouse and yellow-checked apron uniform, she looked as if she'd stepped out of a fifties Norman Rockwell painting. As she was watching the aproned woman walk away, something outside, across the street, caught her eye.

"Excuse me," she told Jeb. "I'll be right back."

He watched her leave the restaurant and walk directly across the street to a girl in a baggy red shirt and jeans. The girl saw her approach and looked for a second as if she might bolt, then she seemed to change her mind and stood facing Pearl with her arms crossed, cupping her elbows as if she were cold.

They talked for a few minutes, then Pearl turned away and weaved and timed her way through traffic to cross the street back toward the restaurant. The girl followed, though it didn't appear that Pearl was aware of her.

Pearl remained unaware until she'd sat back down at the table with Jeb. Lauri was standing over her, looking not exactly angry, but determined in a way that reminded Pearl of Quinn.

"I asked you not to follow me," Pearl said, "and specifically not back in here."

"I only want to make sure you understand I wasn't spying on you," Lauri said.

Pearl looked at Jeb, the man who should have been a spy. "She's been shadowing me all day, staying out of sight while she observes me. Would you call that spying?"

Jeb looked up at the girl—young, attractive, short blond hair, a tiny diamond stud in her nose. "I'd have to say you *were* spying," he told her with a smile. "Unless you're selling magazine subscriptions."

"I'm not."

"Then what *are* you doing?"

"You could call it a learning process."

"She wants to be a cop," Pearl explained. She introduced Lauri and Jeb, who shook hands.

The skinny waitress returned with the Pellegrino. After placing glass and bottle on the table, she looked at Lauri and clasped her hands.

"Nothing for me," Lauri said. "I'm just intruding."

The waitress gawked.

"Sit down," Pearl said to Lauri. She didn't want a scene. She wasn't used to dealing with teenage girls and had a feeling this situation could get out of hand within seconds.

Lauri sat down next to her and looked up at the waitress, who was still gawking and pressing her hands together. "I've changed my mind. I'll have whatever she's drinking."

The waitress broke a jittery smile and retreated.

Jeb was grinning.

"You seem amused," Pearl said, feeling simultaneously irritated and helpless.

"You should be flattered someone like this is following you," Jeb said.

Lauri smiled at him.

"Why do you want to be a cop?" he asked her, obviously charmed. Lauri could spread bullshit almost as skillfully as her father.

"My dad's a cop, and Pearl is. Was. Is again. I guess they're two people I admire."

Now Pearl couldn't help but feel flattered. And like some kind of Grinch because she'd tried to discourage Lauri.

Jeb still wore the amused smile. Pearl thought it was amazing how fast he and Lauri had developed a mutual admiration. Or was it all for show? For her benefit? Two adventurers, chiding the cautious, professional Pearl. Maybe silently laughing at her. Pearl wasn't sure if she liked that.

"Is she breaking any laws?" Jeb asked.

"She's interfering with a police officer," Pearl said. "A homicide detective at that."

"Jeez!" Lauri said. "I only followed you to lunch,"

"Where I went to interview a potential suspect."

"He's awful good-looking for a suspect," Lauri said, grinning at Jeb.

"Not Jeb, the woman I came here to meet first. The woman you saw leave. And she's not a suspect. He's not a suspect. Unfortunately, nobody's a suspect."

"So now you're at lunch? This is just social?"

Pearl sighed. "You could say that."

"Why don't you join us?" Jeb said.

"Love to. If it's okay with Pearl."

"Of course," Pearl said, defeated. "I give up. I can't fight both of you when you gang up on me."

"Ever think of being a journalist?" Jeb asked Lauri.

"Now and then, I have to admit." She gave a little shiver. "It seems romantic."

Pearl thought she might be troweling it on too thick, but Jeb didn't seem to notice.

A lesson here. Unless he's just trying to get my goat.

The waitress returned with a second bottle of Pellegrino. Lauri ordered a vegetable omelet, then ice cream for dessert. Throughout the meal she continued to charm Jeb, knowing he was the way to get Pearl to agree to be her mentor. Or so she thought. Pearl knew better. These two people didn't understand police work and its dangers.

Or its subtleties.

She didn't mention to either of them the presence of Wormy slouching bonelessly in a doorway across the street, waiting for them to emerge from the restaurant. Apparently he'd been following Lauri while she tailed Pearl. Maybe he was trying to protect Lauri. Or assuring himself of her fidelity.

Either way, Pearl wasn't going to confront him. She decided to let the situation ride for a while. She didn't want to get Lauri into trouble by telling Quinn about her persistence in shadowing her. Also, if Quinn learned about this, he'd learn about her assignations with Jeb, and Pearl wasn't quite ready for that to happen. And if Lauri was secretly hanging around Pearl, what harm could Wormy do? The two kids were apparently in love—at least Wormy was, judging by the way he was mooning around. Maybe he should be the one to convince Lauri to pursue something other than a cop's career.

Pearl had to admit there was something about this that amused her, Lauri inexpertly tailing her and not noticing Wormy inexpertly tailing *her*. A procession of incompetents.

When the time was right, Pearl would tell Quinn about this and he'd find it immensely amusing. They'd share a big laugh.

When the time was right.

That night Pearl lay in bed unable to sleep, listening to the window air conditioner humming away in its mechanical battle with the heat. Its low monotone was punctuated by night sounds of the city, muted and diminished in number by the late hour.

Rather, the early hour. Pearl knew it would start to get light outside pretty soon. The dark between the blind slats would become gray, then the gray at the edges of the windows would brighten, and warm sunlight would find its way inside. Pearl, who felt as if she'd had two minutes of sleep though she'd gone to bed at eleven o'clock, would have to get up, shower, and dress.

She wanted to remain comfortably in bed. She asked herself why it was necessary to struggle upright, trudge into the bathroom, and stand nude under running water. Why did people do that? How did that kind of thing ever get started?

Surely there must be a better way.

She rolled onto her stomach, punched her pillow with gusto, and tried to enjoy what little time she had left in bed, but her head began to pound.

She knew what might really have disturbed her sleep. It was the way Ella Oaklie had thought she recognized Jeb when he walked into the Pepper Tree.

Ella had seemed so sure Jeb was the man she'd met with Marilyn Nelson not long before Marilyn's death. And Pearl didn't agree with Jeb that he had the type of face that would cause him often to be mistaken for someone else. Of course, that could be because of the way she felt about him.

Might Jeb actually be the man Ella had met? Jeb using the name Joe Grant?

Pearl punched her pillow again and told herself she was being too cynical. That was why she'd quit the department and become a guard in a quiet, efficient bank where everyone was polite and almost everything worth stealing was locked away in a vault with walls three feet thick. Banks were orderly islands of calm.

Not like the outside mad world where people died horrible deaths for no apparent reason, where questions evoked more questions instead of answers, where a teenage kid followed a burnt-out cop on a dangerous job and was in turn followed by a human worm.

Where a killer might change identities as easily and consciencelessly as if he were changing clothes.

Pearl decided it was time to turn off her mind and turn on the shower. As she climbed out of bed and padded barefoot toward the apartment's tiny bathroom, she wondered if it actually was possible to be too cynical.

She told herself the answer had to be yes. That Jeb Jones and Joe Grant were simply two different people.

The answer had to be yes.

41

Myrna sat in the worn gray vinyl recliner and watched her flickering TV screen. Television wasn't much in the isolated shack. The blues on the screen were greens, and the fleshtones so yellow it appeared that everyone was jaundiced. Myrna didn't have cable, being so far from town, and she couldn't afford one of those new revolving dishes. The beat-up antenna on the house's roof had been struck by lightning and hadn't worked worth a damn since. Sam used to climb up there and adjust the thing toward the signal, but now Sam was gone.

He was sure as hell gone.

And so was Sherman.

Myrna set her beer can on the floor, then got up from the recliner and took a few bent-over steps so she could change the channel and pick up local news.

The truth was, she didn't much care about the quality of the picture. What interested her was information. The TV was at least good enough to receive local channels, and since Sherman had disappeared, Myrna always watched the noon and nightly news.

It had been almost a month now since she'd pursued her son through the swamp, sending piercing spotlight beams into the blackness, calling for him to return, knowing he could hear her or at least hear the rumbling and rattling of the old pickup truck.

But he hadn't replied. When she'd turned off the truck's engine from time to time to listen, her calls were met only with the teeming, vibrant indifference of the swamp. It had been infuriating, almost like an insult.

Sherman had surprised her. He'd been raised at the edge of the swamp and knew what it was, how it could kill. Of course, he also knew what might happen if he returned home. But boys that age didn't think logically. Even after she'd given up and returned to the house, she'd waited and waited, thinking he'd stomp up onto the porch and open the door tired and hungry and hopeless, needing his mother.

Sherman had surprised her, all right. It had been almost a month since he'd run away. He must be dead. He'd chosen his own eventual but certain death in the swamp rather than at her hands.

That puzzled Myrna. Sherman *must* have thought there was some slight chance that he might talk her out of it, that she'd show him some mercy. After all, she was his mother. Yet he'd faced up to reality.

Still, he was a boy.

With a man's balls, she thought, not without some motherly pride, as she sat sipping beer and waiting for a commercial to end.

Myrna was human, and Sherman *was* her son. But if time didn't heal, it at least produced a scab. She went days now without thinking about Sherman. There were some bad ways to die in the dark waters of the swamp, and for a long while after his flight her sleep had been interrupted by dreams. But Myrna was a hard and practical woman. That was what the world required of her. She slept well enough, and thought less and less about Sherman as the weeks passed. It wasn't as if she'd had a choice. She told herself that often. She hadn't made the goddamned rules. The world had. *Men* had.

She settled down into her recliner with a beer to watch the television noon news out of Tampa, as she did every day. It had become so routine she'd almost forgotten why.

"Following up on an earlier story . . ." said the voice from the TV.

One of the regular anchors, a made-up, jaundiced blonde with too much hair and lipstick, was back. ". . . the child who's come to be known only as the Swamp Boy still hasn't been identified. He was found wandering the road in Harrison County yesterday, his leg injured, apparently by an animal, judging by the bite marks. He was carrying no identification and still hasn't spoken. Doctors say that other than the leg injury he's physically healthy but in a state of shock. They're hoping that someday soon he'll be able to say his name and tell us who he is"—the anchorwoman put on a serious pout and leaned toward the camera—"and what happened to him."

A photo of the Swamp Boy appeared on the screen. *Sherman*. Hair long and tangled, face gaunt, eyes wild—but Sherman.

Myrna put her beer can down on the floor and sat back in the recliner, closing her eyes and digging her fingertips into the warm vinyl arms. She couldn't look at the TV screen.

Harrison County. Twenty miles away. My God! He survived somehow, lived somehow on his own in the swamp. All that time . . .

He doesn't know his name. Doesn't remember.

But he will. The doctors will give him drugs. Hypnotize him. He'll remember. He'll talk.

Myrna felt a sudden panic and stood up from the chair.

Then she took a deep breath, waited for her heartbeat to slow, and retrieved her beer and finished it in a series of gulps. She hadn't thought this day would come, but at the same time she'd been waiting for it. It was a miracle that anyone, let alone a nine-year-old boy, could survive the night in the deep swamp, but miracles seemed to attach themselves to Sherman. Sam Pickens used to talk about how odd Sherman was, and how smart. How very smart.

He'll know. He'll remember. He'll talk.

Myrna knew what she had to do. She turned off the TV, went directly into the bedroom, and began to pack.

By the time people learned from the photograph who Sherman was and the authorities came to see Myrna, they found only the empty shack. It was assumed something bad had happened to her, that she'd been killed or had become lost and died in the swamp. It wasn't unusual for dead bodies never to be recovered from the swamp's dark landscape. She became simply another brief story, another unsolved mystery. Not the first to live on the edge of the vast darkness and one day disappear into it.

Over the coming years, from her anonymity and place of safety, she would read and hear about how the Swamp Boy was identified and had finally talked. But his story about how he'd wandered away from home on his own to go fishing and gotten lost wasn't at all what had happened. Myrna didn't know if Sherman couldn't remember the truth, or had chosen to lie. The mind could blank out certain horrors, but Sherman could be devious.

As his biological mother, she admitted to a certain satisfaction as she read from time to time about how intelligent he was, how, as a ward of the state, he'd been tested and found to have an amazingly high IQ. He was given favoritism, scholarship opportunities, as he was shuffled through a series of institutions and foster homes. Sherman made the most of those opportunities.

Myrna knew that by now he might remember at least *something* about the time before the swamp, yet he must not have spoken of it, or surely it would have been on the news. She could understand why he would remain silent, considering how people's view of him would change if he revealed his part in what had happened; the boarders who'd disappeared, and whose Social Security checks had continued to be collected and cashed. He'd been a child and wouldn't be in any legal jeopardy, but still, people would have and share their thoughts.

At times Myrna had her own thoughts about Sherman and smiled with motherly pride. Her son. So smart.

Smart enough not to talk.

42

New York, the present

"This has to stop," Pearl told Lauri.

"You *saw* me?" Lauri's eyes widened in surprise. "How?"

They were in the Hungry U, where Pearl had stopped in to talk to Lauri as she waited tables. It was five o'clock, still early for the dinner crowd, and the lunchtime diners were long gone. Pearl and Lauri were alone in the restaurant except for a touristy-looking couple at a corner table, and whoever was in the kitchen or out by the register. Something in the kitchen was giving off a peculiar but not unpleasant scent, a mingling of sage and cinnamon.

Pearl had ordered only a diet Coke, which she sipped slowly as she carefully formulated her words. She released her plastic straw from between her lips, noticing that it was now lipstick stained. "It doesn't work to follow someone on the other side of the street unless you know what you're doing. It doesn't work to stand around outside someplace like you're haunting it unless you're careful to stay out of sight. And it especially doesn't work if you try to sneak inside without being seen so you can use the restroom."

Standing over Pearl, still holding her serving tray in one

hand, other hand on hip, Lauri said, "What *do* you do if you're tailing someone and you have to pee?"

"If you actually become a cop, you'll go to the Academy and they'll tell you."

Pearl watched as the touristy couple beckoned Lauri over and asked for their check. Lauri smilingly presented it, then carried it and a credit card through the door to the restaurant's entrance area and register.

By the time she came back, returned the card and check to the couple, and walked back to where Pearl was sitting, Pearl had drunk half her Coke. Despite the early hour and having only three customers, there was soft background music in the restaurant. It didn't sound very Pakistani, but how would Pearl know? It bothered her that she'd probably have a hard time getting the nagging little melody that persisted between the overwrought drum solos and the unintelligible singer out of her brain. It sounded vaguely familiar, but it was that kind of melody.

Lauri returned to Pearl's table and stood hipshot, still holding the round serving tray—which Pearl was beginning to figure out was a prop to make her feel more like a professional food server—in her previous spot. The curtain-filtered light from a nearby window made her look even younger and yet somehow even more like Quinn.

"Want a refill?"

"I'm good," Pearl assured her.

"You haven't told Dad, have you?"

"That you're still tailing me? No. But I want it to stop, Lauri. I mean actually stop. Or I will tell him."

Lauri flashed her father's stubborn, defiant expression for a second, then shrugged and nodded. "Okay. If you say stop, I'll stop."

"Your solemn word?"

"I promise you'll never spot me following you again."

Which wasn't exactly the promise Pearl was requesting. *More of Quinn's bullshit. Was it genetic?*

"Lauri—" But something had popped into Pearl's mind. "Now I've got it."

"What?"

"That tune. I *thought* I might have heard it before."

Lauri grinned proudly. "That's right. You heard it here. That's The Defendants' CD of *Lost in Bonkers*."

"They actually sell their music?"

"Not yet, but they will. That's just a demo CD they made at the drummer's brother's apartment studio. Wormy's shopping it around. Well, looking for an agent to shop it around, actually."

"Speaking of Wormy," Pearl said, "do you realize he's following you following me?"

Lauri appeared temporarily confused. Then her face flushed with anger.

It was anger she didn't express in words; she knew what Pearl would say.

"Wormy? Why's he following me?" Lauri admirably kept her voice calm.

"I don't know for sure," Pearl said. "He might think you're seeing someone else. Or he might be afraid for you. The little—he probably loves you and feels protective. Men are like that." *Even worms.*

"He's a musician, not a fighter," Lauri said.

Thinking Lauri had that right except for the musician part, Pearl finished her Coke, which was now diluted by melted ice. "I'm not saying he's a skilled bodyguard, only that he's been following you. I saw him outside the Pepper Tree the other day, trying to be invisible in a doorway across the street."

Lauri couldn't help looking miffed. Pearl figured if Wormy were around he might be beaned with the serving tray, the way Lauri's knuckles were so white on the hand that gripped it.

She stared at a point just above Pearl's head, the way Quinn did when he was angry, as if there were a message written in the air confirming his righteous rage. "I'll put a goddamned stop to that!"

Pearl left enough money on the table to cover the drink and tip and stood up. "You do that, Lauri. You talk to Wormy the way I talked to you. Of course, if you stop following me around, there won't be a problem."

"There won't be a problem," Lauri said, scooping up the money.

Not "I'll stop following you."

Genetic, Peal thought again, as she walked from the restaurant, not realizing she was moving to the infectious beat of *Lost in Bonkers.*

Celandra jogged in place until the traffic signal changed at West Eighty-ninth Street, then crossed the intersection and continued jogging south on Broadway. Heads male and female turned to glance at the tall, graceful woman with the long brown hair, dressed in red shorts that fit her loosely but were nonetheless revealing, and a gray sleeveless T-shirt with a sports bra beneath. When it came to nullifying curves, the sports bra did about as well as the overmatched baggy shorts.

Most New York joggers favored the park or more sparsely traveled side streets, but Celandra loved running down Broadway, taking in the sights and sounds and smells of the city as she worked up a sweat and began breathing hard. She tried to jog every other night, and to push herself. It was good exercise not only for her appearance, but for her endurance in dance numbers. She'd take more dance lessons when she could afford it, but for now her running would have to do.

In the West Sixties she began to tire, and to feel the stitches of pain in her ribs and the burning in her thighs.

Had enough . . . Time to turn around.

She drew admiring stares and a man's offer to run with her as she jogged in place again and waited for a traffic-locked furniture van to move so she could cross the street. Trying not to breathe the van's noxious exhaust fumes too deeply, she began the return run toward her apartment.

She was spent a block from home and began to walk, her shirt plastered to her by perspiration, her head bowed, her hands on her hips; still drawing stares, a marathoner and wet T-shirt contest winner.

By the time she reached her building, her breathing had evened out but was still labored. The burning sensation in her thighs was gone. Her legs felt heavy, tired, good. She smiled. It had been a productive workout. Someday all her hard work would pay big career dividends. She truly believed she'd make it as a major actress. Had anyone ever made it without believing?

She wiped her forearm across her sweaty brow and drew deep, steadying breaths as she waited for the elevator. The ancient brass arrow above the door trembled and hesitated as if struggling against gravity as it dropped from *3* to *2* to *1*, and the elevator's steel door scraped and slid open.

A sixtyish, red-haired woman Celandra knew only as Mrs. Altmont stepped from the elevator with her tiny Yorkie, Edgemore, on a leash. Mrs. Altmont lived down the hall from Celandra and had the tight, stiff stare of too much cosmetic surgery. Her lean features seemed out of sync with her pudgy body. She'd once told Celandra she'd named Edgemore after her former husband. Celandra assumed Edgemore, the husband, might still be paying off the surgery.

The canine Edgemore growled at Celandra, as he always did, and as she always did, Mrs. Altmont smiled at her. As they passed getting in and out of the elevator, Celandra glanced down and saw that Mrs. Altmont already had a small plastic bag like a mitten over her free hand.

She saw where Celandra was looking and her smile widened and became almost apologetic. "Why do we love them so?"

She might have been talking about either of the Edge-mores.

"Sometimes they're worth it," Celandra said, returning the smile.

The elevator door slid closed.

Other than her killer, Mrs. Altmont would be the last person to see Celandra alive.

43

The odor was overpowering.

Quinn wondered if the relentless repetition of the butchery was meant to assail the senses and wear down the killer's pursuers, if it was part of a strategy. If so, it might be working.

Dr. Julius Nift was present for this one. He was dressed for a day in the boardroom, in a black chalk-stripe suit, white shirt, red tie, gleaming black wing-tip shoes. He didn't look as if he belonged in the cracked tile bathroom of this little apartment in the West Nineties, bent over a bathtub and probing at body parts.

Quinn and his team had gotten the call at the office from Renz, so arrived together in an unmarked city car driven by Fedderman. Quinn left Feds to talk to the uniforms who'd been first on the scene, then went inside the apartment.

It was crowded with crime scene unit techs. A police photographer was there, too, sending pops of illumination over the odd sight of people wearing white gloves and assuming various awkward positions so they could see something close up or pluck it up with tweezers and drop it into a plastic evidence bag. So many bodies moving around in the small apartment, it was a wonder they didn't bump into one another. Crime scene choreography was in itself a science.

Nift and the victim were alone together in the bathroom, though. The techs had finished there as quickly as possible and left it to the medical examiner. After a first glimpse, and sniff, not even the most hardened of the professionals present were tempted even to go near the bathroom again.

The little ME didn't actually look back at Quinn and Pearl, but by his head movement acknowledged their presence. They glanced around the beige and white tiled confines. There were the empty cleaning containers—a box of powdered dishwasher detergent, green plastic shampoo bottle, laundry detergent, a couple of gallon bleach jugs capless and lying next to each other.

The raw meat stench was stomach kicking despite the obvious use of the cleansers. Pearl unconsciously raised her cupped hand to cover her mouth and nose, then realized what she was doing. She couldn't appear soft in front of Nift and Quinn, so she pretended her nose itched, rubbed it, and lowered her hand.

Nift shifted to his left and a dim brown eye gazed up at Quinn.

Pearl almost gagged as she returned the dead stare of the severed head resting on its side atop the detached arms.

"Brown hair," she said flatly, of the dead woman in the tub. No emotion. Better to be a cop instead of a horrified basket case.

Nift said, "Let me introduce you to Miz Celandra Thorn. Forgive her if she doesn't shake your hand, but you can shake hers all you want."

Pearl felt like kicking the little bastard.

"Thorn!" Quinn said. "Not the roses themselves. Goddamnit!" He knew it was something they should have thought of; it had been hinted strongly enough by the note about roses. They'd missed the oblique reference in the killer's note

again. It was there for them and so obvious in retrospect. They'd been outsmarted.

"Maybe Celandra is a type of rose," Pearl said, but she knew better. Like Quinn and Fedderman, she'd researched roses named after women until she'd never see roses the same way. It had been *thorn,* and they'd missed it.

Nift straightened up, holding a gleaming steel probe in his gloved right hand, and the entire familiar stack of pale body parts in the bathtub was visible. As with the other Butcher victims, the blanched cleanliness of the victim and the crime scene appeared antiseptic and barren of anything that might prove in any way useful. Probably it would be difficult even to find a germ, much less a clue. There was only the ritual arrangement of meat on display.

"Like the others," Nift said. "Same blades, same saw marks, same technique in reducing the whole to its parts." He flashed his nasty smile. "If you put her back together, you'd have a beautiful woman."

"Would you rather we leave?" Pearl asked.

Nift ignored her. "As you can see, she was facially a knockout. She had the build, too. Very muscular as well as shapely. I'd guess she danced, judging by the impressively developed musculature in her thighs and calves. Or ran cross-country or lifted weights or some such thing. But with her looks, I think it'd be show business."

"Playing detective again," Quinn said.

"Don't you watch those programs on television? We forensics guys solve crimes all the time. We shoot pretty damned straight, too."

"If this was television," Pearl said, "I'd mute you."

"Your partner takes life too seriously," Nift said to Quinn.

"It's death we're talking about here," Quinn said.

"Which brings us to cause of same," Nift said. "Looks like drowning. Also, the usual traces of adhesive from duct tape. Body fluids, what have you, all washed neatly down the drain. Time of death probably early last evening; I'll get you closer after the official postmortem." He bent down and placed his steel probe in his black medical case, then peeled off his gloves and slipped them into a plastic bag, which he also placed in the case.

"So much for the prelim," he said. "Whenever you're done playing with her, you can send Celandra down to the morgue."

They walked with him into the living room and watched him leave.

Fedderman, talking to one of the techs over near a window, noticed Pearl and Quinn and came over. Even though it was warm in the apartment he still had on his wrinkled brown suit coat, and had his notepad stuffed in the coat's breast pocket behind where he had his shield displayed. He'd been taking notes. A stub of yellow pencil was tucked behind his right ear.

"Just a moment," he said, excusing himself.

Quinn knew where he was going, though probably there was no need. It was a professional obligation to call on Celandra Thorn.

Fedderman looked pale and somber as he returned to the living room.

"The bastard!" was all he said. Then, "Like the others. Leaving us nothing to work with."

"Someday maybe he'll drop his wallet with his ID and photograph," Pearl said.

Quinn wondered what was bothering her. He could understand her being sarcastic with that little prick Nift, but why was she riding Fedderman?

Still sobered by what he'd seen in the bathroom, Fedderman ignored her and pulled his notebook from his pocket. He flipped through the pages for a few seconds then stopped. "Victim's name's Cecelia Thorn," he said. "Acted under the name Celandra. A friend she had a breakfast date with came by to get her, found the door unlocked, then let herself in and found what was left of Celandra." He glanced over at Quinn and Pearl. "The name Thorn—"

"We know," Pearl said, cutting him off.

"We should have thought of it," Fedderman said. "It's right there in the note between the lines, just like thorns are between the roses. If you're thinking roses, you're a fool if you're not also thinking thorns. Like coffee and cream."

"Ham and eggs," Pearl said. "The Butcher is probably feeling pretty smart right now."

"The smarter he feels," Quinn said, "the sooner we'll nail him."

"Techs told me not to expect much in the way of useful prints," Fedderman said. "There are various ones around the apartment, but they're sure our guy wore gloves. No blood-work to be done, either. He drains them as best he can before he cuts, and whatever blood gets splashed or smeared around he scrubs away like an honest Dutch maid."

"So we've got zilch again," Pearl said.

"Not quite," Fedderman said. "A neighbor down the hall seems to be the last one who saw Celandra alive, in the elevator about six o'clock yesterday evening."

"According to Nift, that's just about the time she was killed," Quinn said.

"This"—Fedderman consulted his notes again—"Mrs. Ida Altmont was going out to walk her dog and stepped out of the elevator at lobby level when Celandra was coming in. They exchanged a few friendly words, then Celandra got in the elevator. The thing is, when the Altmont woman's dog was finished doing its business, Mrs. Altmont went grocery shopping, then stopped at a Starbucks for a coffee. Got back home about eight o'clock and saw a man leaving the lobby carrying a white box. He had on a gray shirt and dark pants, and she thinks he mighta been a deliveryman of some sort. Not much help on the description. Average height and weight. Dark hair, she thinks, but he was wearing a baseball cap. She remembered him because her dog growled at him even though he was over a hundred feet away, and the man looked what she called furtive."

Quill sighed. "Furtive, huh?"

"You don't often hear a witness say furtive," Fedderman said.

"He was carrying a box," Pearl reminded them. "The Butcher's gotta have something to lug around his cutting tools and power saw."

"And maybe an apron or change of clothes in case he gets bloody," Fedderman added.

"Let's canvass the building," Quinn said. "Make sure nobody got a delivery or had a pickup around eight last night."

"We've also got Debrina Fluor," Fedderman said.

Quinn and Pearl looked at him.

"She's downstairs in the unmarked. She's a dancer and friend of the victim, the one who let herself in and discovered the body. Pretty little thing."

"You go down and get her statement," Quinn said. "I'll tell the paramedics they can remove the body soon as the techs are finished here. Then Pearl and I will see what Ida Altmont has to say."

44

The butcher shop stench came after them as they walked a short distance down the hall. Or maybe they carried it with them.

Pearl wondered with sudden irrational panic if maybe they always would.

The Altmont apartment was three doors down. Quinn knocked, and the door promptly opened.

A small, hairy brown dog ignored Quinn and acted as if it wanted to tear Pearl's leg off. The stocky redheaded woman who'd opened the door adroitly scooped up the dog and clasped it tightly to her breast, saying, "No, no, no, Edgemore. We say no, no, no to naughtiness."

Shouldn't we all, Pearl thought, wishing she could have kicked the hairy little bastard.

Quinn was smiling. "Edgemore," he said. "Nice name. Nice dog." He reached out and petted the dog, which became instantly quiet and licked his hand.

"It's sort of a family name," Ida Altmont said. Pearl noticed for the first time that the woman's face and eyes were puffy, as if she'd been crying. Though she seemed younger at a glance, he guessed her age as about sixty. "Such a horrible,

horrible thing that happened to Celandra," she said. "And right down the hall. So horrible."

Naughtiness, thought Pearl.

Ida Altmont sat down in the corner of a graceful blue-patterned sofa with dainty mahogany legs. Pearl noticed there was brown dog hair on one of the throw pillows. She and Quinn remained standing, watching as the distraught woman drew a handkerchief from a pocket of her gray skirt. She didn't use the handkerchief, merely crumpled it and gripped it tightly in her right hand, keeping it in reserve in case grief or fear overcame her.

"Did Celandra Thorn seem her usual self when you and she talked at the elevator?" Quinn asked her.

"Oh, yes. Very friendly. Celandra was always friendly to everyone."

"You told Detective Fedderman about the man you saw leaving the building when you returned from walking Edgemore."

Ida Altmont beamed, obviously pleased that he'd remembered the dog's name. All in all pleased with Quinn, this mature, ruggedly handsome cop favoring her with his attentiveness. "That's right. Edgemore and I had gone grocery shopping for some salad vegetables, then we stopped for lattes at Starbucks before returning home."

"That would have been about eight o'clock?"

"As near as I can remember."

Under Quinn's seemingly casual questioning she recounted how she'd been approaching the building, and when she was almost there an average-size, average-looking man came out and bounded down the concrete steps to the sidewalk. She tightened her grip on the handkerchief and waved it in the general direction of her face. "He was carrying a large white box and looked . . ."

Quinn and Pearl waited patiently.

"Furtive," Ida Altmont said.

Pearl had been expecting *average*.

"What size was the box?" Quinn asked.

"Oh, I'm a poor judge of such things, but I'd say it was about as wide as it was high, maybe eight or ten inches, and quite long, maybe twenty-four inches. It looked like one of those white boxes florists use for long-stemmed flowers, only somehow heavier, sturdier."

"A very good description," Quinn said. "Are you a trained observer?"

Ida Altmont fidgeted about, made uneasy by the compliment. "Oh, no, no. It was still light out, and I do watch things when Edgemore and I go for our walks. We like to notice what's going on around us."

Quinn smiled at her. "If only Edgemore could talk."

Pearl was pretty sure what Edgemore would say, and didn't like it.

"Sometimes," Ida Almont said seriously, "it's almost as if he can."

"What would he say about the man you two saw?" Quinn asked.

Pearl was impressed. She'd thought he was simply buttering up the woman.

"Edgemore wouldn't have liked him," Ida Altmont said immediately. "He would have said the man was in too much of a hurry and looked furtive."

"Maybe he was running late and had more deliveries," Quinn suggested. "So why would Edgemore be suspicious?"

"Why, because he's a dog. They know things about people; they notice things we don't."

"Such as?"

Ida Altmont sat back, frowning, and her eyes widened. Then suddenly she smiled, as if memory clicking into place had tickled her. "Well, it didn't seem that he was from a nearby restaurant, making a takeout delivery on foot. It wasn't that kind of package, and he simply didn't look the type. And Edgemore and I thought it odd that a deliveryman would be dashing about so when he was leaving, and carrying a package he'd apparently failed to deliver. Also, we could see up and down the block and there was no delivery truck. Surely if the man we saw was there to make a delivery of such a large package, he would have parked his truck or van nearby. There were available spaces right in front of the building, I'm sure."

"My, my," Quinn said, "you're an *excellent* observer!"

Ida Altmont batted her false eyelashes at him. "We do try."

"What *was* parked on the block?"

"Oh, cars. Lots of cars."

"Do you remember which of them was closest to your apartment building?"

"A white one, I think. Large. With stickers plastered all over the bumpers advising us to vote for the wrong people. It belongs to Mr. Cammering downstairs. Why aren't those political stickers ever pasted on straight?"

"I don't know, dear. Were there any unfamiliar cars?"

"Many of them. I really can't remember much about them. But I am certain that Edgemore and I saw no delivery truck, yet there was a deliveryman." She said it as if they'd observed an impressive magic trick.

"Might the man have gotten into one of the cars?"

"No, no. When Edgemore and I entered the building, he was near the end of the block, still walking."

Which wouldn't necessarily mean he lives nearby, Pearl thought, only that he traveled by bus, subway, or cab, or that he had the good sense not to park his car near the building where he intended to commit murder.

"Did you notice any lettering or a company logo on his jacket?" Quinn asked.

"No, but I might have been too far away to notice. And it all happened rather fast."

Quinn thanked Ida Altmont for her time and her help, then gave her his card and asked her to call if she remembered anything else about last night.

Now that he was finished with Ida, Pearl spoke to her. "You said the deliveryman wouldn't have parked far away with such a large package. Did it appear heavy to you?"

"Why, yes. Yes, it did. More heavy than large, actually, if that makes sense."

"It does," Pearl said, thinking steel blades and a portable saw.

Quinn was thinking the same thing, and looking at Pearl with approval. It annoyed her that she found herself almost blushing with pleasure at having pleased him. She wasn't a sap like Ida Altmont. Men were such . . .

"I'm sorry I couldn't have been more help," Ida Altmont said, getting up from the sofa slowly, as if her legs hurt. She did some more eyelash batting, and then stuffed her handkerchief back into a pocket of her skirt.

Quinn smiled and waved for her not to bother letting them out. "We'll find our own way. And don't assume you haven't been a great help to us. You never can tell when some seemingly minor piece of information will turn out to be exactly what we need in a homicide investigation."

"I do hope you catch the animal who did that to Celandra."

"We will, dear. Perpetrators always make a mistake."

"Is that actually true?" Ida Altmont asked seriously.

"Often enough," Quinn said with a grin just for her. "And that one mistake is all we need in order to put them where they belong." Quinn, protector of the city.

"One mistake . . ." Ida Altmont said thoughtfully. She seemed intrigued by the idea. More eyelash work. "Might I interest you in some tea or milk and cake?" she asked. Pearl could see, with some irritation, that the woman was entirely smitten with Quinn.

"Next time perhaps," he said. "It would be my great pleasure."

He actually gave a little bow, somehow managing not to look foolish. Pearl had to admire how he so skillfully disguised his cynicism. It was something she'd have to work on.

Since Quinn, finding his own way out, had turned away from her, Ida Altmont went to the door of the room where Edgemore was safely locked away, instead of the door to the hall.

As Pearl and Quinn were leaving, Edgemore emitted a low growl, then began yapping frantically and charged at Pearl. His teeth were exposed to the gums. The nails on his tiny paws scratched the polished hardwood floor, seeking traction.

Pearl moved quickly out into the hall, almost bumping into Quinn, and shut the door behind her. On the other side of the door, Edgemore continued to bark. They could hear his nails scraping on the door.

"What the hell's that dog got against me?" Pearl asked.

"Dogs know people," Quinn said.

"They know *more* than some people."

"Don't be discouraged," Quinn said. "Perpetrators always make a mistake."

And sure enough, this one had made a mistake.

But not one Pearl was going to like.

45

The day got progressively hectic, making Quinn wonder if he was cursed.

When his desk phone jangled that afternoon, he was surprised to hear Renz's voice. It was too early for the postmortem findings on Celandra Thorn.

"You'll have to speak up, Harley," Quinn said. Con Ed had begun tearing up the street right outside, and the intermittent clatter of a jackhammer punctuated everything said in the office. When the jackhammer wasn't chattering, the muted shrill whine of a dental drill from Nothing but the Tooth made its way through the wall.

Pearl was at her desk, rereading witness statements about the Thorn murder. Fedderman was just coming in through the door, no doubt with additional statements. Quinn planned on the three of them sifting hay for the needle the next several hours.

But Renz wasn't calling about autopsy reports.

"We have a print that might prove useful," he said in a loud telephone voice. "Middle finger, right hand. A bloody fingerprint, no less."

The jackhammer chattered. Quinn came hyperalert. *One*

mistake . . . Maybe the Butcher had made his mistake, just as Quinn had described to Ida Altmont.

Might it really work that way?

"It's the only print that doesn't match any of the seven sets we've found and identified. An obsessive tech discovered it in the bathroom, beneath the front edge of the marble vanity top." Renz gave a satisfied chuckle. "And it couldn't be more clear."

Amazing, Quinn thought. His mind flashed an image of the killer washing up after the murder. He'd removed his latex gloves, or one had torn, and he absently gripped the edge of the vanity while leaning forward studying himself in the mirror, looking for other bloodstains. The kind of small, casual action that could lead straight to hell.

But something was nagging Quinn. "Have you run the print?"

"We're doing that now. I'll fax an enlargement to you when I hang up. If the print's in NCIC or any other data bank, we'll have the name of our killer. He finally got careless. Sickos like him always do, eventually, and they get collared or go out in a blaze of glory. The needle or the gun."

Still . . .

Quinn suddenly realized what was bothering him. "Harley, there's no marble vanity in Celandra Thorn's bathroom."

"The bloody print wasn't found there. It was found in Marilyn Nelson's bathroom, and the blood was hers. Does it matter which murder this asshole gets nailed for?"

"Not if he gets nailed." Quinn looked across his desk at Pearl and Fedderman, who were staring intently at him. His side of the conversation must have sounded pretty good. Quinn was aware of the fax machine gurgling and clucking over in the corner. Renz sending the fingerprint image even as he was talking on the phone. "Keep me informed, Harley. Once we ID him, he's our meat."

"And mine," Renz said, no doubt keeping in mind the political ramifications of the killer's arrest.

"I want the killer. You get the press conference."

"That was pretty much the deal," Renz said, and hung up.

Quinn replaced the receiver and related to Pearl and Fedderman what Renz had said, pausing whenever the jackhammer blasted off on a riff. Dust was somehow filtering into the building. The grit coated his teeth. He watched the other two detectives as he talked. He could almost feel the heightening of their senses, the increased voltage of their energy. At that moment they knew they were all in the right business, and in it together. If a clue dropped like a feather outside, they would all hear it.

Something primitive here? Hot on the scent? Hunting with the pack?

Whatever, it was a hell of a feeling. One worth living for.

"Asshole like that," Fedderman said, "he's bound to have a sheet somewhere. The print'll be on file."

Quinn knew it wasn't a given that psychosexual killers probably had prior brushes with the law. They weren't like burglars or confidence men; in fact, they tended to be closeted and law-abiding, if you didn't count torture and murder. He didn't mention this to Fedderman, who, after so much time retired, should enjoy the hunt.

"If he was ever fingerprinted anywhere," Quinn said, "including the military, we'll have him."

Quinn picked up on a subtle change. Something wasn't right. He wondered why Pearl suddenly didn't seem as enthusiastic as Fedderman. She was seated back behind her desk, looking despondent. She sensed Quinn staring at her and glanced up to meet his eyes.

"What?" she said.

"You read my mind," he told her. "That's exactly what I was going to ask you."

Fedderman walked over to stand near Quinn, adding his own curious and baleful stare.

Pearl knew the time had come when she had to reveal her relationship with Jeb Jones. If the bloody fingerprint was

Jeb's, he'd be arrested for the murder of Marilyn Nelson. And Pearl had been sleeping with him, even confiding to him about the investigation.

Was her luck with men still all bad? Had he been playing her for a fool?

She wanted to believe in Jeb, but now it wasn't so easy. Her cynicism again. It could destroy a relationship, or catch a killer.

Jeb had spent time with Marilyn Nelson, but he claimed he was never actually inside her apartment (except for the brief interview on the sofa), so his prints shouldn't be there, especially with her blood on them.

Pearl wondered, did she trust him enough to assume the print wasn't his? That was the question, the kind of question that had destroyed most of her relationships.

Can I trust him enough?

She couldn't answer right now. She didn't have the clarity of mind. Couldn't stop her thoughts from whirling. She did know that once she spoke up, be he guilty or innocent, her relationship with Jeb was finished.

Not yet, not yet.

"What are you two goons gaping at?" she asked angrily.

Quinn continued to stare for a moment, then busied himself with some papers on his desk. Fedderman turned away and walked over to the machine to get the fax. The image of a bloody fingerprint Pearl didn't want to see.

An hour later, Renz called again. The print hadn't triggered a match, not in the NYPD database, NCIC, VICAP, or the FBI's all-encompassing IAFIS system. Apparently the killer had never been fingerprinted by the police, the military, or by the government for a civilian job.

They couldn't match this print with any of the others in Marilyn Nelson's apartment because the killer wore gloves, except perhaps for the one time when he was cleaning up and got careless. All of the other usable prints in the apartment were obviously women's or had been matched to Marilyn, a previous tenant, an electrical repairman, the super, and three of her neighbors.

So Jeb's prints weren't in the apartment because, just as he'd said, the only time he'd been inside was when he approached the door after her murder. The day Pearl had first questioned him. She was positive he'd never gotten past the living room sofa, and hadn't touched anything other than upholstery material that wouldn't hold a print.

Definitely he hadn't been in the bathroom.

There'd been no need to fingerprint Jeb, so they hadn't. He was a one-time visitor, after Marilyn's death, who hadn't gotten more than ten feet inside the door.

Pearl was sure of that.

She looked at the disappointed expressions of Quinn and Fedderman, her fellow cops.

Sure or not, she owed them something. Owed it to herself.

When they weren't paying attention to her, she picked up her phone and called Ella Oaklie's work number.

When Ella came to the phone, Pearl identified herself and said, "The evening you saw the man who resembled Jeb Jones with Marilyn, are you sure the two of them were coming out of her apartment?"

"Positive," Ella said. "I think they'd just come down the steps to the sidewalk."

Pearl knew how the minds of witnesses could play tricks. "You think? Is it possible they'd just met outside the building?"

"No. Marilyn even told me they were on their way out for drinks and invited me along."

"Maybe she was simply being polite?"

"Well, I suppose that's possible."

Possible. Dangerous word.

"Is it possible the person you saw actually was the same man I was with in the Pepper Tree?"

"Sure. I told you to begin with I thought it was him. You didn't seem to want to believe me."

Pearl cringed when she heard that. She knew Ella was right; she hadn't wanted to believe. She still didn't want to believe.

She thanked Ella Oaklie and hung up the phone. Pearl knew the answer to her question was no, she didn't trust Jeb enough.

Maybe she couldn't trust anyone enough, and maybe that was her problem. But there it was.

She decided she had no choice but to reveal her and Jeb's relationship *before* the bloody print might be matched to his.

The jackhammer chattered and she waited for silence. She cleared her throat.

"There is someone we should try to match with that print," she said.

Quinn and Fedderman looked over at her as if they hadn't understood.

She repeated what she'd said, and then said so much more.

46

Quinn was obviously angry. When Pearl was finished talking, he stood up and started pacing around, not looking at her, clenching his teeth so hard his jaw muscles were flexing.

Pearl and Fedderman sat watching him. The office was warmer than usual, and humid, and the grit from the construction or destruction outside hung in the air. The jackhammer had let up, and the only sound in the office was the faint shrillness of the dental drill on the other side of the wall.

"Should we pick up this Jeb Jones character and print him?" Fedderman asked.

Quinn stopped pacing and faced them. His features were now calm and thoughtful. If he was going to be furious with Pearl, it could wait. His mind was on his prey. "I don't want to move on the basis of one print," he said. "Let's tail him, find out more about him."

"Give him some line," Fedderman said, "while we set the hook deeper." He made a sudden jerking motion with both hands wrapped around an imaginary rod. Showing some signs of all that Florida retirement fishing.

"You latch on to him first, Feds," Quinn said, spoiling the fish metaphor. "Pearl and I will work the computers to see if Jones's prints are in any of the minor databases around the country, then one of us will spell you. Check in every few hours, let us know what's he's up to." There was, other than the large, official websites that afforded the best possibilities, another layer of smaller, lesser-known sites. There were social services, corporate employee sites, backwater police or sheriff's departments, that hadn't merged their files with larger databases. Combing through them was the computer age equivalent of what used to be known as police legwork. It seldom paid off, but often enough that it had to be done. The only way to do it was relentlessly.

"I don't think searching any more databases will do much good," Fedderman said. "A name like Jones."

Fedderman had a point. They'd wasted a lot of time following up on Jones computer hits that had led nowhere productive. There were plenty of people who simply had never been fingerprinted. Jeb Jones was probably one of them. But considering the time they'd put in, a little more wouldn't hurt. Learning everything possible about Jeb Jones before he was picked up could be essential.

Renz called again and told Quinn the blood on the fingerprint had tested A-positive, same as the victim's, so there was no reason get any hopes up over DNA evidence. Still, if the killer and victim had the same blood type, and it *was* a common type . . .

But Quinn doubted if that line of inquiry would lead anywhere. In order to leave a sample of his own blood, the Butcher would have had to cut himself, and he was a killer ever so careful. The fingerprint was almost certainly made with the blood of the victim.

Quinn fixed narrowed eyes on Pearl. "Did he ever act like Jeb Jones was an alias?"

Pearl was losing her fear and getting angry now, at herself

mostly, and also at Jeb. But anyone would do to take it out on.

Out of love, back in the real world, back in the shit . . .

Maybe she should do as her mother suggested and meet Mrs. Kahn's eminently eligible nephew. What was the geek's name . . . Milton?

"Pearl?"

"When we were having sex and I came and said 'Oh, Jeb!' he didn't seem to think I was talking to somebody else."

Quinn stared deadpan at her. Behind her, Fedderman was trying not to laugh.

Quinn, still with a straight face, said, "Get out, Feds."

Fedderman picked up his suit coat from where it was draped over the back of his chair and went to the door. He looked back at Pearl. "The Waverton Hotel. You remember the room number?"

"You can figure it out," Pearl said. "You're a detective."

Fedderman shook his head with mock sadness. "You actually got off in a hotel room with a guy named Joncs."

"Get out, Feds," Quinn said again, before Pearl could answer or reach her gun.

Fedderman managed not to grin until he was out the door.

"Asshole!" Pearl said.

Quinn was already at his computer, scanning the fingerprint image into their system so they could search for matches in unlikely places. He started with remote and small-town police departments that hadn't merged their files with national data bases.

The NYPD tech whiz had set them up for something like this so they could work separately on their computers through different connections. Quinn said he'd take the eastern half of the country, and Pearl should take from the Mississippi west.

Sure, that covers only a couple of time zones.

She rolled her chair closer to her desk and began the Internet search. It wasn't likely to produce results, but staying busy was the best thing for her.

After three hours they'd gotten nowhere. If Pearl's stomach hadn't been so knotted, she would have been hungry.

She sat back, pinched the bridge of her nose, and bowed her head.

"Want to break for lunch?" Quinn asked. He still didn't seem angry.

Pearl didn't look up. "I'm sorry. I really am."

She was hoping he'd reassure her, tell her it was all right, that she hadn't known Jeb Jones would become a suspect, that who she slept with was personal and her own business

What he said was, "It's done. We go from here."

"That's goddamned obvious," Pearl said.

"Then let's do it. I'll buy you a pizza."

She knew that was all she was going to get from Quinn for now. She needed loving, holding, comforting, forgiveness. She'd get pizza.

When they were settled in with pepperoni pizza slices and beer at D'Joes, a tiny restaurant down the street, they made awkward small talk and then lapsed into silence.

Until Quinn took a long pull of beer, licked foam from his upper lip, and said, "Has it occurred to you that if Jeb Jones is the Butcher he might have you in mind for one of his victims?"

Of course it had occurred to Pearl, but she'd been keeping it at a distance. Now she felt her heart turn cold. Her throat tightened and she could only shake her head no, lying to Quinn. Some things were none of his damned business.

"You're a brunette he obviously finds attractive. Why not you as the subject of one of his puzzle notes? Why not you—"

"Enough, Quinn!" She took a vicious bite of pizza and chewed hard.

"Okay, but give it some thought."

Pearl knew what he was thinking. She could be used as bait. Would she be willing?

Would she?

But he never actually suggested it.

The thing was, even though she knew Jeb could be a killer, a part of her still wouldn't accept it. Maybe Quinn understood that, or at least part of it.

When they returned to the office it was still too warm, but mercifully quiet. Con Ed had broken off their work out in the street, maybe for lunch. Quinn and Pearl settled in at their computers to resume their Internet search. Pearl did give what Quinn had said some thought.

She phoned his daughter, who'd just reported for work at the Hungry U.

Keeping her voice low so Quinn wouldn't overhear, she said, "Lauri, I have a question about Jeb Jones, my friend you met at the Pepper Tree. Remember him?"

"Mr. Hot," Lauri said.

Jesus! Teenage girls!

"Have you seen him since?"

Lauri didn't answer right away.

"Lauri, I need the truth from you. It's important."

"I've seen him a few times. We even had lunch once."

Surprised, Pearl actually said, "Huh?"

"Don't get mad at me, Pearl. None of it means a thing. I only did it to make Wormy jealous."

Sure. Why wouldn't any woman prefer Wormy to Mr. Hot?

"How did you happen to get together the first time?" Pearl asked.

"We just happened to bump into each other."

"How? Where?"

Lauri gave a long sigh.

"Lauri, damn it!"

"Okay, I saw Jeb again when I was following you. He was sorta hanging around outside the Pepper Tree when you were inside having lunch with some woman. We talked and agreed us being there would be our secret. Then I saw him again, a few days later, and we talked again and went for lunch. He was sorta in disguise, in jeans and wearing a Red Sox cap. It was almost like he was following you like I was and didn't want to be spotted."

Almost?

Pearl didn't say anything for a while. Quinn might be right. She might be a prospective victim.

"Pearl, you okay?"

"Yeah, Lauri."

"I really gotta get to work."

"Go, and thank you."

Pearl hung up the phone and sat stunned and wondering, trying to come up with some plausible reason other than her impending murder why Jeb might have been secretly watching her.

If he was the Butcher, why hadn't he already killed her?

The answer was obvious—she was useful. He was using her to keep tabs on the investigation.

"Something here," Quinn said, excitement in his voice, but also puzzlement.

He was leaning almost close enough to his computer to take a bite out of it.

"I've got a match on the print."

47

Pearl was up out of her chair and leaning over Quinn, balancing with her hand on his shoulder so she could see his computer monitor.

"It's not a criminal, military, or federal employee site," he said. "It's the Florida Department of Children and Families archives."

Pearl read the information on the screen. The print was a ninety percent match with the right middle finger of the 1980 print of a lost child in Florida identified as Sherman Kraft.

Pearl ran the name through her memory and came up with nothing.

She continued to watch as Quinn played the computer keys and mouse. They followed the thread and the story unfolded:

In Harrison County, Florida, in August of 1980, a boy about ten was found dazed and wandering along a swamp road. His clothes were bloody and ragged. He had an injured leg, was malnourished, and appeared to have been living for some time in the swamp. He also remained in a state of shock and refused to utter a sound.

Local news referred to him simply as "the Swamp Boy" until four days after he was found, when his newspaper photo was recognized as that of Sherman Kraft. He was the son of a woman who lived in a remote house on the edge of the swamp, more than ten miles from where he was found. When authorities went to the house they learned little more. It was deserted, and Sherman's mother, Myrna Kraft, was missing.

Apparently she was never found. There was speculation of foul play, and of her simply running away after losing, or deserting, her son. The archival accounts were concentrated on Sherman, so there was nothing more of substance about Myrna.

Quinn and Pearl kept following the thread, and later, infrequent news accounts told of how Sherman finally began to speak, but never of his experiences in the swamp, or what had led to them. Memory block. Nature's protective device. He was like someone who'd survived a terrible car crash and could remember nothing of it. The rest of his mind was apparently unaffected. Tests on the boy revealed an amazingly high IQ.

Mesmerized, Quinn and Pearl read on about how he'd lived in a series of institutions and foster homes, all the time receiving special treatment and education because of his remarkable intelligence. High academic achievement and scholarship opportunities led him to graduate magna cum laude from Princeton in 1989 at the age of nineteen. He was thought to be brilliant but antisocial and arrogant. After a series of jobs ranging from restaurant manager to bond salesman, he disappeared.

There were photographs of Sherman at Princeton. Quinn placed the cursor on them and clicked them into enlargement.

Pearl gripped his shoulder and leaned in for a closer look.

She was reasonably sure she was looking at the young Jeb Jones.

Suddenly out of breath, she felt her knees gave out. She caught herself and sat down cross-legged on the floor beside Quinn's desk chair.

"Goddamnit, Quinn!"

He looked down at her and ran the backs of his knuckles gently over her cheek. "It's all right, Pearl."

"I really screwed up."

"When you left me, you mean?"

She snorted. *He's making a joke, surely. Just like him.* She began to cry. "That's not what I meant and you know it."

"Yeah," he said softly.

"Such a damned foul-up . . ."

"Not actually, Pearl. And the hell with it, you're human."

"Sometimes I wonder," she said, and bit her lip.

"Pearl . . ."

She sniffled, wiped her nose with the back of her hand, and stood up. Quinn said nothing as she trudged to the half-bath, blew her nose, and splashed cold water on her face.

For a long time she stood leaning with both hands on the washbasin and watching the water swirl down the drain.

Feeling only slightly better, she returned to the office.

Quinn was still at his desk. The printer was whirring and clucking, doling out in glides and jerks the information on Sherman Kraft/Jeb Jones. Quinn was sitting back in his swivel chair, rotating slightly back and forth and watching the printer. When Pearl was near his desk, he looked up at her.

Con Ed was back from lunch or break or wherever they'd gone, and the jackhammer outside suddenly resumed its chattering, only louder. It sounded as if there might be two of them. Reinforcements had been called in to make Pearl feel even more miserable.

"What do we do now?" she asked.

"We call Renz for a warrant and some backup, then we go pick up Sherman Kraft."

Pearl nodded. *Sherman Kraft. Jeb Jones.* This called for a hell of an adjustment in her thinking. In her feelings. She felt like lying back down on the floor, curling into a ball, and trying to process the entire ugly mess.

"You want to be there when we take him?" Quinn asked.

"I wouldn't miss it."

The jackhammers went at it full blast.

Pearl went to her desk and got her gun.

48

They were on their way to kill or capture Pearl's Jeb Jones. Fedderman had the unmarked so they took Quinn's Lincoln behemoth.

Driving fast and skillfully through midtown traffic, Quinn talked with Renz on his cell phone, setting up a rendezvous point near the Waverly Hotel. It had already been determined that Jeb was in his room, and most of that floor was quietly being evacuated. When the time came, SWAT team members would take the elevator to the floor above Jeb and station themselves in the stairwell. Then power to the elevators would be stopped, the stairwell below and fire escape would be blocked by uniformed cops and SWAT members, and Jeb Jones would be trapped.

When Quinn got off the phone and concentrated on weaving his way through stalled traffic, Pearl used her own phone to call her apartment and check for messages. Maybe there was one from Jeb.

My God, Jeb . . .

As she listened to her phone ring on the other end of the connection, Pearl wondered if she'd be able to stop Jeb if he bolted. If he decided to make a fight of it, or commit suicide by cop, would she be able to shoot him? The prospect made her intestines tie themselves in knots. The pain made her actually bend forward in her seat.

Pressing the cell phone to her ear, she listened to her message machine in her apartment click on. One message:

"Pearl?"

Her mother.

"Pearl, are you there? I've had a conversation with Mrs. Kahn, a nice lady, about her equally nice, not to mention handsome, nephew Milton, who comes here and visits with her often. At my suggestion Mrs. Kahn phoned him and he's *extremely* interested in meeting you, dear, so since tomorrow was his regular visiting day anyway, I got together with Mrs. Kahn and set up a lunch in the nursing home cafeteria for the four of us, so the two of you can get to know one another without any pressure. At what would be the proper time, Mrs. Kahn and I would agree that we had to go for mahjongg and you two would be alone so nature could do what nature's been doing best for thousands if not millions of years. That's tomorrow at noon, Pearl. It's pot roast day. Pot roast is the only dish they do well here, but they do it very well and with mushrooms, which are said by some to be an aphrodisiac. If you can't make it, be sure to call me. If I were you, dear, I would wear that navy dress of yours with the matching shoes. Definitely not the red, Pearl. As for accessories—"

Pearl's clamshell phone snapped closed with the force of powerful jaws.

Quinn didn't slow down, but he took his eyes off traffic for a second to glance over at her. "Trouble?"

"Not unless I let it become trouble."

Another curious glance. "Jones?"

"My mother."

Quinn nodded grimly and drove on.

* * *

Quinn flashed his shield for the uniform standing next to a radio car that was skewed sideways in the street and blocking traffic. The cop stepped back and waved for Quinn to drive around the car. This required putting a front wheel up on the curb, but Quinn didn't seem to mind. Pearl placed both hands on the dashboard to keep from getting bounced around.

He pulled the Lincoln in at the curb half a block up and just around the corner from the Waverton Hotel. The cross street was blocked, too, by a black Traffic Enforcement car. More than a dozen radio cars and two unmarked vans were parked at haphazard angles. Half a dozen SWAT guys were standing in a knot. About a dozen uniformed cops in bulky flak jackets were grouped near them. The SWAT people had dark, stubby automatic rifles. Some of the uniforms had shotguns. Quinn recognized Officer Vern Shults and his female partner, Nancy Weaver. Shults was nearing retirement and shouldn't have been there. He was armed only with his regulation nine. The intrepid and promiscuous Weaver was carrying a shotgun. She spotted Quinn and Pearl and waved to them. A small woman with a backpack was standing off to the side, talking into what looked like a recorder.

This was much more backup than Quinn had requested. They were here to arrest a killer, not start a war. What the hell was Renz—

There was Renz, standing near one of the vans alongside a tall, blonde woman Quinn recognized as a local cable TV news anchor. As he and Pearl walked toward them, a brightly lettered news van entered the blocked street and parked at the opposite curb.

"Good," Renz said, as Quinn and Pearl approached. "Now we can get to this."

"Because we're here, or the press?" Quinn asked.

Renz ignored the question and said something into the two-way clipped to his lapel. The anchorwoman, a blonde whose name Quinn remembered now was Mary Mulanphy, smiled faintly but knowingly.

"Who's the woman with the SWAT guys?" Quinn asked.

"Cindy Sellers of *City Beat*," Renz said. "We owe her. She gets the print scoop."

Quinn wondered if newspaper people themselves still used the word *scoop*.

There was activity among the backup cops. A couple of car engines started, and a radio car backed swiftly toward where the one-way street was blocked.

Fedderman appeared out of nowhere and said, "He's still in his room."

Renz tucked in his chin and spoke into his lapel again to relay that information on his two-way. A two-man crew with a shoulder-mounted camera emerged from the TV news van, moving slowly and gingerly under the burden of technology, like a team of almost-drunks walking with exaggerated precision. Staying more or less on course, they crossed the street to get closer. They stopped about twenty feet away, and Mary Mulanphy stood out in the middle of the street and began speaking into a cordless microphone, facing the camera. Quinn knew he and the cops around him were part of the shot's background.

Renz spoke into his lapel yet again, saying exactly what he'd said the last time and apparently getting an identical answer. Was this one for real, or was it for the media?

Quinn looked across the street and saw that the SWAT team and most of the uniformed cops had disappeared, and one of the unmarked vans was gone. Cindy Sellers had disappeared, too.

After a few minutes, Mulanphy backpedaled smoothly in her high heels to where she'd started from, stepped deftly aside, and nodded to Renz. "We're still taping." Quinn noticed she was the only one who didn't have perspiration stains on her clothes. She in no way seemed bothered by the sun's glare or the heat radiating from the summer-baked concrete.

"Traffic has just been interdicted up the block from the hotel," Renz said loudly and with crisp enunciation, looking directly at a somewhat surprised Quinn. "We have all possible escape routes blocked. It's time to start the operation. Main investigators will be accompanied by uniformed officers Shults and Weaver." Quinn, Pearl, and Fedderman glanced at one another. Renz said, "I want everyone to please be careful. I don't want anyone hurt." He looked toward the camera, pretending to notice it for the first time, and raised a palm toward it, shaking his head. "We don't have time for that now." Loudly, back to Quinn: "This is a go."

Quinn motioned for his team to follow, then walked toward the corner. By the time he'd turned it, Pearl and Fedderman were on either side of him. Shults and Weaver, in their bulky flak jackets, Weaver with her shotgun, brought up the rear.

Almost the rear. Actually, Mary Mulanphy and her camera crew brought up the rear, about fifty feet behind the others. Renz had stayed back at the rendezvous point to issue executive orders.

Pearl's throat was dry. She felt like an actor in some kind of eerie movie as they approached the hotel's marquee. The uniformed doorman who sometimes stood outside was nowhere in sight. All traffic, vehicular and pedestrian, had disappeared from the block. She hoped Jeb, up in his room, wouldn't notice the sudden absence of traffic noise from directly below. Then she remembered his room didn't face the street. They could catch him unawares.

They had to.

Without hesitating, they turned and entered the hotel lobby.

It wasn't much cooler inside.

"You okay, Pearl?"

Quinn's voice. He sounded farther away from her than just a few feet.

She nodded.

The lobby was deserted except for a guy in a gray business suit who'd been undercover but now had his shield displayed dangling in its leather case from his breast pocket. He unbuttoned his suit coat, like an Old West gunfighter getting ready to quick draw. There was no one behind the desk. Another plainclothes cop stood stone-faced and unmoving in the archway to the coffee shop.

The elevators were dead so the assault force rapidly took the carpeted stairs to the fourth floor, where Jeb Jones was registered.

"Goddamnit!" Pearl heard the blonde anchorwoman whose name she couldn't remember say behind them, and there was a muffled noise like somebody tripping up the steps. Pearl figured that would be cut out of the tape. Maybe the poor guy who had to lug the camera up the stairs and keep it aimed and focused had tripped. She didn't look back to see what had happened. At the third-floor landing, where there were two SWAT guys with automatic rifles, Pearl drew her nine-millimeter Glock from its belt holster and started concentrating hard.

The fourth floor was unnaturally quiet except for their footfalls on the soft carpet.

As they approached Jeb's room, Pearl said, "I'll knock. If he looks through the peephole and sees me, he'll open the door."

"Don't be a fool, Pearl," Quinn told her. "Let these guys earn their money."

She glanced back where he was motioning and was surprised to see that the two SWAT team members from the third-floor landing had followed them up.

"This is a media show for Renz!" she whispered angrily to Quinn.

"Tell no one," he said to her softly, maybe smiling.

"If they shoot Jeb—"

The two SWAT guys moved out ahead of her and she shut up. They looked back at Quinn, who nodded.

The SWAT guys went in hard. One of them had a weighted battering ram slung by straps over his shoulder and crashed the door open, and the other tossed in a flash-bang grenade. There was a deafening sharp explosion that Pearl knew would do no damage but was meant to temporarily freeze whoever was in the room. Using those precious first few seconds, the grenade tosser charged inside. The door rammer followed. They were shouting over and over that they were police, making all the noise they could to maximize the element of surprise, and because they were revved. Behind Pearl, the blond anchorwoman was speaking frantically. And beyond her, tiny Cindy Sellers had rematerialized and was yammering into her recorder.

Jesus! Pearl thought.

Gotta get in there!

Time was on fast-forward and might leave her behind.

Her heart hammering like a machine gun in her rib cage, she passed Quinn and Fedderman on their way into the hotel room. Weaver somehow squeezed ahead of her, flak jacket and all, smelling of stale sweat and cheap perfume, shotgun leveled.

Don't you shoot him, bitch!

Pearl held her Glock pressed tight against her thigh as she entered and glanced around.

At first she thought the room had been unoccupied, and she felt a great surge of relief.

Then a hand appeared above the narrow space between the bed and the wall, fingers spread wide.

Another hand.

The smoke-fogged room suddenly became silent.

Jeb stood up slowly, surprise and fear on his face, but not panic. When he saw Pearl, his lips parted as if he were about to say something, and his expression of surprise turned to one of disappointment. Pearl felt for a moment as if she might begin to sob.

Damn it, hold on to yourself!

She swallowed, not liking how loud a sound it made.

Pearl knew Quinn had decided to put on a show for Renz. It was, after all, part of the deal. He held his old .38 police special revolver in both hands, pointed in Jeb's direction but low enough so that if he fired, a bullet would go into the bed.

"Sherman Kraft, we have a warrant for your arrest for the murder of Marilyn Nelson. You have the right . . ."

At the mention of the name Sherman Kraft, Jeb suddenly looked stunned, and Pearl knew in heart as well as mind that they had the right man. Her wrong man.

Again.

But they'd solved the case. They'd stopped the killing. And she'd been part of it.

She had her emotions tightly tied and knotted as she listened to Quinn finish reading Jeb—or Sherman—his rights.

Fedderman gripped one of Jeb's raised arms and led him out from behind the bed, then turned him around and yanked both his arms down behind his back.

Pearl stepped forward and handcuffed him.

She had on her cop's face when he was led away and they exchanged glances. She wasn't sure if he knew she was the one who'd cuffed him.

"Have you anything to say?" the blond anchorwoman asked Jeb, dancing nimbly alongside and trying to keep up.

He stared straight ahead. "Only to my attorney."

Pearl thought, *Bastard!*

49

Sherman Kraft sat at a small oak table bolted to the floor in a precinct interrogation room. Behind him stood a uniformed officer with his arms crossed in a way that displayed bulging biceps. Shavers was his name, Quinn remembered. He was a lean-waisted black man who'd won a weightlifting championship while in the academy. Quinn figured he had to be well into his fifties by now, but he didn't look it.

Besides the two unmoving figures and the table in the room there were four hard wooden chairs. They looked and were uncomfortable. It was in one of them that Sherman Kraft sat—uncomfortably.

Quinn, Pearl, and Fedderman were standing outside the room with Renz, looking in through the observation window. Kraft couldn't see out, but he knew they were there, of course, having watched plenty of TV cop shows. From time to time he glanced in their direction.

He'd stuck to his word about waiting for his attorney, but surprised them by asking for a public defender. A call had been made to the Legal Aid Society.

"He doesn't look worried," Fedderman said.

"Concerned, though," Renz said.

Pearl found it difficult to connect this pleasant-featured, mild-looking man with the killer who'd dismembered his victims and stacked their body parts in ritual fashion in their bathtubs. More and more she saw the world as a series of facades, and it scared the hell out of her.

The attorney from Legal Aid turned out to be Lisa Pareta, a woman in her forties with square-cut gray bangs framing a square-featured, ruddy face. She had blue eyes that always seemed to be red-rimmed and swollen, as if they hurt. Quinn knew her to be smart and tough.

Renz glanced over at her approaching figure. She wore a gray pantsuit, sensible black shoes, and was carrying a worn black leather briefcase. She had a confident smile and was swinging the briefcase in her right arm with each stride as if she wouldn't mind bonking someone with it.

"Ball breaker," Renz said in a low voice.

Pearl thought he had a point, but what did he expect?

"Lisa!" Renz's jowly face shaped itself into a smile as he stepped forward to meet her.

Looking serious, flushed, and slightly out of breath, Pareta pretty much ignored him and said, "That my client in there?"

"The one without the uniform," Renz said. Before she could ask, he handed her the arrest warrant and she scanned it and gave it back.

She looked at all of them as if they were the suspects and said, "I'm assuming he's been read his rights and hasn't yet been interrogated."

"We tried," Renz said honestly. "He's been silent as the furniture, waiting for his champion."

Pareta moved closer to the observation window and seemed to study her new client for a moment. Pearl wondered what she was thinking.

"I want to talk with him alone, without the muscle," she said.

"If you're brave enough," Renz said. He unlocked the

door and held it open for her, kept it open after she went inside, and motioned for Shavers to come out.

They watched Pareta sit across from her client, and the two of them talked for a few minutes with their heads close together, as if worried that the bug in the room might be activated. They were right, of course, but as every criminal attorney knew, the system wasn't sensitive enough to eavesdrop on attorney-client whispered conversation.

After about five minutes, Pareta sat back and motioned for her unseen audience to come into the room.

Quinn, Pearl, and Fedderman went in. Renz stayed outside and listened.

Fedderman remained standing and let Quinn and Pearl take the other two chairs. Pareta had moved around to sit alongside her client. Pearl was in the chair farthest away from him.

"My client says he has alibis for the times of some of the Butcher murders," Pareta said.

"*Some* of them?" Quinn said. "It only takes one murder charge to convict."

"If you're not interested in convicting the right man."

Quinn looked dead-eyed at Sherman Kraft as he spoke. "Your fingerprints are being matched with the killer's right now. You left a bloody print in your victim's apartment, which means we have your DNA. It will be matched with the DNA on the swab we took when you were brought in."

That wasn't exactly true, of course, as the blood might be the victim's.

Kraft looked at Pearl as if in appeal. "I've killed no one."

"And your name isn't Sherman Kraft," she said bitterly.

"It isn't," said the suspect.

"Then you've got no worries," Fedderman said. He smiled.

"My name isn't Sherman Kraft and I got no worries. I'm not even lawyered up."

"It's a wonderful world," Pareta said, "where no one is named Sherman Kraft or has worries. We should all go out for egg creams."

"How about going for murder one instead?" Quinn said. He focused more intently on the suspect, who now didn't seem able to look away from him.

Quinn explained how they'd learned his identity, from the time Sherman had been found wandering the swamp road in Florida to when he disappeared from his last job after leaving Princeton.

"Your client's a smart one," Fedderman said to Pareta. He'd noticed her perk up at the mention of Princeton.

"Not so smart we don't have him cold," Quinn said.

Pareta sneered. "Like you'd have a ham sandwich if you had some bread and mustard, if you had some ham." She glanced at Pearl. "You don't have much to say."

"I'm a good listener," Pearl said.

Pareta blatantly took her measure, smiled faintly, and turned her attention back to Quinn. "I reviewed the evidence. You think a photo taken at college when he was nineteen years old is going to convict my client? You coulda fooled me into thinking it's a photo of my nephew Homer."

"If Homer's fingerprint and DNA are at the crime scene, like your client's, he's in some kinda trouble."

Pareta dug into her briefcase and came up with a copy of the Princeton photo from the file on Sherman Kraft that had been faxed over to the prosecutor's office. She peered at the photo, then at Sherman. "Doesn't look like the same guy to me."

Quinn pretended to yawn. "Like you said, he was nineteen when it was taken."

"I didn't go to Princeton," the suspect said. "Went to Yale."

"Is that where you learned to be a journalist?" Pearl asked. Her voice was weary but level. She had herself in check and knew she could handle this now.

"I'm not a journalist," the suspect said.

"Then you were lying."

Pareta laid her hand gently on her client's arm. "There's no need to say anything at this point. You're better off maintaining silence until we know more."

"It doesn't matter," the suspect said.

"Maybe he doesn't remember committing those murders," Fedderman said.

Pareta looked thoughtful. "It's happened before."

The interrogation room door opened and Renz stuck his head in. "Talk to you for a minute, Quinn?"

Quinn noticed that Renz was sweating. Pushing back his chair, he said, "I'll be right back." To the suspect: "Don't go anywhere."

"Aren't one of you people supposed to be the good cop?" Sherman asked, playing the smart-ass now as Quinn was leaving. He must be pretty confident, or was running one helluva bluff.

Quinn had to credit him with balls, even though he felt like grabbing him by the throat and taking the quick route to justice. (But was he thinking of the murders, or of Pearl?)

When he went outside and closed the interrogation room door behind him, he saw Renz standing down the hall by the water fountain. He was splashing cool water on his face, not seeming to mind that he was messing up his shirt and tie.

He straightened up when Quinn approached. Quinn didn't like the expression on his face that was still beaded with water.

"Prints came back," Renz said. "They don't match."

Quinn was astonished. "They must!"

"Must but don't."

"Sweet Jesus!"

"Not only that," Renz said in a choked voice. "It's too early for DNA analysis, but the lab says they got some blood off the swab used to extract a culture from the suspect's gums. It's type O. The blood on the fingerprint is type A, same as the victim's."

"Meaning it's not from the killer and the DNA isn't going to match, either."

"Right. Just like the prints don't match."

Quinn felt himself getting light-headed, short of breath. He understood now why Renz was splashing cold water on his face. Though it hadn't seemed possible until a few minutes ago, they had the wrong man.

He went to the water fountain and got a drink, trying to slow down his thoughts so he could consider each separately and somehow fit them together to form a reasonable whole.

"He *has* to be our man," he said, straightening up and wiping his lips with the back of his thumb. "He's tricking us somehow."

"I don't see how," Renz said hopelessly. "Nobody's that smart."

"He's pretty goddamned smart."

Renz looked at him and said seriously, "So are you, Quinn."

Quinn felt the slow anger in him quickening, building in heat and strength. He charged up the hall and yanked open the interrogation room door. Burst inside. Behind him he heard Renz yell, "Quinn!"

Without remembering crossing the room Quinn was standing over the suspect, his huge right fist balled and ready to strike. He was aware of Pearl staring wide-eyed up at him.

Pareta jumped up, looking indignant and terrified. "Detective! Think what you're doing! Damn it, think!" She'd seen plenty of hard-ass acts in interrogation rooms, and knew this was real.

Quinn hadn't touched the suspect yet, knowing if he did touch him the game would change, his world would change. The system protected scum like this one, who was gazing up at him unafraid, confident.

The system that failed again and again.

"Who the hell are you?" Quinn demanded in a soft voice that made the flesh on the back of Pearl's neck crawl. She knew Quinn. She knew what the gentle tone and stillness could portend.

"I'm not Sherman Kraft," the suspect said calmly. Fear didn't seem to be one of his emotions.

"I didn't ask who you weren't."

"This has gone far enough!" Pareta said. She darted a glance at the one-way window, knowing Renz, somebody, should be out there somewhere and might stop this.

Pearl looked at Fedderman, who looked at Quinn, back at her, and shook his head no. Pearl was breathing hard. If Jeb Jones wasn't Sherman Kraft, who was he?

"Jeb!" she said sharply, the name flying out of her without thought. "Who are you?"

"You don't have to answer that," Pareta said. "You don't have to say a goddamned thing to these people."

These people? "Screw your lawyer!" Pearl said.

"Pearl!" Fedderman waved an arm, cautioning her to be quiet, his unbuttoned shirt cuff flapping like a sail.

The suspect continued looking only at Quinn, matching Quinn's unyielding stare with one of his own. There was a hardness in him Pearl was seeing for the first time, yet she recognized it. She'd seen it in people who'd bottomed out, entered the abyss and returned from it; and accepted that they were someday going back. She truly understood then that she didn't know Jeb, not at all.

He said, "I'm Sherman Kraft's brother."

Quinn backed away and stood looking at the wall behind the suspect and his attorney. Pearl couldn't take her eyes off her former lover who'd just become someone else again. Fedderman nervously paced, absently trying to button his loose shirt cuff.

Pareta snapped her shabby briefcase closed and stood up. "I have to know who I'm representing."

"You're representing me," the suspect said, "but you

won't have to for long because I haven't done anything illegal."

Pareta thought it over, then sat back down.

"What are you doing in New York?" Quinn asked the suspect.

"As your attorney—" Pareta began.

"We're doing the same thing you are," the suspect said to Quinn, ignoring Pareta and cutting off his legal advice. "We're looking for Sherman."

"We?" Quinn asked. "You and who else?"

"Sherman's not my brother, actually. He's my half-brother."

"You and who else?" Quinn asked again.

"Our mother."

50

Now that Maria Cirillo had decided to give up on New York, her mind was at ease. She was simply tired of struggling in this city that moved so fast in the same place, that clanged and chattered constantly inside her head and heart, pressuring her, pressuring her . . .

Losing her part-time job yesterday as an optometrist's receptionist on Tenth Street was the final and decisive blow. Dr. Wolff said he was retiring and was winding down his practice, and his daughter was going to act as receptionist and file clerk for the next few months. He offered to give Maria the highest recommendation, and told her this had nothing to do with her work—it was simply time for him and his ill wife to leave the city and retire to Florida. Maria had received a generous severance check, but in New York it wouldn't last long.

She'd used most of her severance pay to buy an airline ticket to within driving distance of Homestead, Arizona. With her three years at John Jay, she could find work in the town's small police department. Maria had grown up in Homestead, had friends and family there, and had been the high-school sweetheart of the chief of police. The chief, she'd learned in her last letter from her mother, had recently filed to divorce his wife.

Maria didn't actually plan on reviving her old romance, but she knew it was one of those things that seemed ordained and just might happen. She was only twenty-six to the chief's twenty-eight. They were both young. He was handsome, and Maria, with her shoulder-length dark hair, pale complexion, and wide-set brown eyes, was beautiful and knew it. Her small, lithe body hadn't changed from her high school days. The chief would recognize it. High, firm breasts, a tiny waist, legs not long but muscular and shapely, a strawberry birthmark near her left nipple, like a second nipple . . . the chief would remember.

Maria hadn't had any problem getting dates in New York, in between fighting off the creeps.

She thought about the chief as she stood beneath her lukewarm shower with her head tilted back, facing away from the needles of water that were rinsing shampoo from her hair.

Don't get ahead of yourself.

But despite her attempts to control her optimism, Homestead sure looked better to her than New York. It could get hot out there, the dry heat, but today was more proof that it could be just as hot in New York, and it was a damp heat. Not like Arizona. She found herself humming as she ran her fingers through her hair to hasten the rinsing process.

Events and circumstances made it clear to Maria that it was time to give up her struggles in New York, to use what she'd learned and return home, if not in triumph, in contentment.

Her flight to Phoenix left in two days. Her lease on her tiny Lower East Side apartment expired in a month. She wasn't going to argue with the extremely difficult real estate management firm about refunding her month's rent deposit; she would simply not mail the last month's rent and forfeit the money.

Maybe she'd finish her schooling at the University of Arizona, close to home, or maybe she'd go to work as a uniformed police officer in Homestead and work her way up through the ranks. She wanted to earn some money. Maria was tired of being poor.

She squinted through running water and turned the faucet handle so the shower got cooler.

The water was almost cold when she turned it off, stepped out from behind her plastic shower curtain, and began toweling herself dry.

When she left the bathroom, still nude, her hair damp and stringy, she immediately noticed the long white box lying in the center of her bed. She stopped and stood staring.

Flowers? Who'd send—

The right side of her head exploded into a pain so white and bright that it blinded her.

She could feel rough carpet nap on the left side of her face.

Must have fallen . . . Odd . . .

The pain intensified, and now the room was dark, darker, was floating away from the pain, away from everything . . .

When Maria regained consciousness she was lying on her back on her bed, where the box had been.

The white box . . .

She had a headache, and she was cold. Something else . . . Why was she having difficulty breathing?

She could only breathe through her nose. Something was clamped over her mouth, sealing her lips.

Maria panicked and tried to cry out, to rise from the bed, and realized she couldn't move her arms or legs, couldn't make a sound loud enough to be heard more than ten feet away.

Calm! Damn it, be calm!

Her struggles, which had rocked the bed violently but

gained her nothing, gradually stopped, and she lay still, taking stock.

I'm taped! Tape over my mouth, around my legs and arms, wound tight enough to stop circulation. Head still hurts, not thinking clearly yet, I know it . . .

Maria had read about the Butcher, and there'd been plenty of speculation about him at John Jay, but she refused to make any connection with what had happened to her. It was the sort of thing she studied, that happened to other people. Lecture material or newspaper grist for reading over breakfast. She craned her neck, staring around her, listening. She appeared to be alone in the bedroom.

But not in the apartment.

She could hear something . . . a soft, persistent sound. Water running in the bathroom.

It stopped.

The light changed in the bedroom and suddenly someone was there. Maria raised her head from the mattress and saw a medium-size, muscular man enter the room. He was reasonably handsome, mid-thirties, and also nude.

Mustn't be. Can't be.

He smiled at her, then bent over her and worked his arms beneath her back and bound legs.

Mustn't be!

He lifted her gently and held her as if she were a bride about to cross a threshold, and carried her toward the bathroom. Her mind was still numbed by pain and confusion, and she had the crazy idea he was rescuing her. She knew it was crazy but clung desperately to it.

Until he placed her in the almost full bathtub, lifted her ankles, and pushed her head down and some of the cold water went up her nose.

Full awareness came then. An awareness more acute than any she had known.

Please!

She tried to raise her head, but his hand was on her forehead, as if he were checking for a fever, and she had no leverage whatsoever. The laws of physics were on his side. He lifted her ankles slightly higher and she felt her nude buttocks slide on the slick tub bottom as she went deeper. The man held her head steady inches beneath the surface.

Please! It isn't fair! Why are you doing this? For God's sake, why?

Through cold, clear water, drowning, she watched him watching her.

Please!

51

Jeb Kraft said, "I told you I wouldn't need a lawyer."

The interrogation room was getting warmer, from body heat and because the precinct detectives liked to keep it warm in there. Desperation seemed to rise with the temperature, and desperation struggled to find its voice.

"Don't be so sure," Pareta said to Jeb. "I might as well stay here. You're still talking to the police and need legal counsel, and I'm here *pro bono*."

He smiled. "I guess you're right. You're a bargain."

Pearl knew he was turning on the charm for his lady lawyer, and knew she was falling for it.

Quinn shifted his weight in his uncomfortable chair, making wood creak, and looked expectantly at Jeb. "We're waiting for the truth, and God help you if it isn't."

"There's no need for that kind of talk," Pareta said.

Quinn didn't have to tell her she was there because she'd been the on-call attorney next in line. Pareta had been overjoyed to find that she might be defending one of the city's most notorious killers until a high-priced, high-profile criminal attorney inevitably displaced her. Now she was simply defending a man wrongly charged. Everyone ignored her.

She acted as if she'd expected to be ignored. Just getting in her licks.

Moving forward slightly and resting his elbows on the table, Jeb cleared his throat, and began:

"My name is Jeb Kraft, and I was born in nineteen-eighty-one in Slidell, Louisiana. My mother is Myrna Kraft. My father was Samuel Pickett, now deceased. I attended Yale, not Princeton. My mother's other son, ten years older than I am, is Sherman Kraft. When we—Mom and I—read in a Louisville newspaper about the Butcher murders, we knew it was Sherman. It had to be. He was . . . never what you'd call normal. Mom said he liked to kill animals and cut them up, dismember them and clean their body parts, as if he were purifying and justifying his act. We knew we had to do something, but we didn't want to see Sherman killed, or kill himself rather than be captured. Blood really is thicker than water, even thicker than the blood of women we never knew. We came to New York to find him and stop him, Mom and I."

Quinn unconsciously fingered the Cuban cigar in his shirt pocket. (Not that he could smoke it here.) "This is the same Sherman Kraft who was found wandering alone in Harrison County, Florida, in nineteen-eighty, and became a ward of the state?"

"It is," Jeb said.

"Where's your mother now?"

"She's staying at the Meredith Hotel, on the East Side."

Quinn knew the Meredith. It was a large hotel and old, but still elegant, the kind of place where mid-level diplomats and airline personnel stayed, as well as tourists who wanted to see the United Nations, which was only a few blocks away. He glanced at Fedderman, who nodded and slipped from the interrogation room. Jeb Kraft didn't seem to notice, but Quinn was sure he had. Jeb didn't miss much.

"Why did you use an alias in your search for your brother?"

"We decided it would be easier that way, for us and for

Sherman. We didn't want to attract attention if the police learned his name and it became public. We wanted to get to him first, to talk him into surrendering to the law, to keep him from killing again or being killed himself."

"So you found a way to monitor the investigation," Quinn said. "You established a relationship with one of the detectives."

Jeb glanced at Pearl. "I guess you could call it that. Or I let her establish a relationship with me. I pretended I'd known Marilyn Nelson so I might pique Officer Kasner's interest, and . . . our friendship developed into something deeper."

Pearl felt her stomach turn over.

"While pretending to give Officer Kasner evidence, you were secretly eliciting evidence from her," Quinn said.

"You could say that."

"Do you say it?"

Another glance at Pearl. "Yes, I do. You have to understand, the entire purpose of our visit was to find Sherman before the police did. To save his life. I'm not saying I wasn't—I'm not—fond of Pearl."

"And all the while Sherman continued to kill."

"We wanted to save the lives of any future victims, too. Of course. We thought we were going about it the right way, letting the police lead us where they were going anyway, then maybe there'd be something we could do for Sherman, make taking him into custody easier and no one would be hurt. Our intentions were good."

"Have either you or your mother had any contact with Sherman since you arrived in New York?"

"No. I swear we haven't."

Quinn wearily dry-washed his face with his big hands and sat back. The wooden chair creaked forlornly again under the strain of his weight. "Do you have any actual proof that your brother Sherman Kraft committed the Butcher murders?"

Jeb blinked at him. "Proof? In the legal sense? No."

"Then why are you so sure of his guilt?"

"Because Mom is."

Pearl saw a subtle change in Quinn; he'd picked up on something. He no longer seemed tired.

"Are you still single, Jeb?"

"Yes. I've had live-in relationships with women, but I never married."

"Any special someone now?"

Jeb looked everywhere other than at Pearl. "No. I'm afraid not anymore."

Pearl wondered how she could ever have been in love with this creep.

"Do you still live with your mother, Jeb?"

"Of course not. I live in an apartment in Boston, where I have my office. I mean, I work out of my apartment. I'm an arbitrageur."

"What is that?"

"It's complicated. I make money off the differences in the exchange rates of currencies and in the fluctuating prices of certain commodities."

"You're a trader."

"Put simply, yes."

"Your mother lives alone in Louisiana?"

"Yes, but we're close in ways other than geographical. We talk on the phone almost every day."

"Why is she staying at one hotel and you at another?"

"I wanted to stay somewhere more suited to my identity as a struggling journalist."

"Your cover."

"Yes. Is there something illegal about that?"

"About inserting yourself in the middle of an active homicide investigation? You bet there's something illegal about it."

"He was searching for his brother," Pareta said. "Attempting to help."

Quinn laughed. "Spare us, counselor. But please tell your

client that his best chance of extricating himself from the mess he's in is to tell the truth."

"My advice to my client would be to say nothing more. You've threatened to charge him with a crime."

"He's still charged with a crime—homicide."

Pareta saw this as her turn to laugh. She made a pretty good show of it. "And where's the evidence of that?"

"The point is," Quinn said, "the murder charge hasn't been dropped."

"Then as Mr. Kraft's attorney—"

Jeb raised his hands for silence and as if to calm everyone. "It's okay. The police know about us now. If talking helps to find Shorman, I want to talk. He has to be stopped."

He looked down the table at Pearl, this time meeting her gaze directly. Trying to con her again, she knew.

She looked at the new Jeb the way Quinn was looking at him.

"What do you think, Pearl?" Jeb asked sincerely.

"I think you're guilty as hell. Of a lot of things."

"Let's get back to where we were," Quinn said.

"Which was where?" Pareta asked.

"Mom."

52

An hour later, Quinn and Pearl met Fedderman in the cavernous lobby of the Meredith Hotel. Aside from poor acoustics, it featured lots of gray-veined marble and darkly polished paneling, a field of maroon carpet, and fern-adorned groupings of brown leather armchairs. You had to look closely to notice the fine cracks in the marble, patched areas of carpet, and that some of the armchairs were slightly worn. The ferns, which were artificial, looked new and not very much like ferns.

"She's not back yet," Fedderman said. He'd informed them by phone on the way over that Myrna Kraft, registered under her own name, wasn't in her room. "The desk clerk's going to give me a nod when she comes in."

Quinn glanced around the lobby. One of the elevators opened and a couple who looked like teenagers emerged and headed giggling for the street exit. Two elderly women were sitting in armchairs and talking on the far side near a closed shop that sold incidentals and travel supplies. The desk clerk, a slender African American man in advanced middle age and going bald unevenly, was standing and leafing through some papers. A uniformed bellhop lounged just inside the revolving-door entrance.

"Let's wait for her here, then let her go up to her room before we confront her," Quinn said.

The three of them sat in armchairs. Quinn's sighed and enveloped him seductively, and a nearby reading lamp warmed one side of his face. If he weren't so pumped up he might have fallen asleep.

"How long—" Pearl began impatiently, and was quiet as a tall, slim woman in tan slacks and blazer with a yellow blouse pushed in through the glass revolving door. Pearl noticed she wasn't wearing heels; she was simply tall. Her long arms swung freely and she wasn't carrying anything. Not even a purse.

Fedderman, who'd looked over at the desk clerk and gotten the nod, said, "That's her."

She didn't notice them among the almost-ferns as she strode past. Though she was well into her fifties, she moved with a natural grace that couldn't be taught in modeling school, and she had the kind of cheekbones and jawline that aged well. Her dark hair was slightly touched with gray. Her eyes were dark, deep, and widely set. Movie star eyes.

"Jesus!" Fedderman whispered.

Quinn and Pearl knew what he meant.

"She looks like the Butcher's victims," Pearl said. "The same type."

"Almost the same damned woman," Fedderman said. "If ever a serial killer was offing his own mother over and over . . ."

They watched as Myrna stood at the elevators and waited. She didn't seem at all nervous or on guard. Quinn guessed she hadn't seen or heard the news about her son Jeb being arrested.

When she'd entered the elevator and its door slid shut, the three detectives stood up.

"Room six-twenty," Fedderman said.

They crossed the lobby toward the elevators. The desk clerk was back to shuffling though his papers and didn't look up at them.

"He gonna warn her we're on our way?" Quinn asked Fedderman.

"Not unless she's got a third son. This isn't the kinda hotel where the policy is to warn clientele about the police."

Quinn wasn't so sure about that, but he let it go. Myrna Kraft probably wouldn't try to avoid them anyway, even if she knew they now had her identity and her son. She had the appearance of a woman who had never run from much of anything.

They rode the other elevator to the sixth floor. A maid pushing a linen cart with a squeaky wheel passed them with a shy, polite smile. Otherwise the carpeted hall was deserted.

Quinn knocked softly on the door to room six-twenty. Light behind the peephole changed, then the door opened, and Myrna Kraft looked out at them inquisitively.

He was surprised that she wasn't as tall as she'd appeared from across the lobby. It was an illusion because of the way she was built, her regal posture. There was something else about her, a kind of energy that was almost palpable, and her dark eyes were the kind that would hold whatever they were fixed on. Pearl thought that as a younger woman Myrna Kraft must have been quite something.

"Yes?" she said. In that single, drawn-out word was a trace of Southern accent.

"Myrna Kraft?" Quinn asked.

"I am."

"We're police, ma'am." Quinn showed her his shield, which she looked at carefully. Then she looked expectantly at the other two detectives, who also showed her their identification. Only then did she invite them inside. Quinn was hit with a faint acrid scent, almost like insecticide or disinfectant. The room was orderly and spotless. He remembered the maid in the hall.

"We have your youngest son, Jeb, in custody," he said, not mentioning that Renz had only promised he could detain Jeb a few more hours, with Pareta nipping, niggling, and threatening.

Something changed in Myrna's eyes, but you had to look closely and quickly to notice. A good actor, Quinn decided, like her son. Probably like both sons. Talent in the family.

"You have my son Jeb? Why? On what charge?"

"Murder." Quinn was still technically correct, still legal, until informed that the warrant was officially withdrawn.

Myrna didn't respond at all to his shock tactic. "That would be impossible. I know my son. Why, Jeb wouldn't harm anyone, much less take their very life." Laying on the southern charm now. The accent was still subtle, but what there was of it was pure molasses and used sparingly. She could turn it on and off. How much of Myrna Kraft was real?

Pearl and Fedderman remained silent, letting Quinn drive the conversation.

He decided to drive right over Myrna.

"Apparently you haven't seen the news lately."

"Tell you true, I'm usually not interested in the news. It's nothing but unpleasantness."

"Jeb Kraft is under arrest for the murders of six women, but the charges will be dropped. We know your oldest son, Sherman, is the killer."

She looked thoughtful rather than alarmed, and took a few steps back then sat down hard in the wooden chair that matched a small desk.

"That can't be."

"But it is, and you knew it before we walked in here."

She aimed her wide-set eyes at Quinn, full wattage. "If we all know that, then why hasn't my Jeb been released?"

"He will be, Mrs. Kraft. His attorney's working out the technicalities."

"Attorney?"

"The court appointed one. She's looking after your son very competently."

"I'll take your word for that, Detective Quinn." She smiled. "You have an honest face."

"Faces can be deceptive," Pearl said.

Myrna turned her head slightly and stared at Pearl. Faces might be deceptive, but Pearl thought the message in Myrna's eyes was clear. It was a kind of detached hatred remote from any kind of empathy, much less mercy; the exterminator observing the insect. It made Pearl's flesh break out in goose bumps.

I slept with this woman's son.

"We know about Sherman's time in the swamp, and your disappearance after he was found," Quinn said. "We know quite a bit about Sherman."

"Not enough to find him, to stop him. You don't know him like his own mother does, Detective Quinn."

"Maybe I know him better."

He thought he might get a rise out of her, but she remained calm. "I do doubt that. Blood ties are the strongest, you know, especially between mother and child."

"Jeb told us about how you and he came to New York, and how he dogged the investigation into Sherman's murders."

Another glance at Pearl with those deep, dark eyes. Maybe a shadow smile. Myrna looked again at Quinn. "You know a lot, but not enough to apprehend my darling boy."

"Why did you desert your darling boy?" Pearl asked, before she might gag. She knew Quinn was supposed to be controlling this interview, but she couldn't stay silent.

Quinn's cell phone beeped. Everyone stared at him as he fished it from his pocket, as if the noise had interrupted a Broadway hit. He saw that it was Renz who was calling.

"Excuse me." He walked toward the far side of the room as he answered the call, keeping his voice low. "What is it, Harley?"

"You made contact yet with the mother?"

"Yes." Quinn moved closer to the window that looked out at an air shaft. Old brick, lots of recent tuck-pointing.

"Okay, can she hear you?"

"Somewhat."

"Jeb Jones has been sprung. Pareta went on a tear and made us drop charges so he could walk."

"Figures."

"Best we could do without evidence, not to mention that he's most likely innocent. Why I called is, I had him tailed and he's making a beeline for Mom. My man called just before I contacted you and said Jeb was getting out of a cab and about to enter the Meredith Hotel."

"Okay, I'll take care of it tomorrow. I'm busy on another matter now."

"I hired you because you're such a nifty liar," Renz said, and hung up.

Quinn folded his phone and slipped it back in his pocket. And there was a knock on the door.

"Busy, busy," Pearl said.

They watched Myrna go to the door and open it about six inches. "I don't think—"

But an agitated Jeb pushed his way inside.

When Jeb saw the three detectives his jaw dropped, but he recovered his composure nicely. "You don't have to talk to them, Mother."

Myrna ran her fingertips gently down his upper arm and smiled. "I'm afraid I do, Jeb. We both do." Her brow knit in sudden concern. "Did they hurt you anywhere?"

Pearl waited for her to wink, but she didn't.

"No, Mother. They followed the rules."

"We interrupted you," Quinn said to Myrna.

Jeb spread his feet, crossed his arms, and stared at the floor. Fedderman was the only one sitting down, on the edge of the bed. His arms were at his sides, his palms helping to support him on the soft mattress. His loosened right cuff was pinned beneath his hand.

"I was explaining about Sherman," Myrna said. To Jeb: "You might as well hear."

Jeb didn't look at her. She faced Quinn, her main inquisitor, and began:

"When Sherman was a boy he liked to spend time in the swamp, right near where we lived. From time to time he'd come home with dead things."

"He hunted?" Quinn asked.

"Sometimes, but other times he'd just find things already dead. For some reason he liked to dismember them. Tell you true, it gave me the creeps, but I told myself it might be natural boy curiosity, like maybe he'd grow up to be a doctor. The thing he'd do was cut up these creatures in the bathtub, then clean their parts real well and kind of stack them up, doing the same things to them that Butcher killer does. I'd already told Jeb about Sherman, about him doing this, and when we saw on the news about the Butcher, we both knew it had to be Sherman, all grown up."

"Detective Kasner asked why you deserted Sherman," Quinn reminded her in a neutral tone.

"I didn't desert him. I was talking to him about what he was doing to those animals, why he even wanted to do such a thing, and he attacked me with his skinning knife. I managed to fight him off and he ran away into the swamp. I didn't know what to do. Didn't want to contact the sheriff's department, knowing he might do harm to Sherman."

"What about Sherman doing harm to somebody else?" Pearl asked.

"I didn't think he would. Far as I knew, I was the only person he ever attacked. I decided to wait, a few days if necessary. I kept a shotgun nearby and didn't sleep for two nights. Then it became three days, and I knew it was too late to contact the law because they'd have too many questions. Sherman knew the swamp and I figured he'd be okay for quite a while there, but when a week had gone by, I gotta say I figured him for dead."

"Didn't you go looking for him yourself?" Pearl asked.

Myrna shook her head no. "Nothing didn't wanna be found in that swamp ever got found. Besides, Sherman took the knife with him when he ran." Myrna drew a deep breath and touched her fingers to her eyes as if they were tearing up, but no tears were evident. "About a month passed, and I saw on the TV news that Sherman had been found. They were calling him the Swamp Boy, didn't know who he was, and he was traumatized, they said, and wouldn't speak. I decided I'd keep my silence, just like Sherman. But next night on TV news they showed a photo of him, and even wild-looking like he was, I knew somebody'd surely recognize him." She glanced at Jeb now, and maybe those *were* tears glistening in her dark eyes. "Tell you true, I was pregnant by a man who'd recently deserted me. I wanted that child to have a chance in life, so I ran. I admit I panicked, but thinking back it mighta been the best thing I coulda done. I moved to Courtney, Louisiana, got a waitress job, and sacrificed for Jeb. I don't regret a second of that time." Jeb was looking at his mother now, his own eyes moist. "My boy Jeb was bright as a new dime, a scholar, and 'cause he was a brilliant student he went to the best schools even if I only made a poor working woman's wages."

"What about Sherman?" Quinn asked.

"I never knew. Tell you true, I made it a point to avoid watching or reading the news entirely in those Louisiana days. Never learned a thing about his whereabouts nor whether he recovered his memory. Far as I was concerned, that time was past. I had to look ahead, for myself and for Jeb. But I knew I'd hear about Sherman someday, and when I just happened to look at a New York paper in a store near a motel in Louisville, right there on the front page was a story about the Butcher, about what he did to his victims. I knew it had to be Sherman, so I phoned Jeb and told him everything. We decided the two of us best come to New York and try to find Sherman before you people did. We were gonna try to stop him from what he was doing and have him give himself up."

"Why?" Quinn asked simply.

Myrna stared at him as if he must be insane to ask the question. "He's my own flesh and blood."

"He's also police business."

"Blood's much more important than business."

"Not if that business is to keep more of it from being shed."

"You are twisting my words, sir."

She bowed her head and the tears came, dropping and leaving trailing marks on the front of her yellow blouse. Pearl wondered if Myrna could will herself to cry; Pearl had seen people who could.

Jeb moved over and stood close to his mother, making cooing sounds, and very near tears himself. The doting son. He lovingly put his arm around Myrna, then hugged her and rocked her gently.

Pearl remembered that same arm around her and shuddered.

Unmoved by the scene before him, Quinn wondered what the Butcher would think when he learned his mother was in town.

53

Nobody knew for sure how it should be handled, but they all knew where it was going.

They were in Renz's office, sitting in front of Renz's desk. Quinn and Pearl were in the chairs that were usually there. Two folding chairs had been brought in for Fedderman and the police profiler. Fedderman slouched in one of the tiny metal chairs as if numbed by exhaustion. The profiler, Helen Iman, ignored her chair and stood near the window so she was silhouetted in front of the open blind slats and was painful to look at.

She was a tall, lanky redheaded woman Quinn had worked with before, who looked more suited to beach volleyball than to police work. While still not a hearty advocate of profiling, Quinn had to admit that Helen was one of the best.

"They're both staying at their respective hotels," Quinn said of Jeb and Myrna. "Now they're making noises like family members who have a right to all our information."

"Where's the media on this?" Renz asked.

Quinn thought he caught a whiff of burned tobacco and wondered if Renz had been secretly smoking cigars in his office again. "They know Jeb was released, and they're still in the dark about Myrna." Quinn glanced at Helen, squinting. "That's why I requested this meeting."

"You requested it because you want to use Mom as bait," Renz said.

"Sharks aren't often used for bait," Helen said

"Move over a few feet so I can see you better," Quinn asked her.

She did so, smiling. Her features were strong, bony, almost masculine. But Quinn knew of a dead cop who had loved her.

"You want to know if it will work," she said in her throaty voice.

Renz laughed. "She's got you profiled."

"So what are the odds?" Quinn asked.

"I don't usually quote odds," Helen said, "but the Butcher is a killer who's classic in that his victims are all, in his mind, his mother. She's iconic to him." She couldn't suppress an eager grin. Lots of teeth. They all looked sharp. "It's pure textbook. This is so rare. They usually don't get a chance to kill the real thing, the archetype, the woman they know is behind their compulsion. She's the fuel for his fire. Will he be tempted to kill her when he learns she's in New York?" The grin widened. "The way a junkie who needs a fix is tempted by heroin. I'd say the odds are about even he'll go for her."

"Only even?" Quinn was disappointed.

"The variable in this is the exceptional intelligence of the killer. He'll have read the literature and know that we know the real object of his deadly desires is his mother. He'll almost surely suspect she'll be used as bait."

"If he does suspect that, will he still try for her?" Pearl asked.

"Maybe, but he'll be very, very careful, as he is in all things."

"If he knows it's a trap," Fedderman said, "why will he enter it?"

"If a rat's starving, it will go for the bait in a trap," Helen said.

Quinn said, "I think we should take a chance on this one."

"Your call," Renz said. "Your ass."

"I'll approach Myrna with the idea. She isn't as educated as either of her sons, but my impression is she's every bit as smart. If she goes for it—"

"She will," Pearl said. "Smart's got nothing to do with it."

Helen nodded. "There's a certain connection between killer and potential victim, almost a magnetism. Some even say that sometimes the victim is, in subconscious ways, complicit in her own murder. That might prove true in this case."

Quinn wasn't sure if he bought into that one. *Profilers.*

"If she agrees," he said to Renz, "you could set up a press conference, make sure a photo of Myrna gets to the papers and TV news. Use Mary Mulanphy for local cable. Give her a scoop."

"Cindy Sellers for print media," Renz said. *"City Beat."*

"How could we forget?" Quinn was amused by the notion that Renz thought he was using Sellers, when actually it was the other way around.

"Also use that old shot of the Swamp Boy," Helen said. "The one taken in Florida right after he was found."

"Great idea!" said Pearl.

"When he sees it side by side with Myrna's photo," Helen said, "it'll take him back in time and tug at more than his heartstrings. Family photos do that."

Quinn gave both women a look. The ladies were into it.

"Family's the most powerful component in these murders," Helen said. "Family's what serial killers are almost always about."

"What all of us are about in the end," Fedderman said. Wisdom from a disjointed anti-fashion model.

Renz's desk phone buzzed. He glanced at it in irritation,

then snatched up the receiver and punched the glowing line button on the base unit. Said, "I thought—"

Then he shut up and the expression on his face became grimmer and grimmer.

He scribbled something on a piece of scratch paper, then replaced the receiver.

"We've got another Butcher victim. Lower East Side. Name's Maria Cirillo. Neighbors noticed an unpleasant odor coming from her apartment and called the super. The ME's already there, puts the time of death somewhere between five and midnight evening before last."

"Evening before last?" Quinn said.

"You heard me right."

"That's when we had Jeb Kraft in custody," Quinn said. "If he wasn't cleared before, he is now." He stood up to get the address Renz had scribbled on the slip of paper. He could hear Pearl and Fedderman standing up behind him. There was a clatter as one of them, probably Fedderman, knocked over one of the metal folding chairs.

Renz looked up at Quinn. "This is gonna make for a lively press conference." There was a note of real trepidation beneath his mock enthusiasm.

"When we're done at the crime scene," Quinn said, "I'll call and bring you up to speed, and then go talk to Myrna Kraft."

Renz started drumming his fingertips, maybe having second thoughts.

"She'll go for it," Helen said. "Blood calling to blood."

54

He was always alone.

He'd come into the Hungry U a few times before, pretending to listen to the music. Lauri had noticed him because he didn't seem to actually like the music. There he'd sit, handsome in a pleasant sort of way, the kind of guy you didn't notice unless you looked at him closely, and then what was there not to like? He had blond hair, was average height and weight, and looked good in clothes. Lauri thought he was probably a young executive of some sort, or maybe a high-tech wiz with his own company. He looked intelligent. And he looked vaguely familiar, but she didn't know why. Another thing about him was he seemed interested in her.

She brought his second glass of milk over to his table.

"Lunch was delicious," he said, smiling up at her, "but I have no idea what I ate."

"At least you're honest about it," she said, liking his smile. It made him seem more familiar. Then suddenly she had it—he reminded her of Pearl's friend Jeb. That was something Lauri counted in his favor. "Lots of our customers like the food and pretend they're gourmets. Like they know more about food than our cook—chef."

"I know what I like," he said, aiming his smile at her in a way that left no doubt as to what he liked right now.

"People say that about art," she said

He shrugged. "There are all kinds of art. Beautiful women are art."

"I guess they can be."

"You should have said 'we can be.' "

Lauri felt her face flush. To the best of her recollection, Wormy had never referred to her as a woman—much less a beautiful one. Compliments didn't trip off his tongue. "Baddest squeeze" was as close as he'd come.

She cautioned herself. This guy was definitely hot for her, but he was too old for her, possibly way into his thirties. *Look at those crinkly little lines just beginning at the corners of his brown eyes.* But maybe that was what appealed to her— his maturity. Maturity was something Wormy definitely lacked. Sometimes he was difficult to talk with, as if he were in another dimension. Maybe he was. Lauri knew she didn't really understand musicians, didn't hear exactly what they heard, or at least not in the same way. So possibly it wasn't just Wormy's lack of maturity; maybe he was as mature as he was going to get. And the man smiling up at her wasn't *that* old. Crinkly little lines or not, he had nice eyes. They said he was a decent, compassionate person, and eyes didn't lie.

"When you get off after the lunch crowd leaves, maybe we could go have a coffee somewhere."

It took her a second to fully comprehend he was speaking to *her*.

"I, uh, don't get off after lunch. We start getting ready right away for the dinner rush."

"After dinner, then? Maybe a drink."

Should she tell him she wasn't of age, and she might get carded?

Lauri didn't have to think long or hard about that one. *Jump in,* she told herself. *Swim!* Wasn't that why'd she'd come to New York? And Wormy had a club date with the band in

Tribeca. What he didn't know wouldn't make him sing off-key, and if he did somehow learn she went someplace after work and had a drink with a male friend, maybe it would do their relationship some good.

"I think I'd enjoy that," she said. "I get off work at eleven. But I don't even know your name."

"You're Lauri," he said. "I've heard people call you that."

She smiled. "I already knew *my* name."

"My last name's a little embarrassing," he said. "It's Hooker. I'm Joe Hooker."

Lauri was careful not to smile. "I've heard lots more embarrassing names. I knew a girl named Ima Hore."

Not true, but he'd never know. And if it made him feel better about his name, what was the harm?

He laughed. "Yeah, I guess I shouldn't complain. My name happens to be famous, too. Joseph Hooker was a great Civil War general."

"Then you oughta be proud of it."

"Tell you true," he said, "I am."

The crime scene was, as Pearl saw it, exactly like the others as far as potential leads were concerned. The only real difference was the noxious stench of corruption. It was as if this victim had been dead for a long time.

When they got near the apartment, Fedderman paused and drew a small jar of mentholated chest rub from his pocket. He unscrewed the lid, got a dab of cream on his fingertip, and applied it beneath his nose. He handed the jar to Pearl, who did likewise. Quinn refused.

When they entered, Pearl understood the stench. The apartment was stifling, at least eighty-five degrees.

The techs swarming over the place wore white face masks to go with their white gloves, like movie bandits who were the good guys. Pearl envied them their masks.

When she and Quinn entered the blue-tiled bathroom, she

was glad to inhale the menthol. She knew what had happened here. Like the other victims, this one, Maria Cirillo, had been bound and gagged with duct tape, drowned in her bathtub, then disassembled like a helpless doll, her body parts stacked in ritual order in the tub. There was the head resting on its side on top of the severed arms, sunken eyes closed, as if Maria were napping.

Nift was playing with the doll now. He'd removed his suit coat and had the sleeves of his white shirt rolled up, but he was the only one in the apartment not sweating.

"Though you wouldn't guess it now unless you had a trained eye," he said, "this one was a real beauty." He straightened up from where he was crouched froglike by the tub. "Best rack in the house, present company excepted."

"You're in the wrong end of the medical business," Pearl said. "You should be a patient."

Nift smiled, glad to be under her skin.

Standing beside Pearl, Quinn said, "Give us the particulars."

Nift shrugged somehow without moving his shoulders, an illusion he managed to create just with his mouth and eyebrows. "Trauma wound to the head consistent with being knocked unconscious with a blunt object. Tape marks and adhesive traces on her arms and legs, and across her mouth. Death by drowning, then she was dissected with what my guess is were the same instruments—or similar ones—used on the previous Butcher victims. The killer then cleaned her body parts, making them more sterile than any cadaver I ever handled during medical training." He motioned with his head and waved an arm to encompass the tiny blue-tiled bathroom. "It's a wonder he didn't melt her down with all that stuff."

Or she didn't melt away from the heat, Pearl thought.

Quinn glanced around at the cleaning agent containers lying capless and empty on the floor—a shampoo squeeze bottle, a box that had contained dishwasher detergent, bottled hand soap with a plunger, a spot remover bottle. There was an empty white plastic bleach jug on the floor, another upright on the porcelain top of the toilet tank.

"It'd smell good in here if it weren't for Maria," Nift said.

"Don't you have the slightest respect for the dead?" Pearl asked.

"Never had any complaints."

In the afterlife, asshole.

Nift must have read her thoughts. "When we all meet again in the great hereafter, we won't take death so seriously."

There was a sadness in the way he said it that threw Pearl. If violent death could become so matter-of-fact to a cop, how must it seem to a medical examiner? Was crossing the line between life and death more significant than stepping outside to flag a cab?

Pearl looked at the woman in the bathtub and told herself *she* hadn't thought death mundane. Something precious and irrecoverable had been taken from Maria Cirillo. Stolen by a monster.

"Time of death," Nift said, "was around seven P.M. evening before last, give or take a few hours."

More or less what Renz had said.

"Why's the odor so strong?" Quinn asked.

"The air conditioner was turned off, probably by the killer."

"Jesus!" To Pearl: "Go out there and make sure the techs have examined it, then turn the damned thing back on."

Pearl squeezed past him to leave the bathroom and made her way toward the living room.

"My guess is," Nift said, "the killer wanted this body to be found earlier rather than later. They can be home alone for more than a week sometimes before anyone notices, if the conditions are right and the place is tight. So he switched off the air conditioner so Maria would get ripe faster and attract attention."

Quinn's guess was the same, but he merely nodded, then left the bathroom to join Pearl and Fedderman—if Feds was done talking to the uniforms and neighbors.

He wasn't, so they waited for him out in the hall where the odor wasn't so bad. Pearl peeled off her crime scene gloves and hoped Fedderman hadn't used all his menthol cream.

He hadn't, and when Fedderman arrived ten minutes later she dabbed some more beneath her nose.

The three of them walked another twenty feet down the narrow hall, toward some fire stairs, to be out of earshot of the uniform standing outside the apartment door.

"Neighbors saw and heard nothing," Fedderman said. "Mrs. Avarian, old woman who lives in the adjoining apartment, smelled something, though, and notified the super. He let himself in, saw the victim, then backed out and tried not to touch anything. He upchucked on the carpet, though, about six feet inside the door."

"I noticed that," Pearl said, "and assumed it was one of the cops."

"We'll tell Nift to check it," Quinn said, "just in case the victim or killer vomited."

Pearl smiled. "I'll tell him before we leave."

"This victim's the same type as the others, but she followed the last one more closely, and there was no note beforehand to challenge and antagonize us."

"He's changed his MO again," Pearl said. "Even changed his timing."

"More likely this one was a target of opportunity," Fedderman said.

Pearl looked at him, thinking he was a good cop despite being a sartorial disaster. He could be surprising.

"The killer knew we had his brother in custody," Quinn said, "and killed Maria Cirillo then switched off the air conditioner to make sure she'd be discovered soon. His way of letting us know Jeb wasn't the Butcher. He didn't have time to do much research on her. He might have simply latched onto her as she was walking along the sidewalk and followed her home, made sure she lived alone, then killed her."

"Talk about being in the wrong place at the wrong time," Pearl said.

"And having the wrong hair color," Fedderman added.

"And looking so much like Mom," Quinn said.

"I don't know," Pearl said. "Maria's such a good example of type, it could be that she was slated to be his next victim and he moved her time up."

"Either way," Quinn said, "the message is the same—set my brother free."

"Sounds almost noble," Fedderman said.

"Not even close," Pearl told him. She borrowed Fedderman's jar and rubbed more mentholated ointment beneath her nose. "I'm going back in and talk to Nift."

Quinn thought Nift would probably tell her to instruct the SCU team to bag a sample of the vomit on the floor, then who knew how Pearl would react? She was on tilt already, after their visit with the late Maria Cirillo.

He told Fedderman he'd be right back, and then went inside the apartment so he could be there to extinguish any sparks between Pearl and Nift.

Looking out for Pearl was an old habit hard to break.

55

"I often think of all that precious time lost between mother and son," Myrna said to Quinn, "and my own boy Sherman out there somewhere hunted and frightened."

Myrna had more of a southern accent today. It wasn't so much on the edges, and it still dripped pure molasses. She'd been trying to hide it before, Pearl thought, trying to make herself seem as educated as her sons.

She was seated in a wooden chair at the small desk in her room at the Meredith, her body shifted sideways, one elbow on the desk. Her posture caused one of her shoulders to rise sexily so she looked like a femme fatale in an old movie. She was wearing a midnight blue silk robe that made her hair and eyes look darker. Her hair was brushed out so that it appeared longer, a hint of bangs on her broad, unlined forehead. The scent of soap hung in the air, as if she'd just shampooed and dried her hair.

Quinn had left Fedderman to do more legwork at the Cirillo murder scene and brought Pearl with him to the Meredith, thinking the woman's touch might come in handy in convincing Myrna Kraft to act as bait for her son Sherman. Not that they'd use the word *bait*.

"Did your dear son ever try to contact you during all those lost years?" Quinn asked. *Dear.* Pearl saw that Quinn was wearing his compassionate attitude, the one that evoked confidences and confessions, as if he were a priest with the power to heal. While it struck a phony note with Pearl, it might score with Myrna.

"Why, I'd have no way of knowing," Myrna said. "But, yes, something in my heart tells me he tried. Yes, he *must* have tried. Whatever awful things happened to Sherman during that time in the swamp, they must surely have put him in deep shock, as they would any normal nine-year-old boy. I read it was months before he even uttered a word."

"I read that word was *Mother*," Pearl said.

There was no change of expression in the hard, handsome planes of Myrna's face, but something primal moved behind those dark eyes.

"I never read or heard that," she said, "but it wouldn't surprise me that a lost boy's first words would be of the mother he loved."

"It's because you love him that we came to you," Quinn said. "And because he must love you."

Pearl tried not to look at him as he doled out his unctuous Irish charm. Why didn't these people see through such bullshit? But Pearl knew they seldom did.

Seldom, but sometimes. When Quinn encountered someone not so unlike himself.

"He must indeed," Myrna said, "and in a sense I suspect I failed him. All I can say is I did it for Jeb. I was forced to make a mother's terrible choice. I believed so fiercely that at least one of my sons must be saved, and I lived my new life according to that belief. Tell you true, in those days and beyond, there wasn't anything I wouldn't do for that boy. It was like he was both my sons become one."

"Do you still feel that way about Jeb?"

"I'd have to swear I do."

"And now God's given you a chance to help your other

son," Quinn said. He walked over and sat perched on the desk, so Myrna had to look up at him, into his sincere gaze. "I shouldn't tell you this, and certainly I'm not referring to myself or Officer Kasner, but you're correct in your fear that some nervous trigger finger might twitch and take Sherman's life. The police are human, after all, and this killer has taunted them. Most of us act as professionals, but as in every profession, there are those who have their own agenda."

"I do understand," Myrna said. She hadn't blinked in the force of Quinn's charm attack.

Quinn persisted. "Hard as it might be for you to believe, you and Jeb aren't the only ones who want to see Sherman taken into custody unharmed. He's a sick man—to you a boy still—and he desperately needs the proper treatment."

Myrna gnawed on her lower lip for at least a minute. Then she sat back in her chair, stared down at her lap, then back up at Quinn. "Explain exactly what you'd expect of me."

"Of course. We want you simply to remain in your room here as if you were an ordinary guest at the hotel. You won't see us, but we'll be there and we'll have you under our protection at all times." His smile was incongruously beatific on such a rough looking man. "We'll be your guardian angels."

"My angels haven't always been on duty in the past, Detective Quinn."

"We're more professional and closer to the ground," Quinn said. "I promise you'll be safe."

"Oh, I'm not so worried about myself. No woman fears her true son. But you must know how smart Sherman is. Won't he be suspicious of such a plan, especially if I stay here holed up in my room?"

"If he knows where you are and loves you enough," Quinn said, "he'll try to reach out for you."

"Or if he hates me enough," Myrna said. "That's what you really think." For a second it seemed she might actually cry. "Oh, how you must see me . . ."

Quinn gently patted her shoulder. "I don't think, dear,

that your own true son would hate you after all these years. And you won't be strictly confined to this room or even this hotel. You should go out, just as anyone might who's visiting New York. Shop, sightsee, walk about, take a cab. You'll be safe out there. Your angels, invisible to you or anyone else who might be looking, will be with you every step."

"You mentioned shopping," Myrna said. "Will I have a shopping allowance?"

That brought Quinn up short, and he almost stood up from where he was perched on the desk. *What kind of woman is this? What kind of wheels turn in her mind? Her own son might be stalking her to kill her, and she has her sights set on sales and merchandise.*

"She should do a lot of shopping if her movements are going to appear normal," Pearl said, pitching in. To Myrna: "You're a woman in New York. Even under the circumstances, it would make sense that you'd shop."

If you were a homicidal psychopath with your own sick reality.

Quinn settled back down and gave Myrna the old sweet smile. "Of course you'll be given money to shop. At taxpayer expense. That's only fair, because in the end you're doing this for the taxpayer as well as for Sherman, for other people as well as yourself."

"Something else I want's a gun," Myrna said.

"We'll be protecting you, dear."

"Oh, it isn't for self-protection. It's to protect Sherman."

"But you'd use it if you had to in order to protect yourself," Pearl said.

Myrna gave her a cold glance that made Pearl wish she hadn't spoken. She and Myrna understood each other too well for comfort. Monster slayer and monster—was there that much difference once the battle was joined and blood was spilled?

"I'll see that you have a small handgun to keep beneath your pillow," Quinn said.

"I spent my girlhood and much of my womanhood in or near the swamp, Detective Quinn. I'd be most comfortable with a shotgun, as I owned one as a youngster."

"A shotgun . . ."

Myrna smiled at him in a way that seemed to hypnotize him. "If you think this whole thing is a bad idea—"

"No, no, dear. You can have a shotgun. I'll bring one next time I see you."

"Thank you so much. I'll feel a lot safer for Sherman and for me."

"I don't think it will come to gunfire," Quinn said. "You have my solemn word I'll do everything possible to see that no harm comes to you or to your boy."

"If I do agree, what's the next step?"

"We'll see that your presence in the city is leaked to the media, to make sure Sherman knows you're here. The danger to you would begin late tonight or tomorrow morning, with broadcast news and the appearance of the newspapers."

"The danger to Sherman, you mean."

"To both of you," Quinn said. "We know we're asking a lot of you."

"However much it is, I do agree. I'll do as you suggest."

Quinn smiled widely and patted her shoulder again, this time slightly harder and more reassuringly. "That's the best thing, honestly."

"We're very good at what we do," Pearl said, "and we'll see that you stay safe."

"My uppermost thought is safety," Myrna said, "but Lord knows, not for myself."

Lauri knew she was going to sleep with Joe Hooker. She wasn't sure exactly when she'd decided, and it hadn't been sudden. And she knew it was the result of his subtle but persistent plan of seduction. In small but intimate ways he was moving their still young relationship in that direction; in the quiet way he regarded her, the amusing double entendres, the casual but suggestive touching of her arm, her shoulder, her neck. In a way, that was what fascinated her, watching an older, experienced seducer work, being the object of his efforts and moved inch by inch by him. She knew it was happening, it was deliberate, yet she let herself be moved, *she wanted it,* even knowing it was like drifting farther and farther into a strong current that would inevitably claim her completely. This guy wasn't Wormy, who was usually so wrapped up in his music he didn't seem to know she was around unless he wanted sex.

Sex, music, sex, with little time left over for companionship and tenderness.

It didn't have to be that way. That was what all of Joe's actions, all of his thoughtfulness and smiles, and his slight but unrelenting pressure, were telling her. It didn't have to be the way it was with Wormy.

Not that she wasn't still fond of Wormy. But she was an adult and could have a relationship with more than one man. (Was Wormy really a man?) Wormy was takeout food, cheap weed, and wine, and frantic trysts in his dump of an apartment he shared with two other members of the band who weren't away often enough. Joe promised dinner at nice restaurants, leisurely walks in the park, Broadway plays, and . . . what was inevitable. Joe was a Mercedes. Wormy was . . . transportation.

Lauri feigned a headache and upset stomach after work and didn't go with Wormy and the others to a club in the Village. Instead she walked around the corner from the Hungry U, where a cab was waiting, and inside the cab was Joe Hooker.

When she climbed in the back of the cab he pecked her on the cheek and briefly touched her arm.

"Hungry?" he asked.

She laughed. "I just got off work at a restaurant."

He grinned in the darkness. "I know; I had to ask. If

you're not hungry, you must be thirsty. I know a little piano cabaret where we can have some drinks and talk about my favorite subject."

Lauri didn't have to ask what his favorite subject was. Should she tell him she might be carded?

"They know me there," he said, as if he read her thoughts. Then he added, "So we can get a good table. Besides, I already gave the cabbie the address."

She was wearing jeans and a white blouse with a small floral design. She'd changed from her food-server shoes to heels, though. "Am I dressed okay for it?"

"Beautiful women are always dressed for wherever they are."

She laughed, trying to keep her tone low and sexy. Adult. "You know something, Joe Hooker? You're dangerous."

He glanced over at her as if caught off guard, then smiled. "Spice of life, danger."

"Live fast, die young," she said, not knowing what else to say and finding herself temporarily tongue-tied.

He appeared alarmed. "Good Lord, Lauri, I hope you don't think I'm dangerous *that* way."

Why did I have to tell him that? Hurt him? Why am I acting like such a fool?

She snuggled closer to him in the rocking, jouncing back of the cab as it took a potholed corner. "There's dangerous, and then there's nice dangerous," she said, looking up at him. "You're nice dangerous."

He kissed her lightly on the lips.

They held hands.

56

"Is a photograph truly necessary?" Myrna asked, not very sincerely.

She actually seemed enthralled by the idea that her photo was going to be in the papers and on TV news; but at the same time, she was afraid. Pearl didn't think Myrna was afraid of what she was about to do, of her son Sherman, or what might happen to him. It was more that she'd spent almost her entire life playing down her beauty and avoiding being noticed, and now here she was in New York, wearing the smart gray linen pants suit she'd bought at Bloomingdale's and posing for a news photographer.

Well, Quinn had dropped mention that the man was a news photographer. He was actually an NYPD employee who photographed mostly crime scenes. Still, these photos would find their way into the news.

"You look wonderful, Mom," Jeb said.

He'd moved from the Waverton into the Meredith, in a room on the second floor, to be nearer to his mother. It was Myrna who'd negotiated the deal. Apparently, to Myrna, an agreement merely meant the commencement of negotiations. While they were at the Meredith, Jeb's expenses were also being picked up by the city.

Myrna continued to warm to the proceedings, seated in the small wooden desk chair, swiveling her body, striking exaggerated poses. The NYPD photographer, an acne-scarred, hard-bitten young man with an emaciated body and shaved head, glanced at Pearl and Quinn, then got into the spirit and shot from a slight crouch, giving Myrna a lot of meaningless patter so he could catch her "off guard." Quinn had seen him at some of the crime scenes, glumly snapping his body shots, and thought his name was Klausman. Today you'd think the guy was shooting supermodels in Paris.

Quinn had seen and heard about enough. "I want one taken downstairs on the sidewalk," he said. "Out in front of the hotel."

"A candid shot," said Klausman. "We can pretend we've caught her by surprise as she's entering the lobby." This sure beat photographing corpses. It was fun working with a live woman who moved around and smiled when he said *say cheese*.

Out on the sidewalk, a few people walking past slowed down and stared, wondering what was going on, thinking Myrna might be some kind of celebrity. Myrna seemed to be thinking the same thing.

"My hair all right?" she asked, barely touching it.

"Perfect," Pearl assured her, not mentioning the strand sticking almost straight up like a horn.

"You got some sticking straight up," Klausman said, dancing forward and deftly smoothing back the hair the breeze had mussed.

Myrna glared at Pearl.

"Except for that one strand," Pearl said.

"I can pretend I just got out of a cab," Myrna said.

"Sure," Quinn said to her and to Klausman. *Why not?*

Myrna flagged down a cab and worked her poses, momentarily confusing the cabbie and showing a lot of leg.

That seemed to disturb Jeb. "Better not overdo it, Mom."
She ignored him.

"Say 'Kate Moss,' " Klausman told her, evoking a wide
grin.

"Lord Almighty," Pearl said under her breath.

"I want one of her going into the lobby," Quinn said to
Klausman, watching the irate cabbie drive away, "but I don't
want the name of the hotel to be in the shot."

"Why's that?" Jeb asked.

"We don't want to be sued."

In truth they'd decided not to make finding his mother too
easy for Sherman Kraft. They didn't want him to become
suspicious. It was better to leave it up to him to figure out
which hotel was in the photograph.

There were two low marble steps leading to a weather-
proof carpeted area beneath the marquee. Myrna took them
like a young girl.

"Gotcha! Good! Perfect!" Klausman kept saying, as
Myrna struck one pose after another, moving only slightly
for each shot, like a figure on a film skipping frames. "*You
should* be a model. Gotcha! Okay, that's it. Nope, gotcha one
more time—that'll be the best one, most natural. Really, *you
should* be a—there, one more—model."

"It did cross my mind when I was much younger," Myrna
said.

Jeb silently turned away.

He's embarrassed, Pearl thought. *She's embarrassed him.*

Myrna didn't seem to notice. "How long will it take before they're developed?" she asked.

Klausman was surprised. "No time at all. They're digital." He went over to stand near her. "Here. You can review
them."

Quinn let her *Ooh!* and *Aah!* over the camera's tiny digital display for a few minutes, then decided it was time to re-
take charge of this operation from Klausman.

"Take those back and make sure Renz gets them," he said

to the photographer. "Ask him to call me so I know he has them." He turned his attention to Myrna. "Let's get back up to the room, and I'll give you final instructions."

Myrna nodded. "I like that third one," she said to Klausman.

But Klausman had caught something in Quinn's tone and was already hurrying to his double-parked car. The E-mailed photos should be in the hands of Mary Mulanphy and Cindy Sellers within the hour.

No one spoke as they rode up in the elevator. Jeb went with them, passing the floor where his room was located.

Quinn wondered what Jeb thought of the police using his mother for bait. Did he know what Quinn knew, that a psychosexual killer like Sherman probably wouldn't be able to resist not simply the type of woman who was his usual victim, but the archetype. Mom herself. Every serial killer's dream. A Freudian, or police profiler, might say "wet dream."

Something like this had never happened before in Quinn's career, and it would surely never happen again.

The elevator door slid open and they all strode down the carpeted hall toward Myrna's room. The hall was comfortable but noticeably warmer than the lobby.

Quinn fell back a few steps, watching mother and son. These two, Jeb and Myrna, were tricky. They were both intelligent and used to playing a double game. And they both came from a hard place.

Nothing they said could be trusted to mean or suggest anything. They might be smarter than the police and certainly were more desperate. They were not what they seemed and could misdirect or lull you.

They came to room 620 and Myrna used her key card dexterously to unlock the door on the first swipe.

Quinn rested a restraining hand on her shoulder and moved ahead of her to enter first while Pearl held the door open.

Nobody joked or made a crack about being overcautious.

As soon as they closed the room's door behind them, Myrna went to the window and gazed down at the street, as if to watch Klausman the police photographer drive away.

She absently raised a hand to make sure her hair wasn't too mussed.

"We should have had him take one of all of us together."

57

Killing could stimulate the appetite. The Butcher had finished his breakfast of scrambled eggs, bacon, and toast at a diner over on East Fifty-first Street. He was walking along Third Avenue, using the tip of his tongue to try working a stubborn morsel of bacon from between his molars, when he stopped suddenly in front of a news kiosk.

A brick anchored a stack of *New York Posts* from the morning breeze. The brick, which had a red ribbon tied around it in a bow so that it resembled a wrapped gift, was slightly off center, revealing a color photograph beneath the large caption "BUTCHER'S MOM."

He stood motionless, ignoring people bumping into him, some of them glaring or cursing at him as they hurried on. It took all his effort to move closer to the kiosk and slide the top paper out from beneath the brick.

She looked so young! So beautiful! As he remembered her, only more so. She'd aged as did most truly beautiful women, in a way that made them look simply more the way they'd appeared as young girls, a way that preserved the magic.

The black magic.

Very much more themselves. Every artifice stripped away by time. Very much more themselves.

The ancient magic.

Mom.

Not in grimy jeans or a housedress with her hair a tangle. Not barefoot. Not bloody.

Not nude and bloody and screaming my name. Not dragging a black plastic trash bag across a wooden floor . . . thumping black trash bag. Reaching into it . . . into it . . .

Sam!

Oh, Christ! Sam!

"You gonna buy that or just memorize it?"

Jarred from the swamp of the past, the Butcher stared at the old man in the kiosk in a way that made the man blink behind his thick glasses and back up a step.

"They're for sale, you know," he said in a more moderate tone.

The Butcher tucked the folded paper beneath his arm, then worked a ten-dollar bill from his wallet and stuffed it into the man's hand. He then picked up a *Times* and *Daily News*. They also made note of the fact that Mom was in New York. They also featured at least one photograph and promised more on the inside pages.

What was he feeling, staring at her *Post* photograph? He didn't understand. This beautiful woman who'd given him life . . .

Pride? An insane pride?

Hate?

Rage?

He turned away abruptly and strode toward the intersection, where it would be easiest to hail a cab. He needed to get back inside the protection of his four walls, *safe inside the womb,* to recline in his chair, almost in the fetal position, with a Jack Daniel's over ice, back to where he could read.

No, to where he could look at the photographs, stare at them, etch them with fire into his memory.

Mom . . .

"You want your change?"

He ignored the voice calling from the kiosk behind him.

Too late for change.

He understood now that he hadn't escaped the swamp. He never would.

He walked faster and faster, elbowing people out of his way, and finally broke into a run.

Quinn and Pearl were in room 624, two rooms down the hall from Myrna Kraft's. From there Quinn could observe the street and at the same time stay close to Myrna. Fedderman was outside running things at ground level according to Quinn's instructions. He was in an unmarked car, from time to time changing parking spots, while he kept in touch with Quinn or the undercover cop posing as a bellhop and hanging around the hotel entrance with the real bellhop. The undercover cop's name was Neeson and he hadn't liked climbing into a bellhop uniform. On the other hand, he'd garnered some tips just holding the door open for arriving and departing guests. The last time Fedderman had checked on him, Neeson said he was considering changing occupations.

The bearded homeless man across the street, seated on a folded blanket in the shadow of a building recess and holding a cup, was also NYPD undercover. Probably making a little extra money today, too, Fedderman thought, as he sat in the car half a block down and waited for the overheated engine to cool enough so he could restart it and turn the air conditioner back on.

Two more undercovers were in the lobby, looking like a tourist couple, and another—Officer Nancy Weaver—was hanging around Myrna's floor in a maid's uniform. Quinn had requested Weaver. Pearl thought it was maybe to aggravate her, Pearl, because of her short-lived affair with Jeb Kraft. He'd even mentioned he thought Weaver looked cute

in her maid's outfit. Pearl told him Weaver should change
linens and scrub toilets as part of her cover. (And maybe fasten another button on her maid uniform blouse.)

Fueled by three cups of coffee, Pearl was pacing, while
Quinn sat in a comfortable chair he'd dragged across the carpet so he could sit by the window. A set of earphones was
draped over the back of the desk chair. Myrna's room was
bugged, but she was out now, probably shopping, and being
tailed by the rest of the unit Renz had assigned the task of
protecting her.

As Pearl paced, she thought she smelled stale tobacco
smoke. Every hotel room she'd been in lately smelled as if
someone had been smoking in it. Had New Yorkers been
driven to skulk like addicts or adulterers and appease their
filthy vice in hotel rooms?

"I'm sorry about that Weaver remark," Quinn said.
"About her looking cute. I was trying to make you jealous."
He was addressing Pearl but continued gazing out the win-
dow as he talked.

"You only made it to *annoyed*," Pearl said. "Does it smell
to you like somebody's been smoking in here?"

"No. You're always thinking you smell tobacco smoke
where there is none."

"Maybe I do smell smoke, and you can't because you've
burned out your sense of smell with those illegal Cuban cigars you suck on."

"You're testy. Is it the coffee?"

"It's you."

"What you should do," he said, "is only have relationships with other cops."

We're back on that, are we? "I'm no longer a cop, except
temporarily."

"Bank guard, then. More or less the same thing."

"No," Pearl said. "If I were a bank guard I wouldn't be
here."

Quinn continued to stare out the window, silently.

Pearl figured she'd better set things straight. It wasn't that she didn't feel *something* for Quinn. It was more that she knew *something* about herself. It wouldn't work for them.

Maybe nothing would work for her with anyone. It was easy to think that way after Jeb Jones—Kraft. Her psyche was still bruised and confused. She did know she could no longer trust her emotions. *Build a wall around your heart . . .*

"We're friends," she said. "Colleagues. That's all, Quinn."

"I don't want to leave it at that. Not with you."

If it was supposed to be a compliment, it hadn't worked. "You've got a hell of a nerve," Pearl said.

"I won't give up."

"If you don't mind, I'd like to concentrate on the stalker *outside* the hotel."

Quinn turned away from the window just long enough to smile at her. "I meant I won't give up hope."

"That's your concern," Pearl said, "and none of mine."

"At this point," Quinn said, "I know you're not seeing anyone else."

"Don't be so sure."

He smiled again. Didn't turn his head, but she saw his cheek crinkle up just beneath the corner of his eye. She'd seen that enough times to know he was grinning. Anger rose in her.

"Milton Kahn," she said venomously, as if casting a spell.

Quinn looked over at her curiously. "Who?"

"Never mind. He's nobody you're ever going to meet."

Me, either, with any luck.

"I happen to like my life the way it is," Pearl said. "Once I get back to the status quo."

Did that lie even make sense?

Quinn was silent for a while. "I don't think he'll come tonight," he said. "He's more the sort to take his time."

Pearl knew he wasn't talking about Milton Kahn. "He's also the sort to spring surprises. We seem to have everything taken into account, Quinn, but I still can't shake the notion that this killer might figure a way around us. You ever get that feeling about him?

"Yeah."

Quinn's cell phone, lying on the windowsill, beeped the first few notes of "Lara's Theme" before he snatched it up, pressed it to his ear, and said, "Yeah," again. "Okay, Feds."

He cut the connection and laid the phone back on the sill.

"Myrna's back."

Pearl instantly stopped pacing, sat down at the desk, and slipped the headphones back on.

"I happen to like being a bank guard," she said, with a sideways glance at Quinn.

"Probably the uniform," Quinn said.

No mercy.

58

"You have other things to do all the time," Wormy told Lauri.

They were in the kitchen of the Hungry U, a busy place full of spicy aromas, the blur of motion, the clink and clatter of dishes and flatware.

"Not all the time, but tonight," Lauri said. She was checking on a customer's order of *shahi korma*, wondering what the delay was. She had to have something to tell the man, who was a valued regular, meaning he'd been in the restaurant at least twice.

"Be ready jus' about three minutes," said Jamal, the African American–Pakistani chef.

"Lauri—"

"Really, Wormy, you don't have a title proving ownership of me. Women aren't chattel any longer."

"Cattle?"

"Chattel. It means we don't have to spend every minute together you want to spend, but not a single moment you don't."

Wormy seemed puzzled by her phrasing. Or indignant.

Maybe he was still thinking about chattel. Lauri didn't have time to sort it all out.

"Damn it, Lauri. Ain't any call to be so hard-ass. You know you're my woman."

Jamal, racketing a whisk around in a metal bowl to whip up a sauce, gave him a look.

Not half so withering as Lauri's. "I'm nobody's woman. And you don't have any business in the kitchen, Wormy."

"She be right on that one," Jamal said. "Them two."

"I know what you're doin'," Wormy said, ignoring Jamal. "You're goin' out with somebody else."

"Whee-ooh!" Jamal said.

"If I were seeing someone else," Lauri said coldly, "it'd be none of your concern. You think I don't know about you and your friends, and what goes on at those clubs when I'm not around?"

Jamal stopped with the whisk and looked from Lauri to Wormy.

"That kinda thing's nothin', Lauri. Nothin'! I don't feel about any of those girls the way I feel about you. You're everything in the world to me."

Nodding approval, Jamal began whisking vigorously again.

"You don't act like it," Lauri said. "And that's the operative word—act!"

"Girl's education showin'," Jamal said.

Wormy stepped toward him, the upper half of his body seeming to move much slower than the lower half. "I about had it with you!"

Jamal smiled. "C'mon, I stab you with this whisk."

Wormy took another threatening step toward Jamal, but Lauri stopped him, grabbing his stringy upper arm. "You're going to get us all fired," she said, squeezing hard enough to make Wormy wince.

"Screw that! Sometimes you gotta—"

"And no place in the Village will hire you again to play music."

That gave Wormy pause.

"I don't like what's happenin'," he said, wrenching his arm from Lauri's grip and turning his back on Jamal.

"Nothing's *happening.*"

"*Shahi korma*'s happenin'," Jamal said. "Right there ready to serve an' startin' to cool."

Wormy glared back over his shoulder at him, then said again to Lauri, "I don't, goddamn it, *like* it!"

"Like there's some law," Jamal muttered.

Wormy stormed out of the kitchen, not bothering to check and see if anyone was coming the other way through the swinging doors. Fortunately, no one was.

Lauri picked up the plate of *shahi korma* and placed it in the center of a circular tray, then lifted the tray so it was perfectly level.

"You should be ashamed of yourself," she said to Jamal.

"That Joe guy been around askin' for you," he said, deadpan.

"When?"

"Now an' again."

She carried the tray from the kitchen, careful to go up on her toes and check through the tiny window to make sure Wormy wasn't lurking outside the swinging doors.

No sign of him. But that didn't mean he'd left.

"Ever think of goin' out with me?" Jamal asked behind her. "Shed yourself of that worm man?"

If Wormy was still in the restaurant, Lauri didn't know it. She looked neither left nor right as she bore the *shahi korma* to its table with the regal bearing of a queen.

It didn't take the Butcher long to locate the hotel. The low marble steps, the dark lower edge of the marquee, the glass revolving door set in a wall of brick and smooth white stone—all were like features of a face.

He'd spent a while at his computer, visiting the websites

of New York hotels, before he'd found the right one—the Meredith—and compared it with the newspaper photograph to make sure. It was a mid-priced—which in Manhattan meant merely astronomical—business hotel, with all the amenities to make it competitive. He took a virtual tour of several rooms, as well as the restaurant and coffee shop. Most useful.

Later that day he rode past the Meredith in a cab in order to see it in three dimensions and get a feel for the place. Then he got out and walked around the surrounding neighborhood, terrain into which he might someday have to escape.

It had been only hours since he'd learned this morning that his mother was in the city, and already he knew her exact location. Knowing it somehow made her even more real, more menacing. Her presence haunted him like a specter as he walked the streets, mulling over what to do. Even in a city this size, it was possible they'd pass each other on the sidewalk, perhaps not even glance at each other.

Or one of them might glance. The thought gave him a chill.

He was surprised when he looked at his watch and saw that his research had taken most of the afternoon. Though he wasn't hungry, he had a tuna melt and coffee in a small diner before returning to what he increasingly thought of as his lair.

He did feel somewhat better since gaining the essential knowledge of his mother's whereabouts when she slept. The Meredith Hotel. Now what? Time to practice to deceive?

Not yet. Time to learn more.

He poured a Jack Daniel's, walked to his recliner, and situated himself where he could see out the window at the darkening city. Such a long way from that time years ago in the swamp, but time could be folded like an accordion. More and more lately his dreams carried him back, his nightmares that weren't as horrifying as the actuality that gave them birth. The swamp had invaded his mind and become a part of him, and there were things living and crawling there he didn't want to touch. He thought he'd escaped them but they'd been there all along.

Some nights he lay in bed staring into darkness, terrified of falling asleep. Was it only because of his dreams, or was he feeling the pressure the literature on serial killers proclaimed them to feel as their victim count climbed?

None of us ever escapes.

Perhaps his mother wouldn't escape. The things that crawled in the darkness of his mind crawled in hers.

It had been so long since they'd seen each other, but he was sure they understood each other.

He also understood Quinn.

Of course the Meredith would be a trap. He knew his nemesis, Quinn. He'd followed him, studied him. As Quinn had studied *his* nemesis. They'd crawled into each other's brains. He knew Quinn's mind better than Quinn himself knew it.

Quinn had his own miasma of problems, his own dark swamp. A record of harsh justice and violence, a stained reputation, an alcoholic past, a failed marriage, a troubled daughter, a woman he loved who didn't love him. An insatiable need and talent for the hunt.

None of us ever escapes.

Do we really want to?

There was no doubt in Sherman's mind that his mother was bait, an archangel of evil that had to be slain. That she was being used to lure him to destruction was fitting.

Quinn certainly had to understand that the Butcher wouldn't be able to resist the lure of the very demon he'd been trying again and again to slay, the angel demon that wouldn't stay dead. But Quinn didn't understand Sherman's mother as well as he thought. She was bait, but she was deadly bait. She wanted to kill her son as badly as when she'd tried all those years ago in the swamp, only now she'd be even more determined.

Deadly bait.

Sherman would have to plan carefully. Move carefully. He felt like a spider walking the web of a much larger, much deadlier insect. One that was waiting for him and would sense his slightest misstep. One that could paralyze him with a glance and suck him dry of life even before his heart stopped.

Mom . . .

Nine-year-old Sherman took a sip of Jack Daniel's and told himself things had changed and he was grown up now, an adult. With an effort of will, he ignored his fear and engaged his mind.

He was nothing if not a problem solver.

The Meredith Hotel wasn't precisely a spiderweb. There were different ways to approach it, and different ways to move within it.

Quinn's trap was a problem that could be solved. That *must* be solved.

It was a family matter.

59

Something new. Something exciting.

Lauri didn't get to the Upper East Side very often. She tried not to let it show that she thought Mangio's was one of the neatest places she'd ever seen. She and Joe shared a tiny round table near a wall, away from the small dance floor. A band, guys in matching jackets and ties, not like The Defendants, were playing soft syncopated music that she guessed was rumba. Other than the dance floor, the place was carpeted in plush red, contrasting with the white tablecloths and glinting silverware. The long-stemmed glass from which Lauri was sipping a vodka martini, straight up, was fine crystal that glittered in the light of the single candle in the center of the table. She supposed this was what people called class.

She looked around at the women seated at tables or dancing and was glad she'd worn the dress Joe had bought for her. It had been a gift from an exclusive shop on Madison Avenue and was obviously expensive. Since her father was busy in the evenings he hadn't seen her leave in the dress, which was a good thing, because it might have required an explanation. She really should have her own apartment. Her world was opening up like a flower warmed by the sun. If this thing with Joe continued to work well . . .

"You look happy," he said, smiling across the table. "That makes me happy."

"The only thing that would make me happier," she said, "is if this—being someplace like this with you—would last forever."

"No," he said, "There's something else. I know what would make us both infinitely happier."

She reached across the table and lightly dragged her fingernails over the back of his hand. "Joe—"

"I'm going to teach you how to rumba."

She couldn't control the expression on her face. From the inside it felt like disappointment.

He laughed. "Oh, you thought I meant something else."

"I think we both know what you meant," she said, laughing along with him but still maybe showing her disappointment.

"Maybe you already know how to rumba."

"No."

"You will in five minutes. I have a foolproof teaching method."

He stood up, holding her hand gently by her fingertips and guiding her up out of her chair and toward the dance floor. She found herself having some difficulty walking, which was strange since she'd had only one drink

They weaved their way through the tables and reached the parquet dance floor, which wasn't crowded. His timing was right—the band was only halfway through the rumba number. Joe held Lauri close in dance position, her right arm bent up at the elbow, his left hand clasping her right. His right arm was around her waist, his fingers spread near the small of her back, pressing her into him.

"We'll do a simple box step," he said, his breath warm in her ear. "Follow my lead and you'll pick up the rhythm and hip movement."

He was right. She was soon dancing without worrying about getting her toes stepped on. Then he held her even closer so the rhythm flowed through his body into hers. The experience as a whole was making her light-headed.

"Looser in the hips and we're there," he whispered. "That's good. Great! Great!"

She willed her body to relax as he held her more firmly. Now she had no choice; her body had to sway in precise syncopation with his. Fine with Lauri. She swung her hips freely, feeling his hand slip lower on her back to rest on the rise of her buttocks. She wanted so very much to please him.

"I might be slightly . . ."

"Slightly what?" he asked.

"I don't know."

"You okay?"

"Oh *what*?"

"Kay," he said, grinning.

"Oh. I'm that. I think."

"Very good," he said of her dancing. "Just relax. Trust me and follow my lead."

That was his best advice. He loosened his grasp on her slightly (though not on her rear, so they remained pelvis to pelvis) and she let her body respond to the gentle guidance of his hands and the subtle shift of his body against hers. Her body became even looser, her movements more fluid. She could trust him and relax.

He smiled down at her. "Now you're an expert just like me."

She smiled back at him. (Was he going to get an erection? She would know if he did.)

The music stopped and he kissed her.

The Hungry U, The Defendants, Wormy, were all far away and in a different world.

"Trust me and follow my lead," he whispered again in her ear.

* * *

In the back of the cab she surprised him. It had taken only a brief kiss, the slightest fondling. He didn't think he'd slipped that much ketamine into her martini. Just enough to disorient her slightly, confuse her a little bit. He wanted her to enjoy and remember. Maybe he hadn't even needed the stuff; he'd only resorted to it because time was important here. Maybe it hadn't even kicked in yet. The stuff was actually made for veterinarians to give to cats. Pussy. There was an amusing thought.

Within a block away from Mangio's she had her arms snaked around his neck and the warm wedge of her tongue probed his ear. He felt a tightening in his groin, and her hand was on him as they kissed.

"I don't want to wait, Joe," she whispered in his ear. "I can't wait."

"Your place?" he asked, toying with her, stringing this out to make sure, letting it build in her.

"Can't. I don't live alone. With my father. He's not home now but he might walk in on us."

He grinned, knowing she couldn't see in the dimness of the cab. The desperation in her pleased him. She was disassociating somewhat, not too much. He'd gotten the dosage about right.

She snuggled closer to him. "Might . . ."

"What?"

"Don't know. Can't remember. Don't care. What're you—"

Holding the slender nape of her neck, he kissed her hard on the lips, using a thumb to play with her earlobe. His other hand was beneath her hiked-up skirt, exploring her warm wetness. He felt her respond to his kiss with her lips, tongue, teeth.

"Jesus! I can't wait!" she whispered hoarsely when he released her. "I don't know . . ."

"What?"

"Just don't know . . . Only had one drink."

"You had three, darling. I was counting."

"Three?"

She pressed her body hard into his.

He leaned forward, toward the Plexiglas divider that separated passengers from driver. "Take us through the park."

The cabbie had been there before. He glanced quickly in his rearview mirror then veered right and made a U-turn.

Passing headlights of oncoming cars shuffled the light in the back of the cab and made her blink in mild confusion.

"It will be a slow drive," he whispered

"Have you got something?" Lauri asked, clinging to him.

"Of course," he said. "A condom." He kissed her perspiring forehead, working the hand that was beneath her skirt, manipulating skillfully with his fingers. "You don't have to worry, darling, I'm careful. You've never met anyone more careful."

60

Sherman as usual read the *Times* over breakfast. He'd bought the paper from a vending machine at the corner, inserting his coins and thinking with a smile that the paper should be paying him. After all, he was giving them something to write about that was more interesting than their usual gray wire-service pap. He was selling papers. Every time the circulation of one of his victims stopped, the *Times*'s circulation increased.

The morning was so beautiful that he'd skipped his favorite diner in favor of a small restaurant with green plastic tables outside. Pedestrians walked nearby, just on the other side of the black wrought-iron railing separating the outer sidewalk from the dining area. Beyond them, traffic locked in the morning rush rumbled and lurched forward about ten feet at a time. But the cool morning breeze carried the vehicle exhaust away so it didn't interfere with his appetite, and the sun sent warm rays angling in beneath the green canvas umbrella above Sherman's table.

As he forked in his scrambled eggs and nibbled at his toast, Sherman read in the paper that Jeb, the brother he'd never seen, was a currency trader. Something like family pride crept into Sherman's mind. So Jeb was smart, like his half-brother, and like Sherman made his money in the world of finance. Sherman had made his fortune in tech stocks, systematically getting out just before the bubble burst, and then compounding his wealth by selling some of the same stocks short, cashing in as they plummeted in value. Possibly Jeb had gotten rich during the same wild market volatility. Sherman thought—no, he knew—that heredity meant much more than most people suspected. Heredity was destiny, and impossible to escape.

A gust of summer breeze flipped the top newspaper page, and there was the now familiar photo of Mom climbing out of a taxi in front of the Meredith Hotel.

Sherman stopped chewing and stared at it for a long moment, into the dark eyes above the smiling lips. It seemed to him that the eyes were not smiling.

The photo also made him think of last night in the cab with Quinn's daughter. *Quinn's daughter!* Now Sherman was the one to smile. What would Quinn think if he knew? As he *would* someday know—Sherman would take care of that. As for Lauri, she'd remember last night, what she could of it, fondly. He was sure he hadn't used enough ketamine for her to suspect she'd been drugged, so eager had she been to sleep with him even without a little chemical enhancement. And even if she did suspect, she'd probably forgive him for it. Little Lauri wasn't nearly as innocent as she pretended. How could she be, bedding down with that tall, skinny junkie—the musician, so-called?

After finishing breakfast and paying his check, Sherman scraped his metal chair over concrete, away from the table, and stood up, careful not to bump his head on the umbrella. He felt full and satisfied, and sexually sated from last night, as he strolled toward his apartment. He was expecting a fax from a connection to a connection he had in Atlanta, an architect who a few years ago had found himself in a financial tangle Sherman helped him to escape. The man had later landed a plum job in City Planning and Development. He was not only in Sherman's debt, he was a bureaucratic animal who knew the jungle. More specifically, the New York City archival records jungle.

The disentanglement of the man's financial affairs were of questionable legality, and if revealed would at the least be embarrassing if not ruinous. Sherman expected cooperation.

He wasn't disappointed. As he closed his apartment door behind him he glanced over at his fax machine and saw several messages in the arrival basket. He knew what they were—the 1947 blueprints of the Malzberg Plaza Hotel, which in 1964 was renovated and became the Meredith.

Faxed blueprints of the renovation plans were included.

He removed the pages from the fax machine to confirm what they were, and then laid them out on his desk to peruse later. He'd worked up a sweat walking back from the restaurant, so he decided that before anything else he'd take his second shower of the morning. Besides, he'd noticed earlier that he needed to touch up his blond hair.

His dark roots were showing.

Less then five minutes after showering and applying additional dye to his hair, Sherman was seated at his desk. He was dressed only in his robe and slippers, and was poring over the 1964 Meredith Hotel renovation blueprints. Already he'd formulated a plan. It only needed a bit more time, a little more research and attention to detail.

And, of course, some cooperation, but that would be easy enough to obtain. Even a pleasure.

Problem solved.

No riddle in the mail this time, Quinn. No note. No game. No rattle before the strike.

Only the surprise.

If it weren't so early in the day, he'd pour a generous Jack Daniel's and congratulate himself.

The surprise. The revelation.

When they would share the terrible knowledge.

Maybe, in the few last terrified seconds of her life, Mom would be proud of him.

61

Lauri hoped she'd pecked out the right phone number. She still felt woozy from last night. That would teach her not to drink too much. Or love too much. Three drinks. She remembered Joe telling her that had been her total. There was a lot of last night missing from her memory, but what she did remember she liked.

Joe ... What a wonderful lover he was ... wonderful everything!

Sitting on the edge of her bed, listening to Joe's phone ring and ring on the other end of the connection, another dizzy spell made her sway slightly. Was this what it was to be lovesick?

Three more rings.

She was about to hang up when he answered the phone.

"It's Lauri," she said. "Remember me?"

"Forever. I was hoping you'd call."

"How come you took so long to pick up?"

"I was in the shower. Slept late this morning. I was really tired. Can't figure out why."

She smiled. "Try harder and I bet you'll remember."

"You're right. It must have something to do with why I was hoping it was you on the phone. You sleep okay?"

"Deeper than I ever slept in my life."

"Any regrets?"

"God, no!" She sounded choked. She could see the taut material of her blouse over her breasts vibrating in time with her beating heart. "Now I'm sitting here thinking how much I miss you."

"What a sweet thing to say!" His voice broke with sincerity.

She was glad to know she wasn't the only one with a tight throat. "It's only been nine hours and twenty-six minutes."

"Way too long," he said. He always seemed to know exactly what to say. Unlike . . . someone else.

"We can do something about that," she told him.

He laughed softly. She saw in her mind's eye the promise in his brown eyes, the curve of his soft upper lip. She had his face memorized and wanted the image never to fade away. "Problem is," he said, "I have to take a flight out of town shortly on business. I'll be gone for a few days."

She swallowed her disappointment. Her alarm. Was he brushing her off? Lying? "I could go with you to the airport and see you off." *Don't sound like such a fawning fool!*

"Too late for that. I've already got a car coming." He was silent for a few beats while her heart plummeted. Then: "Lauri, I was thinking of something special for the evening of the day I get back."

"It can't be more special than our last evening together."

He laughed again. "This would be a different kind of special. Dinner at one of the best restaurants I know, the Longitude Room in the Meredith Hotel. It's not the Hungry U but I think you'll like it."

"Will I like afterward?"

"If I have anything to do with it."

"You'll have everything to do with it."

"Not another cab ride," he said. "You deserve better than that. I'll reserve a room. We can wake up together and order room service the next morning."

Her heart was on the rise now, soaring. She was determined to seem calm and sophisticated. "Sounds wonderful." *That was good, not too eager. Very adult.*

"I noticed you have a cell phone. Give me your number and I'll call you when I'm back in the city."

She did, in her newfound calm voice. Her emotions were still whirling, but not so fast. She had a handle on the situation now.

"Don't mention this to anyone," he said. "I don't want any trouble for you while I'm out of town."

"Trouble?"

"You might not have noticed, Lauri, but a certain someone is almost as hung up on you as I am."

"Wormy? I can't see him causing any real trouble. He's not much more than an annoyance."

"You might be surprised."

"Now you sound like my—"

"Who?"

"Nobody. If you think it's wise, I'll keep quiet about us. I'm not the blabbermouth type anyway."

"I know you're not. I'll call you soon as I get back, darling."

"I'll be waiting."

They hung up without him saying he loved her. That was okay. *Darling* would do for now. Lauri wasn't discouraged. She knew something about men. He'd get around to the L word. She'd see to that.

"He'll make you wait," Helen the profiler said. "He's tantalizing you. Stringing out the suspense."

"This isn't a mystery novel," Quinn said.

"He thinks it is. And he's the main character."

"Doesn't the main character usually get the girl?" Fedder-man said.

"He's gotten the girl too many times already," Renz said. He was seated behind his desk, chewing on a dead cigar, maybe trying to get across to them that he obeyed regulations and never smoked when he was in his office, which was a crock. He carefully propped the cigar in a thick glass ashtray converted to a paper-clip container, as if the cigar were burning and he didn't want it to go out. "This is the morning of the fifth day for our Myrna-as-bait operation. Pretty soon I'll have to reassign some people so they can chase down criminals who aren't shadows."

"Smooth move," Pearl said. "It'll go over great in the media if Mom gets snuffed."

Quinn threw a glance her way. They'd all been thinking the same thing, but she had to say it.

"I don't intend to let that happen," Renz said, looking hard at Pearl, "and I don't appreciate the sarcasm."

Pearl said nothing.

"I'll take your silence as an apology," Renz said, after about a minute and a half of nothing but traffic sounds from outside.

Good as you're going to get, Quinn thought. He glanced over warningly at Fedderman, who looked about to swallow his tongue. Fedderman seemed to find nothing in life so funny as Pearl being Pearl.

Renz pressed on. "I came up with an idea. Thought I'd run it past you."

Helen the profiler, who'd been leaning with a bony hand on the window frame, straightened up her lanky body and paid closer attention.

"Let's hear it," Quinn said, shifting in his chair and trying to sound enthusiastic. He reminded himself that Renz was a good cop when he wasn't trying to think too hard. His shrewdness seemed to be confined to his political maneuvering.

"We need to get this psycho off the dime," Renz said. "Get him to bust a move. I think Helen would agree that psychologically he needs some kind of jolt."

"Sort of maybe," Helen said cautiously. She crossed her long arms, an impressive show of muscle and tendon.

"He's feeling the increasing pressure, you said," Renz told her. "Especially now with Mom in town."

"True," Helen said.

"So it might not take much to prompt him into action."

"True."

Quinn was thinking that so far he hadn't heard an idea, hoping Pearl wouldn't point that out. He glanced over at her and she favored him with a razor-thin smile. *Mind reader.*

"I think we need to use the media again," Renz said. "Just a short piece about Myrna still being in town, along with a photograph. It could be taken in an interrogation room, or maybe even in this office, and we say she's given a deposition, quote her as pleading with her wayward son to give himself up."

"Nothing new so far," Quinn said, getting impatient and also figuring he might beat Pearl to the punch. He could almost hear Pearl ticking.

"You'll be standing over Myrna," Renz said to Quinn. "Maybe with your hand on her shoulder, and you and she could be looking into each other's eyes. Drive our sicko killer wild."

"Hint at a romantic attachment?" Pearl asked.

Renz nodded. "You got it. Hint broadly."

Fedderman rubbed his chin thoughtfully, his white shirt cuff just beginning to come unbuttoned. "Myrna's still a good-looking woman," he said. "It'd be easy to believe an attachment."

"Maybe you should be it," Pearl said.

Fedderman looked aghast. "I'm hardly in her league."

"Such modesty, when it's convenient. Other times you're Brad Pitt."

"It's Quinn he hates," Helen said. "Quinn is his great nemesis, maybe even the lost father figure who deserted him. Our killer simultaneously hates and respects Quinn."

Many do, Pearl thought.

"So he's all the more likely to respond," Renz said.

"It's possible he'll respond with an oedipal rage," Helen said, "vented at his mother rather than Quinn. When it comes to people he loves, hates, and fears, all at the same time, Mom's at the top of the list. It's Mom he's repetitiously killing."

"Isn't this all getting way too complicated?" Pearl asked.

"Maybe not," Fedderman said. "We're dealing with a complicated psycho."

"It'll all seem simple when the cuffs are clicked on him," Renz said. He stuck the dead cigar back in his mouth.

"Or a bullet brings him down," Fedderman added.

"I di'n' hear 'at," Renz said around the cigar.

Quinn wasn't sure he liked this at all. Still, if it might work . . .

He glanced over at Helen, who was idly rocking back and forth simply by flexing her long muscles, looking more like a decathlon champion than a psychologist. He knew her background. She wasn't just Helen Iman, NYPD. She was Dr. Iman, Psy.D. The expert in the room.

She caught him looking at her, misreading him. Maybe.

"Have you ever secretly thought of sleeping with Myrna Kraft?" she asked him.

"If I were a spider."

Pearl was silent.

There was a mood in the office no one quite understood.

Renz removed the dead cigar from his mouth. "So whaddya think?" he asked the room in general.

"I think it's a brilliant idea," Helen said. "But be ready for whatever you wake up."

62

The sun cleansed, purified, burned away whatever festered and gave pain.

At least for a while.

The Butcher sat on a bench at the Seventy-second Street entrance to Central Park and tilted his face up to the warm sunshine. He'd dreamed again last night and had been in no mood for breakfast this morning. He was tired from lack of sleep, and there was a sour taste beneath his tongue that persisted no matter what he did.

Not that he couldn't shrug off his dreams when he was awake.

Not that he couldn't at all times differentiate dreams from reality.

Except during his dreams, of course.

He almost shivered with the chill he felt even in the warm sun.

After his morning shower, he'd taken a walk, thinking that might stir his appetite and then he'd stop somewhere and have at least orange juice and coffee. And of course he wanted to read the morning *Post* he'd picked up at a kiosk during his stroll to the park. He was always interested in what the media had to say about the killer who so baffled the police and intrigued the public. Even the grand gray lady, the *Times,* the paper of record, sometimes ran news items on the Butcher, and right on the front page, above the fold.

Sherman smiled up at the sun. He'd found fame, in an anonymous way. Had he always sought fame? Or had it only been after he'd begun to act on what he'd known, what he'd felt?

He cautioned himself that it could be dangerous, this hunger for publicity. It was a hunger that at times consumed its own compulsion. Sherman had read the literature on serial killers and knew as much about them as Quinn. Well, maybe not that much. Quinn had actually met serial killers, whereas Sherman merely . . . *was one.* His smile broadened and he almost laughed out loud, sharing the joke with the sun.

He was still tired and his legs felt heavy, but he was definitely feeling better. He'd sit here a while, read the paper, and enjoy the day in its full and early bloom. After glancing around the park and then out at the busy avenue, he drew his reading glasses from his shirt pocket, slipped them on and adjusted the frames at the bridge of his nose, and opened the paper in his lap.

Ah! Interesting.

He leaned over the paper, peering at the photograph on page two. Not merely interesting. *Astounding!* Mom and Quinn, in some kind of room, perhaps an office. Mom was seated at a table, a sheet of paper before her, and a pen in her hand. Quinn was standing close by, just behind her, his hand resting gently on her shoulder near the curve of her neck. She was staring not at the paper or camera but up into Quinn's eyes.

And the way he was looking at her!
How dare—

Sherman felt a cold, cold pressure just beneath his heart. He closed his eyes and waited until it went away before he looked again at the photo in the *Post*.

Now he smiled. Making himself arrange his facial muscles at first, but then the smile became genuine. Reason had supplanted emotion.

This photograph was obviously a trick. He laughed out loud, a kind of strangled giggle. Quinn! He didn't hate him, didn't want to kill Quinn. After all, he'd chosen Quinn. And Quinn hadn't let him down. Sherman laughed again, this time in admiration at the wiliness of his opponent. The old "Killer's Mother Signs Statement" trick, but with a twist. Wonderful! Audacious! Mom as bait while having an affair with the lead detective. All a lie, of course. Quinn had come up with something new, something innovative, that could be added to all the other misdirected claptrap written and spoken about serial killers and their mothers.

Misguided and unhappy professors in musty classrooms or lecture halls half full of bored students, TV chatterhead pop psychologists mouthing the tired phrases of others, spoon-feeding pap in sound bites to the millions, what did they know? Who were they to presume?

Well, let Quinn be smug for a while. Sherman knew better. Who was this asshole detective really? And how innovative *was* he? Did he think he'd invented flush toilets or the forward pass?

He realized he was clenching his jaw. *No anger. No need and no reason for anger.*

Sherman knew the police were getting anxious, wondering if he'd actually rise to the bait and confirm their cleverness. *They* were the ones feeling the pressure. *They* were planting staged photographs in the newspapers. *They* were the sources of amusement being laughed at for their futility. *They* were the ones lost in the swamp.

As he stood up from the bench, he folded the newspaper,

then walked over to a nearby trash receptacle and dropped it in with the rest of the detritus of humanity.

Then he began to walk, still not hungry.

Around two that afternoon he fell asleep in his recliner and dreamed of Quinn and Mom gazing at each other . . . that way. Of them doing other things. Of Sam Pickett and the sounds that had come from Mom's bedroom, the squeal of the bedsprings and crashing of the headboard against the wall, over and over and over until it became like distant thunder that wouldn't quit, that wouldn't allow peace or safety, that remained fear on the horizon.

The squeal of the bedsprings!
The squeal of the bedsprings!

There was no way to stop it, or to stop the distant thunder from moving closer and closer.

The past threatened like a summer storm, roiling the darkness of his mind, and other sounds and images rose unbidden to the surface of Sherman's memory: the lapping of black water in moonlight, the persistent droning of insects, the smooth dark movement in shadowed glades, the shrill scream of the power saw cutting through—

The squeal—

The storm grew in intensity and roared in on him like a hurricane.

It gathered him struggling to its bosom, and he surrendered to it.

He expected darkness when he opened his eyes, but light flooded in through the window. He sat for a while staring out at the city, still there and not a dream, miles of soaring stone and glass and angular stark shadow and bright sunlight. The past was over and gone. Outside the window was the present.

Now! Real!

He swallowed his fear and the bitterness of sleep and dreams.

A trick. The photo in the newspaper looked real but it was a trick.

But the dream echoed and flashed in his mind and Sherman was furious, perspiring, his heart hammering.

Calm, damn it! Calm . . . A trick . . .

He recalled fishing in the swamp, the bait taken, the hook bare. Sometimes a gator would yank at the line, breaking it and sweeping away hook and bait with an invisible awesome power. Quinn would learn there were creatures you didn't fish for. Quinn could never imagine. He'd never been where Sherman had been, or learned the hard lessons. You didn't stalk creatures that regarded bait and hunter as gift and prey.

Quinn could never imagine.

Sherman reached for his cell phone and pecked out Lauri's cell phone number. *Cell to cell, like a living organism.* His heart slowed its pace and he was breathing evenly at last.

She answered on the third ring.

"Hi," he said. "Miss me?"

63

Undercover officer Jack Neeson was playing the bellhop, pansy uniform and all. Shakespeare or whoever the hell had said it was right—life was like a stage and we were all actors. Sometimes Neeson was a bum, sometimes a drug dealer, sometimes a straight-arrow WASP with a smile and a line, sometimes a low-life asshole in the rackets. Always he was a cop.

He was hanging around just inside the entrance to the Meredith Hotel, trying to remember a joke he'd recently heard, when he recognized Quinn's daughter. She was on the arm of a guy in a well-cut blue suit and carrying a white box that looked as if it might have flowers in it. He and the girl made a good match. She was a looker, though still young and not as filled out as Neeson liked them. The guy she was with was a nice enough looking sort, with a medium-size, athletic build and a head of full wavy blond hair worn a little too long.

Neeson figured Quinn might already know she was here. She could even be on her way upstairs to see him.

But she and her date—looked like a date, anyway—made a left turn away from the elevators and walked down the corridor leading to the hotel's pricey restaurant, the Longitude Room.

A date, then. Neeson envied the guy. He recognized Lola, Laura—whatever her name was—from seeing her hanging around Pearl Kasner. Pearl acted like she wanted the girl to scram, but Neeson would have taken just the opposite position, even though the kid wore that glitter thing screwed in the side of her nostril. Why the hell did they do that?

There was a joke about those nose studs, but he couldn't remember that one, either. He maintained a large repertoire of jokes because it helped to keep the memory sharp, which was useful in his work. If only he could remember the damned things . . .

For a few seconds Neeson thought it might be worth calling upstairs and letting Quinn know his daughter was in the building, just in case, but what was the point? The guy she was with must be okay, if Quinn's own daughter was going out with him and could vouch for him.

Movement over by the lobby entrance caught his eye.

Here came a little guy with a carry-on slung by a strap over his shoulder, wearing baggy khaki pants and a black golf shirt, an airline ticket folder sticking up out of his breast pocket like a badge saying, "I am a rube tourist." *Yeah, sure.* He fit the description and like a lot of other men resembled the old photo of the suspect, only he was probably too short. *Way* too short.

Still, it paid to be thorough.

Neeson knew dozens of short guy jokes. His vertically challenged partner had once filed a complaint against him. Neeson was soon transferred out of the precinct. He kept an eye on this short guy checking in, waiting until the man had shooed away the real bellhop, who wanted to carry his bag, and strode off toward the elevators.

Soon as the elevator door closed on the guy, Neeson was at the desk. Getting information fast on these mopes was major in this operation.

The guest's name was Larry Martin. He was from Sarasota, Florida. Neeson used the phone to call in the information to Fedderman, who called back within minutes and said the name and address checked out, and reminded Neeson the suspect was medium height, an estimated five-feet-eleven inches tall. The information on Martin's Florida driver's license had him at five-feet-five inches.

"Didn't look even that tall," Neeson said. "But maybe his legs weren't all the way out."

"I don't follow," said Fedderman's voice on the phone.

"A joke, a joke," Neeson said. He had to struggle not to laugh.

"You're a smart-ass for a bellhop," Fedderman said, and hung up.

Two hours later, Neeson didn't notice Lauri Quinn and her date emerge from the restaurant corridor and walk toward the elevator.

Lauri was tired but happy, and hanging on Joe's arm this time for support as well as show. One of her high heels turned in slightly as she walked. Her date still carried the long white box. A gift he'd promised to show her after dinner, when they were upstairs in the room he'd reserved.

She sat on a small bench for a minute or so, while the elevator made its way down. He still held the white box beneath his arm. She thought he looked amazingly handsome, standing there. The finished product.

Neeson came in from talking to the doorman outside and observed them getting into the elevator but didn't think much of it. They were probably on their way up to the sixth floor to see Quinn, or maybe they were going to a room and the guy was going to be doing what Neeson wouldn't mind doing.

He told himself not to let his imagination run away with him. This was the daughter of one of the shrewdest, toughest homicide detectives the NYPD had produced. Better to get crossways with tyrannosaurus Rex. If the blond guy didn't know that and was going to tap the kid, good luck to him.

Neeson leaned with his back against a wall, almost out of sight over by some potted palms, and paid attention to the other guests coming and going, to the real bellhops hustling to get their bags and stack them on luggage carts. It looked to him like a hard job. Those guys deserved their tips.

Not that they didn't also have some fun. There must be a thousand jokes about bellhops.

Pearl was in 624, the room down the hall from Myrna Kraft's, seated at the corner desk and wearing the headphones again. Not that there was much to hear other than what might be the faint sound of Myrna breathing deeply in her sleep. Myrna had gone to bed and didn't even snore. Which kind of aggravated Pearl, who'd been told that she, Pearl, softly snored, at times.

Quinn was standing at the window again, peering out at the night and using his cell phone to check on positions since their two-ways didn't work worth a damn in the pre-war building with its thick walls. Pearl could hear him talking, but with the bulky earphones on her head had no idea what he was saying. Her back was getting sore from sitting so long, and she was getting bored.

She kept one earphone on and used her own cell phone at her other ear to check her machine at home for messages.

There were two. The first was a reminder of a standing appointment for a mammography next Monday. The second was her mother, berating her for not calling or showing up for her lunch with somebody named Milton.

Milton? . . .

Then Pearl remembered—she was supposed to be introduced to Mrs. Kahn's incredibly eligible nephew at lunch at the assisted living home. Pearl had stood him up, along with her mother and Mrs. Kahn.

Pearl breathed hard through her nose. Damned complications! She didn't need this crap. Not now. Not ever.

Screw it! Screw all of them!

Pearl refused to let her anger rise. She had her life to live. She didn't need coercions and complications from her mother or Mrs. Kahn or her nephew Milton—from any of them, especially her mother. She didn't deserve it and wouldn't put up with it. She felt like spitting out her guilt.

"Something?" Quinn asked, noticing the puckered expression on her face.

"Nothing!" Pearl said.

Screw all of them! You, too!

He turned back to the window and his cell phone.

Sherman glanced at his watch and saw that it was past midnight. Time to move.

He'd used a larger ketamine dose this time, figuring it just right. Lauri had made it okay on the way up in the elevator, and into the room. She couldn't have gone much further without her legs giving out.

She'd slept deeply at first, but now she was conscious again, if barely, seated in a wooden chair, her arms and legs taped to the chair's arms and legs, a rectangle of tape firmly fixed across her mouth. She wasn't going to make a sound. She wasn't going anywhere. She and the chair were one, as if they'd been manufactured together out of a single piece. The white box was on the floor behind the chair, where she couldn't see it.

So far, he was pleased. Everything was falling neatly into place.

Her fearful eyes followed him as he moved about the

room. He thought she'd still be unconscious if she weren't so terrified. He smiled at her. She looked back at him hazily, bewildered. Poor girl. In her mind, time had slipped a cog. Was maybe still slipping. There was so much she didn't understand.

He slipped off his suit coat and laid it carefully folded, lining out, on the bed. Then he removed his shoes and tucked the legs of his suit pants into the tops of his black socks. Her eyes watched him, wondering.

Let her watch.

He swiveled her chair slightly so she could see in through the open bathroom door.

After winking at her, he scooted a second, smaller armchair into the bathroom, placing it just so. Then he returned and from the white box withdrew a nine-millimeter handgun, a key-chain penlight, a long screwdriver, and a large folding knife with a thin blade. He preferred to use the knife, but the gun was an added measure prompted by the fact that he knew full well he was entering a trap.

Though not the way his pursuers anticipated.

The hotel renovation plans had made it simple. Many of the building's original air vents had been retained, and additional ductwork was installed to facilitate air-conditioning. The ceiling vent in the bathroom was twenty-eight by thirty inches, and led to a steel duct that connected to other ductwork, including that for the bathroom vent in the room one floor below and one over, room 620. The rectangular ducts were lined on the outside with insulation beneath three-quarter-inch wallboard, so not only were they spacious enough to crawl through, they would allow for fairly quiet passage.

Sherman stood up on the chair and used his screwdriver to remove the vent cover, then propped the steel enameled grate against a wall.

With knife in pocket and gun and screwdriver tucked into

his belt, he took a long last look at Lauri, whose eyelids were fluttering.

She'd make the perfect hostage, if he needed one. But either way, later, at his leisure . . .

With the brimming confidence of the chosen, he lifted himself into the vent.

64

Lauri opened her eyes wide and watched the dark pants and socks disappear as Joe wriggled his way up into the ductwork.

She was exhausted but able to stay awake—mostly due to fear. That time she'd drunk too much with Joe and gotten sick had stayed in her memory. No way was she going to let it happen again. She'd thought they were not only going to have sex tonight but that it would be something special. He'd told her as much, took her to a swank restaurant, then a hotel room. She didn't want to mess things up by getting so drunk she'd be sick. So before and during dinner, when he wasn't watching, she'd transferred most of the contents of her vodka martinis into her water glass.

Most but not all.

She understood now the missing segments of her memory, her unnatural weariness, her nausea. She'd been drugged, and it wasn't the first time. If she'd consumed all the contents of tonight's drinks, she'd probably be unconscious now.

Lauri had no idea what Joe Hooker was up to, but she knew who he was. She'd heard Pearl and her father mention the Meredith Hotel. And of course she knew what case they were working on.

She decided not to use what energy she had blaming herself and trying to figure out how she got here, how she could have been so naïve. She'd instead use her time and energy trying to get away.

She was taped so tightly she couldn't move her arms or legs even an inch, and there was no way she could use her tongue or jaw movement to work the tape across her mouth loose.

The Butcher was a professional. She'd heard her dad, Pearl, and Fedderman speak of him almost in admiring terms. She shuddered, cold even though he hadn't yet undressed her. That would come later. Whatever his plans, they wouldn't include her surviving the night.

She craned her neck and saw the phone on the nightstand by the bed. It seemed far away.

Desperately she tried to shift her weight, rocking the wooden chair back and forth. Several times she almost toppled, making her catch her breath, but eventually she captured the knack of using momentum to move the chair gradually across the carpet, toward the phone, inch by inch.

And when she got there?

She'd worry about that when—if—it happened.

He was cautious moving through the ductwork, occasionally using his penlight to see ahead of him. Progress was slow, but it wasn't difficult for him to propel himself forward using his elbows and knees. Mainly, he didn't want to make too much noise.

And he didn't. He soon developed the knack of not lifting his elbows and knees, only sliding them and then increasing and decreasing pressure, as he used them to gain traction.

Once he heard voices from below, a man and woman arguing, like a distant radio or TV playing too loud. Another time he heard a phone faintly ring, once, twice, then silence. He reasoned that if he could barely hear these sounds, anyone near them wouldn't be able to hear the slightest of sounds he might make in the ductwork.

While the duct provided enough space for movement, it was still cramped. Confining. No place for someone claustrophobic. Or less determined.

There was some difficulty in quietly dropping to the ductwork for the floor below, but he was careful, bracing with his arms against the sides of the duct so he didn't lower himself too quickly, breaking his fall with his hands. There was no way to change position; everything had to be done headfirst. He began lowering his weight.

Quiet! Knees or toes mustn't bounce . . .

There! Perfect! Hardly any noise at all.

He was just above the sixth floor now, and could see yellow light where bathroom fixtures glowed up through the ceiling grates. His mother's room should be the first haze of light, about twenty feet away. It was late and she should be sleeping. Was she awake, with the light on, afraid of the dark? Of monsters from the past?

Sherman had been holding his breath. He let it out now and began breathing evenly. He wasn't afraid. He was part of the dark. *He* was the monster.

She had created him.

He tucked the penlight into his pocket and worked the screwdriver from beneath his belt, holding it before him as he began squirming again toward destiny and toward the light.

Twenty feet.

Ten.

Blood calling to blood.

He was almost there.

* * *

Down in the lobby, Neeson was saying to the real bellhop, "Did you hear the one about the bellhop who . . ."

It was late, and the bellhop, a middle-aged Asian man named Vam, was the only one on duty. Not that he had anything to do except listen to this red-faced cop tell bad jokes, after each of which Vam would laugh politely.

". . . tip? I thought you said 'trip,' " Neeson said, and grinned hugely.

Vam laughed. "Good. Very funny!"

He was a part-time student at NYU, going for a psychology degree. Neeson interested him in a way the blustery cop wouldn't have liked.

Across the street, in the dark doorway of a luggage shop, undercover officer Frank Weathers, part of the NYPD's Fugitive Apprehension Team, sat on a blanket in his ragged mismatched suit and raised a brown paper bag to his lips. The bag didn't contain a bottle, though; it concealed his two-way, which he could slip up an inch or so out of the bag. The reception wasn't good enough to carry on a real conversation, but he could report in to Quinn and let him know everything outside the front of the hotel looked okay. It was late enough that most of the activity in and out of the lobby had slacked off.

Weathers was tired. He'd been at his observation post for hours and wasn't due for replacement until 3:00 A.M. He bowed his head so his ear was near the mouth of the bag and he could hear Quinn's static-marred reply: ". . . 'Kay.' "

He heard a car engine and glanced to his right. There'd been no need to contact Quinn. Fedderman was approaching in his unmarked.

The car barely slowed as it passed Weathers' OP, and the

two men exchanged looks and slight nods. Myrna Kraft was still safe in her bed.

In her bed, anyway.

Staying in character, just in case he might be under observation himself, Weathers pretended to take a long pull from the imaginary bottle in the bag.

The night was warm, there were roaches on the sidewalk, and Weathers was sweating profusely and itched under the ragged clothes.

He wished he could have a real drink.

65

"Maybe he isn't going to show," Pearl said. She slid one of the earphones back a few inches so she could hear Quinn's reply. He was still at the window, where he spent almost all his time except for when he was pacing restlessly or using the bathroom. Pearl thought he must be feeling the same doubts that had crept into her mind.

Quinn turned away from the view outside to look at her. His face, never a thing of beauty in the conventional sense, was a series of rugged, worn planes that would have put Lincoln to shame on Mt. Rushmore. "You think all of us are wrong?"

"All of us being us two, Feds, and Renz? That's not so many."

"You forgot Helen," Quinn said.

"Yeah. The profiler. I thought you distrusted those people."

"She's got a pretty good track record," Quinn said. He turned back to the windowsill and picked up the cup of coffee he'd made with the brewer that came with the room. He took a sip, regarding Pearl over the rim of the paper cup.

When he lowered the cup and swallowed, it made a noise suggesting that his throat was dry. "Remember Haychek?"

Pearl remembered, though it hadn't been her case. Three years ago, Brian Haychek had killed six women in New York and New Jersey. He also turned out to live in the same building as Helen Iman, had even served with her briefly on the co-op board. "Helen had him wrong," Pearl said.

"She had him right, far as the profile went. She just didn't know it was Haychek."

"Her neighbor," Pearl said. "They knew each other. Helen should have figured it out."

"That's why she didn't figure it," Quinn said. "You can be so close to somebody you don't see them."

"That's awful metaphysical for"—Pearl glanced at the bedside clock—"well past midnight."

"Not at all. It's like you're sitting alongside somebody and observing them from only a few inches away, then trying to identify them from a distance. From so close up, you haven't really seen the symmetry of them, and it can blind you as to who they really are."

"Sounds good when you say it fast."

"It happens all the time. Strangers walk up and shoot someone, or a guy on the next bar stool punches somebody out, and the witnesses can't pick the perpetrator they've been face-to-face with out of a lineup."

Pearl smiled. "You should have been a public defender, tried that in court."

"I guess it is a little theoretical," Quinn admitted.

"Well, what I meant simply and directly is that it's possible the killer is too smart for us again."

"But our—"

"Shh!" Pearl slipped the loose headphone back on.

She kept her forefinger raised so Quinn would be silent, and she listened . . . listened . . .

The sound she heard might have been Allsworth, the veteran cop stationed in Myrna's room. But it was the bedroom that was bugged, and Allsworth was in the suite's outer room, on the other side of Myrna's closed door.

The mikes were sensitive and might simply have picked up Myrna stirring in her sleep, turning over in bed, bumping an arm against the headboard. But Pearl was familiar with those sounds. What she'd heard hadn't been any of them.

What she thought she'd heard.

Finally she began to breathe again. "I thought I heard something, but it was nothing."

"I heard it, too," Quinn said. "I think it was a vent or pipe rattling in the wall. What I was about to say is that our killer will show because of the woman in the room down the hall. This kind of compulsion doesn't have anything to do with IQ."

"Get me some coffee," Pearl said, "and I'll agree with you."

She watched Quinn cross the room, then adjusted her headphones and leaned again over the desk. It was difficult to concentrate, listening to nothing. Difficult just to stay awake.

Gifted criminals, she thought. There weren't many of them, but they could be hell.

66

Quietly . . . This had to be done so quietly.

He lay on his stomach in the duct and peered down through the vent cover into the dimly lighted bathroom. He could see an angled slope of white plastic shower curtain, falling away, a corner of a marble vanity top like the one in his own room, the pattern of the off-white tile floor.

Undoubtedly there would be someone standing close guard over Myrna, but they wouldn't be in the bedroom with her. They'd have the suite bugged, though, and the slightest irregular sound would bring them running. Almost certainly Quinn himself was somewhere nearby, controlling the surveillance, maybe in another room on the same floor, listening. Sherman hoped so.

Of course there was always the possibility that Mom's bedroom was unoccupied, that the bait wasn't actually in the trap.

No, that would be risky for them. He might somehow tumble to it and bolt without making a try for the prize. After everything that had happened, they wouldn't chance that. They were too smart.

He smiled and reassured himself. They were the way God made prey animals, just smart enough and no more.

Sherman turned his head, pressing his cheek against the steel grate of the vent cover, and lay listening.

Silence. Complete silence.

Then, very softly, someone breathing. The slow, steady rhythm of deep sleep.

His heartbeat kicked into high and he heard his blood rushing in his ears. For a moment he felt light-headed.

She was there. Like the queen in her nest.

He could *feel* her presence nearby.

He pressed his cheek harder against the cool steel and was surprised to find himself crying.

A tear worked its way through the grate and he heard it strike the tile floor.

It did nothing to lessen his resolve.

Sergeant Al Allsworth was twenty-six years on the force and had done this kind of duty before. Ten years ago, in a Times Square hotel, he'd taken a bullet for a state witness and preserved testimony that helped to put major organized crime figures in prison.

Fifty-one years old now, Allsworth wasn't regarded as a genius and would never advance far in the NYPD, but he had a rarer and more valuable commodity than intelligence. He was one hundred percent certified reliable, a cop in every cell of his body. He would do his duty and would preserve Myrna Kraft's life even if it meant giving up his own. That was what he was about and he was respected for it.

Allsworth sat now on the small sofa in the anteroom of Myrna's suite, a *People* magazine fanned cover-up over his knee. He was a big man, bald but for a dusting of buzz-cut gray hair around his ears. He had bunched muscles, a stomach paunch, and a slab-sided face with a thin scar that ran through both lips near the right corner of his mouth.

His eyes were half closed but he was nowhere near sleep. The only light in the room was from the reading lamp on the table beside him. His uniform tie was loosened, as was the top button of his shirt, and his eight-point cap lay on the nearby table, alongside a half-full coffee cup.

Allsworth thrived on caffeine on this kind of duty; it was what kept him awake and alert while he was in the stand-down-but-aware state that every cop on steady stakeout duty learns to accomplish. He drank his coffee black and was on his second pot. The room reeked of overheated stale coffee, but he was used to the acrid aroma and didn't notice.

It seemed he wouldn't notice if a gunfight broke out in the room, but the part of Allsworth that listened was somehow made more alert and sensitive by the reduced activity of the rest of his body. He looked like a weary, middle-aged cop of the sort who might help lure a kid's cat down from a tree, gone somewhat to seed and slumped almost dozing on a sofa, but Allsworth was much more than that.

He was ready.

Shifting her weight back and forth violently, Lauri managed to work the chair she was bound to across the carpet until she was within a few feet of the nightstand by the bed.

Now what?

She couldn't reach the phone, but her fingers weren't taped together, so maybe she could maneuver the chair around so she could clutch the cord and pull it closer.

It was slow, difficult work, making her perspire heavily, which at least somewhat loosened the tape. And it was delicate work, because if she didn't manage enough control over her movements, the chair would tip over and she'd never be able to right herself.

Finally she managed to angle the chair correctly, then she worked desperately to move it the final six inches she needed if she might touch her fingertips to the tantalizingly dangling cord.

Each time the chair tipped toward the phone, she scissored her right middle finger and forefinger. She felt the tips of the fingers brushing the cord. One more rocking motion might be all she needed.

She held her breath, and shifted her weight to tip the chair as far back as she could without falling.

Now forward.

She felt the cord *between* her fingers and brought them together hard and held them, gripping the elusive cord.

As the chair's momentum reversed and it began to tip back the other way, she worked her fingers so the cord was wrapped partly around one of them.

Something wrong!

She knew immediately that in her eagerness to draw the cord closer and hold it, she'd thrown her weight back and to the side too vigorously.

The chair was tipping too far.

Toppling.

Oh, God! Falling . . .

Turning!

She clenched her eyes shut and bumped her shoulder and head on the floor as the chair swiveled on one rear leg and hit hard on its side.

But she'd held on to the cord. In fact it was wrapped even more tightly around her forefinger.

She remembered a brief dinging sound as she'd fallen, and knew what it meant. She'd pulled the phone off the nightstand. The receiver had bounced out of its cradle and was lying on the carpet. Her shoulder felt broken. Her head ached and throbbed, but she could move it to the side and see the phone's base.

The problem was that it was at the other end of the chair, near her feet.

Lying in a seated position on her left side, she struggled

to move her left foot closer to the phone. The force of her fall had caused the tape to loosen even more, and she managed to clench her toes and wriggle the foot until she'd worked off her left high-heeled shoe.

It was a small accomplishment, but now she didn't feel completely helpless. She had a real shot at alerting someone to her plight, at getting free. She had actual hope.

She adjusted position to take as much weight as possible off the left chair leg and dug her toes into the carpet.

It took her several minutes to find the technique that would let her edge her taped nylon leg over near the phone's base. The way she was lying she couldn't actually see the phone's keypad, but she could reach it with her heel.

Drawing a deep breath, leaning her upper body as hard as possible into the carpet, she fought the pain in her shoulder and used her nyloned heel to press again and again on the phone's keypad.

Though it wasn't likely, she told herself she might coincidentally tap out a number that was valid, that would somehow summon help. The numerals nine and one, she remembered, were diagonally opposite each other on the keypad, so she tried to adjust each press of her heel to increase the chance that she'd hit the right keys. After a while, she moved her heel in patterns of three with a pause between each effort. *Nine-one-one.*

She hoped.

As she fought her bonds and pain and the cramping of her muscles, Lauri wondered what the odds were that she'd actually reach the emergency number with her thumping heel.

She decided they were long enough that they didn't merit thinking about, but they were the only odds she had so she went with them.

In room 624, Pearl leaned slightly forward, rested a fingertip on her right earphone, and smiled.

"What's funny?" Quinn asked. He'd dragged one of the upholstered armchairs over to the window and was slumped in it with his legs extended and crossed at the ankles.

"She snores," Pearl said. "Not very loud, but at last she snores."

"So what?"

Pearl looked over at him, thinking he'd better not mention that she also snored, though not very loud. Quinn seemed to know what she was thinking and looked away. Did the bastard smile?

"It isn't fair," Pearl said, "that somebody looks like Michelle Pfeiffer and snores and men think it's sexy, but when other women snore it's a turn-off."

"Myrna Kraft doesn't look like Michelle Pfeiffer."

"I wasn't talking about Myrna Kraft, I was talking about Michelle Pfeiffer."

"It isn't fair," Quinn said, "that somebody looks like Michelle Pfeiffer."

God, we're getting tired. Too tired.

He stood up from the chair, stretched, and worked his arms back and forth to get up his circulation, then stepped over to the window to observe the dimly lit street below with its sparse vehicular and pedestrian traffic that never disappeared altogether. New York at night.

"Looks innocent enough out there," he said, not turning around.

"We know what that means."

"Uh-huh." Quinn glanced at his watch and sat back down.

Pearl thought they were probably wasting their time, but she knew better than to say so.

Four floors beneath Quinn and Pearl, Jeb Jones sat in a chair he'd moved over to his window. He was watching the homeless man across the street. The police had allowed Jeb to be in the same hotel as his mother, but they didn't want him to be any part of what might happen if Sherman came calling. They wanted him out of the way.

Jeb wanted to be here. As far as he was concerned, he had every right to be here. He'd pretended to go along with the idea that he wanted to be nearby so he could comfort his mother only *after* Sherman had been captured. But only pretended.

He already knew the route he'd take to her room four floors above his own. Out his door, turn left, and run up the stairs. There was a cop on the sixth-floor landing, but Jeb knew that if Sherman was thought to be near his mother all of the cops would converge on her room as fast as possible.

Jeb would be right behind the cop on the landing.

The key was the homeless man across the street. His clothes were ragged and he was seated on a blanket in a dark doorway, slouched backward against the closed door, his head bowed as if he were sleeping. There was a begging cup on the corner of the blanket, but Jeb knew the man wasn't a beggar. He was an undercover cop.

Jeb had even seen the beggar speaking into a brown paper bag that was supposed to contain a bottle, and once he was sure the man had used a cell phone.

Like all the cops in and around the hotel, the beggar would get the word as soon as something was happening. They were all in touch with each other, ready to act in unison, ready to converge like a trap springing closed. The beggar was a tooth in a trap's jaw.

The beggar who was a cop.

The instant he moved, Jeb would move.

67

Working only by light filtering in from below, Sherman slowly and quietly used the blade of his long screwdriver to begin prying loose the grate covering the ceiling vent. He knew it was held by a large screw at each corner of its steel frame. Experimenting with the vent cover in his own room, he'd learned he could pry out one side, then move the cover back and forth so the two opposite screws would bend and work as makeshift hinges.

But he wouldn't use them as hinges more than once. They'd soon break anyway.

After prying loose the nearest side of the vent cover, he delicately removed the loose screws and worked them into his pocket. Then he twisted his wrist while holding the partly lowered grate, extended his other arm, and loosened the first of the bent screws, catching it so it wouldn't drop to the tile floor.

Carefully he removed the remaining screw with his fingers, clasping the steel vent cover so it wouldn't drop.

He deftly put the screw in his pocket with the others and held the cover with both hands. He rotated it diagonally so he could lift it and place it on the bottom of the duct, on the far side of the vent where it would remain out of his way.

The white tile floor of the bathroom was just below him now, easily accessible. All he had to do was lower himself carefully headfirst from the duct, catch himself with his hands, then land silently in his stocking feet on the tiles.

He poked his head over the opening and then down into the bathroom. The door was open about six inches to allow illumination to spill into the bedroom, a night-light so Mom could find her way if she had to get up during the night.

He lay silently waiting, wanting to make sure the slight sounds he'd made hadn't been noticed. With the vent cover removed he could hear Mom's light snoring. Good. He hadn't disturbed her sleep. Or was she pretending? He knew she of all people wasn't above pretending.

He'd come this far, so he forced himself to take the time to be careful. He continued to lie motionless, listening to hear if there was any sound other than Mom's soft snoring coming from the bedroom. Watching to see if a light appeared on the other side of the door.

The judgment and the blood were near. It would soon be time to act.

He wasn't even thinking about what might come after. His knife was a silent killer, and he would simply leave quietly the way he'd arrived.

If something went wrong and he couldn't get near enough to use the knife, he'd use the gun, then make his escape back into the bathroom, leaving the door locked behind him to slow down his pursuers just enough so he could climb back into the ductwork. He would lay the vent cover over the opening and they might not even notice he'd escaped that way. Not at first, anyway, and he only wanted to divert and delay. That was the heart of his secondary escape plan—divert and delay. Once he made his way back to his room and down out of the ductwork, he would replace the vent cover. After that he would improvise. And, if necessary, use his hostage. If the police thought this was going to be a suicide mission, they'd learn otherwise.

For Sherman there was only the firm belief that the next few minutes would go exactly as planned.

And the desire that was like pain.

He'd wait a few minutes while he managed to stop breathing so hard from the effort and tension of working with the heavy steel vent cover. He had the situation under control now. He simply wanted that control to be complete before the next step.

Or maybe he wanted to savor the moment, the anticipation. This was an opportunity he'd never dreamed would come. Of course he was breathless with anticipation. Who among those who understood could blame him?

Mom, just on the other side of a door partly open.

Mom!

He was, after all these years, surprised to be so close to his mother.

68

In the lobby, Gerald Goodnight, the aptly named night desk clerk, noticed the switchboard blinking. Not a regular, steady blink, but intermittent and frantic.

Probably nothing to get excited about. The switchboard had the high-tech heebie-jeebies and was always sending crazy signals. The blinking would probably stop soon.

It wasn't a real switchboard, but a simulated one on the computer screen. Goodnight, a tall, gray-haired man with a receding chin and a drinker's bulbous red nose, had been at the Meredith for more than ten years. He didn't drink, and for that matter didn't sleep well, so his looks and his name were both deceptive.

Goodnight was, however, good at his job. He was diligent and provided the deft touch of inoffensive snobbery the management desired.

His diligence was the reason why he was about to walk over to the computer and check to make sure all the wake-up calls for the coming morning had been entered correctly. Even though it was years ago, he remembered well the apoplectic anger of a wealthy corporate type who'd left a wake-up call for his room at 8:00 A.M., and received it just before he'd checked out in a rage in the P.M. He'd later tried to sue the hotel because he'd missed a crucial business meeting across town. The Meredith had settled with him and avoided litigation. Goodnight thought the man should have backed up his wake-up call with his own travel alarm clock or even wristwatch alarm. That was what Goodnight always did. He knew about hotel staffs.

It wasn't the first time he'd worked at a hotel in cooperation with the police, either. The last time, the undercover cops had been easy to spot, like actors in a bad gangster movie. But he had to admit these people were good. The phony doorman looked genuine, and the cop pretending to be a bellhop had even managed a few tips. Goodnight had told the guy if he ever needed a different job to drop by. The guy had given him a cop look, and Goodnight knew the man was already in the right business.

The switchboard light was still flickering.

Goodnight thought it would be a neat idea to send the bellhop cop upstairs to see about the blinking phone connection. He could scare some rowdy kids or an unruly guest. But he knew that was only whimsy. Riley the genuine bell captain was the one to handle it.

The phone was in a room on the floor above where the woman the cops were guarding was staying; and this kind of thing happened all the time at most hotels. It would be kids, probably, playing with the phone. Or a drunk. Maybe a violent one. If that was the case, Riley could call down and the cops would be there in seconds. If they'd bother with such a thing in the middle of their important assignment.

As if sensing something was wrong, Riley looked over at him from the bell captain's station. Goodnight gave him an almost imperceptible nod, and Riley ambled across the thick carpet and over to the desk.

Riley was a big man with a bear walk, in his sixties but still strong and fit. He was of good humor but had a combative disposition if necessary. While in the Navy he'd been third ranked in the fleet heavyweight boxing division. He was confident he could handle anything that came up in the hotel, and the hotel had confidence in him. This was why he'd held the difficult position of bell captain for more than seven years.

Riley's only flaw as bell captain, as far as Goodnight could discern, was that he thought he had a sense of humor. He was the only one who thought that. He could be trying.

"We've got a blinker on the seventh floor," Goodnight said, motioning with his head toward the computer monitor, visible in the alcove behind the desk.

"Want me to send my new bellhop?" Riley asked, throwing a glance in the direction of the undercover cop in his bellhop uniform. He knew the cop bellhop—Neeson—also thought he was a funny guy, and saw him as competition. Maybe someday they could have a laugh-off.

"Don't try to be funny," Goodnight said. "Just go upstairs and see what the problem is."

"Probably the phone," Riley said. "They act up when the moon's full. Something to do with the tide. I mean, the same gravitational force only on electronic stuff."

"Are you serious?"

"No," Riley said. "It's probably kids. That's what it usually is. What's the room number?"

"Seven-twenty-four. Guest's name is John Brown. It's a single."

"Or was when he checked in," Riley said. "Did you know there are more Browns than Joneses?"

"Yes," Goodnight said, though he neither knew nor cared. Nor was it any of the hotel's business if the man had checked in under a phony name, as long as the guest paid cash or had secured credit.

"We'll charge him for a double only if she's ugly," Riley said.

Goodnight ignored that one. "I don't have to tell you not to tromp around up there and make a lot of noise that might disturb the other guests."

"You did tell me," Riley said. "And just in time. I have my harmonica with me."

"Harmonica?"

Riley grinned. "A joke, George."

Goodnight shook his head. "Harmonica. The moon."

"I was trying to be funny," Riley said, accepting the pass-card master key Goodnight handed him.

"Stop trying," Goodnight told him. "Really. It's sound advice. Stop trying."

He could see Riley's shoulders quaking with laughter as the uniformed bell captain strolled toward the elevators. The dancing fringed epaulets made it quite apparent.

Over by the potted palms, Detective Jack Neeson, in his jerk-off bellhop uniform, saw the prissy desk clerk who was probably a secret drinker talking with Riley the bell captain. Riley might erroneously see himself as a comedian, but he was no priss, Neeson could tell. He could probably handle whatever was wrong—if there even was a problem.

Riley took something from the clerk then turned away from the desk and swaggered toward the elevators. He had his back muscles bunched in an odd way. Neeson knew that kind of walk—man on a mission.

Maybe I oughta go over and see.

He walked toward the guy behind the desk, Goodnight, who saw him coming and stood in a waiting attitude. Over by the elevators, Riley was pressing the Up button.

Neeson figured it would take a while for an elevator to arrive. If something *was* wrong, they might as well go up together, a couple of guys in funny-looking uniforms. Neeson thought they'd look like characters in a costume movie or one of the operas his wife dragged him to, the general and his adjutant. Riley, with the fancier uniform, was obviously the general. Neeson didn't like that. He was no second banana.

"Trouble with one of the phones," Goodnight said, not even waiting for Neeson to ask. He wasn't sure if he wanted the cop and Riley in the same elevator at the same time. Two giants of comedy in such close quarters. "The receiver's off the hook and somebody's playing with it. Probably some kids or a drunk."

Or a killer, the adjutant thought, and veered and walked faster toward the elevators and the general.

This was nothing to get excited about yet, but certainly it was something to look into.

He saw that he'd figured wrong. This late, the elevator traffic was sparse and there must have been one waiting at lobby level.

The general was gone.

69

Riley stepped out of the elevator on the seventh floor and saw the guy immediately. He was outside the door to one of the rooms facing the front, possibly 724, where the phone problem was, and hammering on the door with his fist. He wasn't strong enough to be making much noise.

Single my ass, Riley thought, figuring there was somebody else in the room, probably a woman. The guy was a weirdo he recalled entering the hotel about twenty minutes ago, way over six feet tall, with springy-looking long red hair and weighing not much more than a hundred pounds. As Riley watched, the weird guy began yelling and flinging himself over and over against the door. He looked like a human snake or something standing upright and didn't weigh enough to budge the door even if it had been cardboard.

He yelled again: "Lauri!" *Blam!* Against the door, causing him to bounce back about three feet, only to coil his long body and hurl himself again. *Blam!* Useless. "Lauri!"

"Hey, sport!" Riley said, when he was about ten feet from the man.

Weirdo noticed him for the first time. His eyes were wide,

maybe afraid, and he looked young. Riley wondered if the skinny guy was on drugs.

"You gotta help me get in there!" the guy yelled. "My girl's in there and I think she's in trouble."

"Whaddya mean, trouble?"

The man splatted himself ineffectually against the door again.

"Stop that!" Riley said. "You're gonna hurt yourself."

"Then help me get in! I think somethin's goin' on in there. A rape or worse!"

"What makes you think so?"

"I followed my girl here. Saw her go in there with this guy I don't trust!"

"And?"

"And what?" The weirdo's long body moved in a kind of springy wave, like he was about to charge the door again.

"Are you John Brown?" Riley asked.

"Huh?" The weirdo paused and stared at Riley.

"Is he the one with your girl?"

"I'm not him an' neither is he!" the weirdo said.

Riley gently touched his bony shoulder, preventing another assault on the door. "We'll see," he said, in the face of such determination. He knocked on the door. "But you say and do nothing, understand?"

The weird guy nodded, but Riley didn't for a second believe him.

There was no reply to his knock.

"I don't want the other guests disturbed, you got that?"

Another nod from the spring head. "Yeah. Yeah."

Riley knocked again. Louder.

Still no response.

"Okay," Riley said. "You stay out here and I'm going in and take a look. For all we know somebody might be in there taking a shower."

That seemed to really disturb the weird guy, but he said nothing.

Riley used his pass card on the lock and the door opened, which struck him as wrong, since usually by this time of night the guests had fastened their security locks.

He stuck his head in. The light on the desk was turned on. "Hello? Anybody?"

Then he noticed the desk chair was gone. Then he saw it lying sideways on the floor near the bed. Then he saw the woman taped to the chair, and the phone off the hook and lying near one of her feet.

Riley charged all the way into the room, the skinny guy right behind him, almost pressed to his back. He heard the guy cry, "Lauri!"

She was alive, at least, Riley saw, as he stooped beside the girl. Her eyes were wide and staring at him. As gently as possible, he peeled the duct tape from across her mouth. She drew in a deep breath through her mouth, worked her lips, licked them. Then she said something odd.

"Wormy?"

Riley pulled the small pocket knife he carried from his pocket and began cutting the tape that was binding her arms. The blade was dull from cutting cardboard and envelope flaps, and he had to saw with it frantically. It was slow going, but he was getting there.

"Call my dad!" the girl said, looking pitifully up at him. "Please! He's in the duct."

He frowned at her. "Duck?"

"Duct!"

Riley stared at her. "Your dad's in a duct?"

"Not my dad! *Call* my dad!" She spat out a phone number.

Riley wasn't listening. He was concentrating on cutting away the tape without damaging flesh, making sure the girl was all right. She was young like the skinny weirdo, probably not even twenty. Talking like she was on drugs.

"My dad's Detective Frank Quinn," she said

Riley stopped cutting. "Give me that phone number again."

She did, then glanced beyond the ridiculous fringed epaulet on Riley's shoulder and saw Wormy wriggling his way up through the bathroom ceiling vent.

Neeson stepped out of the elevator on the seventh floor and looked up and down the long, carpeted hall.

No sign of Riley.

The elevator door closed behind him with a soft rushing sound.

Neeson turned left, toward room 724. The hall was softly lighted by fancy-frosted glass sconces every ten feet or so. His shoes made no sound on the plush carpet as he walked swiftly and observed the even room numbers, making sure he was going in the right direction, unconsciously counting cadence.

Seven-sixteen.

Seven-eighteen.

Seven—

He saw that one of the doors ahead was open and he walked even faster, no longer observing numbers.

Now was the time.

Sherman somehow knew that all his celestial luck was with him in this single moment. When he felt like this, he'd never failed.

Careful to make as little noise as possible, he eased his body forward, lowering his head through the vent opening into the bathroom of Mom's suite.

Take your time . . .

He stuck his left arm through the vent, letting it dangle, and touched, barely touched, the white plastic shower curtain, simply to acclimate himself, to begin the process of becoming one with his surroundings so he could move with the necessary sureness and stealth.

The only sounds he could allow himself to make now would be his bare hands contacting the tile floor when he eased his way headfirst through the vent opening and the balance of his weight shifted, and then the soft thud of his stocking feet landing on the tiles. He had to manage to keep his balance. That would be the only real challenge.

It would be almost done then.

He'd move silently, through the partly open door to the bedroom, avoiding touching it so as not to risk even a hinge squeaking and alerting Mom.

Then the knife.

The knife.

70

Neeson entered room 726 cautiously, his gun drawn, and saw Riley kneeling alongside the bed. Then he saw the girl taped to the overturned chair.

Riley was pecking out a number on the phone, which was on the floor. He glanced over at the girl and said, "You're gonna be okay, sweetheart. You're safe now."

The girl, who looked familiar to Neeson, stared at him with wide eyes and said, "Duck."

"What?"

"*Duct*," Riley said. "She's Quinn's kid. Says whoever did this to her is in the ductwork."

It took Neeson about three seconds to process this.

He holstered his gun as he crossed the room

"Give me the phone."

Sherman emerged halfway from the ductwork, his upper body dangling from the vent opening.

Things had to happen fast now. Quietly, but fast.

He inched his body forward, and was about to lower himself into the bathroom, when he felt his right pants leg snag on something.

What the hell?

Cautiously he moved the leg, maintaining his precarious balance. He needed to free the material of his pants leg from the nail or screw or whatever it had caught on.

Wha—?

Something was trying to clasp his ankle now. *Ouch! Sharp!* Fingernails? Teeth?

Something about to clamp down on him in an alligator grasp?

Jesus!

He panicked, kicking both legs furiously, not caring now if he was making noise. He only knew he had to get out of the duct, away from whatever had him. He felt the soles of his stocking feet brushing something. His left foot made solid contact and he pushed with it while continuing to kick as hard as possible with his right. There was no pressure on his ankle now, but his pants cuff, worked out from where it had been tucked beneath the band of his sock, was being tugged. He could feel the tautness of the material.

He kicked even harder, bruising his heels and bending back a toe.

Free!

Suddenly free!

He'd managed to yank his leg away from whatever had it.

But with freedom came a sudden shift of weight, and he fell to the bathroom floor too abruptly to get his hands properly positioned for a soft landing.

He landed with a thud and a clatter on the hard tile floor, rolled painfully onto his left shoulder, and lay sprawled with one leg up on the commode. The leg must have dragged across the vanity top, too, because several cosmetic bottles were on the floor, even a small tube of toothpaste.

Knife won't work. She'll be awake! Cops on the way. Not the knife now.

He was glad he'd taken precautions. Immediately scrambling to his feet, he reached for his gun.

Not there!

The gun was no longer tucked in his belt.

Damn it!

There were sounds outside the door, which in his fall he must have kicked all the way closed. Someone running! Voices!

He glanced around desperately.

There was the gun. On the floor, half concealed by the skirt of the shower curtain.

He dived for it.

Allsworth flung open the door and ran into Mynra Kraft's bedroom without knocking, gun drawn.

Only Myrna.

The expression on her face, where she was looking . . .

Without hesitating, he made for the bathroom door. He remained aware of the startled figure in the bed, sitting bolt upright and staring, and held up his free hand palm-out in a signal for her to stay put.

Noise, like glass or plastic clattering, coming from the bathroom!

Allsworth clenched his jaw hard enough to break a tooth, gripped his nine-millimeter with both hands, and kicked the door open.

Quinn and Pearl were the first to approach the door to room 620. Neeson was sprinting down the hall toward them. Quinn was aware of the uniform who'd been posted on the landing converging from the other direction, a heavyset man laboring, not moving as fast as Neeson.

Behind Neeson was someone else.

Jeb Jones. Quinn had forgotten he was in the hotel.

Quinn didn't knock. He kicked open the door to suite 620 in the same manner Allsworth had used to enter the bathroom.

The anteroom was empty. A *People* magazine lay on the floor beside an armchair near a floor lamp with a crooked shade.

Quinn knew the suite's layout. He charged toward the bedroom, feeling Pearl's presence close behind.

Myrna was sitting up in bed, still in shock from being jolted from sleep. Quinn saw the shotgun she'd requested leaning against the wall near the bed.

Her body didn't move but her dark eyes slid toward where light was spilling from the bathroom.

Two shots roared echoing from the bathroom, brightening the light.

When the bathroom door had sprung back, Allsworth kicked it again, all the way open, and saw the man sprawled on the tile floor near the tub and shower curtain. White T-shirt, dark pants with one leg tucked into a black sock, *something in his hand!*

Gun!

Allsworth knew he was in for it and let out a roar. Sometimes a sudden loud noise stopped them. Made them hesitate just enough.

Sometimes.

Sherman was waiting and ready. He was surprised by how fast the cop got there, but his gun was held high, in both hands, and the cop was slightly off balance from kicking open the door. It would be instantaneous, but Sherman knew he had the instant.

The gun in the cop's hands couldn't drop fast enough to

sight in on Sherman. And Sherman wasn't at all distracted by the noise. Now noise of any kind was no longer a factor.

He squeezed off two shots even before the cop's gun was at shoulder level, their combined roar drowning out that of the cop before he dropped lifeless to the floor.

The damaged door was wide open now, the doorway framing Mom sitting upright in shock in bed.

Gun in one hand, knife in the other, Sherman vaulted the fallen cop who had half a face and ran toward her.

Quinn and Pearl paused when they saw the fleeting figure burst from the bathroom. They knew it wasn't Allsworth.

Still, they'd been caught by surprise and they stood paralyzed.

Sherman almost made it to the foot of the bed.

Pearl fired first, and kept firing. Beside her, Quinn opened up with his ancient police special revolver, feeling it buck like something alive in his hands.

Sherman took two sideways, wobbly steps and stopped as if in confusion. His gun slipped from his grasp. His legs trembled, and he dropped to a kneeling position.

Pearl lowered her gun. She felt weak and thought she might drop like Sherman. The Butcher.

She swallowed the coppery residue of fear beneath her tongue and found her resolve.

Work to do.

Damn it! Work to do!

The bedroom was suddenly full of noise and motion, Neeson, Jeb, the uniform from the landing.

They diverted attention only for a second.

Neeson was pointing. "He's up!"

And Sherman *was* up, moving like a zombie, propelled by sheer will, knife raised, lurching toward Myrna, who seemed too shocked, or mesmerized, to move.

Quinn knew they'd never be able to react in time. Sherman would reach her, stab her, and probably kill her.

Even as he thought this, there was a deafening roar and Sherman spun away, spraying blood across the room.

He lay motionless and silent in the reverberation of the shotgun's thunder, blown almost in half by the massive force of the gun at such close range.

Jeb, racing toward his mother the moment he'd entered the room, had reached the shotgun in time to save her life.

Everyone stood motionless, more in awe and exhaustion than shock. The handcuffs Pearl was about to clamp on Sherman still dangled from her hand.

After the incredible flurry of motion and noise, the only sound now was the regular hissing of heavy breathing.

Until a thud, clatter, and yelp of horror from the bathroom.

Gun at the ready, Quinn moved to the door and peered inside.

Wormy.

71

Myrna lay curled into a ball near the headboard, where she'd waited for almost certain death. She looked small there, and vulnerable.

Harmless.

She smoothed her hair back from her eyes, then climbed out of bed and stood with her arms crossed tightly across her body, squeezing herself as if for reassurance that she still existed. But she no longer appeared to be in shock. Her deep-set dark eyes were moving about slowly, taking everything in, assessing. When they met Quinn's gaze she averted them and stared at her son Jeb, who was standing over his dead brother, obviously distraught by what he'd done. Tears were streaming down his cheeks.

Tension had suddenly drained from the room, leaving the acrid stench of cordite, the reverberations of gunfire, and a heavy sadness. The air seemed weighted and stilled by death.

Jeb wasn't quite sobbing, but Quinn thought the convulsive breakdown might come at any second. And who could blame Jeb? He'd just saved his mother's life by killing his brother. The two brothers might not have met before tonight, but they were of the same blood. Quinn knew from other homicides what a devastating effect that could have. It wasn't like killing an unconnected stranger, which was enough of a horror in itself.

He moved toward Jeb. "You did the right thing," he said softly, but Jeb seemed not to hear.

Instead he looked over at his mother, still standing hugging herself.

He racked another round into the shotgun, brought the barrel up, and swung it around to point at Myrna.

She saw it and knew it was too late and knew what was coming. She stood taller, dropping her arms and staring defiantly at her son.

Quinn's gun had barely cleared his shoulder holster. Around him he sensed the sudden uncoordinated motion of the others redrawing or raising their weapons.

The shotgun fired first, filling the room again with thunder, and Myrna flew back against the wall, bouncing in the corner as she went down.

Quinn wasn't looking at her. He'd been concentrating on Jeb beyond his gun sight, like the others in the room, praying he could get off enough shots in time to stop him. Watching Jeb do the same awkward dance his brother Sherman had done as the bullets tore into him.

When he was down, Pearl reached him first. She kicked the shotgun away, under the bed, so hard it felt as if she'd broken a toe.

Jeb could see only white ceiling at first, and then watched the dark forms advance toward him. They still seemed afraid and were keeping their weapons aimed at him. He would have tried to reassure them only he didn't have enough strength. What he'd had to do was done.

He was thinking about the swamp of the past, how you

could never escape it entirely. It was always with you, awake or asleep, tooth and claw. And eventually . . .

A voice from far away: "She's dead. Shotgun from that range, there's not much left."

The big cop, Quinn, was bending over him, blocking the light, saying something.

"Why'd you do it? Why kill your mother?"

The big man's voice was unexpectedly gentle, puzzled. Jeb felt compelled to answer, and he knew there wasn't much time.

"When Mom and I lived in Louisiana," he said in a hoarse whisper, "we were dirt poor. Lived by the swamp. We took in boarders."

"What?" Quinn asked, kneeling to get closer, still puzzled.

Instead of answering, Jeb started to close his eyes. They didn't make it all the way.

"He's gone," Pearl said.

"Holy Mary!" one of the cops said. "Shot his own mother."

Quinn looked down into Jeb's half-closed eyes, as if there might be an explanation there. But nothing was there, no one behind the eyes.

Quinn sighed and straightened up. He could hear sirens outside, one of them nearby that abruptly ended its shrill singsong yodel below in the street. They'd be on their way up soon. More uniforms, plainclothes cops, a crime scene unit, paramedics, the medical examiner, all to shape the wild violence and death that had occurred here into something categorized, comprehensible, and not nearly so horrifying—on the surface. Cop world.

"What did he tell you?" Pearl asked.

"I don't know. Something about being poor in Louisiana and taking in boarders."

"Boarders?"

"I have no idea what he meant. Maybe he didn't, either. He was shutting down."

"Long time ago," Pearl said. "I guess it doesn't matter now."

Quinn looked down and saw blood on the toe of his shoe, from when he'd knelt over Jeb.

"Guess not," he said.

72

It was late the next afternoon when they found themselves driving back to the office in Quinn's Lincoln. The sun was still hot, and traffic was beginning to build, but Quinn knew the rhythm of movement and alternate routes in the maze that was his city, so they were making good time.

There was still plenty of work to do. It would take them a few days to clear everything out and officially close the file. And of course they'd have to handle the media, though they could put that off for a while, maybe avoid some of it altogether. Just maybe. The media had tumbled to where the office was and would be lying in wait for them there.

"What next?" Quinn asked.

"Goddamned paparazzi," Pearl said.

"I mean after all of that?"

Fedderman, in the backseat, said, "I'm going back to Florida. Maybe take up fishing again."

"What about golf?"

"Screw golf."

Quinn avoided a pothole and smiled. "I hope it works out this time."

"If it doesn't, there's always hunting."

"You've already done that," Pearl said.

Quinn glanced over at her. "You, Pearl?"

"I don't golf or fish." When no one commented, she said, "I think I can get my job back at the bank."

She thought Quinn might try talking her out of it, maybe even *hoped* he'd try, but he remained silent, staring straight ahead out the windshield. Mister Mt. Rushmore. She understood his silence and it made her angry.

He doesn't think he needs to talk me out of it. Doesn't think I can do it. That I can live a quiet life and stay away. The bastard doesn't understand.

"What about you, Quinn?" Fedderman asked from the backseat.

"Me? I'm a retired cop."

But Quinn knew better. His retirement wouldn't last. And neither would Pearl's job as a bank guard. And Fedderman would be more than relieved to give up fishing.

Pretenders, all of them.

That evening at his hotel, Fedderman told the desk clerk he wanted an early wake-up call and would be checking out in the morning.

While that was happening, Quinn was seated in his leather armchair with his feet propped up on a matching ottoman. He was smoking a Cuban cigar and feeling pretty good.

When Pearl finally got back to her apartment that evening, she downed half a bottle of Pellegrino, then removed her shoes and padded in her stocking feet to the phone.

She pecked out her mother's number at the assisted living home.

Blood calling to blood.

Lauri and Wormy resumed their relationship, with Quinn's grudging approval.

Wormy's sudden fame garnered The Defendants a record company contract, and their CD of *Lost in Bonkers* debuted on the charts as number 473 with a bullet. Wormy remained afraid of Quinn. Quinn never told him he sometimes found himself humming *Lost in Bonkers* when he was in the shower.

Maybe Lauri really would someday be a cop, Quinn thought, while he waited patiently for another phone call from Renz.

He was sure there would be one.

Don't miss John Lutz's next spine-tingling thriller . . .

NIGHT KILLS

Coming from Pinnacle in 2008!